JANE

GRACE WILLIAMS

Jane

ISBN: 9781089970392

Copyright 2019

Cover design Grace Williams

Photo Grace Williams

First Edition

Disclaimer

This is a work of fiction. Names characters, places and incidents either are the product of the author's imagination or are used fictitiously, and are no resemblance to actual persons, living or dead business establishments, events or locales is entirely coincidental.

Contents

Dedication

Without you this story would never have been told, thank you for believing in me and always being there.

Beloved

The minutes go by, tick tock, tick tock,
With you time stands still, there isn't a clock

I gaze at your soul through your eyes I do see,
There is no other but you, only you are for me

A moment, a second, a minute, an hour,
Your heart beats are rhythmic with infinite power

It began with hello and some innocent banter
Then picking up pace with a more vigorous canter

Wheedling my way to your inner space,
Hoping I'll consume all your thoughts and take over their place

No matter where I am or what part of the day,
I close my eyes and envision, you are there to stay

I picture your face and can smell of your scent,
Every moment with you is a moment well spent

The taste of your lips, the warmth of your skin,
Fueling my desires, I cannot wait to begin

Clutching your jowls and thrusting my tongue ever deep,
taking your breath it is mine now to keep

Gasping for air light headed, aloft in the moons
I caress your breasts, creations of soft dunes

I grab your hips and you feel the weight of my rock
I enter you softly you feel the veins of my cock

A rocket in space your planet to orbit
I brace for re-entry, the thrust you absorb it

Splashing to sea a tsunami of O's
In my arms, you hold tight awash in my prose

I whisper to you the words you must hear,
I love only you, only you I endear

Playlist

Recormmended listening for parts of the book, where indicated.

James Blunt – Youre Beautiful

Queen – You're my Best Friend

Silk – Freak Me

Florida Georgia Line - H.O.L.Y

Eric Clapton – Tears in Heaven

Dan and Shay – Speechless

Queen – I was born to love you

Acknowledgement

Grace Williams

Thank you to Pauline for being my wonderful Editor without your support and honesty I wouldn't have got this far. You are a very special lady.

Thank you to my wonderful beta readers your feedback has been very welcome. Thank you for your amazing support. I love you guys.

To my wonderful helpers for putting up with me and listening to me go on all the time, you know who you are.

 To my dear friend Ben, thank you for your beautiful poem, for "Jane" your work is inspiring. I can't wait to see what you write for the next two books. https://www.facebook.com/BAQuill/

Chapter 1

New Beginnings

Jane was in the middle of packing up her home in the UK ready for the big move. She was in a serviced apartment as she moved around a lot with her job. She loved working in Construction and had worked on some amazing projects she met some great characters from all walks of life and found that Mental Health issues were high in the Industry. She made it her aim to help others and becoming a Counsellor was another step in what she loved. She had trained to be a Counsellor after her own personal issues had led her to need support.

Being in Construction was the toughest job doing what she did, these guys thought they had to be tough after all what big strong builder has emotional issues? Of course, she knew better, although being in the US was going to be a huge learning curve, American men were more in touch with their emotions than that of the Brits so she had a lot of catching up to do. It was going to be a real challenge.

Jane was looking for something nicer to live in when she got to Connecticut, she was going to rent again, and she didn't want to get tied down with her own place, until she decided where to settle.

The Company she worked for offered her a placement for 2 years working on a deluxe apartment development in Connecticut. That was an understatement it was more like a village being built, all were top notch homes and businesses and many had been sold already. She knew a little about the area having had time to look around on the internet see what was about and had found some nice new places to go and look at. She wanted to be somewhere quiet but close to the town. She had also contacted the local Skulls MC at the local Harley Dealer so she could get her trike across before she left, luckily the dealers each side of the pond were taking care of the finer details, Jane just did as she was asked handed over her paperwork and of course the fee.

She couldn't do without her trike for two years not with the open roads over in the US. She had paid a lot for the trike and wanted to get the most out of it for the summer. She was a little short for the bike she wanted and didn't want a chop (one that had been lowered or messed about with) so settled on the Ultra Trike, it was beautiful, full of chrome, cherry red, a good music system, very important for eating up the miles and great storage so she could take off whenever she wanted with enough room for her essentials. A few of the guys from the MC had put her in touch with a guy called Shadow out in Connecticut, he was also VP of the MC, some of her guys had been over a few times to the bike events especially the Veteran events, they were all ex-serviceman themselves and enjoyed the weeks they spent out there. The bike would go out ahead of her so be there when she arrived. She had ridden once on Route 66 so knew the American roads. She was also hoping to get a paint job done on the trike too, a lot cheaper than at home. She just needed to make her mind up about what she wanted, that wasn't her best quality, at work not a problem she could scare the best of them and organised everyone but making a decision about a new tattoo or what to have for tea was bad enough, but deciding what design to have on the trike that was a joke and Moses teased her constantly about it. He knew what she was like being so indecisive.

Jane was reliably informed by Moses who worked at the Dealership and was part of her Chapter that they had a great guy who did their paint jobs out there, she was looking forward to meeting him but giving her baby up to a stranger was making her tummy nervous. She knew the guys in Southampton, they had helped with her bikes in the past and always knew what she expected, and they had the utmost respect for her. They knew she was a tough cookie and wouldn't be messed with.

A few of the younger members had thought she was an easy target as a single biker, the older guys had great fun watching Jane shoot them down in flames, occasionally she would have a wager with Moses they would watch her teach a youngster a lesson. Him and G would do anything for Jane, she was like a sister to them and they made sure she was well looked after. Jane never went too far, of course doing the job she did she knew better but a bit of leg pulling didn't hurt anyone. She never dated anyone from the club, all the old ladies knew her and looked at her as their one ally when things got tense. Only two of the boys knew Jane's story Moses and G they didn't discuss it. She had taken a long time building herself back up to where she was all those years ago before they saw what was happening to her.

She was going to miss the gang, there was a BBQ being held in her honour G and Moses promised to come out and spend a few weeks with her and go on a few ride outs in the summer, she was already looking forward to that, Jane had toughened up over the last 10 years and the boys had been by her side all the way. She wasn't going to crumble not now when she left the security of them. Moses had already laid plenty of foundations for her anyway and she was going to be given a welcoming committee when she arrived. G and Moses did it for their sakes as well as Jane's, they knew she was tough but being away from home in a different Country was a different thing altogether. They knew she loved her job and this chance was huge for her.

Moses was what you expected an old biker to look like, a dirty old grey beard well past its scruffy stage in fact it was wild, she loved grabbing hold of it and threatening to chop it off and shaving his face clean. She was a traditional girl, all her boyfriends had been clean shaven like her Dad, the only bearded men she was used to were the boys, but they didn't get that close apart from Moses but he was like a big Brother, he often nuzzled her to annoy her when she was in a small string tshirt, Moses would leave food in his beard or make sure some beer spilt on it just to annoy her. They would fall about fighting like a pair of kids, but it was all in good fun and Moses always came off worse. He should know better by now, Jane would get her claws out and scratch him to pieces, he would tease her and say "down my back J, you know you want to, and it will give me street cred with the ladies thinking I get laid". He would fall about laughing then get into a state coughing like an old furnace. His jeans hung off his hips, he had a baggy t-shirt on always with a dirty oil mark on it and his leathers nd boots had seen better days.

Hidden behind this messy old guy was a military man, when he dressed up and combed his beard he looked very handsome and could woo the ladies if he behaved himself. He was mid fifties and had seem some action in the military, he had some awful stories to tell. But only to those he trusted, it wasn't easy for him to open up to what he had seen.

Jane continued with the packing, some of the girls had shown up to help her and they decided to have a few bottles of wine while they packed. Jane had a week to go so needed to get sorted, the girls distracting her with wine wasn't going to help but she needed to let her hair down a bit and she wasn't riding anywhere, the boys were coming over in the van to take her boxes to the shipping container, she only had a small one, a lot was going into storage, after all it was only two years, she was sure she could do without most things.

The girls crashed onto the sofa, it was a huge room, with a thick pile carpet and a nice deep old leather sofa and two huge chairs, she was going to miss this for sure, quite often after a tough day she would fall asleep on it and wake up with a crick in her neck, wondering how she managed to pull the blanket around her. As the wine flowed the girls started talking about men, and as with every time you get a gang of girls together the talk got smutty, but as expected the topic of conversation was Jane, Gwen started it. Swinging her glass out a little too wide and lapping the wine against the edge Gwen said,

"Soooo Jane, do you think you will meet a nice man out in the US of A, and get your gorgeous arse laid once and for all?"

The others started to giggle as she continued. the girls got louder. "There must be someone out there for you who isn't too up tight or in the gutter, we just haven't found him yet. But girl we will".

She had this lovely way of waving her hand about and clicking her fingers when she said it, and the walk when she strutted away, it was classic. Gwen was beautiful, she had the olive skin and the dark hair and eyes. Her hair hung down her back so smooth. She was a Mum to a beautiful brood of kids but still looked stunning with a too die for figure. Matt adored her, there marriage was volatile though and when they fought everyone knew about it. Jane was shorter than the other girls, and they enjoyed picking on her, but she had a gorgeous hourglass figure which was envied and lusted after by a few. She had blonde hair that fell down her back in curls but she had recently started to straighten it under the orders of the girls and it had got her a lot of attention. She wasn't confident about her looks and knocked back the compliments she got. She promised the girls she would let them dress her up for the leaving party, she wasn't looking forward to it though, it was going to be a bit like "Sandra D" from Grease.

She had promised to arrive early at the Dealership and let the girls do their "thing". Heaven help her as Gwen was in charge of the make over. The rest of the girls joined in with questions. "Come on Jane, tell us when did you last get laid" Helen asked. Jane just laughed, "behave, why is it my sex lif is always the topic of conversation with you lot". They laughed, "because we need to get you laid" Helen joked. The afternoon continued in the same vain, not a great deal of packing was done but plenty of wine drinking and giggling. Jane loved it, she thought the world of the girls but hadn't had the courage to be honest with them about her marriage.

Chapter 2

Jasper

Jasper was finishing up for the day in the office, he was a good-looking man who looked younger than his years, he hadn't any grey hairs yet and his skin was good and tight. Apart from the wrinkles around his eyes.

He worked out 5 days a week after work and sometimes on the weekend, he was proud of his body. He had lived in Connecticut for 20 years but flew off to do whatever job he needed to do for his own Company around the world, but also the Contract he had with Bates and Co. He was an engineer and a damn good one. He was single, he had been burnt a few times but divorced now. He wore his heart on his sleeve and had been taken in by a Cougar who saw a good time and lots of presents. He was still hurting from it and felt a fool. He wasn't going to be taken in like that again. His job kept him busy enough, so he wasn't distracted.

He was the only one left in the office when he took a call from his boss. He knew this meant he wanted a favour what was it this time, "I bet it has something to do with this new job" this joint venture was already a pain in the arse he wasn't babysitting some Graduate again, let someone else do it he thought".

"Callum Hi, what can I do for you" he said. "I'm just heading out to the gym, this better be quick"

"Ahhh Jasper, glad I caught you".

"Here it comes he mumbled under his breath".

"I wondered if I could ask a huge favour of you? You know we are doing a JV on the new development with Jakes well they have a Counsellor who is coming out for the duration of the build, He's some hot shot who works with the guys, something to do with emotions and all that shit, anyway he is looking for a place to rent and as you know the area I wondered if you wouldn't mind showing him around. He's a bit of a biker by all accounts has some big flash bike they are shipping over for him, so you won't need to babysit him. Just show him a few of the nicer blocks we have built and see if you can get him interested in one" "Whatever Callum" He groaned.

"Hey J look at it this way it's not some totty you need to try and schmooze or a Graduate".

"Fine, fine whatever Callum, when is this happening?"

"He is due to fly out in a week, we are putting him in the local hotel. I will get Joan to organise that side of things, if you will just meet him a week Thursday at the site and show him around, I'm sure we can get that done and dusted in no time".

"Fine" he groaned again and hung up. "The downside to being single you get all the shit jobs to do like babysitting" he moaned as he left the office. He bid goodnight to Harry the Security guard. He was a lovely old boy, he was ex military. Jasper had time for everyone just liked being a grumpy sod. Harry knew him well, he had been at the firm longer than most and had seen what Jasper had been through. He had a soft spot for him.

"Good Night Mr Mitchell, have a nice weekend Sir" Harry said with a huge grin on his face.

"Good night Harry, thank you, Best wishes to the family. I hope Mrs Black is well?"

"She's good thank you, keeps me and the kids on our toes" both men laughed as Jasper raised his hand and walked out into the cool night air, it was warming up; the summer was on its way. That pleased him, he could get the Ferrari out and get the roof off and join his friends for some weekends away. He was a petrol head, his main car was a Ranger Rover, he loved it. But recently he brought himself a white Ferrrari, his friends all had sports cars, they used it as an excuse to get away from the wife for the weekend. They went to a few car shows and liked to strut their stuff like single men, there were always a lot of girls there preening over themselves looking for their next prey, a few of the guys played away Jasper wasn't interested. He worked hard and liked his weekends to himself to join races or talk to other petrol heads. He wasn't interested in women again at the moment. Not for some years now in fact.

Jasper went off to the gym with a few knots in his shoulders now thanks to Callum. He did get frustrated being used like that. But at least it was a guy, a biker too, "I hope he's not some guy going through a midlife crisis with shiny new leathers pretending he knows everything about bikes. Time will tell I suppose". he thought to himself A couple of hours later he was on his way home after a great workout, feeling better and had a quick catch up with a few of his friends. They were planning a weekend away in a few weeks, no ladies allowed, just the boys, he was up for that. Steve had found a local B&B the owner had come highly recommended, her husband had barns for the cars to be locked up in, they were on a farm, it sounded perfect.

Jasper stopped at the local market and picked up a few ingredients, it was early enough for him to spend time cooking which he loved, and his favourite was noodles. He didnt cook that much these days but today he felt like it, he was lucky the local market had some great little places with fresh cooked meals being made, it was like a market stall but inside and all were privately owned, some had seating and he often sat and had a meal, he knew a few of the local stall holders to pass the time of day with and they often stopped at his table to speak, he loved the friendliness of the area, it had been one of the reasons he had stayed in the US, he found his area of London to be cold and unwelcoming.

Jasper got home grabbed his shopping out of the back of his Range Rover and walked into the house. He had all the tech he could want so the lights were set to come on so he could walk in to the house feeling like it was lived in and not dark and unwelcoming. He had brought a nice house, with a large garden he loved gardening but employed a gardener to help him especially when he was away. Ernie was a lovely guy. He certainly made gardening look easy.

His kitchen was one of his favourite places, it was a big room with white wood units, lots of lighting and a huge island in the middle. He had brought himself some lovely kitchen equipment no expense spared, he believed in the best of everything. There was a staircase at the end of the kitchen, a small office off to the right, glass doors throughout flooding the house with light during the day which he loved. He left the shopping on the worktop and went upstairs to have a quick shower before setting about cooking, he pulled on a pair of lounge pants and a white tshirt before going back to the kitchen, he flipped on his music which woke up the house and set about chopping his vegetables for his noodles. He moved around the kitchen like a pro, it was times like this he missed having someone to cook for.

Jasper took his meal into the lounge and flicked on the TV one of his favourite Avengers films was having a rerun that will do he said to himself, he sat back eating his dinner and watched the film for half an hour. Once he finished he washed up his dishes and headed to his office, he had a mountain of things to get through and if he was to show this new guy around then he better get on top of things, he wasn't really a grumpy man but doing a joint venture on a job was going to bring its own issues and he could do without babysitting one of them.

He settled in for a few hours and got a good head start, by midnight his head was pounding so he decided to get some rest.

Chapter 3

Party Time

Jane's alarm went off and she kicked off the covers thinking of all that she still had to do before her flight in a few days time. Her bike had arrived at the dealer, so she was happy. Moses had been in touch with them and all was well. She was going to collect the bike the morning after she arrived so she could get around find her feet before the following week when she started work, it would give her a chance to look around and get over the flight.

It was party day, so she knew time was short before Moses came to collect her. She felt lost without her own transport. Moses offered her one of the low riders, but she was still a little short so declined the offer.

The girls had really helped after all the leg pulling and wine drinking, her apartment was almost finished, G had arranged with a few of the guys to come and collect her boxes before the party. All she had left then was her essentials in her big suitcase.

The day flew by, the boys came for the last of the boxes and Jane looked around her empty home, she had some great memories here, she had moved in after the break up of her marriage, Moses had found it for her, it was secure so she didn't worry so much at night like she used to.It had two entrance doors both of which she had to give access to visitors to. Moses knew how worried she was about anyone getting in so made sure it was a fool proof system, or as good as you could get anyway. She smiled thinking of Moses and the front he put on for others, he was a gentle man really with a heart of gold, she was lucky to have him as a friend, she was going to miss him.

She got herself showered and ready and within the hour Moses arrived to collect her. He buzzed himself in, he had his own key just in case Jane needed him. She opened the door and was surprised to see a clean Moses, his beard was trimmed, well as good as he would allow, he had his best jeans on and a new t-shirt, Jane smiled "wow who are you trying to impress then, I take it there is some tail there tonight you are after" as she laughed he replied

"Can't a man clean up for a friend, I thought you might prefer it if I made an effort for you"? She hugged him.

"I'm sorry Moses thank you, but I still think some tail will be chased tonight" he slapped her on the arse and handed her his spare crash helmet.

"Move your arse half pint, before I kick it out of the door"

They headed down to his bike, his pride and joy, Moses preferred his older Harleys, he had a beautiful sea green low rider with an amazing paint job, it was in memory of the guys he lost in his regiment out in the Afghanistan. He had his cap badge and the names of the guys spray painted on plus a photo they had taken together.

Moses fired up the bike, the noise neither of them would ever get sick of. They got on and headed out to the club, they were fortunate enough to be on the edge of the New Forest and had a great space for visiting clubs, there was a field that spread a few acres, the guys had built a shower block and toilets on the outside for when they had weekend parties and other clubs pitched up for the weekend, they had a stage too for local visiting bands. The dealership had a great café but on weekends such as this they used the BBQ they had built and the outside kitchen, it wasn't anything special, but it worked. Inside was a commercial kitchen where the girls who ran the café prepared the food it was all stainless steel and filled with fridges freezers and worktops.

The field had started to fill up Jane noticed when they arrived, she wasn't expecting so many people but then she should know better, the boys didn't do anything by half.

Jane went into the kitchen to see the girls who greeted her with hugs and kisses, G was in there interfering and annoying the girls, stealing food as they were trying to prepare it. Jax was slapping his hand as he went to kiss her cheek, she pushed him away "fuck off G, I don't want your slobber all over me, save it for one of the tails later" he grumbled under his breath and walked away as the girls laughed.

G was a lovely man too, they all were. He was another ex Veteran, an old friend of Moses, they were stationed together many times. G was a sharpshooter, quite a slim guy but tall, long legged. But then anyone was tall to Jane. As he came passed her, he kissed the top of her head. "You okay sugar?"

"I'm good G thank you" she replied as he left the kitchen.

The girls whooped with delight, Jax grabbed Jane's hand and the other 3 girls led her to the ladies room, it was a big room the boys had added for them, somewhere nice for events where they could get dressed showered in comfort, they had a few sofas and big mirrors, hair dryers along one wall and every conceivable extra they would need, the guys had done well under the supervision of Gwen though, she had given them her requirements as she saw it and as Matt would say she was high maintenance so probably the best one to advise what was needed. The walls were painted a pale yellow it was flooded with light but had the glass that stopped anyone seeing in even when the lights were on and there were a lot of lights. Gwen knew what she wanted, she had free rain and loved it. Moses trusted her not to overdo it but also allowed her to do what she wanted. He had the utmost respect for her she not only ran the café but had her 2 kids at school and her husband who worked at the dealership too. She organised all of the Charity events and got involved in everything, she was a great cook, and everyone fought for her cakes and goodies.

Jane knew it would be foolish to argue and let the girls do as they wished, normally she was a jeans and t-shirt girl with boots and leather, hair down and straight and a little make up. Obviously if she was going to an event then she would get out her little black dress and heels, but every day wear was different, and she wouldn't want to wear a dress with this rowdy bunch.

Linda covered the mirror so Jane couldn't see what was being done Every surface was covered in lotions and potions, boxes of makeup, there were clothes hanging everywhere. All the lights were on it was like watching a huge production get underway.

Jane sat and the transformation began. Gwen was in charge each girl had her role. Gwen started on her nails, bright red Jane's favourite. Linda was in charge of hair, Jax was feet and Sonja was makeup.

The wine was flowing and the girls were happy singing to the music using their glasses as microphones and bumping hips as they moved around the room. Sonja and Linda got their phones out, any chance of a selfie or a group picture they were there. They loved pouting in fun at those that took it so seriously. Gwen gave them a glare and pointed at Jane, letting them know to get on with transforming Jane.

By the time they had finished Jane felt like she had a tin of hairspray on her hair but felt good, she loved her toe nails it was a first for her, she never saw the need as she was always in boots but she liked it and kept looking at them admiring how nice they looked. Gwen smiled at the others with that look of contentment. They all gave a thumbs up to each other.

The girls didn't know Jane's story, they had heard bits and pieces of gossip, even Gwen and Jax didn't know and their husbands were close to Jane. It's not that Jane didn't want to share it, she felt that part of her life was over and the more she moved on the better for her, she didn't want to think of her past anymore, she was scared enough of being found and stayed close to the guys knowing she would be well looked after.

Moving to America for a couple of years would allow her to relax completely. She didn't do social media for obvious reasons so unless she told anyone where she was, she stayed pretty hidden.

The transformation was complete, the girls were wooing and cheering at their work, Jane stood up in Gwen's sandals they were 4 inches high, sparkly and strappy, definitely not something she had tried before but looking down she liked it, a lot.

Linda came across with a dress bag and Jane was told to close her eyes, they wanted a big reveal.

Jane wasn't confident about her body so the girls wanted to show her how good she could look with just letting go a bit. She had put on weight while she was married and had taken a few years to get rid of it, but she still saw herself as big. The dress was slipped over her head, and she didn't feel any arms, and felt it hug her body, oh god she said to herself feeling nervous and took a deep breath. She opened her eyes and saw the girls grinning at her, all with tears in their eyes. Sonja moved over to the mirror "are you ready Jane" she asked, Jane nodded a ball of nerves in her tummy. "Close your eyes then and I will tell you when to open them again" Sonja said. Jane did as she was asked and Sonja took the cover off. Jane had her head down and eyes closed. "Okay open your eyes" Sonja said as the girls all held their breath.

Jane looked up from her feet, she didn't have stockings or tights on, her legs were bare all the way up to above her knees, she kept on going and saw this figure in front of her that she didn't recognise, her hand went up to her mouth as she took in a deep breath. The dress was a silver shimmery waterfall dress, it hugged her hips and nipped in at her waist, It showed off her hour glass figure perfectly. She had shoestring straps and a scooped neckline that sat just above her cleavage. She turned around and liked what she saw, her hair was half up and down, curls added for extra body and a slight fringe, her lips were a beautiful red that matched her nails and her eyes shone, she had lovely eyes and the girls knew what to do to bring them out more. She stood with her mouth open in awe of what she saw, she felt brand new and a little like her old self before her marriage. She had tears in her eyes and the girls came in to hug her, all echoing the same words, how beautiful she looked and sniffing back tears. She was desperate not to cry and so were the girls they didn't need a panda on their hands after all that work. All the girls chocked back their own tears as they stopped hugging and were gushing with compliments, Gwen smacked her arse and said

"Girl if you don't get laid tonight then I will do you myself" the girls laughed and agreed too, she looked a million dollars.

The girls dashed about finishing getting dressed and doing their own hair and makeup before they said it was time to go and party. Jane suddenly felt really nervous, the guys were going to see her and she wasn't sure if she was ready for that. She started to shake, Linda came up behind her put her hand on her hip and put a gin in her hand.

"Come on beautiful lady drink this, your audience awaits"

The door opened and the noise hit them all, the band was playing and the noise of what seemed like a good hundred people came flooding into the room, Jane felt her knees go weak as she backed into the door, " Oh I don't think so" Gwen said, as she gently moved her forward. They were at the back of the building and there were a couple of corridors to get through before they reached the front.

The girls were dancing to the band as they walked towards the noise. Gwen had sent a text to Moses and G to make sure they came and met Jane at the inside door. Jane stopped at the last door and took a deep breath, as she put her hand on the door it flew open and Moses and G stood there, mouths open eyes out on stalks.

"Fuck me girls who is this gorgeous bit of arse you brought along tonight" Moses asked grinning from ear to ear and whistling loudy, G pushed Moses in the chest and said

"sorry Moses I saw her first she's mine, go find your own" laughing and grinning too not believing what he saw in front of him.

Jane tried to turn around embarrassed by the guys, the girls stopped her telling her they were teasing her, Jane knew better but this was huge for her. Moses walked up to her, grabbed her face in his hands looked her in the eye and said quietly,

"that's my girl, you have been hiding her along time half pint, welcome back, you look a million dollars lady, may I escort you to your party?"

He kissed her on the forehead and put his arm out for her to take. G followed suit and hugged her but not too tight he didn't want to spoil her even though he wanted to hold her so tight, he knew this had taken her so much courage.

"hey beautiful little lady, we've missed you, welcome back" he said kissing her nose softly and put his arm out for her, she took both arms as they looked down at her and she nodded letting them know she was ready. The girls had moved round the front and watched the tenderness from the guys, they all went to jelly, and they knew how much they both loved and respected Jane. The girls led the way with huge smiles on their faces, as they walked through the crowd of people everyone stopped and turned to look at Jane, Moses and G were so proud to have her on their arm like two Brothers giving her away at her wedding.

As expected the wolf whistles started and the comments from the guys, more of the girls that Jane knew came up and hugged her all feeling proud of her. All telling her she looked amazing.

The rest of the gang came together at the bar and everyone grabbed a drink. Shell was behind the bar for an hour they took it in turns so they could all enjoy the party. Once they all had their drinks Moses said "a toast to our not so half pint tonight who has blossomed into a beautiful swan" they all cheered and clinked glasses and bottles,

"let's get this party started" G shouted and a roar went up in the bar, everyone started to move towards the bifold doors where the band and 100s of people were partying outside already.

The BBQ area was lit, there was a hog roast on the spit which had been cooking most of the day, the girls were setting up the last of the tables and sorting the cutlery, there were huge bins around the perimeter for bottles and rubbish, they were a good bunch and cleaned up after themselves until they had a few too many then it was just a pile anywhere and everywhere.

The drink was flowing it was past 9 the evening was still young. Quite a few needed food as they were well on their way to be passing out any time soon. The single men were starting to find any tail they could for the night, it was relaxed and friendly.

Jane headed back into the building feeling a bit lost and wanted to help out. She passed Suzys room who was just finishing a tattoo on one of the guys from another club, she was surprised there was any room left on him he was covered and it was all Suzys work.
Suzy was a short girl, very slim with tattoos all over her, she had dark hair which had the addition of some wonderful bright colours and different ribbons hanging from it, she wore her leather waistcoat all the time with shorts that showed off her arse cheeks or short skirts. It really helped her out having a room to work here, she managed to save the extra money her and Lottie needed to buy their own place. She was indebted to the boys and of course they had their tattoos free. Lottie came wondering in to see how long she was going to be and gave Suzy a huge full on passionate kiss in front of the guy in the chair, he wasn't bothered, everyone knew these two were very passionate regardless of where they were.
"You got one in there for me Lottie" he asked
Lottie bent over him and gave him a huge kiss as Suzy stood watching and laughing. As Lottle pulled away he had the biggest grin on his face. They all laughed. Lottie was a tall slim girl with amazing curves which the boys said went to waste on Suzy, she was blonde and curly, little girls would tell her she had angel air. She had her fair share of tattoos that Suzy had given her.

Jane carried on towards the kitchen to help bring out some tubs of potatoes and coleslaw that Linda had prepared, she hadn't seen her or Steve for a while so assumed, they were busy in the kitchen, Jane pushed the swing door about to say

"what can I carry for you Linda" but as she opened her mouth she shut up and stepped back, instead she was greeted with the bare arse of Steve who had Linda bent over the stainless steel counter her legs wide open, her mini skirt round her waist and her thong pulled to one side as he was riding her hard she screamed
"fuck yes, don't stop you dirty bastard fuck me hard"
This only egged Steve on who was making a lot of noise too. His hands on her top pushing it up so he could get to her nipples, Jane was just moving back quietly as Moses collided with her heading in to do the same thing as Jane, Moses wasn't so quiet, he was used to catching them at it, but not on the counter where food was being prepared. He laughed and shouted,
"unless that pussy is being shared Steve you might want to put her down there are a lot of hungry people out there"
Steve lifted his head and said "Fuck off Moses, I ain't stopping now I have waited all day to fuck my missus, come back in ten minutes". Moses and Jane burst out laughing, walked into the kitchen grabbed the wrapped pots as Steve went back to finishing Linda and they walked out. Jane suddenly relaxed and she and Moses shared the scene they just saw.
"Lucky bastard" Moses muttered under his breath.
Jane thought it's been a long time since anyone did anything remotely like that to me and smiled. She had her toy, which would do until she was ready for a man. They walked outside with the tubs as the girls met them and took them away to start the food.

The party was going well, the food was a success and the bar was getting busier a few of the girls jumped behind to help out Jane slipped in and did the same but was ordered out and sat on a bar stool. This was her night she wasn't working.

Beautiful – James Blunt

The music slowed down and Moses took the opportunity to grab Jane and take her onto the dance floor. Jane had been drinking quite a lot but wasn't drunk just more confident, Moses wrapped his arms around Jane and looked down at her
"How's my girl doing?" She looked up at him with a huge smile

"Im good Moses thank you, I've had a great night, I can't thank you enough for all you do for me and have done for me over the last 10 years and more".

Moses loved Jane to bits he would kill anyone if they tried anything, she was like a sister but more than that. He fancied her years ago but their friendship was deeper than that. Hell he was in love with her but would never do anything about it. She was everything to him. He knew it would kill him if she found someone else, but he couldn't have her. Letting her go to the US was bad enough, he was really struggling with it. Jane laid her head on his shoulder as they moved around the floor, two perfectly beautiful people who couldn't mean more to each other. He kissed her head and they danced together no words were spoken, they didn't need to. He closed his eyes and breathed in her scent. He wanted to get as much of it in his memory as he could. He took a deep breath as G came up behind Jane, he opened his eyes as G nodded letting Moses know it was time to hand her over and get ready for a little surprise.

G took Jane in his arms, as Moses let her go.

"Lady you are beautiful, don't ever forget that. Whatever man gets to win your heart better look after you because he's one lucky Son of a bitch and we want to vet him first".

Jane slapped him in the chest and laughed, "I'm not going forever and not to find a man either G".

The music was interrupted by the lead singer from the band.

"Ladies gents and drunken bums, can we have your attention please". The music stopped and everyone turned to face the front. G put his hands-on Jane's shoulders as they stood together. Moses appeared on the stage and took the microphone, the singer slapped him on the back.

"All yours brother"

Standing to one side with the rest of the band.

Moses looked straight into the crowd at Jane.

"We all know why we are here tonight, to say cheerio to our little lady "Halfpint", who's not so short tonight in those killer heels", a cheer went up and everyone looked round at Jane. She blushed as usual and G squeezed her shoulders.

"Anyway" Moses continued "Would you please come up here with us Jane, G took her hand and led her through the crowd to the stage, everyone was cheering and whistling as she got onto the stage.

She was bright red and laughing nervously. Both men put their arms around her as Moses continued. "We know this is not forever but you leaving us is going to leave a huge hole here. We couldn't let you go without a proper send off and hope you have enjoyed your party tonight, the place wont be the same without you Doc, you have straightened more than one of us out, and turned a few of us into big girls, the crowd roared. Only teasing, you have been part of this club for over 10 years now, damn you are this club, you have held us together through some shit times and shown us true friendship. This club wouldn't be what it is without you". The crowd went quiet, the girls were getting emotional and hugging each other. Jane could feel the tears welling up in her own eyes.
"So, without further ado, we wanted to give you something to remember us by and remind you where home is in case you forget"

Gwen came up onto the stage with Linda both with bags in their hands and handed them to Jane, they hugged her tight and stood to the side wiping their eyes.

G nodded to Jane to open the first bag, she pulled out a leather waistcoat it was black with tassels, which she loved, she held it up looking confused.
"Turn it round half pint Moses said.
As she turned it round she noticed the leather burning that had been done in the back. It had the club emblem with 3 red roses and buds around the outside and across the top of the skull it said The Skulls MC, at the bottom England and "Doc, our Half pint" underneath it.
That was her undoing, the tears started, she hugged the leather no knowing what to say looked up at Moses and then to G and just hugged them both, the crowd cheered. Moses let go and said.
"Sorry half pint there is more". She wiped her eyes and laughed.
The next bag was a pair of boots, She'd had hers for years, they had red flames up the front and sides and got them just right but they had seen better days. She pulled the first boot out and a sob left her, they had the same burning as the jacket. The girls grabbed her and cried together.

Jane was trying to compose herself, at this moment in time she had never felt so loved. These guys were her family and meant the world to her. G gave her the last bag and motioned for her to open it, she looked inside and saw a Tshirt, which she pulled out. It was huge the biggest they could find, on the back was the club emblem and everyone had written messages on it for her, some smutty as expected but as she read through them, she laughed. She hugged it into her chest and said "you guys are the best" as Moses handed her the microphone and held onto her.

Jane looked around the sea of faces smiling at her.
"I really am lost for words, yes I know that's unusual", the crowd laughed, "you guys will never know how important you are to me everyone one of you has a special place in my heart and I will take a part of you all with me". As she held her t-shirt tight.
"I wrote where your tit will be Doc, so I get to be close to you" shouted Simon, "I claimed your arse Doc another yelled" as they all started laughing, it was all innocent banter and Jane loved it.
"Some of you know everything about me and a lot of you don't, yet you have never questioned helping and supporting me, for that I will be eternally grateful, you are my family. Please be kind to each other I will be at the end of the phone and have promised to Skype regularly to keep you updated. I love you guys" Jane chocked back more tears as she handed the microphone back to Moses and a cheer went up from everyone.
It was time for Jane to leave she was emotionally exhausted and it would take a good hour to go round and hug everyone before she could go. She moved around the throng of people, hugging and kissing the guys getting lots of offers of tents for the night which she laughed at and thanked everyone. She got to the end of the row and the girls were waiting for her. They came together in a huge hug and she knew how desperately she would miss them.
She went back into the bar to grab her bag and dashed to the ladies first, it was a good half an hour journey home she needed the loo before she left, as she moved towards the ladies there were people everywhere kissing and making out. Some were better dressed than others, nobody bothered as she walked past them. They still managed to nod at her as she went past, she couldn't help but laugh seeing a guy with his mouth full of nipple and his hand up his girls skirt, or a girl on her knees up against the wall her man stood in front

of her hiding her giving him a blow job. Jane laughed and walked around the corner.

"Ahh", she wondered where these two were. Suzy was on her knees with Lottie stood against the wall, she had the smallest skirt on and crop top, Suzy had it pushed up with Lotties leg on her shoulder and her knickers round one ankle as she was pushing one finger into her pussy and her mouth covering the rest sucking her like it was the last time she ever would, Lottie was pulling at Suzys hair and moaning loudy biting her lip. These two never gave a damn about who saw them, they were highly sexed and were very tactile, One of the guys asked them once in all honesty what it was like for a women to taste another and they both said it was heaven on earth and once started there was no way you could stop. The guy agreed with that statement and said "well ladies we have a lot in common then" which made them all laugh. Jane walked on by and smiled, there certainly was a lot of alcohol and god knows what else consumed tonight.

Before long the taxi pulled in to collect Jane she left the building and waved to the guys and she climbed in, Moses and G held up their beers to her, she wasn't saying goodbye to them they were taking her to the airport in a couple of days and she was all cried out for now, she blew them a kiss and sat back feeling very loved.

Chapter 4

Road Trip

Jasper was packing up his things for his weekend away with the guys, it had been a long week and this weekend was well overdue. He was dressed in his trademark jeans and white V neck t-shirt which hugged his shoulders, he was 6ft tall and had a great chest with a killer smile and the deepest of eyes which you could see the hurt in if you cared to look hard enough, but when he laughed and smiled, he lit up any room. His smile could give any girl butterflies.

He had brought the Ferrari Spyder a few months ago as a gift to himself, well he didn't have anyone else in his life to buy anything for and he had earned it. It wasn't a new one, it was a few years old, he wanted a white one not the traditional red, it was a beauty and he loved it.

They were staying in a new B&B they hadn't used before up the coast, it was a good drive out and a great road to drive. They were going along the Mohawk trail, it was the scenic route with amazing scenery and it was the perfect time of year as everything was coming up for the summer. Jasper loved this road and was eager to get going.

His phone beeped it was Tony confirming they would all meet in the local diner, have breakfast and head out from there.

Jasper packed his overnight bag into the car plugged his ipod in and set off. The boys were there when he arrived, it looked good to see the cars parked up together, Tony and Jasper both had Ferraris, Tony's was red, and John and Sam had Lamborghini's black and silver.

They were all good-looking men, they looked after themselves, they spent time at the gym keeping there bodies in shape, they didn't body build they weren't interested in that. Just wanted to look good and toned and they all did.

Jasper walked into Jacks Diner it was a traditional old place with red and white stripped seats, 50s music playing in the background, it had a long counter to sit at plus tables and booths. They always had the same spot over in the corner booth so Tony could see the tottie coming in. so he said.

Tony was blonde with blue eyes, he had a great smile and a mouth full of teeth. You could see why the ladies loved him. He was divorced twice as he couldn't keep it in his pants. He never wanted children he didn't want to be tied down. He was happy to play the field. He stood when Jasper walked in and hugged him.
"Good to see you J, it's been a while!"
Sam and John stood and hugged him too, the guys were great friends, and Jasper had met them at the gym when he first started going almost 20 years ago, they had been together for one another in good and bad times and now they were all enjoying the good. Tony had spent some time at Jaspers when his second wife caught him cheating, the guys didn't pity him they had warned him enough.

They all sat down and looked at the menu before Jenny came across to take their orders. Jenny knew the guys from old and could take their nonsense, Jasper was always polite but Tony made up for all of them, he couldn't resist. He patted his lap.
"Jen Jen come and sit, take the weight of those gorgeous legs for just a minute" and let's talk about the first thing that comes up.
The guys laughed and so did Jenny, she knew he was a player and didn't fall for his nonsense just took it in good fun.
"Thank you, Tony" she replied "but some of us have work to do so get your minds made up and let me get your drinks"
Tony saluted her, "Yes Ma'am".
Jenny left with their orders and soon came back with coffees for the guys and Tea for Jasper.
"Always the Englishman with the tea" Sam said to Jasper laughing.
"No, I just don't like coffee unless I have to drink it" he replied.
Jenny returned soon later with four plates of full English nothing was missing and silence fell at the table as they all devoured their food. 40 minutes later after settling the bill and giving Jenny a good tip Jasper followed the guys out. The route was decided.
They had a great drive up to the B&B. They arrived mid afternoon, as they pulled up the driveway they saw the house come into view. It

took their breath away, Jasper thought it was just a small place when Tony told him about it, this was quite the opposite, it was a traditional wood and stone built place, with a wrap around terrace, with huge furniture on it, surrounded by trees it was idyllic, the fire was lit as there was a gentle stream of smoke coming from the chimney. The drive was quite bendy, with bushes and trees either side, he saw something out of the corner of his eye and looked round to see a pair of squirrels run up the tree, he couldn't help but smile and felt the stress of the week drain from his body. Jasper loved being out of the city he loved the peace and quiet, not that he would get too much this weekend.

He thought how nice it would be to come here with a lady and relax for the weekend. "Who knows he said to himself one day maybe".
They parked outside of the house and the owners came out to meet them, Lillian and Henry her husband owned the house, they were known locally to be great hosts and loved sharing their house with good people.
Lillian was a traditional looking Grandmother with her pinny on and her silver hair, Henry was a slight man but you could see he had worked hard all his life. They came to the guys like they had known them for years and introduced themselves. The guys warmed to them instantly, they all walked into the house and Henry was explaining how he had built the house himself in the 1970's for him and his family. They had four children two of each and all had moved away to work, they were very proud of them but you could see they missed them. As they climbed the stairs onto the terrace Jasper could smell home cooking, it teased his senses and at the same time as the others, "mmmm something smells good Lillian" the guys echoed his words. "She can't help herself whenever we have visitors she goes overboard" Henry replied. Lillian nudged him in the ribs and blushed.

In front of them was a huge wooden door with a glass panel, it had a stags head in glass it was beautiful, there was a narrow glass panel next to it too. Henry opened the door and ushered the guys in, the main room opened up from floor to ceiling, there was a huge fire place where the fire was burning, the furniture was big to match the size of the room, 4 big leather sofas that looked like you could lose yourself in for days were in a square round the fire. There was a 70 inch TV screen above the hearth which had a picture of the house as a screen saver. At the far end of the room was a 12 person dining table which looked like it was handmade too, the chairs were pure luxury. Beyond that were patio doors which led out to the back of the terrace, you could just make out a stream beyond the trees, Jasper made a note to explore later. Lillian beckoned the boys to sit down and went to prepare drinks for them. She came back with a tray of tea and coffee pots and beautiful china mugs, Henry followed with a tray of cakes and biscuits all home made. They all sat down as Lillian played Mum. The boys went for the fresh cream Victoria sponge first, it was overflowing with fresh strawberries it was huge. She knew how to cook for sure. As they filled up with cake Henry told them how he had built the house from a drawing on a napkin that he had done for Lillian on a date when they first met. They had gone to the bar one night having dinner and he was trying to win her heart and thought by building her a huge house that would do the trick. Lillian interrupted and said.

"Little did he know he won my heart a lot quicker than that, but a girl has to play coy" with a naughty grin on her face. Henry bent across and kissed her head, they had been married for 45 years and still adored each other, it was so clear to see. Jasper thought to himself "that's what I want". He smiled at the couple and asked more questions about the build. He explained he was an engineer and the guys were all in Construction too. Tony was an Architect, Sam and John were Project Directors They all sat chatting for a while, Henry was enjoying the conversation it was a while since he had company like that. His boys were not interested in anything manual which was a great shame.

They walked around the lounge looking at the pictures of the house as it was being built and the family pictures when they were all together.

Lillian showed them to their rooms, they all had huge handmade beds with beautiful throws made by Lillian, they had fantastic views over the grounds and ensuite bathrooms, Henry even made the sinks. Jasper was in awe of this mans talents. He thought what an amazing man he must be as a father. He never knew his own he left when he was very young and his mum had bought him up.

He really warmed to Henry.

Lillian led them next into the kitchen to show them the meals she had prepared for them and a label sat on top of each one giving them instructions for the oven. The fridge was full of food too including beer and wine, they were truly being spoilt. The kitchen wasn't small either, it had workspaces right round the room and a huge island in the middle, and much like Jasper had.

They couldn't thank their hosts enough they were all overwhelmed with the place.
Henry said "we are only a call away, if you need anything at all just call us". Jasper spoke.
"Where are you staying?"
Henry replied, "I built another smaller place some years back for Lil and I, it seemed silly to keep this place warm just for the two of us, we have a small cottage at the back of the property, its only a mile away and we have an off road vehicle to get us back and forth. There are also four quads in the garage if you boys fancy some fun in the field, it's a bit muddy so keep Lil happy you will have to shower down in the barn after".
Lillian gave them all a knowing look and they laughed. The smiles on there faces said it all. They really had found a jewel of a place and it wouldn't be the last time they would be here.

Henry and Lillian left and gave the boys the keys.
"We wont bother you again unless you need anything, have fun, there is Karaoke on in town tonight it gets quite busy and a lot of fun, there is a taxi number on the wall Jerry will come and collect you when you want him too" Lillian said. They said their goodbyes and left, Jasper watched as they walked away, Henry held Lillian's hand as she went down the terrace stairs. It made his heart ache a little. He turned back into the room and the guys were deciding what to do next, they talked about going into town for a few beers, so decided on a bit of TV for a while before eating dinner and heading out. There was some football on and motor racing so the afternoon was sorted.

Jasper decided to have a wander and explore the property. He headed out the patio doors and down the back terrace stairs. He followed the pathway to the trees and out onto the bank of the stream, it was magical the sun was shining through the trees and it was making beautiful pictures on the water. The birds were singing obviously talking about the stranger that had wondered into their wood, he looked into the water and it was crystal clear, he could see fish swimming around happily, he felt completely at peace here. He walked along a short distance and found a huge rock which was half in the water and climbed on top of it and sat down, he took a deep breath and let it out slowly. This was just perfect. He could sit here forever. He heard a noise in the bushes and looked round to see a stag watching him, he was frightened to move in case he scared it, but he was mesmerised by it and desperate to get a picture. He slid is phone out of his pocket slowly and lent it on his leg, he wasn't sure what kind of picture he would get but tried anyway, he moved the phone back and forth hoping he could line the stag up. Something else moved and before he knew it the stag ran off. He quickly looked at his phone and most of the pictures were no good but a couple were great with a little tweaking. He stayed for a little while longer enjoying the peace and tranquillity of the place.

"This is something special. I could live her myself with the right girl" he said outloud.

He set off back to the house after an hour, feeling relaxed and happy. When he got in Sam was sleeping John and Tony were cheering on the football. Jasper went into the kitchen to warm the oven up to get the dinner in, if they were going out tonight, they needed to get on with it.

He found some wine on the shelf and opened it to let it breath. He enjoyed a good red wine from time to time and as he wouldn't be driving until tomorrow night he was going to have a few drinks tonight, it was a bottle of Brown Brothers, he had this before it was a mid range wine and it was a good all rounder for the lamb shanks they were having tonight he was the sensible one of the group, maybe he needed to let his hair down, its not something he had ever done though.

They all went and got ready to go out, each showering and getting changed, Tony and Jasper were finishing off the dinner as Sam and Tony came in, they knew the bar they were going to was very casual so all had jeans and shirts on, nothing special. They sat down to what can only be described as an incredible meal prepared lovingly by Lillian. It was lamb shanks in a red wine gravy with root vegetables and roast potatoes. The smell filled the house they were all hungry and ready to feast. They dished up and sat down together, they clinked their glasses and toasted their hosts and wished them good health. When they were done apart from clean bones nothing was left, they all sat back rubbing their stomachs. They loaded the dishwasher and Tony rang Jerry to organise the taxi to the bar.

Within twenty minutes Jerry was knocking on the door the boys booted up and walked out ready for a good night. Jerry had a 7 seater Mercedes, plenty of room, the guys nodded in approval.

Jerry talked to the guys about their cars and what they were doing out this way, they explained they did this regularly and they would be back for sure. Jerry gave them some more stories about Henry building the house and what he had gone through to do it, the boys were listening intently.
They arranged to be picked up just after midnight, according to Jerry that's when the bar would kick you out anyway.

They paid him for both journeys and gave him a good tip, he thanked them and drove off for home.

The boys walked into the bar it was already rocking, the music was loud the bar was full and it had a great vibe about it. They all looked at each other with big smiles and headed for the bar.
Chainsmokers was playing and Jasper nodded in approval he had been listening to them on the journey up. He was bobbing his head to "Closer" singing the chorus to himself. "So baby pull me closer in the back seat of your Rover that I know you can't afford". The boys patted him on the back laughing he wasn't as quiet as he thought he was. They grabbed their beers and moved to a table.

Karaoke was about to start, get a few more beers inside them and they would probably get up, Jasper wasn't so sure but he knew he needed to chill a bit. They were having a great night, some awful singers got up and crucified some great songs. The waitress had been back and forth to the table. She hadn't gone unnoticed by Tony. The other three just raised their eyes at each other, they could see what was going to happen. Beth the waitress was pretty, dressed in a short denim skirt and a check blouse which was open low enough to show her ample cleavage. You could just see a small love heart tattoo on her right breast. It sparked interest from Tony, he was determined to see more of it. She had mid brown hair which was pulled back in a high pony tail, a pretty face. Tony kept asking her to bend down to whisper in her ear so he could slide his finger down her neck into her blouse, Beth was taken in by him and enjoyed it.

Sam got up and decided it was time for them to have a go. Their go to favourite was "you've lost that loving feeling" by the Righteous Brothers.Corney yes, but it got everyone singing. He registered with the guy behind the desk and went back to the table. Before long they were called and all four of them got up, well and truly full of beer which had them giggling like school boys, Tony insisted Beth sit down so he could sing to her, she did as she was asked and sat at their table. They were ready as the music started, they were sharing two microphones, "You never close your eyes anymore when I kiss your lips" they sang, all the time Tony was staring at Beth, he knew he had her hook line and sinker. They continued "And there's no tenderness like before in your fingertips. You're trying hard not to show it, (baby). But baby, baby I know it" As the chorus started they threw their arms in the air to get the bar to join in which they did, Tony was pointing at Beth now, she was blushing and holding her hands against her face. Tony was loving it.

As the song ended the bar erupted clapping and cheering the guys, they took their bows and stepped off the stage, Beth threw her arms around Tony and he kissed her full on the lips. She came up from it a bit flustered looking round to see if her boss had noticed, he just walked away shaking his head. He had seen this before. It was nothing new.

The night came to a close Tony told the boys he was staying to talk to Beth after her shift and not to wait for him, he would find another cab to take him back. The three left without him and climbed into Jerry's car. They had a fantastic night and were relating the story of the night to Jerry who enjoyed the guy's happiness with them.

They headed into the house and went their separate ways to bed, they had had a great night, and tomorrow was another day. They were heading out on the quads to get muddy.

Sometime later Jasper woke up to shushing noises, he came out of his room rubbing his eyes to see what was going on and saw Tony and Beth disappear into his room, he raised his eyes and went back to bed. He climbed into bed layed on his right side puffed up his pillow and pulled the quilt up his body.

He was just dropping off when he heard a thump and a giggle. Then followed more giggles, he punched his pillow.
"For fucks sake. Another sleepless night".
He turned over pulling his pillow over his head to drown out the noises as Beth started to moan, Tony got vocal too, she was obviously riding him Jasper thought. Then the slapping started, he knew Tony well and knew what he would do next. Before long she would be on her knees. Tony had lived with him too long and he was used to hearing the same set from him, did girls really enjoy this, he was never any different he thought.
"Time for a drink".
He threw back the covers grabbed his jumper and walked out of his room into the kitchen, he put on the kettle and made a cup of tea, took it into the lounge and laid on the sofa. He took out his phone and started flicking through the news and other inconsequential websites. He hadn't been on Social media for some time after being hacked, but went onto his facebook and changed his picture, a friend had taken some great shots of him when he thought he would join a dating website, he picked one of him in his dinner jacket, he liked that one, it made him look confident. He removed all access to anything else along time ago and just left the picture, maybe one day he would come back on. He logged out drank his tea and laid flat on the sofa, popped in his ear buds and put on some blues, he would go back to bed when Tony and Beth went quiet.

Jasper screwed his eyes as the sun shone in through the front windows. He had fallen asleep on the sofa, there was a blanket across him which he wasn't sure where it came from but he recognised it from the back of the sofa the day before.

Sam and John got up and came into the kitchen, seeing Jasper on the sofa they knew what had happened.
"Is she still here?" John asked.
"Christ knows" Jasper replied, "I just woke up".
"Oh, the walk of shame then, this will be interesting" John replied.

Sam started pulling all the ingredients out for their breakfast, Lillian had left bacon, eggs, sausage, mushrooms, waffles and pancakes. They started cooking and John put the coffee pot on. Jasper went to shower, and grabbed a coffee on his way, Sam looked up, "one of those days then J?" Jasper nodded as he went to get sorted. He came out 15 minutes later breakfast was almost ready so he went back up the hallway and hammered on Tony's door.

"You two getting up, breakfast is ready" and walked away, not waiting for a response.

The three of them sat down at the table overlooking the back of the house, it was another beautiful day, the door to Tony's room opened and out walked him and Beth, she had her head down, her hair was a mess, She had Tony's jumper on and his sweats, she looked really embarrassed, they came over to the table and sat down. Tony poured some juice for them both and looked round the table.

"What?" He scowled.

Jasper just shook his head, as Beth looked up, he saw traces of love bites around her neck, and "another Tony trademark" he thought.

They went back to eating and Jasper was the first to speak.

"Would you like some sausage Beth?"

Sam and John burst into laughter, as did Beth and Tony, that broke the ice, they started to chat and went back to eating.

The guys felt sorry for Beth, she seemed to be a nice girl, it was a shame she got messed up with Tony. He didn't know how to love some one and this would be the last time she would see or hear from him.

They left the table as the rest of them cleared up and loaded the dishwasher, they were going out on the quads for a couple of hours and told Tony and Beth to meet them at the barn.

They went out to the barn it was huge. 4 brand new quads sat there gleaming, on hooks were crash helmets with disposable hoods inside to keep them clean and fresh, gloves and wet weather overalls were hanging up too. Henry had been out to make sure the ground was a little wet to give them a bit more fun. As they were ready and about to climb on Beth and John joined them and quickly got ready, Beth climbed onto the back of Tony as they all wheelspan out of the barn and into the field.

They rode straight into the middle where it was wet and started to do circles, they were whooping and laughing as the mud was spraying up all over them, it was exhausting staying on the quad the mud was sticky but they were having the time of their lives. They raced around the field like children. Their googles were the only clean thing as they had to keep wiping them off to see. They were all starting to tire, it had been a couple of hours, Jasper put his hand up and circled it. They all nodded and headed back to the barn. Henry had told them about the pressure washer and to leave the quads for him to clean, but the guys wouldn't do that, they rode round to the drain and parked up, there were two pressure washers, Tony grabbed one Jasper the other, they started to hose down the quads and then each other, they were covered from head to toe. Beth quickly cleaned her hands off and grabbed her phone to take some pictures of them together covered in mud. Before they turned the pressure washers on each other. By the time they had finished the quads and themselves were clean. They returned everything to the barn and headed back to the house. They could smell fresh bread and headed to the kitchen, there was a note on the side and 6 baguettes laid there still warm, Lillian had been in and baked some bread while they were gone she laid the table out with fresh meats, cheeses pickles and sauces. The guys were overwhelmed by the generosity of them both. They washed their hands grabbed the baguettes and headed to the table, it didn't seem 5 minutes since breakfast but they were ravenous after the fun and games in the mud. They all sat around the table chatting and laughing, they would need to leave soon to get back at a decent time, they were back to work in the morning and all of them were early risers. Sam and John wanted to spend some time with their wives before bedtime too.

They began packing up their bags and loading the cars, they had all agreed it had been a great weekend to just kick back and relax, they didn't miss the car show. The house had given them time to relax.

Tony called Jerry and asked him to collect Beth as the town was in the other direction and would take another hour or more out of his journey home.

As Jerry arrived he kissed Beth goodbye promising to keep in touch and see her next time he was this way. The guys bid her farewell and walked back into the house.

Henry and Lillian arrived shortly after, they had cleaned the house up put everything away but were sure Lillian would do it all again anyway.

They thanked their kind hosts for an amazing two days, hugged Lillian she was an amazing lady, and promised they would be back and they meant it, they had enjoyed their time away. Jasper wasn't the selfie type but suggested taking a picture of the six of them together, he had really warmed to them, they all stood together and smiled as he took the picture, he promised to send a copy to them both and he would.

Jasper made a mental note to send flowers too, he wanted to show Lillian how grateful they were for all the care she had shown, he would get the picture framed and send it later in the week by courier.

They said their final goodbyes got into their cars and made their way home.

By 8pm they were back, they stopped at the diner car park to say goodbye and arranged to see each other at the gym later in the week. Jasper suddenly remembered he had the new boy to show around and said as much to the guys.

"Don't know if I will make it, we have some bloke coming over from the UK who is joining the job for 2 years, he's a counsellor works for Jakes Construction. The boss wants me to show him around and help him find an apartment. Hes a biker by all accounts and is shipping his bike across too".

Sam replied "well he can't help being a biker but why don't you see if he wants to come to the gym, introduce him to a few people, at least you get to come aswell?"

"Good plan" Jasper replied, "I will test the waters with him and drop you a text and let you know"

They all agreed and went their separate ways. Jasper was exhausted when he got home, he put the car into the garage grabbed his bag and went into the house, he had set the lights to come on again and went straight to the kitchen to make a cup of tea. He was ready for bed, so grabbed his laptop off his desk and took it into the bedroom with him. He propped himself up in bed with his laptop on his lap. Had a scroll through what properties they had available for rent for this guy and made a note of which had garages for the bike, he understood how important it would be or the guy to get his bike locked away, he was the same with his cars.

He finished his tea, switched of his laptop, slid down in bed, switched off the light and moved onto his side, within minutes he was asleep.

Chapter 5

Leaving on a Jet Plane

Jane woke up feeling anxious it was D day she was leaving for the states she had a 14-hour flight ahead of her and a 5 hour time difference. The flight was leaving at 11am from Southampton, with an hour stop over in Dublin then onto Hartford arriving 16.35pm their time. She wasn't the best at flying and couldn't sleep in public so this would be interesting. She had loaded new books onto her kindle and packed her charger in her hand luggage. If nothing else she could read. She was being met by a town car whatever that was and taken to her hotel. She had looked at the place online it was very nice, it looked huge. It had its own kitchenette which made her happy, she planned to cook for herself, and she didn't like eating alone and wanted to eat normal food. She had stayed in enough hotels to get bored with menus.

The airport was 30 minutes away she needed to be there 3 hours before, Moses and G were picking her up at 6.30am they wanted to have breakfast with her before she left and went through passport control. It was 5am, she was always an early riser, she got up showered and made a cup of tea, then poured the last of the milk away. She went through her bag again to make sure she had everything in its right place. She wiped off the shower gel, toothbrush and toothpaste and packed it in her bag, with a fresh flannel, she wanted it on the plane to freshen up.
She grabbed the bag of rubbish it was just a few bits, stripped her bed and put it into the washer dryer. Gwen was coming by to take it home and press it before packing it away in her belongings with her quilt and pillows. If needed she would buy new when she arrived. The most important thing had arrived which was the trike. She'd had an email from the dealer letting her know they were checking it over and would see her Tuesday.

By 6am she was ready, she walked round the apartment once again which she had done a dozen times making sure nothing had slipped out of the back of the drawers and fallen to the bottom, checked under the bed and checked the wardrobe, she was satisfied it was all clean. Moses had cleaners coming in to give it the once over before he gave the keys back. Jane could have it back if she wanted but anything could happen in two years.

Moses and G arrived early as she expected, typical military men, they wouldn't leave anything to chance and they all knew what the M3 was like. They grabbed the last of her bags and loaded the car, Jane closed the door and handed the keys to Moses. "Ready half pint?" G said. "As I will ever be" she replied and jumped in the front seat, always the gent G, he let her sit up front.

It took 45 minutes to get to Southampton airport, Moses parked in the short-term parking and G and him grabbed her bags and walked her into the terminal. It was too early to check in, so they went in search of breakfast. They found a café and sat down, G and Moses ordered the full monty they could eat for England, Jane went for the small one, and the boys would finish what she left, she was used to Moses finishing her food he had done it long enough.

They finished up eating, Jane didn't eat much she was a bag of nerves. They headed towards check in. Jane now felt sick, this was it, no backing out now, she was leaving the safe haven of Moses and G and was terrified, they had been her support for 10 years she was hardly ever far from them.

She checked in and the boys carried her bag to the gate, they would go as far as they could with her, they were feeling her loss too, not being able to see her was worrying them both, Moses had spoken to a guy he had met at the dealer a few times, and gave him a bit of background on Jane and asked him to keep an eye on her, he promised he would, she would be one of them in no time.

You're my Best friend – Queen

They arrived at the gate and this was it. She had to go through now, Moses put her bag down, she looked up at him and shook her head, "can't do this Moses please just go" she said backing away as if she would turn and run, he grabbed her and held her tight, she felt the tightness in her throat as she was trying to force the tears back down, it was pointless, she held onto him like it would be the last time he would see her, the tears came, she couldn't hold on any longer, he held her tighter, and smoothed her back, he had held her many times and calmed her when things were bad.

"Come on half pint, this is good this time, we will be over soon I promise, you will be sick of the sight of us"

She was laughing through her tears, he lifted her chin and looked into her eyes, he wiped away her tears and the smudge of mascara.

"No panda moment kiddo come on" he said, she smiled at him, "you are a very beautiful lady, with a big heart and an incredible soul, you have helped so many people and will go on to help more, just think you are spreading the love. Just remember to save some for us back home in blighty, you mean the world to me you are one special lady, if you need us you shout and we will be on the next flight out, you are never alone, don't forget it".

Jane could feel the tears starting again, G appeared behind Moses "Yeah what he said Doc" Jane and Moses laughed. Moses bent and kissed her on the forehead and nose, G came in and they had a group hug, G kissed her nose too and held her head as he did. The call came over the tannoy that she had to go through now, one last hug and kiss and she picked up her bag and walked away.

"No looking back just keep on walking half pint" he knew he couldn't hold onto his tears any longer and if she looked back she would see it and he didn't want to upset her anymore. G wiped the tears away and looked at Moses.

"Damn hay fever", they both laughed and watched her go through until they couldn't see her anymore and turned and left. Moses and G both felt the loss and left with heavy hearts. The drive back to the dealer was a quiet one, they were both sat there with their own thoughts.

Jane walked onto the plane repeating to herself "I can do this. Just put on that mask, keep Moses and G close in my heart easy peasy". She smiled as she sat down in her seat after grabbing her kindle and charger before her bag was stowed away, she had a window seat so she could hide away from everyone, until she needed the toilet of course.

Jane didn't know much about planes, ask her about vehicles or bikes and that was easy, she knew it was a big plane and she had a seat between her and the next person, but this was only a short flight to Ireland hopefully nobody else would get on so she had room to stretch out.

It didn't feel like they were in the air long before landing in Dublin, it was only an hour stopover so they all got off and went into the airport, they had to go through American passport control at this point. They had chance to use the facilities and grab a cup of tea before they were getting back onto the plane. She turned her phone on quickly and sent a text to Moses to let him know where she was and tell him she loved him very much.

They got back on the plane Jane was back into the window seat and the same man sat next to her, he turned to her.
"Here give me your bag I will pop in the locker for you".
"Thank you, I always struggle being so short", they laughed and he put their bags away and sat down, leaving the space between them, he held out his hand.
"I'm Graham Frost"
"Jane Kirkpatrick" she replied shaking his hand, he had a nice firm grip she liked that in a hand shake.
They got themselves ready for the flight watched the in flight emergency procedure and got ready for take off, Graham looked round at Jane and could see she was nervous she was already squeezing the seat like she was on a fairground ride.
"Would you like to squeeze my hand Jane, I don't mind, it might stop you leaving nail holes in that arm rest?" Jane laughed as did Graham "really you don't mind? I am a wimp when I fly".
"Of course not it will be my pleasure", he held out his hand for her and she took it. He had huge hands, she noticed he was very tall at least 6ft they had the wider seats which Jane found funny being so short. When she looked down Grahams legs went under the seat in front where hers only just touched the ground. She looked round and smiled at Graham he had a lovely smile, and kind eyes, he was dark haired with flecks of grey around the temples, she guessed he must be mid 40s, he was dressed smart casual a nice pale blue shirt and jeans with nice brown brogues. He was American so must be going home, she wouldn't ask just yet, maybe later. They were finally in the

air and Jane released her tight grip on Graham's hand, she had squeezed quite tight when they first lifted which made him smile.

"Thank you, Graham, I really appreciate that"

"Anytime you feel the need you just got to ask".

The air hostess came around it was lunch time now, "I suppose this would help to know what time of day it is" Jane thought. A tray was placed in front of her, she had ordered a light snack, she wasn't a big eater and not being able to move about onboard food would just sit heavy for her. Graham had a fish parcel, "healthy" she thought raising her eyebrow. The drinks trolley came, Jane ordered a glass of Rose she thought it might be nice and light followed by a bottle of water. Graham had the same, they clinked glasses and said cheers and ate their meal, Graham spoke first, "would you mind if I asked what is taking you to America?"

"My job" Jane replied, "I'm a counsellor I work for a large International construction company, I am there for two years, it's a huge job we are working with another Company on a joint venture, so it should be quite interesting".

"How about you. Are you going home?"

"I'm a businessman, I travel all over the world, and I'm from Connecticut, I have been in London for a week on business, next week Hong Kong. I get to spend a few days with my daughters first and I can't wait". Jane could tell by the look on his face he adored his daughters. "Can I bore you with a few pictures of them" he asked

"I would be honoured" she said as he got his phone out. There was a picture of the three of them, Melissa was the eldest at 11 she was blonde and curly a real cutie. "She's head of the house" he said, she orders Abigail and I about". Abigail is 9 mousey coloured hair, both so cute, Melissa has that look on her face though you know she is the boss. "They must miss you being away" Jane asked.

"Yes they do, we skype most nights and I get them as often as I can when Im home. Their mum and I have a good relationship it's all about the girls".

"Oh sorry you are divorced, I am sorry I didn't realise" Jane replied.

"It's okay it's been 4 years now, we live close by, the girls have two homes, they have their own bedrooms at both houses and don't go without, they know their Mum and I love each other which is most important, we just fell out of love, we spend their Birthdays together with them, she has a new man in her life who the girls like, and we get on, as long as he treats all 3 of them well I don't have an issue, I still care a lot about her but more like a Sister".

Jane felt a huge lump in her throat, what a beautiful family he has and how lucky that they are still so close she thought, I would love that kind of relationship.

"You are very lucky to be so close still Graham" she said.

"Yes I am and I cherish that"

"Tell me about you Jane, who is the lucky man or women in your life, do you have children?"

Jane thought about it for a few seconds, and decided to give the same answer she always has done, she didn't need anyone's pity.

"I'm divorced, we should never have got married we weren't compatible really, both wanted different things from life so decided we were better off going our separate ways and maybe find that one person we were really destined to be with. No I don't have any children and I am glad we didn't, I want children with the man I am in love with" her heart crushed when she said that, she felt a sob rise in her throat, how could she lie but this man was a stranger, she knew nothing about him she couldn't be honest, she didn't know who else was listening. She locked her thoughts away as she was so used to doing over the years and continued chatting to Graham. He asked about her job and what she got out of it, "that conversation could take hours she warned him once I start talking about mental health and emotions I won't shut up", he laughed

"It's good to meet someone so passionate about it and I believe you will do a great job in the states. She thanked him, he said "I hope you don't think I am being forward but would it be possible to have a couple of your business cards, I promise I wont hound you to take you to dinner or anything I just think it would be helpful to keep some". She smiled.

"Yes of course, I have already changed the number to my new US mobile which will be switched on when I arrive". She went to her bag to find her card box, she always carried a few with her, she was delving in and out and couldn't find it, "that's odd" she said, "I was sure I put it in my handbag".

"Hang on let me get your carryon bag down maybe you switched it across".

"Sure, thank you" she replied.

Graham got up and pulled her bag down, he stood while she looked through it. She was getting frustrated, this was silly. She opened the side pocket and found a package, she frowned and pulled it out. Graham looked across at her.

"You ok Jane" he asked?

"Yeah I think so, I didn't put this in here".

She turned it over and saw a note attached, "not to be opened until you are in the air" and 3 kisses.

She beckoned Graham to sit while she opened it, her heart caught when she saw what it was inside was a silver business card holder and double silver compact mirror. Both were engraved. The business card holder said "Doc you got this, forever in my heart.M". She felt a huge lump in her throat and tears sprang to her eyes, Graham touched her arm.

"Jane are you ok, can I get you anything?" She shook her head and passed it across to him, she was speechless, he read the inscription and smiled.

"This person really loves you Jane"

She nodded and knew she should explain a little. She unwrapped the mirror, it was also engraved. "Half pint, believe what you see in these eyes as we believe in you. Your family", that was it, she sobbed quietly Graham swapped seats with her bag, moved the arm rest and took her in his arms, he couldn't leave her there to cry alone, he wasn't built like that, he knew there was more to her, he saw it in her eyes, Jane didn't pull away she allowed him to hold her which was very unusual, she let it all out crying softly into his chest, he gave her his hankie that he kept for these moments something he had learnt from his Dad, she sniffed and blew and wiped her eyes, sat up straight but stayed close to Graham.

He moved a stray hair away from her face and wiped a tear away, smiled and said,

"How you doing, do you want to talk about it?"

She nodded and sat up. He didn't say anything just sat and listened, he wasn't moving away in case she needed him again.

She took a deep breath and started.

"Moses is a very close friend, like a brother really, we met over 10 years ago when I went into the Harley dealer close to home with my ex husband, he wanted a Harley he thought he could get into the club that I was once part of, he didn't like me having friends.

I was introduced to Harley's years before after meeting a soldier who had one and we used to go all over on it, he treated me well but was only around for a year. I kept in touch with the people at the dealership and promised myself one day I would get my own bike.

Any way we went into the dealer my ex was a big head, thought he knew everything, well the guys brought him down a peg or two which he didn't like and he took it out on me. We brought a touring bike and started to attend events at the club, the guys could see he was a bully and always said if I needed anything they would be there for me, they only talked to him for me. Then Moses joined he had been at another dealer and came in frequently so we knew each other, he was head mechanic and always looked after our bike. I came in one day to the dealer with a bruised cheek my makeup hadn't done such a good job and he saw the way I cowered away from my husband, he took me to one side and told me he would deal with him if needed, I told him it was my fault which made him angry, not at me but the situation, he put his number in my phone and promised he would be there at a drop of a hat if needed.

One weekend we are at an event I dropped my drink which splashed up the bike, he yelled so loud and swung out to hit me I think he forgot where we were, I didn't move quick enough and the back hander hit me across the head and I crashed down to the floor hitting a stand. That made him angry he saw red and kicked me in the side and called me a stupid bitch, grabbed me by the hair dragged me off the floor and threw me at the bike told me we were going home as I had spoiled the day. It all happened so quickly and before I knew it Moses was across the field and landed a punch straight in his face, a couple of the other guys had heard the shouting and came to help, I was begging Moses not to do anymore and told him it was my fault, I knew I would pay for it when I got home. We left soon after, Moses was angry with himself for reacting instead of giving me space to deal with it. He rode home like a complete idiot which I had got used to over the years, when we got in the house he threw his crash helmet at me and stalked across the room, throwing punches at me, I was in the corner protecting myself sobbing and begging to be left alone, this had escalated the normal beatings, I always knew when it was going to happen, he had these eyes that would bore into me. He walked away and calmed down, I went to clean up and he came into the bedroom full of remorse, promised it would never happen again, and that it was my fault, which I always agreed with.

He slept on the sofa that night, but when I got up to use the bathroom I woke him up he was always angry if you woke him, I knew I was pregnant and didn't know what to do, he followed me back to the bedroom and punched me in the stomach then in the face for waking him, grabbed my hand and tried to get my ring off, said I wasn't worthy of wearing it. He broke my finger trying to get it off and just walked out of the room. The next morning I was in the shower, he came in and dragged me out, he bent me over the sink backwards and had his hand around my throat, I really thought I was going to die, he was swearing and accusing me of all kinds threw me to the floor kicked me once more and left. I crawled to the bedroom I could barely breathe or see out of my right eye. I knew I had to get out, he was too angry, he was going to kill me.

I rang Moses within seconds he answered the phone I could barely speak, he told me to get dressed and leave the door unlocked he was coming for me. When he arrived minutes later with G I had collapsed at the door, he scooped me up in his arms, told G to grab my bag and phone and we left.

He took me to his Doctor who helped the lads who got into fights at the MC, the Doctor checked me over and said I needed stitches in my head and cheek, but I need to see the Gyny he was concerned about the baby. My phone rang while I was there and I ignored it, he continued to call it and leave abusive messages telling me he was going to kill me. Moses said he would take care of me and after cleaning me up and G finding me some clothes they took me to the emergency gyny appointment the Doctor had made. When we arrived we were taken straight in, the Doctor did an ultrasound and said the baby was barely hanging on so they needed to keep me in overnight or for a few days. Moses gave his number to the nurse on the ward and promised to be back in the morning with more clothes and anything else I needed, he asked them not to use the details for my husband and to remove them from the system. What we hadn't bargained on was a friend had seen me go in and had seen my husband and told him, he turned up at the hospital late turned on his charm and the nurse let him see me for 5 minutes explaining the baby was at risk. He came into the room while I slept. I woke with his hands around my throat, he spat into my face and said "you think I want you a slut like you to carry my fucking kid I don't think so you little whore how do I know its not Moses who is the Father", and with that he punched me again over and over while covering my mouth so I couldn't be heard screaming, I started to bleed almost instantly he smiled and said "that's sorted that, hes welcome to you. Don't think you will be coming back to me, but I promise you Jane I will be watching you and I will finish you off when you least expect it. You can't hide from me and you don't get to make the decision to leave me". With that he left. Graham put his head in his hand, but didn't speak, just listened, he knew Jane needed to talk. She was doing well holding it together. She went on, once he left, I pressed the call button for the nurse and I was screaming in pain, she came rushing in to see the blood and called for the emergency team. I was screaming for Moses. They put me to sleep and when I came round Moses was sat by my bedside with a tear stained face, G sat opposite him looking ashen, the Doctors had told them I was very poorly had lost a lot of blood and the baby which they had to remove, it had been touch and go if we would both survive. I moved my hands to touch them both when I woke which made them jump, they both lept up shouting for the nurse, they both grabbed my hands and kept kissing them thanking god that I had woken up. The nurse and Doctor came in while the boys left the room but they stayed outside, Moses promised to never leave my side again. They checked me over and the Doctor explained how poorly I was that my body had been giving up with the beatings I had taken and that I had lost the baby, he told me I was 20 weeks and it was a girl. He wouldn't tell me how bad she was but said it was for the best. When the boys came in I just looked into their eyes, Moses nodded letting me know they knew already. He kept apologising for leaving me that night and vowed to never leave me again. We cried together that night the 3 of us, we bonded too, and vowed not to tell anyone else, it was between us, I didn't want the pity from others, we had to make sure I was safe though so they told the club I had been threatened and beaten which they knew but not to the extent or about the past which I had told the boys I needed to tell them so they knew what he was capable of.

Moses and G took shifts while I stayed in hospital never leaving me for a minute, Gwen and the girls came in to see me a week later and brought me some new clothes they knew I had been beaten but nothing about the baby was discussed.

When it was time for me to leave the hospital I was going to Moses's house until he knew I was ready to be alone and to know he was sure he could leave me. I had been given 6 weeks off work, my boss was aware of what had happened and a few of the guys who worked on site from the club so had my back if the chatter got to much.

I was still staying off my feet under orders from the Doctor and Moses ensured it stayed that way, for 6 weeks he did everything for me, when I went back to work the guys were there but Moses and G insisted on dropping me off and picking me up every day they were not taking any chances. I closed down my social media accounts I didn't need any further grief, they had both been hacked anyway and we knew who by, the messages he was sending to people pretending to be me said it all. Moses sorted me a new phone and I sent the other one back. We changed everything and then started divorce proceedings. They told me he couldn't be prosecuted for the death of my Daughter because I had been admitted due to a miscarriage and just because he visited my room there was still no proof it was him. I was told to expect abuse from him once the paperwork was received by him and they weren't wrong, but all through it Moses was by my side. My divorce came through and the same day I changed my name. It has been quiet for a few years but I never take chances. I know given the chance he will try it". Jane went on to say Moses had found her a new place to live after a year he could see she needed to spread her wings and grow. He also helped her buy her Trike, sort her finances and brought her new leathers and boots. She said "I felt very special but didn't realise how special until last week". She brought James up to date and sat back with a big sigh, he said "Jane I don't know what to say, I don't want to show you pity because I know you won't want that, I feel honoured that I am only one of three people that you have told. I know there is more you have not told me, I promise never to tell anyone, I would like to say if ever you need anyone while you are here then please call me", he handed her his business card, "I will do everything I can to help you" he lent forward and kissed the top of her head, he couldn't believe how in a few hours he had grown to care about this lady. He knew he would make sure they kept in touch and became friends though. "Do you want me to move back to me seat he asked her" she shook her head, "No I feel comfortable with you there if you don't mind". He packed her things into her bag and put it back in the locker.

"So where do you go from here Jane?" he asked, "what's next for you". "I will be looking for somewhere to live locally to the site but quiet enough to relax at weekends". She said.

"My Company have organised someone to meet me and show me around and they are going to take me to some of their apartments to find somewhere to live". She told him about the dealer and her bike being ready for her, he smiled.

"I cant wait to see that, it's a huge machine you are talking about, and you are a bit short, please forgive me I am not being rude", Jane laughed for the first time since she left the boys.

"No offence taken, I'm used to that".

They sat chatting a little more light hearted telling stories of growing up and asking silly questions they began to form a great friendship, Jane had no interest in him sexually it was like a switch had gone off 10 years ago it would take someone pretty special to turn that on. Graham wasn't even going to try anything he knew too much and was happy to be her friend and watch her grow and relax in the US, he promised himself to see her at least once a week and introduce her to the girls, and they would love her and her trike.

It was dinner time before they knew it and they sat and chatted with a few glasses of wine, a couple of hours later Jane began to yawn it had been a long few days, she could never sleep around strangers but she was dog tired, blankets were brought round by the stewards and Jane went to clean her teeth and have a wash before she settled down, she took her shoes off and put her fluffy socks on. Graham lifted her legs off the floor and told her to rest back against the window, she would be hidden from anyone then if she managed to sleep.

"But what if I dribble or snore", Graham laughed

"Then I will tell everyone", she hit him on the arm playfully, he said "only kidding cupcake , I can promise you there are more people around us that will do enough for all of us", he covered her legs under his blanket feeling very protective of her and laid his head against the seat, he kissed his finger and pressed it to her nose, she screwed her face up in fun and they laughed. He could see why Moses and G felt so much for her, she was unique and incredible lady that had been through so much and still came out smiling, he knew she had a lot of healing to do and hoped that there was a man out there that could love her as deeply as she deserved to be. Hell he would love to be that person but to be her friend would be good enough for him right now.

Jane reached out and stroked the side of his face.

"A penny for them?" he smiled.

"Oh nothing, just thinking of my girls, I cant wait to get home and hold them", it wasn't a lie as he always thought about them but he didn't want to scare Jane by letting her know how protective he felt towards her. She smiled and closed her eyes. They both slept soundly for 5 hours. They woke to the smell of breakfast, it was only a few hours before they landed in Hartford and the time difference would kick in. Graham changed his watch onto home time, Jane didn't need to she didn't wear a watch. But she changed her mobile. They both went to the bathroom to freshen up and change. Graham came out in jeans and t-shirt she could see he worked out and was impressed by his toned body, she might be dried up downstairs but she still appreciated a good body, he had a great western buckle on his jeans she was impressed. She commented on it.

He said "I enjoy country music and if you ever fancy a change from your normal rock I would be happy to take you to a concert sometime".

she replied. "I would love that".

They tucked into breakfast and they both agreed it wasn't so bad, or were they just that hungry it didn't matter how it tasted. They had pastries too and sat munching them when the tea and coffee came round again. Before long it was all moved away and they sat back chatting again. Jane showed Graham some pictures of the party she had and her pride and joy, James was even more impressed when he saw it.

"If you're nice to me" she said "I might take you for a spin", he grinned from ear to ear, he had never been on a bike let alone anything so beautiful as that and with a beautiful women like Jane.

"That would be amazing, I would love it and I promise not to pass any more short jokes" they laughed and she shared pictures of Moses and G and the gang, he was surprised looking at Moses and G, they were not what he had expected, but what had he, he wasn't sure really. It seemed only minutes later the announcement was made that the plane would be making its decent into Hartford, they packed everything away and buckled up. Graham gave Jane his hand, he knew she was going to be nervous now, he was sad that the flight had come to an end, he had never enjoyed a flight so much before and he knew he never would again unless it was with her.

Jane explained where she was staying and that a car was coming for her Graham said he would see her to the car and they arranged to meet in a few days before she started work, he would have the girls but would love to introduce them to her, she agreed and was looking forward to it.

They got off the plane and made their way through all the guards and passport control, grabbed their bags and Graham wheeled them out. As they came out into arrivals Jane scanned the room for her name. James saw it first.

"Over there cup cake" he said, Jane gave him a funny look.

"Very American" she thought "but cute, I will allow it" she smiled. he laughed he was testing her and she knew it. They walked over to the driver and he said he would take the bag, Graham insisted, he walked her to the car, when they arrived, he loaded the bags into the boot and looked at Jane.

"Right then sweet cheeks", she screwed her face up and shook her head. "Nah didn't think so either" he said they both laughed. He took her in his arms and held her tight, "you have my number, anything at all promise me you will call, I will let you know when I am out of town but my phone will always be on for you". She nodded feeling a little lost now.

"I promise" she replied, he kissed her on the head and she tiptoed up to him.

"Sorry Jane I promise this is the last time I say this, you are damn short lady", she hit him again and they both laughed, he bent down and she kissed him on the cheek holding him for a second and whispered in his ear.

"Thank you Graham, for everything, you are a wonderful man". And pulled away. He gulped as he pulled away from her, said he would see her in a few days but would text in the meantime to check up on her.

Chapter 6

Red Robin

Jane got in the car, waved to Graham and got comfortable, ready for the final part of her journey.

The driver explained it was quite a new place and it was like an apartment, she was looking forward to seeing it, it was now 5.30pm local time, she was 5 hours behind the UK so sent a text to the boys to let them know she had arrived, they replied instantly she told them she missed them, once she was unpacked and sorted she would skype them, Moses said they didn't care what time they just wanted to see her.

The driver Nick stopped outside the Castlewood Suites, it was an 8 storey building, it looked very new and nice, the driver offered to take her bags to the room, but she assured him there would be no need, he gave her his card and said.

"If you need a car at all give me a call"

He worked for her Company and would make sure she was looked after, she thanked him and walked into the main entrance, she took a deep breath before walking in, the guy at reception was very organised he had everything ready for her, he took her bags and gave her a quick tour of the ground floor, There was a small area with drinks fridges along one wall and on the other a coffee machine one with pods of every flavour you could try, there were also packets of crisps and sweets too. Further round was a huge pool and a gym which made her happy, she would make use of that, round another corner was a seating area where you could buy breakfast items including beans and cereals, it made her chuckle to see it, there was a laundry room to with washers and tumbles which was a great idea and a computer room.

She was on the 3rd floor, the door was opened for her by Mark. She made a note of his name from his badge, it was important to her to know all this. She was very surprised and pleased as she walked into her suite, there was a table and chairs to your left, on your right was a kitchenette all in dark wood and over by the window was a desk area and a sofa with a huge TV on the wall, to the left was a door way to the bathroom with a double walk in shower and a double bedroom with two huge beds, which she would need to jump onto to get into it made her chuckled she would remember to show the boys when she skyped later. She thanked Mark for his tour and said she would unpack and settle in, he had left milk bread butter and jelly in the fridge for her as requested. She had brought her own tea bags. She went to give him a tip and he refused.

"No ma'am no need all taken care of".

He walked out leaving the keys on the side. Jane jumped onto the bed and laid like a starfish letting out a big sigh. She did a quick imitation of a snow fairy and messed the bed up before getting off and unpacking, she had no plans to go anywhere tonight but wanted to check out the local market tomorrow once she picked the bike up. She had two days before she would be meeting Jasper her "buddy" for the next week or so. She hoped he was nice and not a grumpy old man, but time would tell.

She unpacked quickly made a huge cup of tea, dropped a text to Graham to let him know she was settled and where she was staying and wished him goodnight and that she looked forward to seeing him the day after tomorrow.

She then sat in front of her laptop and started to call Moses, within a few rings it was answered and a huge cheer went up as a sea of faces greeted her. She suddenly felt so homesick. She waved at everyone as questions were being shouted at her. Moses shouted at them to shut up and asked her how she was, she told him she was fine and asked if they would like a tour of the suite, as she walked round they were whooping and whistling in delight, she then sat back down and chatted answering lots of questions. Moses then told everyone to bugger off out he wanted Jane to himself for a few minutes.

"So half pint, how are you really, you look drained" he said.

She told him about Graham and how it all unravelled because of the beautiful gifts he and G had organised, he was surprised she opened up so much, but understood, she said she hadn't told him everything there was a lot she was ashamed of and nobody needed to know that. Only Moses knew.

Jane soon said goodnight to Moses and promised to check in tomorrow once she had picked up her red robin. She was shattered and needed some real sleep and that big bed looked pretty damn comfy. She closed her laptop put her phone on charge, got a quick shower and climbed literally into bed, she said out loud, "note to self, remember when you need a wee in the night to not fall out of bed, the bed is higher than you think". Then laughed at herself. As she laid on the pillow and pulled the covers up she let out a big loud sigh and said "Oh god that's soooooo nice mmmmmmm", anyone listening in would think she was having sex she thought and giggled again. Before long she was asleep.

The sun woke her up on the following morning it was Tuesday the day she got her Red Robin back, she was so excited, She slid out of bed and went to fill the kettle with fresh water, made a cup of tea and turned on Radio 2 from iplayer, she wasn't ready to miss UK radio yet. She went into the bathroom with her tea and turned on the shower, the roar of the water was immense, this would certainly wake you up she thought and stepped in, oh she was right, it was like a massage, it was heaven, she could stay here all day. She washed her hair and was shocked at how soft it felt and washed her body, she felt alive, she grabbed the towel which dwarfed her and went into the bedroom to dry off and dry her hair. She grabbed her leathers and her club t-shirt out of her case and her new boots, she asked the boys to rough them up a bit she couldn't go in with new leathers and boots looking all shinny.

Within the hour she had eaten cleaned her teeth and was ready to go. She was going to head out on the trike when she picked her up, she wanted to get used to the roads then she would stop at the market get some fresh fruit and food for dinner before she headed back. She called Nick before she showered to see if he was available to drop her at the dealership, he said he would be over in the hour which suited her perfectly. She went down to reception bid them good morning left, when she got outside Nick was there waiting for her. She climbed into the car feeling much brighter and confident than the day before, Nick noticed it too.
"Good Morning Jane you are looking much better today, did you sleep well?"
"I did thank you Nick, I know it will take a few days to catch up but I feel great".
He laughed and said "it will hit you later Im sure another good night's sleep will see you right".

He sat back feeling really excited about picking up the trike, Nick told her it would only take 15 minutes to get her there. When they arrived she was parked out the front, Jane was grinning from ear to ear, Nick looked in the mirror at her.

"Is that yours?" In total astonishment.

"Yes that's my Red Robin" she replied,

"Well, well, that's a beauty Jane".

"Thank you" she replied, Jane went to pay him but he refused.

"All paid for Jane, Im here whenever you need me but by the looks of that you might not want to". She laughed and assured him she would be needing him for work from time to time.

"Okay great, well give me a call when you need me, take care and ride safe" she thanked him and climbed out walking up to her trike with a huge smile. She looked her over grinning even more then walked toward the door.

She walked in up to the counter to see this huge guy looking down at her, this big voice boomed out.

"You must be Doc", he said putting out his shovel hand to her. "Yes I am" she said laughing scared to put her tiny hand in his in case it got crushed, he shook her hand gently and said

"Hi Im shadow, yes you can laugh and yes it's because I'm black and tall", she laughed with him.

"I wasn't going to laugh I promise".

"Moses said you were short Doc but I didn't expect you to be that short" he said laughing, his laugh was deep and it really could crack a few windows.

"Well I could say the same to you shadow", she replied, he laughed again.

"Point taken Doc". He bent down to get closer to her, it was like watching a giant with a child, "how tall are you Doc" he asked, "I will tell if you will".

"I'm 4ft 11 Shadow, and you?" he had a fit of the giggles.

"Im 6ft 8 Doc".

"Well from now on you will be known as HT to me then Shadow", he frowned, "High Tower" she said and laughed, he slapped his leg "Police Academy!!" they both laughed.

"Right back to business, you saw your beauty out there I see, well she is ready to go we checked her over for you, all of your things are in the side panels, your lid is in the box on the back, We have a gathering Wednesday and Saturdays but any day or night there is always someone about, come along one night and let me introduce you to some of the girls and boys, a few of them know Moses and G it would be good for you to meet them. But for now we will let you get reacquainted and find your feet. We are here whenever you need us, here is my number. Moses has given us yours already. Day or night you need anything Doc just call".

"Thank you High Tower", he got on his knees.

"Now can I have one of those special hugs Moses tells me will heal any bad day?" She laughed and walked into his open arms, "bring in that sugar" he said as he hugged her gently, she had never hugged anyone so big he was like a giant teddy bear. He let her go, "I will be sure to tell Moses hes right", she swatted him across the chest, he grabbed his muscle "ouch".

Jane laughed "oh please High tower that was nothing you big baby".

"Go women please before you do any more damage", she laughed waved and walked out feeling really relaxed.

She unlocked the top box and pulled her helmet out, she clipped it on and climbed onto Red Robin, put on Queens greatest hits and pulled out of the dealer remembering to stay on the other side of the road. Now she was grinning from ear to ear.

She was going for a long ride out and would use the sat nav to find her way back, it was still early and she knew if she followed the main road out she would pass the new site.

She opened up the engine sat back and relaxed. I want to break free playing loudy to all who cared to listen.

She was coming up to the new site and waiting at a set of traffic lights they were four way road works, she could see the long delays already, so knew she would be sat her for a good 5 minutes. Her hair was hanging below her crash helmet it was waist length now, she didn't always tuck it up. She was enjoying the breeze through it. A Range Rover pulled along side her, she looked round to see the guy looking at her, he was dark haired, had a short beard kind looking brown eyes a lovely not too muscly neck, with a cute v at his throat, he wore an open shirt with a dark jacket hanging behind his seat, she could see his legs, he was wearing jeans. Both hands on the steering wheel they were big with the veins running through them that protruded, "very manly" she thought. He looked round at her and smiled she suddenly felt butterflies in her chest, his smile lit up his face. He looked her up and down slowly, looked over the bike then back at her. She smiled back their eyes locking. Suddenly she heard a horn behind her, oops the lights had turned to green, they both looked at each other again laughed and pulled away. "Wow where did that feeling come from, he was a bit of alright. Maybe I'm not a dried up old hag and these American men could help me", she laughed again and kept going.

Chapter 7

It's in the eyes

Jasper pulled into the office 10 minutes later smiling like a Cheshire cat, "wow I might of only seen those eyes and body but that was enough, she was stunning and don't get me started on that hair!" He said aloud to himself. His tummy flipped thinking about her, he looked down to his stomach "don't you start, we will probably never see her again. Anyway shes a biker".

He walked into the office, "Morning Harry" he called across to the Security guard, "Morning Mr Mitchell, how was your weekend away?"
"Great thank you" he replied, "and yours?"
"Great Sir thank you, Mrs Black sends her best".
"Thank you Harry that's very kind" he walked into his office, still smiling as he passed Joan the Office Manager. "Morning Joan", "Morning Jasper, good weekend?"
"Very nice thank you, how about you?"
"Great, too, thank you".
 "Good, good", he said smiling and walked on.
"Hmm" he looks happy that smile we haven't seen in a long time" she thought. "I will keep an eye on him I think". Joan liked to think she was Miss Marples but she was right Jasper was smiling seeing this lady this morning had brightened his day.

The day flew by for Jasper he was going to finish on time and go to the market he was cooking again tonight. He left the office wishing good night to the cleaner and Harry on his way out. He reached the market and parked up, the air was full of amazing smells, he wasn't sure what he wanted tonight he would see what took his fancy when he walked through the market.

He got close to the entrance and saw the trike again, his stomach flipped, "she's here" he thought, he forgot what he was there for and started scanning the isles for her, all he knew was she was in black leather had blonde hair and those eyes, it was a bright night and the sun was shining right into the market he had to put his sunglasses on, he walked faster round the isles up and down desperate to see her again, what would he do if he did, just stand and stare at her? He felt like a school kid. "Oh god" he said again, he looked everywhere and couldn't see her, "oh well" he said to himself "I will just get some food and head home". He turned the corner and saw a women in a t-shirt and leathers, "nice bum" he thought but she had her hair up, it didn't look long either, she had sun glasses on so he couldn't tell if it was her or not, there were a few bikes outside too, he let out a big sigh and went to order his ingredients. He picked up hiss normal noodles and headed for the door, he saw the Trike reverse out and head off. He noticed her hair wasn't hanging down her back, "damn it" he shouted "it was her", he was cursing himself when he saw her turn at the top of the road heading out of town, he smiled thinking she must be local. He kept his fingers crossed he would see her again. But hating himself for letting her pass him by.

He drove home and as per usual he went in cooked his meal and went to do some work. By midnight he'd had enough and turned off the light ready to sleep, but all he could see was this woman on the trike, he couldn't get her eyes and hair out of his head. He hadn't felt like this in a long time and over someone's eyes and hair, what was that all about. He drifted off hoping to dream about her.

Chapter 8

New friends

Jane woke the next day feeling fresh she'd had an amazing time on the bike yesterday and she couldn't get that gorgeous man out of her head, even the fact he had a beard, she thought he was handsome which was odd too, she never like beards always thought they were dirty things harbouring bugs, but then when you have spent 10 years around Moses and his beard what else would you think. She laughed to herself got up put the kettle on and jumped in the shower, she was seeing Graham and his girls today, it was her last day before going to the new site tomorrow, she was looking forward to getting stuck in and meeting new people, and finding somewhere to live, her boxes would be arriving in a week and she wanted to be ready with keys when they did or she would be paying for storage too.

Graham called and arranged to pick Jane up to save her taking the bike, she thought that was sweet of him and wanted to show off her suite to him and the girls, she had a couple of hours to kill so decided to watch a bit of TV, her favourite programme Outlander was on so she decided to indulge herself, it was a drama about a women who goes through the stones to the time of Culloden battle, she met a handsome Scot after being picked up by the English and almost being raped by a man who looked like her husband who later she found out was one of his ancestors.

By 12 oclock Jane had seen two episodes and was feeling relaxed, she got her bag ready made sure none of her knickers were left out anywhere, she didn't want to embarrass herself or Graham.

Within a few minutes he arrived, she was really excited to see him and meet his girls the apples of his eyes, he knocked on the door and when she opened it she was saw these two beautiful girls, he was right they were gorgeous and would be heartbreakers one day she was sure of that, she beckoned them in and Graham didn't hesitate he came straight at her for a hug and picked her up off the floor which made the girls giggle. He then said "Jane I would like to

introduce you to the two ladies in my life, Melissa and Abigail", the girls smiled and Graham said "girls this is my good friend Jane".
"Hello Jane they said in unison".
"Hello girls". "Can I get you something to drink?" they nodded.
"Yes please".
"Well I don't have much to offer but we could go down to the reception and find you something out of the fridges, how does that sound, is that okay with you Dad?" Graham smiled "yes of course lets go", they got into the lift and went down to the reception area and the girls faces lit up when they saw the choice they had, they both picked a Ribena in a carton and a packet of crisps, Graham said "well I hope you will eat your lunch girls as well", they nodded grinning at him.

Jane showed them the gym and swimming pool and then took them back upstairs, she gave them the tour of the apartment, the girls loved it and laughed at how high the bed was especially when she showed them how hard it was to get on to, they both jumped on with her and were bouncing around so Jane decided to join it, "well if you cant be a child once it a while then life isn't worth living" she said to Graham as he stood laughing in the doorway he took some pictures it was good to see Jane laughing.

The girls came down and Jane remade the bed, they were heading off to the park and then to the girls favourite burger bar.
One the way out Melissa asked if she could see Jane's Trike, she asked her why it had three wheels, so Jane explained she couldn't touch the ground so needed 3 wheels to stay upright the girls giggled. They were eager to get on and have a sit down so Graham lifted them on he didn't want them scratching it, he took more pictures. He never could get enough of the girls. He then took a selfie of them all stood at the bike. They headed off to the park it was a decent size with swings and roundabouts giant slides and rope swings, the girls ran off squealing give Graham and Jane a few minutes to catch up while watching the girls have fun. Graham asked how Jane was feeling about starting work, she told him she was really looking forward to getting her teeth into the job and finding out more about the guys she was working with. She was a bit anxious about the boss of Bates he was quite an ignorant man by all accounts and didn't believe in stress that was for pansies so there first meeting

would be interesting. Graham was sure Jane would set him straight in no time.

They joined the girls at the swings and pushed them to see how high they could go, of course they didn't go too high, Jane was always nervous about things like that, not having any children of her own she never wanted to take things to far she was afraid of hurting someone, she had 12 Godchildren all of which she adored and they adored her. She loved having time with them taking them out on treat days, but didn't get the chance much these days, she would miss them while she was away. Graham looked over "Penny for them cupcake?" she laughed she had said the same thing to him on the plane, "Nothing, just thinking about my Godchildren back home, they will all be grown up by the time I get home", He smiled.
"I feel the same about these two, being away from them all week they change so much" Jane made a mental note to skype them all regularly even if it was to watch them on their computer games.

They were in the car driving back to Jane's suite, Graham said "Jane I will be away for a few days next week would you like to get together at the weekend if you're free?"
"That would be lovely, thank you, I would like that".
"Great but if you need anything at all please call me, I can come home". She smiled.
"That's very sweet of you Graham I am sure I will be okay, but we can still chat while you are away can't we?" She asked.
"Yes of course".
"Great", she enjoyed talking to Graham he was relaxed and a great listener and it was nice to have a friend here.

It was time for the girls to go to bed soon so Graham said his goodbyes as they all got out of the car, the girls hugged Jane and said they couldn't wait to see her again at the weekend, she told them to bring their costumes just in case she was still here so they could go for a swim and use the jacuzzi, they went home very excited. Graham hugged Jane and left as she went up to her suite for an early night, she had a big day tomorrow and wanted to be fresh. She showered, climbed into bed and fell to sleep quite quickly.

Chapter 9

Can't Take My Eyes off You

Jasper was up early and headed off to the office before he went across to the site to meet the new guy. He had an hour of work to get done before he left. He finished what he needed to do and left the office, all being well the guy would be on time and he could be back in the office mid afternoon, he had an apartment block to show him which had a garage for his bike as requested and it was close to the amenities but quiet. He could get that viewing done quickly once they had looked round site and he showed him to his office. He didn't want to hang around the quicker he could get that done the better.

Jasper was in the car going back to the site and as he sat at the lights he got caught at the other day his thoughts went back to the day before when he saw the women on the trike, he thought about where she could be from and if he would get to see her again, the lights changed and he turned left into the site car park, it wasn't much at the moment just a huge expanse of waste land with hoarding and flags of both companies, Security had been set up already and a turnstile system was in place, temporary cabins were on site whilst they waiting for their more temporary structure to be built. Jack was the Security guard a young guy, very smart and he knew his job well, he had worked with them before.
As he was sorting himself out getting his things together when he heard a rumble come up behind him, he looked up to see the trike, his heart stopped, it pulled up in front of Jacks cabin, he couldn't believe his eyes, he looked harder to make sure it was and oh it was! His stomach did a flip.
"What is she doing here?". His heart started to pound as she got off. She was clad in leather, black tight leather, her trousers had leather lace ties down the legs and her jacket had fringe across the back, her hair was up but he could see traces of it, his mouth went dry as he watched her, she took her helmet off and her hair fell from underneath it. She ran her fingers through it and fluffed it up

"Oh my god look at that hair, oh to have that wrapped around my hand from behind her" he said, his cock was doing a happy dance in his jeans, he had to move in his seat to get comfortable, he looked down at his growing cock.

"You haven't even seen her face, yet and you picked a great time to wake up. Thanks!" he looked back up willing her to turn round, she walked round to the back of the trike and put her crash helmet into the top box, bent over to the back box, her leathers got tighter around her backside and Jasper couldn't take anymore, his cock was wide awake and eager, "Jesus Christ" he yelled, "oh fuck what I would give to have my hands on those hips right now". He didn't know what to do, get out or stay in the car, downside he had a very hard cock and would look really stupid tenting his jeans walking across the car park, he needed to calm down. He was watching her intently, she stood up, she had a pair of site boots in her hand, now he was confused. He needed to get out and talk to her, she started to walk towards the cabin as Jack came out admiring her and the trike, he felt his blood boil, "eyes off Jack shes mine" he said, then laughed at himself "pull yourself together Jasper you haven't even spoken to her you might not even like her" he got out of the car his cock back under control and started walking towards the cabin he could hear Jack talking to her, he was straining to hear her voice, "she sounds English? This is odd" he said. He got closer and heard her laugh, she had a dirty sexy laugh his cock was doing another happy dance, he looked down, "for god sake, don't make me look a complete jerk" as he got closer he could smell her perfume in the air, she smelt amazing, not too much of it either, he hair was being lifted by the wind and the sun was shining on it, it was beautiful. He stood behind her, not too close as to be pervy but close enough, to hear her, "oh my, she's English. She must be in the wrong place, surely someone would have mentioned her to him?" He thought. Jack said "anyway how can I help you".

"My name is Jane Kirkpatrick I am here to see Jasper Mitchell". He thought his legs were going to give way, there definitely was a mistake he was expecting a man, his name was Jay, oh hang on and started to laugh. Jack looked up.

"Oh just the man Jasper this is Jane Kirkpatrick", she turned round to look at him and his stomach lurched, Oh my god she was stunning, those big blue eyes were looking up at him and she had the most amazing smile. His cock was screaming at him, look at those lips!

They just stood and looked at each other, she realised who he was from the other day and they just smiled. Jack cleared his throat, he could see what was going on here.

"Can we sort these passes out then Jasper" he said, Jasper stumbled he couldn't get his words out, he didn't want to take his eyes off her, he had not felt like this in a very long time, in fact he was a young man the last time he did. He just laughed and so did Jane, her cheeks flushed a light pink, that made matters worse in the trousers department, she was adorable and so short, he liked short women. He held out his hand.

"Sorry umm, Im umm", laughing stupidly like a boy, "Jasper, Jasper Mitchell", she took his hand and introduced herself.

"Jane Kirkpatrick. I understand I will be your shackles for the next few days, I am sorry to be putting you out".

"Oh' don't be silly it's my pleasure, you take all the time you need, and my time is yours". Jane blushed again.

"Oh, I like that" he thought, as his cock started to dance again "come to Daddy. You can shackle yourself to me anytime you like he thought".

Jack gave them their passes and Jasper showed Jane through the turnstile and out onto the barren site. There were 30 cabins stacked in twos, the welfare area was in a C shape and had wooden picnic tables outside. The offices were inter-connected and the doors had been removed except for a few which were stand alone. Jane's was one of those, Jasper showed Jane inside and gave her the key.

"Yours I believe Jane, and nobody else will use it. Let me know what you want in there and I will ensure it is done" they walked inside, to the left was a standard desk and chair, in front of it were two chairs, the rest of the cabin was empty, she needed to make it more homely where people could come and relax and not be feeling they were talking to the boss. She looked around thoughtfully.

"I could do with a comfy chair or two, preferably leather so it can be cleaned off if they come in dirty. And a little table for tissues". Jasper nodded, "consider it done, right then fancy a walk out to have a look at the layout" he said.

"Yes, I would love to, but is there somewhere I can change my leathers, I have my jeans with me?". She asked.

"Yes of course, I will show you the ladies PPE room and your locker". They walked out and she locked her office putting the key in her bag for safe keeping. They walked along the cabins and Jasper opened the door and stepped in, the cabin was a bit high Jane felt she had to almost jump to get in, Jasper smiled, "oh she is cute", he thought to himself, "I think I will get another step put in there for you we don't want you falling out on a wet day".

"That's kind thank you, one of the downsides to being so short" she replied.

He smiled "I don't see that as a downside at all", and flashed her one of his gorgeous smiles that could melt a women's knickers off at 50 paces. "I will leave you for a few minutes and go and grab my boots, I will give you a knock, shout if you are not ready".

"Great thank you", he left and Jane started to get changed, she put her leathers in her bag and slipped her jeans on, she was just putting her boots on and tying them up with her foot up on the bench when Jasper knocked. "you ready Jane?".

"Yes" she shouted as he opened the door being greeted by her lovely backside in jeans, "does this day get any better he thought?", his cock cheering again, her t-shirt had risen at the back and he could see something just below her waistband of her jeans, she stretched a bit further and he saw it, a red rose tattoo. He had never liked tattoos on women before but this was sexy as hell, "I just want to touch it" he thought, "with my lips"

"Fuck she is so sexy", knowing if he keeps staring he will get caught. He was imagining her naked bent over the bench pounding into her holding her hips. His cock was getting harder by the minute.

"Fuck i need to calm down" he said to himself.

"Jasper" Jane said again.

"Oh umm yeah, sorry yes".

"Are you ok? I'm ready if you are".

"Oh I'm ready Jane, he says quietly". "Great yeah sorry just thinking about something I need to prepare for" with a little grin on his face. "Jasper handed Jane glasses gloves and hard hat as she's putting on her Hi Viz waistcoat and they head out of the cabin. As they wander round Jasper is telling Jane about the build he can't say anything else his mind is shot to bits on thoughts of her. She is asking so many questions.

"You really are interested aren't you? he said".

"Yes of course I wouldn't be here if I wasn't". She replied, "it's not just about the guys you know I do love working in Construction and finding out as much as I can about the build, I'm here to help out too.

Happy to be a PA or admin person if it helps". He has to stop himself PA, "Jesus I wouldn't get any work done if you were my PA". He thinks

"Shall we head back in then and I will take you to see some apartments? I know you are eager to move so no time like the present".
"If you have the time Jasper, I would really appreciate it".
"Of course like I said earlier my time is yours, lets get sorted lock up and head off, do you want to drop your trike off at your apartment and we can go in my car?", he asks knowing he can then spend more time with her.
"Okay sure I can then leave my jeans on. This is really kind of you", she says.
"My pleasure Jane, and hopefully yours soon he thinks", the little devil in his head has just woke up.

They head out giving their passes back to Jack and tell him they will be back to start tomorrow.
Jasper gets into his car and is transfixed watching Jane get her leather on and crash helmet.
"Suddenly bikes just became sexy" he says out loud. Jane was leading so Jasper pulls in behind her loving what he sees. Her apartment isn't to far away and soon they are there Jane parks up the trike locks up her helmet, grabs her bag and struggles to jump into Jaspers car.
"Nice apartment block", he says.
"Its ok, its not somewhere I would stay long term its too short term type if you get what I mean"
"Yeah I understand" he says. "Well I have a really nice place to show you which is in the West of Hartford, it's not a huge block but its one of my favourites". He was going to take her to one of the mid range but she was better than that, after all she was supposed to be a man then.

They head out and relaxed into their seats. Jasper looks over at her as she looks out of the window and thinks "I could get used to this". He felt comfortable with her, yes she was sexy as hell but he found her good company, he liked that she was interested in what he did and enjoyed working in construction his ex wife hated it and never wanted to know anything about it, it was just rough dirty men as far as she was concerned.

Jasper pulled up outside the apartments waiting for Jane's first impression it was a three-storey building, they looked like tall houses quite a few in a row. They had light cladding at the top and brick at the bottom, there were lot's of windows flooding them with light, Jane looked up.
"Oh Jasper this is lovely", sounding excited.
"Do you want to go in then?" he asked
"Oh yes please, can we?" "it has a nice feeling".
"Come on then let me show you around". She jumped out of the car excitedly.

The apartment was in the middle of the row, it was a quiet building no children so no noisy corridors. They walked in the door and the lounge kitchen diner opened up in front of them, it was tones of cream, yellow and brown, the windows from every angle flooded it with light, it was furnished to a high standard. In one corner was a huge sofa that wrapped around the corner, Jasper could imagine them both sitting on it. To the right was the kitchen with a huge island in the middle and a great cooker with plenty of storage, beyond that in the corner was a dining area, with a generous table and chairs, it was a stunning place. As Jasper turned around he walked through a door way to the left of the kitchen which took them to the bedrooms there were two, both had en suite shower rooms and were very generous with storage, he looked at Jane's face she was grinning from ear to ear. He showed her the cupboard where the washer and dryer were and headed back into the lounge.
"If this hasn't made your mind up come with me" he said, he walked over to the dining area and pulled the door open, they walked out onto the balcony and Jane caught her breath, there was a a huge swimming pool with a beautiful gazebo area and a BBQ with an outside kitchen, Jane spun round and looked at Jasper he could see she was happy.
"Jasper this is beautiful, but", as she said it he put his finger over her lips and smiled.
"Look to your left", she did as he said and saw a huge garage, which would be all hers for the trike. She looked back around.

"Jasper I don't know what to say, its stunning are you sure its available and I can have it?"

He smiled at her. "it's yours if you want it, you can move as soon as you like". Jane jumped up and down and threw her arms around Jasper, he took her in his arms as she squealed with delight and laughed, she was intoxicating he couldn't help smiling and laughing with her. Having her in his arms felt good, too good, it had been a long time and suddenly his body missed the touch of another.

Jasper was thrilled Jane was so happy. "Come on let's get back to my office and get the paperwork done then we can sort out moving you in. Where are your things? Do you have much". He asked.

"Yes, I have some things in storage that will need moving and just my bag from the apartment".

"Okay we can sort that for you". He said

"Are you sure Jasper I seem to be putting you to a lot of trouble". She asked.

"Honestly Jane its no trouble at all". She smiled and they walked back into the apartment. She ran over to the sofa and sat down looking around her. Rubbing her hands across the fabric.

"I think i can be happy here" as she patted the seat next to her.

"Come and try it Jasper".

He smiled "anything to please you" he thought he loved her smile already and that little excited girl that kept coming out. He sat next her and she laid back.

"What do you think Jasper?" she said.

"It's nice". He replied.

"Well you can't tell sitting all stiff and upright like that" she laughed. So Jasper laid back like Jane had and laughed.

"Do you always get your own way Jane?" he asked.

"Yes, most of the time" she replied and they both laughed.

"Right then let's go" she said standing. Jasper sat there looking at her. "Yes boss" he smiled.

"Cheeky" she replied laughing. They headed out and back to the car Jasper opened the door for Jane.

"Would her ladyship like a leg up?". He felt relaxed with her now and wanted to make her laugh. "Oh, didn't take you long to start with the short jokes did it" she replied.

Jasper just smiled "just being a gentleman". She took his arm and he helped her in. He could have turned the engine on and lowered the front of the car but then he wouldn't have had fun with her and felt her. They chatted on the journey back to Jaspers office. When they arrived he came around and opened the door for her and gave her his hand to slide out. He was enjoying this. They walked into the building and Jasper signed her in. Harry was on duty, Jasper introduced them. Jane shook his hand and said how nice it was to meet him. Harry was grinning he could see that smile on Jaspers face. He also noticed he didn't lower the front of the car to help Jane get out. He knew why which pleased him. He couldn't wait to tell Mrs Black when he got home. They both thought a lot of Jasper, had seen him hit rock bottom. If Jane being around could change that then good for him. They walked into the office together and all heads turned to look at them both. Jane followed Jasper into his office. He pulled a chair round to his side of the desk.

"Please take a seat. Can I get you a drink?. Tea, coffee, water?"

"Oh, tea would be nice thank you" she said.

"Oh, I expected you to say coffee"

"No I drink tea". Coffee only when I'm shattered".

"You're kidding right?"

"No, why would I be?" she asked.

"I'm the same" he said.

"Oh really?"

"Tea coming up" he said walking out of the office with a huge smile on his face. He returned with two cups of tea and set them down." I forgot to ask about sugar, so just in case I brought some". "No thank you, Im sweet enough" She smiled. Jasper printed off all the paperwork and they sat going through it when his boss knocked on the door.

"Ahh, Jasper".

"Callum", he replied grumpily.

"I thought you were meeting that guy today the touchy-feely counsellor bloke. I take it he didn't turn up. Did he get all emotional leaving the UK and decided to stay?", Jasper was trying to jump in without success and spoke over him.

"Let me introduce you to Jane Kirkpatrick" as Jane stood putting her hand out and said "the emotional one". Jasper and Jane were holding in a laugh as he squirmed and left the office. Once he was gone, they both burst into laughter.

"I'm sorry you had to hear that" he said.

"Oh, don't worry about me I have thick skin, I have heard worse believe me"

They finished with the paperwork,
"Right today is Monday how does Saturday sound for moving in?"
Jane looked at him, "Really are you sure?".
Yes of course".
"Oh, Okay great. I can see if Graham my friend can help" she said. Jasper felt a knot in his stomach. He made a call to the cleaners asking them to go in and give it a thorough clean the next day. It was immaculate already, but he wanted to make sure it was perfect for her. Then he rang their removal company and arranged to have her boxes collected from the storage company and delivered to the new place Whilst talking to them he said "hang on Joe, Jane what time shall I meet you at your place so I can take your bags and Joe can collect your storage boxes".
Jane looked shocked "oh umm, really?".
"Yes of course".
"Umm whatever you think", she replied.
"Well I will help all day. 8am okay?".
"Yes perfect". He gave instructions to Joe to collect the boxes and said he would meet him at the new place at 9am where he would help bring them in. Jane could then follow on with her trike. Graham wouldn't be needed either, he didn't need outside interference. He didn't know who this guy was but he didn't like him already.

Jasper was happy with all of the arrangements, he was looking forward to spending the day with her unpacking on Saturday, he wanted to get to know all about her and find out what made her tick, why she was single and if she would go out to dinner with him. He was desperate to ask her but didn't know what to say, he was tongue tied and felt like a teenager.

Jasper finished the paperwork with Jane.
"Would you like to see the artists impressions of the build?"
"That would be great" she said. Jasper opened the file and turned his screen a little, but not too much he wanted Jane to move closer. He loved the smell of her. She moved her chair closer and her hand touched his. He felt the electricity go through his body and straight to his groin. He glanced down at his cock and said to himself. "Don't

even bloody think about it. Not now" he had to keep focused. The women was doing things to him and it was driving him crazy.

They went through the pictures of the build and the description of what was being built. They were going to be here more than two years but it was being done in zones. The first of which Jane was part of. Jasper looked at the clock.

"Jane, I'm so sorry we seem to have skipped lunch it's just gone 3pm". That's ok I don't always bother anyway she replied".

"If you're sure" he asked.

"Yes of course" she replied engrossed in the pictures. Jasper looked at her, his palms feeling sweaty and feeling like an idiot,

"Ummmm. If you're not busy tonight, as we haven't had lunch and you have no plans, and ummm you fancy getting out". He stumbled.

"Yes Jasper I would love to have dinner with you" she replied smiling. Jasper laughed and Jane joined in.

"Sorry i dont do this and wasn't sure, but it's not a date" he said worriedly.

"Oh" she replied pulling a sad face and laughed. "I can see you're going to be a handful Miss Kirkpatrick.

"You enjoy teasing me dont you?" "Sorry" she replied "you make it too easy".

"Oh we will see about that" he said as they both laughed. Let's get you home then and I can pick you up later. Say 7pm. Will that give you enough time for a rest and to get ready?"

"Are you saying I need alot of work then Jasper to look decent?" she teased.

"No, no sorry I meant..." he laughed "you did it again" "Oh lord what have I let myself in for" he teased. "Not only short but sassy too" Jane swatted his arm

"hey cheeky less of the short. Just because you grew up in a growbag" she laughed. "If i knew you better Miss Kirkpatrick I would put you across my knee and give you a good spanking for that smart mouth" his cock woke up " down boy", he said to himself. Jane laughed "oh you think do you Mr Mitchell. You would have to catch me first" she said flirting. His cock was wide awake now. So many thoughts running through his head he could imagine her over his knee pulling down her jeans and spanking her hard-leaving lovely red marks that he could kiss and lick better. He could feel himself getting hard this wasn't good. He had to reign in these thoughts.

"Let's go then before we start running riot round the office" he replied Jane laughed and got up. They left the office and Jasper started feeling more relaxed being around Jane. He fancied her like crazy but had to keep himself in check or he would make an idiot of himself. They got to the car and Jasper asked Jane to hang on and he lowered the suspension. She started to laugh. As he walked round the car, she smacked him with the palm of her hand across his upper arm. He let out a little laugh.

"Ouch what was that for." She was laughing.

"You cheeky sod. You watched me struggle to get in".

"I'm so sorry it was to good a chance to miss".

"Hmmmm. You're forgiven this time". She replied glaring at him but smiling. When they were in the car Jane said.

"So what was all that with Callum earlier thinking I was a man?"

"Ahh well. Callum assumed you were a guy because he misheard your name and called you Jay".

"Oh I see, and did you assume the same too" she asked. He smiled, "Well why wouldn't I believe the boss?" He replied

"So when you saw me at the lights then at the market and today on site you didn't register?"

"Honestly? No, I didn't" he said.

"Well I'm sorry to disappoint you both. I hope I won't be a burden to you" she said smiling. Jasper laughed and wanted to say something else but thought better of it and replied.

"Far from it Jane and no you are not a disappointment either. You are a welcome change and I know the guys will find you a great help. Ignore Callum he's an arse" They settled back into the rest of the short journey to Jane's, when they arrived Jasper went to lower the suspension.

Jane said "dont worry I'm used to jumping out now and gave him a huge smile".

"I will pick you up at 7pm then? Do you like Italian?"

"Yes, i do".

"Great look forward to seeing you then". He watched her walk into the building feeling on a high. He was so excited about seeing her again tonight the time wouldn't come around quick enough. He decided to go to the gym and try and burn some of the sexual frustration off. Not that he thought it would work but it would kill some time if nothing else and he may need to pull one off in the shower something he hadn't done whilst thinking of a women in a very long time.He texted his friends to let them know he wouldn't be at the gym later that he was going now he said was busy with the new guy. He didn't want to be bombarded with messages later so would explain next week. Once he mentioned a woman that would do it and he wouldn't get any peace.

He got to the gym as it was early it was quiet too so he put his ipod on and started a run. All he could think of was Jane. What it would feel like to be here with her getting hot and sweaty. Then sharing a shower. "Fuck sake" he said a little too loud. He stopped running and went to do some cardio. Nope she was still there. His balls were aching like crazy it was driving him mad. He continued, he wasn't giving up. After 40 minutes he couldn't cope.

Freak Me by Silk

He grabbed his bag towels and clothes and headed into the shower. He stripped of his pants, shorts and t-shirt put them in his gym bag got his clean underwear out and turned the shower on. When the water started his thoughts went to Jane again. He could feel his cock getting hard. He wasn't stopping it this time. He ran his left hand down his body, past his chest which was firm and toned and onto his stomach. He had a great six pack and an amazing V down to his happy trail. He worked hard on his body and was pleased at how it looked. He moved his hand down to the start of his cock and sucked in through his teeth. Ran his fingers up the length and grazed his hand over the tip sucking in breath imagining it was Jane stood in front of him touching him. "He moved his hand down to his balls and cupped them pulling gently.

"Oh Jesus Christ that feels good" he said. He brought his hand back up onto the underside of his cock and ran his finger up to the top. He was groaning with pleasure, his finger moved over the head which was already well lubricated with his precum. He rubbed it over the head and wrapped his hand around his cock. He stepped into the shower and lent against the wall pushing his hips out. He knew this wouldn't take long but wanted to savour the feeling. He was slowly rubbing from top to the bottom and twisting as he went. He could feel his orgasm building. He imagined Jane on her knees in front of him with her lips wrapped around it and his hand on the back of her head guiding her gently. He couldn't wait any longer and started to rub faster. Moaning loudly "oh fuck yes". He grabbed his balls and pulled them down as he was about to cum and felt his orgasm hit. It had been along time since it felt this good. His whole body trembled down to his toes. He repeated over and over "oh fuck oh fuck oh fuck ahhhhh". Finally it slowed down and he laughed feeling exhausted from it but relaxed. "Fuck me that was intense" he said and hoped he hadn't been too loud. He showered off feeling sensitive to the touch. He turned off the shower dried off and got dressed before leaving the cubicle luckily it was empty. He headed out and got in the car. It was now 5.15pm time to get home shave and decide what to wear.

Chapter 10
Falling for you

Jane walked into her building knowing she was being watched by Jasper so she was trying to pull off the wiggle but felt she was doing a poor job. She needed to practice this in heels. She was so excited she wanted to jump up and down but held off until she got into her apartment. As she walked in and shut the door she did a little girl happy dance jumping up and down stamping and squealing. She couldn't believe she had spent the day with such a gorgeous man and not fallen over her feet or done something else stupid to embarrass herself. She was after all accident and stupid prone it was a good job she had a trike really at least she couldn't drop it. She started running around the apartment so excited. She jumped on the bed and started bouncing like the girls did a few days ago. She was whooping and laughing then flopped down and spread herself out like a snow angel doing the actions and making the bed a complete mess. Suddenly she stopped and jumped up onto her knees "Oh shit what am I going to wear?. Oh god, oh god" She lept off the bed and dashed to her wardrobe pulling at everything, "jeans, jeans, trousers, more jeans, leathers. Oh crap! "" she said to herself, "I don't even have time to go shopping and wouldn't know where to go either", then she spotted the little black dress, "you will have to do, my go to emergency dress, at least he hasn't seen you before" she said to the dress as she held it up. "Shoes what shoes?", then she remembered those strappy shoes had been squirreled away in her bag for those emergency moments she shouted "I love you girls, "this isn't a date remember Lady Jane , its just dinner with a friend so why are you getting so nervous?" She went and got into the shower washed her hair, shaved her legs under arms, "I really need to get into this waxing thing it would be much easier" she chastised herself, she looked down at her pussy, "sorry I know its been a while and you might feel the chill but a girl has to be prepared for every situation". She was happy now knowing the hair on her head her crowning glory was the only hair left on her body.

She was done with the shower, got out and dried off and cleaned her teeth. Her toenails still looked good which was a relief if she was wearing those sandals. Her hair took a while to dry, "up or down, that's the big question?", she held it up, "hmmm, now I look like a school teacher and if I have to put my glasses on to look at the menu that will be worse", "nah forget it, leave it down" she said huffing at herself. "Where are the girls when you need them, Gwen would have had me waxed and done up in no time at all". Gwen, I miss you" she shouted

Gwen had given Jane an emergency make up kit including all she needed for eyes, cheeks, lips and nails so she went to work remembering what she had been told to do, as she still had red nails and toes she went with red lips too, she looked in the mirror, "not bad if I say so myself", she pouted at herself in the mirror striking a pose with her hand on her hip and her bottom sticking out, she started laughing at herself. "Gwen you would be so proud" she looked back at herself stood naked "Tart" blew a kiss to the mirror and went to her underwear drawer remembering what Gwen had told her along time ago, "if you feel beautiful in gorgeous underwear then the rest will feel the same, always wear matching and sexy, you never know when you will be grateful", she pulled out the red lace knickers and red bra and Gwen was right she did feel sexy in these, she adjusted her ladies into the bra properly so they sat in the same place and slipped her dress on, it had a sweetheart neckline which showed a little cleavage, short sleeves, it tapered in at the hips and hugged her perfectly showing off her figure without being slutty and stopped just above her knees, she smoothed it down did a turn to the side and nodded she liked what she saw. She slipped on her sandals and went from gorgeous to stunning and sexy. She grabbed her pashmina it was black and red with big red flowers, her clutch was black to match, she put on her tiny necklace that was a love heart with a pale purple stone in the middle and tiny diamonds round the outside. She was ready, it was 6.50pm her tummy was doing somersaults, her mouth was dry, she needed a drink before Jasper arrived and she embarrassed herself not being able to talk.

The buzzer went of and it made her jump, "oh crap he's here, oh crap and he's early" she said dashing out of the kitchen, "well I'm impressed". She checked herself in the mirror again and ran her tongue along her teeth to make sure no traces of lipstick were there, smoothed her hair down took a deep breath and opened the door. Her legs went to jelly, she held onto the door handle to steady herself. Jasper stood there with a huge smile on his face which made her melt, she loved how his eyes crinkled at the sides and how they twinkled. He had the most beautiful brown eyes she got lost in everytime she looked at him. He had trimmed his beard, she loved his hair the way it was cut short at the sides but he had the top brushed back, he had funny nose that was slightly round but very cute and those lips, she could imagine being kissed by them and her body being devoured, she guessed they were soft, the bottom lip was quite full, she had to squeeze her legs together she could feel herself getting wet. Her nipples hardened, "oh damn you body this isn't the right time or place you traitor!, I can't sit with wet knickers all night". She looked down his body, he had a dark suit on with a pink shirt and black boots, not big boots they were more like a shoe thickness. His shirt was open at the neck she could see the v at his throat, "oh Jesus how I would like to kiss that" she thought. She could see his chest was bare, "he obviously waxes with that much dark hair he must be naturally hairy chested" she continued talking to herself, she did like a hairy chest but bare was even better too especially when you are kissing it. "I wonder if he is bare all the way down, she thought raising her right eyebrow, she felt her knickers get wetter "for gods sake women pull yourself together".

Jasper spoke which brought her out of her fantasy about his body, "Wow, Jane you look beautiful" she heard the emphasis on the "wow", "this had to be good she thought". She blushed and looked into his eyes that was her undoing, he was drawing her in, if she didn't leave her apartment now she would end up dragging him in and devouring him. She was aching to be touched, her body had not felt like this in a very long time.
"Are you ready?"
"Yes I am, let me just grab my bag and keys", she turned and picked up her bag from the table behind her and looked in the mirror at Jasper, his eyes were on her arse she watched as he adjusted his trousers.
"Really?" She thought, "nah he can't fancy me, oh my god what if he does?", now she was a mess, "control yourself Jane you know this is when you do stupid things, take a deep breath and relax. RELAX, how the hell am I supposed to relax, there is a gorgeous man staring at my arse and you are telling me to RELAX!. You can do this" She was

arguing with herself now. She turned around as Jaspers eyes met hers and he smiled.

"Let's go then" he pulled the door closed, took her keys from her and locked the door. He gave her the keys back and put his hand in the small of her back as he led her out of the building, his touch warmed her whole body and went straight down to her pussy.

"Christ" she said quietly.

"You ok, did you forget something"

"No sorry just my shoe dug into my toe".

"Do you want to sit in reception and I will take a look?"

"Oh, Jesus" she thought "I can't have him touching my leg that will finish me off". "No its fine honestly".

"As you wish, nice shoes by the way". He replied, when they got outside Jane was looking for the Range Rover, he put his hand on her back again.

"Just over here", and he pointed at the Ferrari.

"Oh, wow that's lovely, yours aswell I take it?" she asked.

"No, I thought I would steal it from the garage for the night to try and impress you" he laughed. She tutted and raised her eyes at him.

"Being stuck in a Police cell with you all night is not going to impress me", they both laughed.

"Good job its mine then" He opened the door for her and took her hand as she lowered herself into the seat very elegantly, she lifted both legs and swivelled herself in.

"You've done that before" he said.

"Once or twice" she teased, "but not in a Ferrari".

Jasper closed the door and got in.

"This is nice, unusual to see a white one, didn't you fancy red?"

"No, it's too common, it's my favourite colour along with black but fancied white instead". She looked down at herself dressed in black and red.

"You must have known" he teased her with a glint in his eye.

"You're joking right?" she asked. "No Jane, I'm not honestly. Like my favourite flower is a rose, red ones actually", she felt her cheeks flush, "this man was a tease".

"Mine are yellow roses" she said

"But any rose I filled my last garden with them, they remind me of my Grandad he was a great gardener and had many roses, we used to put the thorns on our noses and run around the garden pretending to be rhinoceroses, oh god did I really just say that out loud" she laughed putting her hands over her face with embarrassment, Jasper took her hand and moved it away from her face. She looked at him.

"I feel honoured you would share such a precious memory with me, and I think it's really cute" that made her melt.

"How sweet was this man, was he for real?" She asked herself.

Jasper turned the stereo on low as Closer was playing by the Chainsmokers, "how odd he thought this was the last song I listened to the other day", Jane was tapping her fingers and in unison they both sang the chorus, he laughed "you like this one too", "yes I do", they sat back chatting easily for the last couple of miles.

"Do you like long drives Jane?, I suppose you must with a trike?

"Yes, I do, I get lost in myself, it clears my head just to be out on the open road, I put my music on depending on my mood and take off".

"I understand that", he said. "I enjoy this in the same way, I love my Range Rover but this gives you a different buzz. My friends and I go away for weekends, sometimes its to car shows others it just to have a long drive and stay somewhere nice just to chill out. A couple of them are married or living with and enjoy the freedom. I don't understand that myself though, yes its nice to go away with the boys but enjoying the freedom doesn't make sense to me, maybe I am just old fashioned".

"That's nice to hear, its rare these days". she said. "I am a member of an MC (Motorcycle club) called The Skulls (England)its attached to the dealership that I use, I have known the guys for over 10 years now, we do weekends away but ours is more camping or glamping for me, and we go to bike shows they get quite noisy and rowdy, but are fun, a few of the guys are coming over later in the year to attend a few, they are veterans and like to do the runs with the vets here".

"Sounds great" he replied, "yes, it is, Moses is my best friend, he looks after me. We met about 15 years ago when I went to get my first trike conversion. Life took a turn and he ended up being my saviour really and since then he has looked after me"

Jasper frowned, "sounds like you had a rough time, I won't ask, but if you ever want to talk, I am a good listener" he offered.

"Thank you, yes something like that but let's not bring this lovely evening down". She smiled at him.

"Well we are here" he said as he pulled up outside a small restaurant. Jane waited as Jasper came around and opened the door for her, he gave her his hand as she lifted her legs and swivelled out and stood. They were so close almost touching, she could feel the heat from his body so he must have felt hers. Her heart was beating like crazy, they were close enough to kiss. Jasper looked at her for a second and stepped back, she let out a sigh quietly missing that closeness. He took her hand and moved her round the front of the car and then let go placing his hand once again in the small of her back, she loved how he was so attentive.

"So gentleman like, he must have had a good teacher". She thought

The owner opened the door as they approached.

"Jasper, good to see you again", Marco said as he shook his hand.

"And who may I ask is this beautiful lady?" Jane smiled.

"Marco may I introduce you to Jane she is from the UK she is here working with us for a couple of years unless we can persuade her to stay" Jasper replied, Marco beamed at her took her hand and kissed the back of it.

"Jane welcome to our humble restaurant, please come in" As they went through the door Jane looked round it was a small restaurant unless you knew it was there you would miss it, very understated from the outside, it was family run over many generations, it was half full each table had beautiful white linen and candles, it was quiet and very intimate with low lighting. Marco showed them to their table it was in the rear of the restaurant it was a cozy table more for lovers. Marco pulled out Jane's chair beating Jasper to it.

"Can I get you a drink while you look at the menu?" he asked "Jane what would you like to drink?".

"I actually fancy a glass of wine I don't normally drink but as we are here, Marco would you choose for me please?" she asked".

"It would be my honour Jane" he grinned.

"I will have the same then please" Jasper said.

Marco smiled and walked away to get the wine. Jane looked around "It's very nice, you must come here a lot to know Marco".

"I have known the family for many years, I helped when they built their home, I normally come alone unless we are entertaining clients and we bring them here". He replied

They sat looking at the menu Jasper asked

"What kind of pasta do you like Jane. Whats your favourite?",

"Oh, it has to be Carbonara I think and Lasagne.

"Oh, really",

"What about you?" she asked

"I like squid, Linguini and Carbonara also you can't beat a good Lasagne".

Marco came back a few minutes later to take their order.

"So beautiful people have you made a decision?"

"Ladies first" Jasper said to Jane as he directed with his hand to Marco. "Thank you, I think I am going to have the carbonara please Marco, but no garlic bread thank you"

"Okay Carbonara for the beautiful lady, and for you Jasper sir?"

"I think I will join the beautiful lady too Marco please" Jasper said smiling at Jane. "I will have the Carbonara and no garlic bread".

"2 Carbonara hold the garlic bread coming up" Marco said as he walked away.

"Oh Marco" Jane called after him, "and a bib for us both please" she said laughing, Jasper frowned, "I am not making a mess of myself and looking stupid in a bib so you can join me" she sat grinning getting her own back. Jasper almost spat his wine out with laughter.

"If it makes you happy then I will".

"So why did you leave the UK Jasper?" Jane asked. "Pretty simple really, I was offered a job I was single it seemed like a great idea the money was better, I wanted to see a bit of the world and what a great place to start. Once I got into the job I really enjoyed it, the Company are great, I then met my wife and got married, then divorced. Set up my own Company as I am only a contractor here and I come and go as I please, so if I get another job elsewhere I will fly off and do it. Of course I give plenty of notice to Callum, I don't step on his toes, all my private work is consulting, and occasionally I will do a large house and stay on site with the guys for as long as I am needed, I have my own team that work for me as and when I have something"

"Wow" Im impressed Jane replied, "sorry to hear you got divorced, its never easy is it?"

"No, it was messy, but let's not bring this lovely night down as you said earlier" smiling. "Tonight is about getting to know each other more". "What about you, what's your dream Jane".

"Well I'm halfway there, I am passionate about mental health which is why I trained to be a counsellor so I could help more people. My dream is to have my own practice but still work within Construction instead of being employed".

"I'm impressed too! Don't you get fed up listening though?" He asked, "thank you that's kind, not at all, no, knowing I can help someone to stop feeling ill mentally makes me happy". She replied. Marco arrived back at the table with their meal, he put Jane's down first.

"For the beautiful lady Jane" he said, Jane looked up smiling,

"Thank you Marco your very kind" he then put Jaspers down.

"For the handsome gent Jasper".

"Thank you Marco, you are too kind".

"Now can I get you both another drink?"

"Water for me please Marco" Jane said.

"The same for me to I'm driving".

"Oh, if you want a glass I don't mind driving" Jane said, "I have a spare room if you want to stay over? I'm sure I can handle the beast out there" she said grinning. Marco gave Jasper a huge grin and walked away.

"While the offer is wonderful to sleep in your spare room Jane I will decline. I don't need to drink to enjoy myself and I would like to stay sober to enjoy my evening with you, however if you would like to drive I would be more than happy for you to take it for a spin, but maybe in a better pair of shoes?" Jane stuck her foot out from under the table, wiggling it round so he could see all of it.

"And what may I ask is wrong with my footwear Mr Mitchell?"

"Well let's start with nothing is wrong with your footwear Miss Kirkpatrick, they are beautiful shoes, sorry sandals, but do you want to get your foot stuck under the accelerator or clutch and damage those pretty feet or shoes?" He said looking down at her foot.

"No, I don't". She wiggled her foot at him again "Well thank you Mr Mitchell you are so kind", putting her foot onto his leg, she was flirting now, one glass of wine and she was anyone's. He put his finger onto her toes, ran it across the nails.

"Pretty toes too, and my favourite colour as you know Miss Kirkpatrick"

Jane started to get hot and very turned on, she wanted to slip her sandal off and push her foot into his groin, but that was a little too much for the first night. Marco came back to the table with plastic bibs for them both and they started laughing. Jane took her foot down.

"We better eat before it gets cold", putting her bib on.

"Jasper please could I take a picture you look so funny", Jane asked laughing. Jasper joined her laughing.

"Under one condition Jane", he said as he pushed his chair back put his napkin on the table, got up from his seat walked round the table and crouched behind her "as long as you are in it with me? Jane got her phone out and tried to take a selfie, they were both in hysterics seeing themselves with bibs on. They were trying hard to compose themselves, they managed to snap one. She took a chance as they laughed and turned to his face and as she took another picture, she kissed his cheek, he turned and looked at her.

"What did I do to earn that?"

"Thank you Jasper, for making my first day such good fun and for looking after me so well, I cant thank you enough".

He stood up put his hand on her shoulder bent and kissed her on the head.

"Miss Kirkpatrick it has been a pleasure and the night is still young, now eat".

"You're so masterful Mr Mitchell" she replied laughing.

He walked back to his seat sat down with a huge smile on his face.

"I will take that as a compliment Miss Kirkpatrick" and started eating, Jane was feeling quite flushed, very turned on and confused. She was feeling things she had not felt before this man was so gentle and kind, so thoughtful and playful. She continued to eat and was enjoying her food without a spillage which was typical had she not used the bib she would have dropped something down her cleavage and that would not be a pretty sight for anyone when she started digging around trying to dig out wet pasta.

As she had eaten enough Jane pulled her napkin off her lap and wiped her lips pulling her bib off. Jasper was just finishing up his plate.

"Had enough love?" he asked, Jane's body tingled all over.

"Love, love, oh my god, he called me love, calling me Miss Kirkpatrick was a turn on this was as bad if not worse, this was one step forward arghhhhhh" she was driving herself mad talking to herself in her head. "Yes, thank you it was delicious".

"That's good, I'm glad, we will have to come back then and try the lasagne". She blushed and replied

"That would be lovely thank you" Marco came over, looked at Jane's plate.

"Lady Jane you are not hungry? or you didn't enjoy it?"

"Oh no Marco it was beautiful I just don't have room for more".

"Oh, I see you are saving yourself for dessert then?" he said rubbing his hands. Let me take your plates and get you a menu. Jane looked over at Jasper, he raised his eyebrows.

"Don't look at me, you tell him you're full. Tell him you will have takeaway dessert that will keep him happy".

"That's a good idea" she said, Marco came back with a menu.

"Can I get you a Tea or coffee".

"I'm fine thank you Marco, and would it be possible to have my dessert to take away, I don't think I have room for it at the moment" Jane asked.

"Of course, of course, Jasper"? asked Marco looking at him.

"The same please Marco, we don't want to spoil our dinner". Jane looked at the menu.

"it has to be Tiramisu for me please Marco".

"Make that two please".

Marco nodded and left to get the desserts to take away, Jasper took his bib off and noticed he had dropped a tiny bit of sauce, Jane spotted it to just before he went to hide it .

"Not so fast Mr Mitchell I saw it" she teased.

"So who was it that needed the bib this time. Hmmm?" Jasper laughed with Jane.

"Okay you win. Lady Jane".

"Oh, you've pinched that have you from Marco?"

"Yes, I think it suits you".

"Why thank you kind sir" she replied. Marco returned with a paper bag containing a sealed dish and gave it to Jasper.

"Dessert, enjoy both of you".

Thank you Marco, could we have the bill please?"

"On the house tonight Jasper, to welcome the beautiful Lady Jane to our restaurant"

"Oh no that's too kind" Jane said reaching for her purse.

"It's our pleasure and we hope you come back with Jasper and see us very soon".

"That's very kind Marco" Jasper said, "are you sure?"

"Absolutely friend" Marco replied, he took Jaspers hand and hugged him, he came to Jane, she stood and he hugged her and kissed her on both cheeks.

"It has been a pleasure to meet you, Jasper please take good care of this beautiful lady and come back soon".

"We will" they both answered in unison.

"Now get this lady home at a decent hour Jasper, and see you soon" Marco ordered. They both thanked Marco again and left with their dessert. Jasper guided Jane to the car with his hand in the middle of her back, when they reached her side he opened the door for her, took her hand so she could get in, once again she lifted her legs and swung round, he passed her the dessert. Jane looked up at him, "thank you Jasper".

"My pleasure Lady Jane" he replied with a little grin. He walked round the car and got in. "ready?"

"Yes Sir" she replied laughing.

"Thank you again Jasper, I have had a wonderful night".

"The pleasure has been all mine Jane you have been wonderful company, you must send me the pictures. I would like to keep a copy" oh I don't have your number", he reeled off the number as she put it in her phone.

"You do now".

"I will send them once we get back and I am on wifi, I only have a cheap sim at the moment once I move, I will sort out a contract I think". "That's fine. Let me know if you need any help with that".

"You really are too kind Jasper."

"Like I said the pleasure is all mine".

"What have I done to deserve this incredible man" she thought to herself, "and damn sexy too"

Within a few minutes they were back at Jane's apartment, Jasper came round the car opened her door and put his hand out again to help her out, as she stepped out trying to hold the desserts with her other hand she caught her heel in the door rubber and fell towards Jasper, her foot still stuck in the door she fell straight into his arms.

Jasper caught her under her arms and stood her upright on one leg still holding her, she winced, as her foot hadn't moved from the rubber.

"Are you okay?, have you hurt yourself?" he said looking down, it was dark so he couldn't really see what had happened.

"I'm stuck Jasper" she said he ran his hand down her ankle and unhooked her foot. Once he put her foot down he looked up at her. "How does that feel are you okay? ".

"It's just smarting a little it will be fine".

"Well let's not take a chance he said standing up, hold on tight to my neck and don't drop the desserts". She grabbed her clutch and held him round the neck.

"There is no need honest".

"Do as you are told" he said, Jane laughed as he scooped her up in his arms, "push the door closed please", Jane did as she was asked.

"You are so masterful Mr Mitchell". they both laughed.

"Get ready to push the door". He said as they got to the main door Jane let go of him and pushed the door open. He walked towards the lift as Jane pressed the call button, and he walked them in.

"You okay?" he asked.

"Yes, thank you", she replied blushing.

"Good".

"Are you sure I'm not too heavy Jasper?".

"If you were Jane I wouldn't be carrying you, stop worrying" he said smiling at her, the lift door opened as Jane was trying to balance her clutch on her legs to get her keys out.

"Wait until we stop we don't want you dropping that or we are in trouble"

They reached Jane's door and she managed to get her keys out and open the door. She flicked the light switch on as they headed in.

"Well it's not the end to the evening I expected he said carrying you over the threshold" Jane swatted him on the shoulder.

"Cheeky".

"Now where would Lady Jane like to sit?, we need to take a look at that foot first?", Jane pointed to the sofa, "good idea", Jasper walked her to the sofa gently sat her down so she was propped up and pulled the cushions from the chair and put them under her leg to elevate it. "Right then, give me the dessert and your bag", Jane did as she was told, Jasper put the dessert into the fridge and her clutch onto the table in front of her.

"Let's have a look at you" he said.

"Jasper there is no need you have done enough already"

He just smiled went down to her foot.

"I will be judge of that and if I want to do something then I will do it, so behave and let me see this pretty foot". Jane laughed.

"Okay serious now, I am going to take off these lovely sandals so I can take a better look", Jane nodded. "I need you tell let me know where it hurts okay?"

"Yes boss" she replied

"Good", he ran his hand down her left leg from the knee just in case she had twisted it,

Jane's body responded he had such soft hands and it was driving her nuts, "no don't go down go up she was screaming in her head" he reached her ankle, and she flinched "ouch that hurts".

"I can see you have a slight swelling already, compared to the other one, its probably a sprain and we need to keep you off it"

"I wish you had a slight swelling" she thought, "Jane pull yourself together you're supposed to be in pain not letching after him", said the good side of her brain, "oh hush your noise" said the naughty side "you need to get laid and chill out".

"Earth to Jane" Jasper said laughing.

"Oh sorry" She said, blushing slighty.

"Let me get you some ice so we can help with the swelling and then I will make a cup of tea and we can have our dessert; how does that sound?" Jasper asked.

"Perfect actually".

"Good". He went to her freezer, no ice, he did remember seeing a machine in reception, he grabbed her keys.

"Do not move I will be back in a few minutes, she smiled.

"Yes boss". While he was gone, she grabbed her phone and sent the pictures to him, she giggled looking at them, what an incredible day and now it's been spoilt because I am so accident prone. She thought annoyed with herself.

Jasper came back into the apartment, holding up the ice.

"You okay Lady Jane?" he asked smiling.

"Yes Im fine thank you kind Sir" making him laugh.

"Where do I find a tea towel?" he said opening cupboards and drawers.

"Bottom one" she pointed,

"It's always the last one huh?", he wrapped the ice up and walked back to her "okay then, now 20 minutes at a time, every couple of hours and we need to strap you up to support it or and you need to keep the weight off it".

"I'm sorry to have put a dampner on our evening Jasper".

"Don't be silly I'm still enjoying myself, its not every day I get to help a beautiful damsel in distress is it?".

"Did he just call me beautiful, omg omg!!" She said to herself blushing, "Thank you Jasper"

He took his jacket off and hung it over the back of the chair. "Would Lady Jane care for tea and dessert now?", she nodded with a smile "yes please".

"Coming right up", as he got up and went into the kitchen.

"Jane said tea is above your head and cups are in the right hand side, spoons are in front of you and plates are down to your left".

"How did you know I was going to ask?"

"Oh, you know a wild guess".

Jasper continued to make tea and put the dessert onto plates. He went back over to the table put down the teas and went back for dessert. He pulled the table in closer so Jane could reach.

"I need to lift your legs to sit down is that okay?"

"Yes sure", he lifted her legs sat close to Jane and laid them over his and her ankle back onto the cushions, he put the ice on top and passed Jane her dessert.

Bon Apetit he said, as they both tucked into the Tiramisu. Jane moaned with pleasure, and put slightly too much in her mouth.

"Oh wow this has to be the best ever" Jasper smiled

"Yes it is". He didn't tell her she had left some on the side of her face he wanted to have some fun with her about it and going by what she said it may not be the last, he laughed to himself.

"What's so funny?" she asked

"Nothing I was just thinking about the pictures you took earlier"

"Oh, I sent them to you while you were getting ice", "oh great thank you, I will turn my phone on shortly and take a look."

"Why did you turn your phone off?"

"I didn't want to be disturbed, I don't believe in using a phone whilst in company, especially when it's a beautiful lady".

Jane blushed "you are so sweet".

"Just being honest Jane" he replied.

They finished desert Jasper took Jane's plate and put them down on the table. He was right, she did have a little more on her face. He smiled.

"In for a penny in for a pound". He lent towards her.

"umm, miss mucky pup you have some dessert left around your lips"
Jane's tongue shot out running around her lips trying to find it Jasper
was laughing.

"Has it gone, I am so embarrassed?"

"No love its still there come here"

She moved towards him, they were inches from each others faces,
suddenly the air changed and became hot and sexy they were both
breathing hard now, Jasper put his finger onto her lips and brushed
the dessert away, then slid his finger into her mouth, not once taking
his eyes from hers, as his finger went into her mouth Jane ran her
tongue around it, sucking, Jasper caught his breath and had to move
slightly in his seat. Jane continued to lick as Jasper let out another
moan."Oh my"

Jane smiled and let go of his finger, Jasper could see another tiny
piece so lent into her further, put his hand on the left of her face slid
his fingers into her hair and brought her to him, Jane's heart was
pounding out of her chest as was Jaspers, he looked her in the eye,
slowly he licked the corner of her mouth, moaning he said

"mmmm you taste good, I think you have more all over your lips,
would you like me to get it off for you?"

Jane couldn't breath her knickers were soaking wet and her pussy
was aching, all he did was lick her lip. She just nodded, Jaspers other
hand went to the right of her face and into her hair as he gently
pressed his lips to hers, Jane thought she would pass out, he had the
softest lips, he ran his tongue along her lips and pushed it slighty in,
willing her to open and she did without any pressure from him, their
tongues met as they both moaned, Jane's hands went into Jaspers
hair, she ran her fingers into it grabbing, it pulling him to her, Jasper
let go with one hand and moved it down her body round her back to
pull her closer, their tongues making love to each other, Jasper
stopped for a second and sucked her lip gently into his mouth, Jane
came undone. She whispered breathlessly.

"oh Jasper"

Their kissing became more passionate, Jasper left her lips and moved
her hair away from her neck pushing her chin up, he was working his
way down and left a little nibble and a soft kiss on her chin, licked
across to her ear, Jane was hot and completely lost to him, he teased
her ear with his tongue moving around the outside nipping at it, he
sucked it gently, she could feel him breathing into her ear, her legs

opened she was desperate to be touched by him. He moved down her neck nibbling and kissing.

"Oh god Jasper, please don't stop, she moaned grabbing a handful of his hair. Her nipples were rock hard and she knew they were pushing into him, he reached the bottom of her neck and kissed along to her shoulder, he pulled the dress away as best he could.

"Oh, Jasper take me please, I want you" she begged in a hushed voice. Jasper stopped and looked at Jane.

"Are you sure about this Jane, its been a long time for me I don't do this lightly, but you are intoxicating"

"neither do I" she said, "yes I'm sure."

Chapter 11

Two become one

Jasper pushed the table away so he could stand up, he needed to carry Jane to the bedroom, he was aware his cock was rock hard but what did she expect, from the moment she opened the door to him tonight looking absolutely stunning and sexy without even knowing it, he wanted her, and those sandals wow!. She had driven him mad all night long, all he wanted to do was kiss her, "she is so damn cute and very beautiful" he thought. He looked down at Jane.

"Let's go to the bedroom where it will be more comfortable for us both and especially with your foot".

Jane nodded.

"Hold on then"

He scooped her up like there was nothing of her and as she turned to look at him, he kissed her again, she held his face and said.

"Take me to bed Jasper".

He didn't need telling twice.

"Yes ma'am your wish is my command".

They both laughed, Jane pointed to the bedroom and Jasper carried her in, he sat her on the bed and kissed her.

Jane started to unbutton his shirt he was smiling while kissing her, his hands went to the sides of her dress he knew he had seen a zip earlier, he found it and unzipped her, he climbed onto the bed in front of her, she pulled at his belt buckle to undo it then went to his trousers, she pulled his shirt out so she could open the last few buttons, she stopped and caught her breath when she saw his chest and fanned herself. He was perfect in every sense of the word. She couldn't help staring at him.

"My turn" he said, "lift your bottom please".

she did as she was asked and he pushed her dress up over her bottom, she put her arms up as he lifted the dress over her head. He threw it onto the chair. He stopped and just looked at her, she was so beautiful, she wasn't skinny, she had the perfect hourglass figure and she was wearing red lace, he could feel his cock straining now to get out, he kissed her gently on the mouth.

"I want you Jane, last chance to change your mind".

She shook her head.

"Okay but at anytime you are not happy tell me to stop and I will, I promise".

with that he pushed her back down onto the bed devouring her with his kisses, Jane undid his trousers and put her hand inside finding his cock, he was rock hard and huge, she could feel the vein running all the way down as her thumb moved down to the base. He stopped kissing and got off the bed, took his trousers off and folded them over the chair as quick as he could, he knew this wasn't what he should be doing but he had nothing else to put on, he took out a condom from his wallet, not that he had any plans for this, it had been in there a while. He dragged his shirt off and put it over the back, Jane sat up laughing, he pulled his socks off and as he pulled his boxers down his cock sprang out, the laughter stopped as Jane gasped in delight, he laughed and went to the bottom of the bed. He climbed on and pulled Jane down by her thighs, went back up to her head and asked.

"Comfortable?"

"Yes, thank you" she smiled. He bent and kissed her nose, mouth and decided to tease her. He kissed her hard left her lips, and moved down to her neck, Jane moved her hair away as he was nibbling licking and kissing moving round the front of her neck, she was panting and moaning.

"Oh god", he smiled as he moved further down, he wanted to kiss her breasts.

He pulled on the straps so her bra cup would come loose, ran his tongue down her cleavage, and across to her left nipple, they were rock hard and waiting to be licked, his tongue circled one through the fine lace and he bit it gently, Jane arched off the bed.

"Oh, god yes" she moaned.

He smiled and did it again, then moved to the middle of them and left a soft kiss as he slid his lips towards the other.

"Oh Jasper" she whispered.

He slipped his hands round her back and she arched as he found the clasp and undid it, she slipped her arms out and he threw it across the room. She laughed.

"Not going to hang it up then?".

"Nah passed that" he smiled.

He looked down and saw the most gorgeous breasts he had ever seen, they were perfect and real, nothing false about them, this was going to be a first for him, he bent down and licked across the tip of the left nipple, Jane moaned again, he ran his tongue around it, another moan, he was going to savour this, his balls were aching and he wanted to be inside her but he wasn't spoiling this first night, he took the nipple in his mouth and sucked gently.

"Oh God" Jane said out loud.

Her hands in his hair. He sucked harder she tasted incredible and her smell was intoxicating, he was hooked on her. He moved across to the other nipple and did the same. He licked down her body, kissing biting all the way down to her belly button, he circled it, kissing around it, he continued down, he was getting harder if that was possible, he came to the lace thong, he ran his lips across her skin just above her pussy where the lace started, Jane opened her legs wider, she was so wet and horny for him desperate to feel him inside her.

"Oh christ yes" she said.

Jasper moved his lips further down kissing as he moved down the lace was so soft it was teasing his senses too. He moved across to the side of her pussy licking the skin in the seam of her leg, he couldn't get enough of her. He moved across to her pussy the lace barely covered it, he could smell her arousal it was like a drug as it hit him he felt high, he went down and covered her pussy with his mouth and sucked her, his tongue wetting the thong, she was bucking towards him, he slipped a finger into the side of the thong and pushed it deep inside her.

"Oh Jasper" she said loudly gripping his hair hard "oh god".

He pushed his finger in deeper in and out making love to her with it. He slid in another.

"Oh God, Oh God yes" she moaned.

He kept sucking her through her lace but wanted to taste her properly, he slipped his fingers out of her and smelt them.

"Mmmm Jane you smell delicious".

He put his fingers into his mouth and sucked them, she tasted amazing as good as she smelt, he wanted more, he grabbed the sides of her thong.

"Lift your bottom Jane"

She did as she was asked and he pulled them down lifting her legs above his head and pulled the thong off, throwing it onto the floor, he opened her legs and put them back down on the bed, he bent down to her pussy, he was going to eat her up.

He grabbed her left leg, kissed and bit along it gently, she was moaning and screwing her fingers into the bedclothes, he loved how it made her feel, she opened her legs wider as he reached her pussy, it was beautiful, clean shaven tight and he knew she smelt and tasted amazing, he looked up into her eyes she was watching every moment of this not believing how lucky she was. He smiled lowered his head and licked her from the top to the bottom of her pussy, Jane moaned, he looked up at her questioning her, she nodded biting her lip. He moved back down, ran his tongue back up again and slipped into her opening, as he reached the top then he found her clitoris, his tongue teased it gently, Jane thought her head was going to explode. He continued to tease it, Jane bucked into him, pressing herself against him. her hands in his hair.

"Oh god please don't stop" she begged.

He had no intention of stopping. He continued to lick her clit slowly, delving in and out with his tongue, he moved up to the hood and sucked harder sucking in her lips, his tongue was darting in and out her the more she moaned the more he continued, he could do this all night he loved the noises she made she got wetter, he could see it glistening out of her lips he lapped it, up it was pure nectar to him, she started to mewl he slipped two fingers back in he wanted to find her G spot and make her cum so he could drink her.

"Oh God Jasper" he was fucking her with his fingers he had hit her jackpot he wanted to do so much to this beautiful woman he just wanted to please her.

He continued licking and sliding his fingers inside he was rubbing against the wall of her pussy.

"Oh, Oh, Oh Jasper Im going to cum" she screamed, he sucked and licked harder, she gripped his head harder one hand was on his shoulder her nails digging into him she didn't care if she left marks in him, Jasper felt her orgasm hit her and Jane yelled

"Im cumming, oh fuck yes".

Her whole body trembled her eyes closed everything went white, she kept pushing against him needing the pressure to ride this orgasm, she had never felt one like this it was so long, Jasper kept sucking and rubbing her, he wanted more.

"Oh my god" Jane screamed. "Jasperrrr.

She sang his name.

"Fuck another one"
She came and came he kept sucking he wasn't missing a drop he was slurping he didn't care he wanted it all, he was pushing his tongue in as another hit her.
"Oh fucking hell"
She screamed, Jasper grabbed her legs and pulled her closer to him his tongue was deep inside her lapping it up, Jane finally slowed down feeling exhausted she had never had so many orgasms at one time her body tingled all over and his touch now was like a tickle her body was too sensitive, Jasper slipped his fingers out, she let go of his hair and shoulder, she pulled his head towards her.
"Come here please"
He moved up to see her with a huge smile on his face.
"You okay love?"
She just laid there looking stunning and well and truly satisfied, but now he wanted her to look well and truly fucked, she pulled his face down seeing her juices in his beard, she pointed.
"You have umm, you know in your beard".
He smiled "that's afters".
Bending to kiss her, she could taste herself on him, he kissed her gently.
"I'm not done with you yet".

She laughed.
"Good I want that cock".
He didn't need to hear that twice, he lifted her legs putting them on his shoulders, he rubbed his cock up and down her pussy while he reached for the condom, he ripped the packet open and rolled the condom on, he looked into Jane's eyes as he slid his cock into her pussy. Her eyes grew wide and she gasped.
"Oh God Jasper".
"You ok love?"
"Yes, I am....... oh god yes I am".
"Oh, fuck this is heaven, you are heaven Jane" he said.
He felt his balls hit her arse and knew she had taken all of him. She clenched her muscles around him.
"Oh, fuck Jane" he said throwing his head back.
He slowly started to pull out of her and got into a slow rhythm Jane joined him as the slowly made love.

"Oh, fuck yes", he lent forward and kissed her breasts, and then her lips, he pushed harder his balls slapping against her.

"Oh, fuck yes right there Jasper". Jane screamed.

She dug her nails into his back and scratched down.

"Oh god," she clenched around him again, he put his hand down to her clit and rubbed her with his thumb he wanted her to cum again, "oh Jesus Jasper, you're going to make me cum again".

He grinned "that's the plan".

She pushed hard against him and started to clench and unclench around him which made him push faster. Jane looked him in the eye, "Fuck me hard Jasper please".

"Oh fuck Jane", it was like flicking a switch, he pushed her legs off his shoulders went onto his haunches rolled her onto her side.

"On your knees Jane".

She got up quick and put her head into the pillow, he spread her legs and rubbed his cock up and down her pussy and rammed it into her, she screamed.

"Fuck yes, fuck me Jasper".

He grabbed her hips and pulled her into him, he spanked her, she screamed out

"Ouch".

"Don't you like that Jane?"

"Yes" she replied.

"Good", and he spanked her again. "Fuck this women is hot I'm not letting her go" he thought , he had left a huge red mark on her arse, and wanted to kiss it, he was looking at her rose, he loved it, it was so beautiful just like she was. He started to fuck her hard, they were both moaning as Jane pushed back at him as he pulled and pushed into her, they were both sweating he could see the sweat forming on her back he lent to lick it she tasted so good, there was nothing he wouldn't do for this women. He felt his orgasm building.

"Oh Jane I'm going to cum, I want you to cum with me", she started to play with her clit.

"Yes Jasper, oh god yes make me cum, oh fuck"

That was it, he was done, he felt it hit him.

"I'm cumming Jane" he yelled.

"Me too", she screamed.

"Fuck"

He exploded like never before into the condom wishing he was filling her up instead, his body trembled he felt her cum and it washed around his cock they were both trembling and sweating, their hearts pounding, they both laughed as he lent over her back and kissed her again. They started to slow their breathing down, ready to fall into a heap on the bed he pulled out of Jane slowly.

"Ohhh"

She felt his loss straight away and felt empty, he bent to kiss her tattoo.

"My rose lady", he said.

He kissed her red sore bottom too as she winced. Jane then collapsed onto the bed exhausted, Jasper hopped off to go and deal with the condom, he came back from the en suite with a huge grin on his face, climbed into bed, Jane turned and snuggled into him, he wrapped his arms around her. She looked up at him and he kissed her nose.

"Well I didn't plan that Jane honest it's not something I have ever done before".

"Me either, I hope you don't think bad of me in the morning?"

"Hell no" he said, "you must be joking".

They both laughed.

"How is your foot feeling?"

"Its ok a bit sore".

"Do you need the bathroom at all?"

"Yes I think I do".

"C'mon, I will help".

He got out of bed scooped her into his arms and carried her, she laughed.

"I can walk".

"Not while I'm around you wont until that has heeled. You do want to move on Saturday don't you?"

"Yes of course".

"Well then do as you are told", he said and laughed

They got to the bathroom door and he sat her onto the toilet, she looked up and kissed him.

"I will leave you until you are done, do not put weight on that until it's strapped up in the morning, I will help you with everything".

He stood outside the door giving her privacy but next time he was going to be in there with her, he didn't want barriers between them he wanted to know every little thing about her. He wanted to share everything with her even his past.

Jane called out she was ready, he went back in she had balanced on one leg to freshen up.

"Hold on then" he said

As he scooped her up and took her back to bed, he climbed in with her, brought her back into his arms bent down and kissed her gently, "Goodnight Lady Jane".

"Goodnight Mr Mitchell" she replied.

She kissed his nose and snuggled in. it wasn't long before they were both fast asleep.

Chapter 12

Moving day

Jane woke up the following morning to an empty bed.
 "Surely this wasn't just a horny dream?"
she looked at the floor and chair and his clothes were still there.
"Oh, thank god, oh, hang on, I need a mirror, he can't see me like this".
she moved to get out of bed and Jasper appeared at the door.
"Going somewhere?"
He came around the bed.
"Don't look at me, I must look a mess".
"Too late Jane I have been laid watching you sleep for the last hour" he said laughing.
"Oh noooo" she moaned.
He put his finger under her chin and lifted her head.
"Look at me Jane, do you know how beautiful you are first thing in the morning with your bed hair, smudged mascara and that happy fucked look?"
She laughed "no".
"Well let me get you a mirror" he said kissing her on the nose.
"Now back into bed, I made tea and toast and I haven't had enough cuddles with you yet".
"Oooh, where have you been all my life Jasper, you are too kind and so sweet?"
"As are you Jane"
He said climbing into bed with her, putting a tray down on the foot of the bed. He propped himself up dragged the tray onto his lap and pulled Jane into him and passed her a mug of tea.
"Good Morning Lady Jane"
He said bending and kissing her on the lips.
"Mmmmm you taste wonderful in the morning" Jane blushed a little, she felt a mess and was sat in bed naked with her breasts on show next to Jasper with his gorgeous body out.

Jasper passed Jane a piece of toast let her take a bite and put it down for her so she could keep snuggling into him and drink her tea.

"I could get used to this" she said. "I like being waited on"

He smiled "me too Jane I feel like I have known you a long time, its been 24 hours but I just seem to relax with you, its like we have been doing this along time".

"I know I feel the same", she replied. "its strange".

He pulled her in closer and kissed her head.

"Jane would you mind if I gave you another nickname?, I know you have a lot already" he laughed. She looked up at him.

"If you want to".

"Yes".

"Its not rude is it?"

He laughed "no love it's not rude."

"Okay then"

"Well you know Marco calls you Beautiful Lady Jane, well I like that but that's his name for you, and I want something shorter, sorry no pun intended, you are so beautiful and I would like to call you Belle"

"Isn't that French for beautiful?" She asked.

"Yes, it is".

"Ahhhh I love it Jasper". She said and reached up to kiss him.

"That's settled then". He said with a huge smile on his face.

"So if you call me Jane I will know Im in trouble?" she said laughing,

"Yes most definitely" he replied.

"Okay then, note taken"

Jasper took Jane's cup away from her and moved the tray onto the floor.

"Come here Belle"

Jane grinned from ear to ear.

"Awwww I love it".

He picked her up and sat her on her knees across his legs, his cock was hard and he had to have her before they got up, he didn't tell her he wasn't going into work today, he was going to help her pack and move her in this afternoon, he got out of bed early to make a few calls, he didn't want her on her foot to long, he could see how sore it was and the new apartment had a great shower big enough for both of them with a ledge she could sit on.

He was going to pop home and quickly change and grab a change of clothes for the following day.

He pulled Jane towards him and kissed her.

"You are so beautiful my Belle".

Jane smiled and melted inside.

"This man is something special" she thought, she didn't want to be away from him today she was hooked. She fell into him, kissing their tongues finding each other. His cock was rock hard but he had no condoms, Jane moved down his legs looking into his eyes, as she moved down she bent and licked across the top of his cock.

"Oh Jesus Belle" he said, "come here".

She shook her head.

"No its my turn".

She ran her tongue around the top and down the inside, wrapping her hand around it.

"Oh, fuck Belle you will make me cum so quick doing that".

Jane just shrugged her shoulders. Jasper fell against the bed head.

"Oh, fuck yesss, don't stop" he said, hissing through his teeth. Jane covered his cock with her lips and slipped down over him teasing him with her tongue as she moved down.

"Oh, fucking hell Belle, jesus".

She looked up at him and continued. He pulled at the bed clothes as Jane moved her hand down to his balls and cupped them, she squeezed them.

"Oh god, oh god, don't stop Belle please don't stop".

Jane loved her new nickname it spurred her on hearing it from Jasper, She moved faster up and down his cock and sucked him harder.

"Oh Fuck Belle stop I'm going to cum you better move if you don't want me to fill your mouth".

Jane just moaned with her mouth full of his cock waiting for it. She felt him get harder she was loving every minute of this.

"Oh shit Belle he screwed the bed clothes up and felt himself cum hard, it hit Jane in the back of the throat she swallowed and swallowed he kept cuming, his whole body trembled, Jane ran her tongue up his cock which made him laugh as it tickled and didn't help the sensations going through his body.

"You are in big trouble Belle! he said, laughing.

As his body continued to tremble. She came back up the bed licking her lips. Grinning like the cat that got the cream. She went straight to his mouth to kiss him and share the remnants of his orgasm with him, as she got closer, he spanked her hard.

"You are such a bad girl".

"Owww what was that for?" she asked. "You going to my cock, I wanted to fuck you".

"Well you should have said so" she replied grinning.

He went to spank her again, but she moved to quickly. Giggling.

"I have never cum as hard and much as I have in the last 24 hours Belle, what are you doing to me?"

"Oh, you're asking me?" Look what you have done to me too"
she replied laughing.

"Okay let's call it quits shall we?".

"Yes let's".

"Now come here and kiss me again before we shower".

"Mmmmm" she said crawling up to him and sinking into his arms.

"I have a confession to make Belle,"
Jasper said as they stopped kissing, and he moved to the edge of the bed.

"I have arranged for you to move today, I don't want you on your foot and the new place will be easier for you, it has that huge shower with the ledge so I know you wont fall over trying to sho'wer if I'm not there. I'm not going to work but will need to dash indoors and get changed and grab some clothes if that's okay on our way?" Jane was quiet, she looked up with tears in her eyes.

"You did all that for me?"

"Umm yes, are you mad? Just one other thing, I rang the trike dealer and spoke to Shadow, he is coming across with one of the boys to move your trike too".

Jane launched herself across the bed at him and hugged him so tight, she started to cry and he just held her in his arms,

Im sorry Belle, I didn't meant to take over, I am just worried about you and didn't want to leave you today and this seemed the best option, I want you to get checked by the Doctor too, I know its probably a sprain but to be on the safe side, the Doc will come to you too".

He sat her up and looked into her eyes wiping away her tears with his thumb, she looked at him pinched him and then herself.

"Ouch what was that for?" he moaned.

"Just making sure you are real".

He laughed, "yes Belle I am real, after all you just sucked my cock it can't get any more real that that".

She laughed through another sob.

"Come her Belle", she climbed onto his lap, and cuddled into him, he held her for a little longer until she pulled away.

"Cmon lets get us showered and you can sit there and direct me to where everything is that needs packing and we can get going. I want to get you settled as quickly as possible"

"Hold on tight" Jasper said picking Jane up again and took her to the shower, he already wanted her again but knew they had a busy day, he would wait until later at the new place, he had arranged for Joan from the office to get some shopping organised and delivered for Jane, it would be there mid afternoon, he would then cook for her tonight. He knew he needed to reign in his excitement and not take over her life she was going to want some time alone too. But while she was off her foot, he wanted to be there for her. That was his excuse, he just couldn't bare to be away from her. She was his drug and he was addicted.

Jane pinned her hair up it didn't need washing again just a good brush which she could do after her shower, Jasper grabbed her shower gel as she was propped up against his body, he was going to enjoy this. "Belle let me take your weight he was kneeling on the floor and rubbing shower gel up her legs, he was trying so hard to be good, Jane had hold of his shoulders he got to her pussy.

"Open wide Belle", she giggled.

"I promise to be good I don't want you falling and we don't have time. But believe me I want you so bad". They teased and giggled through the rest of their showers and Jasper carried Jane back to the bed so she could dry off and get dressed.

Jane got dressed and sat on the bed trying to get her long hair under control while Jasper watched in awe.

"Before I get lost in you and your hair put me to work Belle, tell me where to find your things".

Jane pointed out the cupboards that needed emptying so Jasper went round opening all the doors found the bags and put them on the bed, he started to fill the bags and Jane joined him.

"Just put it in a pile I can pack while I'm sitting here" she said.

Jasper opened Jane's underwear drawer.

"Ooooh nice, I like these" he said "I hope you are going to wear them for me soon?"

Jane laughed "what have you found?"

He turned around holding out the biggest pair of knickers in her drawer, they were control pants that she had kept from when she was bigger, it was a reminder of how far she had come.

"Oh my god, no" she shouted, covering her face laughing nervously, "oh the shame", Jasper was laughing with her.

"They are sooooo sexy Belle. Im disappointed you didn't wear them last night", she was now bright red giggling with embarrassment, "please Jasper give them to me"

He was waving them around.

"What's it worth?" he asked

"I will suck your cock again", he laughed.

"Oh, it's going to be like that is it, you are going to bribe me with your body?"

"If it will work, yes",, they both laughed and Jasper threw the pants at Jane.

"I will hold you to that Belle" he said grinning.

They finished packing the bags, "I think I should be able to get these in my car, anything else can go in the trike. If anything is left, I can get Joe to pop in and collect it when he brings the boxes over".

Jane was getting excited about moving, Jasper grabbed a bin bag and went into the bathroom, wiped down the contents of the shower and toothbrush and packed them away, he went round the apartment making sure everything was packed, he poured the milk down the sink and bagged up the rubbish.

"Right Belle what are we going to put on your feet".

"Can I try my boots they are flat and will support my ankle, I left them by the front door?"

Jasper went to collect them, it was the first time he had noticed the logo and the name on the side, her hair covered the jacket so he hadn't seen it before. He smiled.

"Half pint and Doc, I like that" he said.

Jane smiled "that was Moses he had that done for me".

"They must think the world of you, and I can understand why" he said, Jane blushed. "Thank you, Jasper."

He bent and kissed her, "lets try then".

He got onto his knees at the edge of the bed and undid the zip.

"No forcing it if they don't fit then its site boots for you."

Jane had only thin socks on so hopefully she should get them on, she slid her foot in wincing but it went in, the zip wouldn't go up properly but it was something, Jasper wasn't letting her put weight on it anyway, it was just so she was covered and didn't knock it. Once they got to the new apartment, he would call the Doctor and get him to call over, if it needed strapping he would do it for her then.

"Ready then" he asked.

Jane nodded excitedly.

"Hold on then, I will take you down first and get you settled then come back up for the bags"

Jane wrapped her arms around his neck, he kissed her on the nose and headed to the door, as they opened it Shadow was stood there.

"High tower" Jane exclaimed.

"Hey Doc, I hear you've been in the wars, were you trying to break the car?"

She laughed "no cheeky".

"What else can I help you with, this man here tells me you are pretty special and so did Moses so I have to do all I can to help or the two of them will be having my balls on a plate". They all laughed.

"There are bags behind me" Jasper said

"If you wouldn't mind bringing some down, I think between my car and the trike we can get them done in one hit".

"No sweat J" he replied

"Animal is here with the van to follow me so we can put them in with him."

"Great" Jasper said, "I need to stop at my place and grab some clothes first if that's ok."

"No sweat, we will follow you. Do whatever you need brother".

"Thank you, Shadow," Jasper said

"I really appreciate it".

Jane fell quiet, she was feeling emotional again. "these people don't know me, yet they are treating me like a queen" she thought and felt a few tears run down her face. Jasper noticed as they walked out of the door, he just kissed them away, no words were needed for Jane.

Chapter 13

Feeling loved

The van was loaded Jane was safe in the car, strapped in and Shadow was starting up the trike. Jasper and Shadow had both been round the apartment to check everything was taken and Jasper grabbed the rubbish.
"That's it then, lets get her moved".

Shadow looked at Jasper, "be good to her brother I don't know what's happened to her, but I know Moses and G have looked after her for over 10 years shes very precious and has a past that isn't so good". Jasper looked up at Shadow he replied.
"I have no intention of hurting her and if anyone tries I will be the first to protect her but by the sound of it there will be plenty of you by my side".
Shadow nodded "for sure Brother, you need anything you just call, we will be there like a shot. Come down to the club one night when Jane can ride again, I will introduce you to the rest of the guys and girls, I know it probably isn't your scene, but they are good guys and will do anything to help".

Jasper felt like he had made another friend in Shadow.
"Thank you Shadow, we will definitely do that".
Shadow slapped Jasper on the back and they walked outside where Jane and Animal were talking at the car, Animal was on his knees with the door open laughing with Jane.

"Hey you two" Shadow called "what did we miss". Jane looked up, "Animal was just telling me some stories of Moses and G when they were here last".
"Ooooooh I see" Shadow laughed.
"Jasper walked up to join them after putting the rubbish in the bin he frowned.
"Long story brother, we will fill you in later, lets just say girls bottles and lots of drink". Shadow said.
"Maybe I will skip that one then".
"Wise move" Shadow laughed.

"Let's get this show on the road then."

They pulled out together Jasper looked across at Jane his heart filled with joy seeing her happy and smiling, he was determined to keep her smiling every day. He wanted to know what had hurt her in the past but wasn't sure if he could cope knowing, he really did feel a lot for her already. That scared him, he had been burnt before and couldn't go through it again, but his Belle was different he knew it.

Within 10 minutes they were at Jaspers. Jane's mouth dropped open, it was a huge house with a double garage, he blipped the garage door and it opened, the lights on the Range Rover came on, he was going to swap cars, the Ferrari wasn't practical and if he need to get anything he would need the Range Rover, then he wouldn't have to come back before work tomorrow, if he went in, he could work from Jane's if needed.

Shadow came along side, "all okay J brother, you swapping cars?"
"Yeah it's more practical, I just need to grab some things and I will swap Jane over and put this one away".
"Give me your keys brother I will move the Range Rover out, you put that one in and I will help the Doc while you grab your things".
"You sure Shadow? That would be great".
"Of course, let's do it"
Jasper opened the other garage door and reversed in, Shadow pulled the Range Rover out and went back for Jane as Jasper went into the house.
"C'mon Doc, bring those gorgeous arms around my neck and give me some of that sugar, we can't let Jasper have it all can we?"
he said laughing, Jane put her arms around his neck.
"You are sweet High Tower", Jane said.
He laughed a real belly laugh it was so deep.
"Anything for you little lady".
He scooped her up making sure he didn't knock her head getting her out and carried her like a doll to the Range Rover. He put her onto the seat and she got comfortable.
"That better Doc?"
"Yes much, thank you High Tower".
Animal got out of the van and came across to chat to the two of them while they waited for Jasper.

Jasper was dashing round the house grabbing things he may need, he packed a couple of day's worth of clothes just in case, his laptop from the office and put it into his workbag. He called Joe to make sure the van was still going to be there when they arrived and called Joan to make sure the shopping was on its way. He was happy everything was coming together.

He locked up the house set the alarm and walked out with his bags, Shadow turned round as he got to the car.
"We are going to wait until the Docs boxes arrive and give you hand up to the apartment brother".
Jasper was overwhelmed with the generosity of these guys he knew it was because of Jane but even so it was incredible.
"If you're sure that would be great, I really appreciate it guys, I know Belle does too".
Jane smiled all teary eyed, "Hey Doc none of that we look after our own, and you girl are one of ours".
Jasper got in the drivers side and lent across, kissed Jane on the head. Shadow and Animal went back to the trike and van.

"Let's get you home shall we" he said.
Feeling a pull on his heart strings, he would have loved to take her into his house and show her round, see how she felt about it, he loved his house and wanted to share it, he wanted it to be a home. He knew he was being daft, for godsake he had only known her 24 hours, but he still felt so much for her already.

He grabbed Jane's hand as they pulled out and kissed it. He wanted to devour her and he couldn't wait to get her on her own later. Jane kissed his hand and smiled at him.

It didn't take long to get to the new apartment. Shadow and Animal parked up, Jasper went over and showed Shadow the garage that was Jane's, he put the trike away and he went to meet Animal at the van to collect Jane's bags.

Jasper went round to Jane's side of the car, gave her the car keys she automatically wrapped her arms around his neck and he kissed her

nose as he scooped her out of her seat, Jane pushed the door closed on the car and locked it.
"Ready Belle?", she nodded.

Jasper had so much going through his head the cleaners had been in he hoped the other delivery had arrived already he wanted to see Jane's face.

They got up to the apartment door and Jasper told Jane the key was on his, she found the key and opened the door, Jasper carried her into the lounge and as she looked round she felt at home, the sun was streaming in the windows she couldn't help smiling.
Sat on the kitchen island was a huge bouquet of yellow roses and right in the middle was a red rose. They were already in their own glass vase so all she had to do was enjoy them. The tears started she couldn't believe it. She didn't remember the last time someone had brought her flowers that weren't because she had taken a beating and it was an apology.

She wrapped her arms around Jaspers neck so tight, "Oh Jasper they are so beautiful please let me see up close", he walked her over to them, the smell was intense, she counted 24. She turned to him and peppered his face in kisses, he couldn't stop laughing. "24?" She asked, "Yes well 25 really including the red one, a yellow one for every hour I have known you and the red one to match your beauty and your tattoo". He kissed her tears away again, this was becoming a habit, he was just glad it was happy tears. He lent in and kissed Jane she grabbed his face. "Thank you, thank you, and thank you".
They heard someone behind them clearing their throat, they turned around and Shadow, Animal and Joe stood there. Anymore of that to go around Animal said and everyone laughed.

Jasper put Jane down on the sofa and took her boot off.
"Sit and don't move, do you hear me?"
he said.
"Yes yes, I know", he took her phone out of his pocket.
"Why don't you skype the girls or Moses and G the wifi code is here look".
Jane looked up at him with a huge smile on her face.
"Do you mind if I do?"

"Of course not silly we are going to unload the van".
He kissed her head and left her too it.

The boys were in and out with boxes and then bags began to arrive, "What's that" Jane asked as they put the bags on the kitchen counter. "Its food shopping Belle, Joan organised it I asked her to so you didn't need to worry about it, and I will be cooking tonight".
Jane couldn't stop grinning.
"Come here please".
She said, Jasper walked over to her, she grabbed his t-shirt and pulled him down.
"You Mr, are wonderful and I don't deserve you". She said and kissed him, "thank you Jasper you really are spoiling me".
"You're worth it and you deserve so much more Belle"

They boys came up with the last of the boxes, Jane had labelled them as she packed them, so they were put into the right rooms ready to be unpacked.

"That's it brother, everything is in, what's next?", Shadow asked.
"I think you have done enough", I really am so grateful" Jane said.
"Oh no we are here for the duration Doc, you are not doing anything, we can unpack for you just don't ask us to do the bedroom" and he laughed.
"I don't want to see things I'm not supposed too"
Jasper laughed, "Yeah had some of that trauma this morning, think I need some counselling for that" he said laughing.
Jane threw her cushion at him and they all laughed.

"Let's start on the kitchen and lounge" Jasper said, "Belle you tell us where you want things to go".
"Put me on a stool then please so I can make a drink for everyone".
Shadow was closest and went and picked her up.
"Thanks Shadow" Jasper said.
"Where do you want to sit Doc?" he asked her.
"In the middle so I can see around the room please", no problem Doc, Animal moved a stool round and Shadow put her down, they gave her all the cups and tea coffee and milk so she could make a drink.

They were busy unpacking when Jane's phone rang, it was a skype call, she answered and the girls all squealed when they saw her, Jane was ecstatic, the boys were busy behind her putting things away, Gwen started throwing questions at her.

Where are you Jane? It looks different?"

It's my new place" she said, then Jasper shouted.

"Belle where do you want this?".

The girls all came close to the phone.

"Belle? Who is Belle?"

Jane blushed oh god she had so much to tell them.

"Umm that's me" she said laughing.

"Spill right now girl" Gwen demanded.

"I met someone", Jane put her fingers in her ears as the girls screamed at her, the boys came over to see what was going on, the noise was so loud, Jasper was stood in front of Jane.

"Everything okay Belle?", "yes" she laughed "I think they are excited". Jax shouted "whoever that voice is coming from get your sweet arse round this side of the camera so we can see you".

Jasper laughed, Jane beckoned him over, he came and stood behind her and gave them one of his smiles, they squealed again and Jax wolf whistled, Jasper blushed.

"Ladies may I introduce Jasper". They all spoke at once, and everyone started laughing.

Moses, G and Matt appeared to see what the noise was all about. Jane introduced Jasper to them, Shadow and Animal heard Moses's voice and came up behind them.

"Well I'll be fucked" G shouted.

"Where the hell did you two reprobates come from?".

"Half pint you have a lot of explaining to do lady".

They all laughed.

"Okay a quick update, Jasper found me this apartment we went out to dinner last night I got my heel caught in the rubber on his car and have sprained my ankle so instead of moving at the weekend Jasper organised everything for today and High Tower and Animal moved the trike and stayed to help Jasper".

"Right okay" said Moses laughing. "Jasper thank you Brother I can see she's in good hands I hope we will get to meet you in July when we are over for the Vets run?"

"Yes for sure I will be here" he replied.

"Shadow, Animal thank you both, we really do appreciate it, looking forward to seeing you both and riding out with you again".

"Half pint" he said looking straight at Jane, "You okay kid?"

He was talking to her like nobody else was around.

"Have you seen the Doc yet?"

"I'm good thank you Moses, no Jasper has organised for him to come later today". "Okay, you need anything you call me you hear?".

"I will, I promise but I think with these 3 I am covered right now, they are really spoiling me".

"As you should be" he replied.

"We will let you get back to unpacking, and catch up over the weekend, guys thank you for everything, please take good care of our girl. Jasper get my number from Jane we need a chat sometime and if you need any help call me".

"Sure thing" Jasper replied.

Everyone said their goodbyes for now and Jane hung up, she felt a little home sick, but it wouldn't last long with these guys around.

Jasper saw the way Moses looked at Jane he could see how much she meant to him he saw the love in his eyes for her, he knew he had a lot to live up to and would show them all how much he cared, he would drop Moses a text and call him soon. He was expecting a lecture from him and he was happy to take it, he would do the same in his shoes.

He looked down at Jane she looked melancholy, he moved her hair away from her neck snaked his arms around her waist and nuzzled into her neck, kissing her, she held onto his arms and bent her neck to let him kiss her more.

"Mmmmm that feels good, don't stop"

He came up to her ear and whispered.

"I want you on here right now Belle".

Jane giggled "I don't do audiences" she said.

he laughed "I just want you all to myself now".

Shadow and Animal came back into the room a few minutes later with more empty boxes, "right then you love birds we are done, the only boxes left are bedroom, everything else has been unpacked."

Jasper went to them both and shook hands they both pulled him in for a hug.

"Guys I can't thank you enough we really do appreciate all your help today".

"Hey brother its no problem, we look after our own, we will leave you in peace but you need anything, anyone of us will be here to help, remember what I said earlier get yourselves down to the club and meet the rest of the guys and girls soon". Shadow said. He really was a larger than life character and a gentle giant. Animal had been quiet, but Jasper was sure that he would come into his own as they got to know him.

They both went over to Jane, "give me some of that sugar Doc" as he bear hugged Jane.

"Mmmmm your hugs can really heal the soul little lady" he said.

"Out of the way Shadow, I want some of that sugar too" Animal said laughing.

Jane hugged Animal he was a tall guy, dark haired clean shaven and a handsome man, your typical American looking boy, he was a body builder in his spare time and had won some medals over the last few years. He was a Vet too and done his time in Afghan with Shadow, he was a Helicopter pilot. He had seen his fair share of the war and missed the comradery of his unit but had a great bunch of friends at the club most were Vets from every unit of the military, they were brothers regardless.

"I think your right Shadow, them their hugs are pretty special Doc" Animal said.

"Sorry Jasper brother but it looks like you will be sharing this little lady. Well for hugs anyway" They all laughed and Jane swatted Animal, "ouch Doc, that's some slap you have there" pretending to be hurt.

They all laughed said their goodbyes and Jasper promised they would be down soon and he meant it, if all the guys at the MC were like this then they were a great bunch of people who got a raw deal and were typecast. He was probably guilty of it too. But not anymore, he was actually looking forward to getting on the trike with Jane. But he wouldn't tell her that, he wanted to tease her first.

The Doctor knocked soon after the boys had left and Jasper let him in, he was the Company Doctor so he knew Jasper well. He was a short man quite portly his name was Doctor Adams, he was a very cheerful man.

"Well hello you must be Jane?" he said, I hear you had a fight with a car?"

Jane laughed "yes something like that".

"Okay let's take a look at the damage"

Jasper picked Jane up off the stool and took her over to the sofa, he sat her up and the Doctor sat at the end, he could see it was swollen, he felt up and down her leg and moved the joint to check how good it was. Jane winced and he apologised.

"Well its not broken Jane but a sprain can be just as bad, stay off it for a few days, if you can get some crutches to help you get around then great, but if Jasper here is going to carry you everywhere then you wont be needing them" he said laughing.

"It will take a couple of weeks to completely heal but just a few days off it and then you are good to go, just don't overdo it. No heels for a while, flat boots are best for at least two weeks.

Paracetamol for the pain and Ice every few hours".

"Thank you, Dr Adams".

"It's nice to meet you Jane" he said as he stood. "I hope next time it's under better circumstances".

"Could I trouble you to wash my hands Jasper?"

"Of course Doctor"

Jasper showed him to the bathroom. He came out shortly and bid them goodbye as he left.

Jasper saw the Doctor out.

"I will look after her Doc, I will work from here for the rest of the week then we are on site together so I can drive her around anyway".

"Great just watch she doesn't over do it especially with all this unpacking".

"Not a problem Doc, most of it has been done by friends anyway".

"Take care Jasper any problems give me a call".

"Thanks Doc I will" he said as Dr Adams left.

Jasper went back into the lounge Jane looked tired.

"Do you want to have a lay down Belle?" he asked her.

"That might be nice, will you join me?"

"If you want me too yes".

"Then yes I do" she said with a naughty grin on her face.

Jasper carried her into the bedroom, he'd had the cleaners put a new duvet on the bed and used one of his cover sets. As there wasn't enough time to get a new one laundered in time.

He sat Jane on the bed and Jane started to undress.

"Do you need a hand Belle?" she looked up coyly

"Yes please" knowing full well she wanted him.

He bent down and kissed her, pulled her t-shirt out of her jeans.

"Arms up Belle"

She did as she was told, he pulled her t-shirt up over her head and threw it onto the chair, she had her light blue lace underwear set on, it was a front fastening bra, he bent forward and Jane laid her head back, he licked down her neck into her cleavage and kissed her, he had a little trouble with her fastener but mastered it quickly, he opened it slowly, he loved her body, her breasts fell out, they were so firm. She had the most amazing nipples, he bent back down to her and sucked her left nipple moaning. Jane laid back flat on the bed, Jasper moved to the other nipple and circled his tongue around it before biting it gently, Jane arched off the bed.

"Oh god yes", Jasper ran his tongue down her body to her jeans and undid them slowly.

"Lift Belle" he said in a husky whisper.

Jane could see his hard cock desperate to push out of his jeans, she loved that sight, he pulled her jeans down and took one leg off at a time. She laid there in just her blue knickers looking so perfect, he bent down towards her again and licked down the rest of her body to the top of her knickers, he grabbed them with his teeth and pulled them down, she lifted her bottom for him and they moved all the way down her legs, he let them drop to the floor and stood up.

"Oh Belle you are so beautiful".

He pulled his t-shirt off over his head and undid his jeans, he let them drop to the floor and stepped out of them, his boxers followed, they stayed where he stepped out of them too. He pulled back the covers and lifted Jane into bed, he climbed in behind her and spooned into her back. She moved her hair and piled it at the top of her head. Jasper kissed her neck and her ear, working his way down to her shoulder. He bit her shoulder gently, he wanted to taste every bit of her but wasn't in any hurry they had plenty of time. He slipped his hand down her side and onto her thigh, pulling her leg back over his, opening her pussy, his hand rubbed up and down her leg slowly, Jane was mewling softly, her hand came up and she wrapped it round the back of his head pulling his head further down onto her skin. His hand moved forward and slid down into the inside of her hip and down to her pussy, as his fingers skimmed across the top of her pussy. Jane moaned louder and spread her legs wider, his cock was hard again and pressing into her back. Jasper slipped his middle finger into her hood and found her clit, Jane moaned quietly.

"God Jasper, yes", his fingers moved lower and he found her wetness, he slid a finger inside her and pressed against her pussy wall, she was mewling louder now as he slowly slid his finger in and out of her. She could feel her orgasm building.

"My god already?" she thought to herself. Jasper felt her get wetter and stopped, he pulled his fingers out and brought them to Jane's lips, he ran his wet finger along her bottom lip.

"Taste Belle", Jane licked her lip and moaned, she tasted good, Jasper sucked the remaining juices from her finger.

"Belle I can't get enough of you", she turned her head towards his lips and he kissed her. He moved her body further up his until he felt his cock slide between her legs, he slipped his cock inside her slowly, they both moaned in unison, he slid in and out of her slowly while kissing her, they were both overcome with intense pleasure, he didn't want to come inside her they hadn't discussed protection he just needed to feel her, feel her completely, it was heaven. He pulled out and Jane moaned at the loss of him as he kissed her shoulder.

"I don't have any protection Belle I'm sorry that was wrong of me".

"It's okay I'm clean and on the pill, you are my first in many years".

"As you are mine Belle. Are you sure?" he asked.

"Yes I'm sure".

He rolled Jane onto her back, he wanted to look her in the eyes as he made love to her slowly. He bent down and kissed her, she opened her legs for him, he moved himself closer to her and slid inside her, he loved watching her eyes open wide, it was such a turn on. Jane wrapped her legs around him to pull him in deeper, they both moaned together as he slowly made love to her, he really couldn't get enough of this incredible women. Jane moved with Jasper, she could feel his cock against her pussy wall and she knew her orgasm wasn't far off, "Jasper I want to come" she whispered.

"Fuck Belle yes".

He moved a little faster but gently he wasn't far off either as Jane's legs tightened around him. He felt Jane cum as her juices flooded her pussy and hit his cock, that was his undoing knowing he could do this too her. He came with her and buried his head into her shoulder biting her, he wanted to leave his mark, make her his, claim her forever, as their orgasms slowed Jasper laid onto Jane's chest, he didn't want to squash her so rolled off her and took her with him, she laid on his chest her legs between his, this was perfect, he kissed her on the forehead as she went to sleep nestled into his arms. Jasper dropped off soon after. Completely sated.

Chapter 14

Home

They both woke a couple of hours later, still in the same position as they went to sleep, Jasper kissed Jane.

"Hi, did you have a nice sleep?"

Jane nodded "yes thank you, did you?" with a big smile on her face.

"I did thank you. Hungry?".

"Mmmm yes I think so".

"Let's get you something to eat then".

Jane lent out of bed fishing on the floor for her t-shirt and came across Jaspers, she smiled to herself, he wasn't getting this one back, she pulled it on it was huge on her but fitted like a dress she loved it. Jasper turned to see what Jane was giggling at an saw her in his t-shirt.

"Oh, don't you think that belongs to me?".

"Nope, not now anyway it looks better on me".

Jasper grabbed her face in his hands and kissed her mouth, rubbed noses with her.

"Darling Belle, anything will look better on you, keep it, I have another in my bag".

Jane cheered, "Yesss!!".

Jasper laughed at her, he really loved her silliness it was so cute.

He grabbed his boxers while Jane grabbed her knickers and he fished around in his bag for another t-shirt, he pulled a blue one out, when he put it on Jane sucked in her breath, it hugged his muscles and arms, it was tight across his chest.

"I have died and gone to heaven" she thought. Jasper looked round, "You okay Belle, did you hurt yourself?"

She chuckled "No Im okay honey thank you" grinning to herself, she wasn't about to admit she had the hots for him 24/7.

Jasper got out of bed and Jane came to the edge, he put his arms out, "Your chariot awaits my lady".

Jane laughed and put her arms around his neck as he scooped her up, he walked her into the kitchen and put her on the stool, he went back to his bag and grabbed his Ipod and connected it to the wifi speakers, they had been fitted into all of the apartments so you could have music throughout.

"Anything you fancy listening to?" he asked.

"I don't mind, easy listening maybe?"

"Good choice" he said. "Do you have an Ipod Belle?"

"Yes love, it's in my bag wherever that is" she replied,

"Great I will pair it with the speakers for you then later".

"Thank you honey that will be great. Can I still get Radio 2?"

Jasper laughed, "How old are you Belle?"

Jane swatted him, "younger than you Mr anyway" she said.

"Hmmm really." He teased

"Right then, tell me what you don't eat Belle so I know what to avoid". "Apricots, lots of plain pasta, liver and offal".

"Okay that's easy then". He said grinning

"So, beans on toast is good for you then", he said laughing.

"Oh, you tease" she said looking for something to throw at him, he couldn't resist, she was so easy to tease she fell for it everytime.

"Im kidding Belle, sorry".

He went to her, kissed her, she caught his bottom lip as he went to pull away, he opened his eyes wide at her, and tried to talk, she let go and laughed.

"Naughty girl Belle, did you want another spanking? I will put you over my knee if you're not careful".

Jane squirmed in her seat knowing she couldn't run. And laughed nervously.

Jasper laughed and kissed her head. "How does chicken noodles sound with stir fry veg?".

"Perfect".

"Good", he turned to the fridge to get everything out. He covered the countertop with veg.

"Can I help chop anything honey?".

"Of course, as long as you promise not to chop your fingers off?"

"I won't do that, I'm not daft you know".

"No, you're not daft Belle far from it just an accident waiting to happen" he replied laughing.

She pouted pretending not to be impressed knowing he already knew her so well. He passed her the chicken.

"How about chopping this up and I will do the veg and get the wok on".

"Do we have a wok here then?" she asked.

"No, I brought one for you today, Joan added it to the order for me".

"Oh Jasper" she crooned "you are just too perfect". She grabbed his face and kissed him, "even if you do have a beard".

His mouth dropped open, "I beg your pardon young lady".

"Well I don't like beards, I only ever dated men who were clean shaven, I suppose you can't be 100% perfect".

Jasper roared with laughter, "and what may I ask is wrong with my beard".

"Well it tickles for one", "oh, I didn't hear you complain last night when I was licking your pussy".

"Well it's been trimmed so that's probably why".

He moved in behind her pulled her hair away from her neck and rubbed his beard down her neck, tickling her, she started squealing at him and started giggling, Jasper joined her she was infectious.

He stopped. "I won't shave it off Belle".

"I don't want you to either honey, it does make you look hot and sexy actually, just promise me you won't let it grow like Moses".

Jasper laughed "hmmmm I will think about that, as long as you behave then I will keep it trimmed".

"Deal" she said and got on with chopping the chicken.

Jane watched Jasper as he moved round the kitchen like a pro cooking for her, she was seriously impressed, "is there anything this man can't do?" she thought, "hes too perfect" and laughed. She was so surprised at how she was feeling she hadn't been this happy in a very long time, if ever really, she thought, she didn't feel nervous with him, he said what he thought and he was a lot of fun. "Long may it last".

Jasper finished cooking and dished up.

"Where would you like to sit Belle?".

"Can we sit at the table please?".

"Of course.

He took their meals across and the wine he had poured for them, "Ma'am".

He said putting his arms out for her, she wrapped her arms around him and he carried her across the room, he put her in the chair opposite him so she could see out of the window, it was a nice corner, roomy and cozy especially when the nights drew in, but this time of year you could open the balcony door and enjoy the evening air. Jasper held his glass up to Jane.

"Here's to you Belle in your new home".

"Thank you honey, here's to us too".

Jasper smiled. "To us", that made him so happy to hear. He had so many questions to ask but didn't want to pry, she would tell him in her own good time, he wasn't about to upset her for anything, he knew there was something though.

Jane sat looking at Jasper as he ate, he put his hand out across the table and she took it.

"You okay Belle?"

"Yes thank you, just in awe of you, where did you come from?"

"London" he said teasing her.

"I know that silly".

"I know Belle". He replied laughing.

"Im serious Jasper, why are you single, you are so kind, thoughtful, caring, honest, seriously hot and…" giggled "oh and good in bed" blushing.

"Oh, I didn't think I was single anymore or are you just abusing my body?" He teased.

"Grrrrrr, you know what I mean ratbag", he laughed.

"If I'm honest Belle, I have had a rough time and I wasn't interested anymore, I had my fair chance a couple of times but just walked away, I didn't want to get hurt or turned over again so it was easier to stay single, my job keeps me busy and I travel too, but to be honest the day I set eyes on you in the traffic all that changed, you set my tummy full of butterflies and your eyes spoke to me, you certainly reeled me in, the leathers and hair helped too" he teased, "I have never seen a more beautiful women in charge of a bike like it. I needed to know more about you".

Jane felt her cheeks flush, "and now she asked".

"Now, I can't get enough of you, I don't want to swamp you I know you have your own friends but I just don't want to be away from you for a second, you have brightened my life in the last 24 hours Belle, I can't believe it". She looked at him.

"If I could get up I would come round and kiss you but I can't so this will have to do".

She blew him a kiss. He put his hand up and caught it.

"How about you Belle, whats your story, I don't mean all of it, why is a beautiful woman like you moving across the other side of the world and single?"

Jane took a deep breath, "it's a long story which I will share with you but not here, I don't want my past to taint what we have or this place". "Okay" he said.

"In short I am divorced, he was abusive and a bully".

Jasper squeezed her hand, "when you're ready Belle maybe we both need to offload".

She nodded "yes we will".

"We can always go somewhere we don't want to go back to, like a seedy hotel".

She laughed, "that will do it".

They went back to their meals and Jane cleared her plate, it must have been good she never did that.

She sat back feeling very full. "Jasper that was delicious, thank you so much, that's a first for me I hardly ever clear my plate".

"I noticed last night" he replied, "and thank you that's very kind of you to say".

"Looks like you will be cooking all the time then" she teased. She was a good cook herself and loved to cook for others but to find a man who was and who wanted to cook for her was unheard of.

"Would you like to go back to the sofa now love?"

She nodded "yes please I could do with putting my foot up, my legs are hanging from the chair".

He was trying not to laugh.

"It's ok you can laugh, get it out of your system", he came round the table took her plate and came back for her, he didn't wait for her to hang on just scooped her up into his arms and kissed her, she wrapped her arms around him as he carried her towards the sofa, he laid her down and got on next to her they snuggled up together, with their legs up on the sofa. Wrapped in each other's arms, from where they were they could see the sun setting, it was a perfect evening.

Jane fell asleep just after 10pm so Jasper picked her up and took her to bed, he left his t-shirt on her and her knickers as he didn't want to wake her, he stripped off and got in next to her spooning with her.

They both slept soundly all night, it was unusual for them, they both had trouble sleeping but together they didn't.

It was Sunday morning and a bright sunny day again. Jasper thought it be nice to get Jane out for some fresh air, he didn't want to get up until she woke up, he enjoyed watching her sleep, Jane stirred shortly after, Jasper bent down and kissed her nose.
"Good morning Belle". She opened her eyes.
"Good morning handsome man of mine, I could get used to this". She moved round and cuddled into him.
"I love waking up next to you" she said.
"I do too Belle. "
"Hang on, I don't remember coming to bed last night, oh no did I fall asleep on you?".
"Yes Belle, it's ok I just carried you into bed, I didn't want to undress you in case you woke up".
"You are just too good to me Jasper.
"Tea?".
"Oh yes please" she replied.

Jasper got out of bed and made tea for them both and came back to bed. "How did you sleep Belle? He asked.
"Better than the night before last".
"That's great".
"How about you?". She asked
"Really well too Belle. It seems you're good for me".
He lent down and kissed her.
"What would my lady like to do today? I know we can't go far but you mentioned your friend Graham and his daughters were going to come over. Why don't you invite them? The girls might enjoy the pool and I will make myself scarce if you like". "No i dont want you to go. It would be lovely for them to come over and meet you. Unless you have things to do?"
"No Belle only you" he said laughing and rubbing her nose with his.
"That's settled then give him a call. We can have a BBQ if you like?".
"Oh, Jasper thank you baby. You are good to me" she squealed.
"Let's go get some breakfast and then you can call Graham".
It was a warm start to the day so Jasper decided not put on any clothes. He loved being naked around Jane and seeing her naked, she

looked so relaxed around him and he loved it, he could use the pinny when cooking.

"Did you want any clothes Belle?" he asked.

"Are you?"

"No, it's warm enough".

"No thank you then". She replied taking her t-shirt off from the night before.

She scooted across the bed to Jasper put her arms around his neck and he picked her up. He walked into the kitchen and sat her down on the stool and went back for their cups.

"So, Belle what is it to be?" He asked.

"What are my options".

Jasper laughed "eggs anyway you want them cooked. Waffles with fruit and chocolate sauce or pancakes".

"Hmmmm eggs, I think. Scrambled on a piece of toast."

"Coming right up".

He grabbed the pinny off the hook it was very frilly and floral, big red and white roses with a black frill and pocket very feminine. He shrugged and put it on. Then decided to prance around like he was on high heels in front of Jane. When she looked up from her phone, she was sending a message to Graham she burst into fits of laughter. That just egged him on even more. He went about getting the eggs and mushrooms and didn't stop his act. As he turned away from Jane she span on her stool and spanked him across his bare bottom. He yelped "Ouch! What was that for?".

"Well I couldn't resist, isn't that what happens to women in the kitchen they're fair game".

He grabbed the tea towel twisted it and flicked it lightly at her.

"Ouch, what was that for?"

"Women fight back too you know" he said pretending to flick his hair over his shoulder the way Jane did. She started to giggle. Jasper followed suit. They both ended up laughing so much they couldn't breath. Jasper took Jane's face in his hands and kissed her lips.

"Thank you for coming into my life and brightening every single moment". Jane kissed him back.

"I think you came into mine and swept me off my feet". Jasper kissed her again and smiled, "these eggs won't cook themselves" he said and went back to cooking.

Jane couldn't help staring at his bottom. It was so perfect. "Nice and pert. In need of biting she thought". That would have to wait until she was allowed on her feet then she would catch him when he least expected it.

While he stood next to her cooking the eggs, she started to rub his back and run her fingers down to his bottom. He moaned in pleasure wiggling his bum at her.

"If you want to eat you better stop that" he said.

Jane continued, with her nails grinning. Jasper moaned a deep animal moan.

"Final warning Belle. I mean it. She looked down and could see his cock was tenting her pinny. She stopped. He pouted which made her laugh.

"Not while you're cooking, we don't want you to be burn't do we?"

He turned off the gas pushed the eggs away turned around and pulled the pinny off picked Jane up by her bottom and spread her legs either side of him. Their lips crashed together, their tongues fighting with each other. Jane's hands were in his hair he was squeezing her bottom and pushed her against the wall.

"You are such a bad girl Belle". He lifted her a little higher opened her pussy and slid her down onto his cock. Jane screamed out.

"Yes, yes fuck me Jasper". He rammed himself into her lifting her up and down. He bent and bit her nipple.

"God i can't get enough of this woman" he thought and pounded into her. They were both panting and moaning. There was no gentleness about this, he wanted to fuck her hard, he was lifting her up and down the wall, pounding into her, Jane was moaning loudly as he rammed his cock into her, he loved being inside her, feeling her wetness wrapped around his cock over and over again he slid in and out of her, she was so wet, he couldn't wait much longer, she drove him mad. "Cum with me Belle" Jasper moaned.

"God yes Jasper dont stop".

He pounded faster until she went quiet and let out an "ooohhh, ooohhh Jasper" she dug her fingers into his shoulder as she came. As soon as Jasper felt her release her juices he came too.

"Oh, fuck Belle yes, Im cuming". They were both panting Jasper was trying to stay upright his head was laid on her shoulder as he kissed her neck his cock still inside her , his legs were getting weak, after that orgasm he walked her into the bathroom and put her down in the shower on the ledge and turned on the water.

They both washed each other slowly, massaging the shower gel into each other, it was very sexual but without the sex, every touch was to tease and show adoration for each other. When they finished Jasper carried Jane back to the bedroom, he was going to miss this tomorrow when she walked again, it somehow brought them closer, if that was possible.

They dried off and put on some clothes, Jane had received a text from Graham they would be over in a couple of hours, they went back to the kitchen and Jasper started on the eggs again, this time Jane watched and they chatted easily.

As they were eating Jasper asked

"Belle, can we go somewhere this next weekend and talk, I want to know everything about you if you are ready, I want to know when you are sad and why, when to just hold you and let you cry, what to say and not to say, I want to know every little detail about you the way I am getting to know your body?. "I want to share my demons with you too, I don't want anything to be between us".

Jane nodded "okay, can we go on the trike?"

"Yes of course if that's what you want, I have to do it sometime" he smiled.

"Great we can go down to the dealer and get you kitted out on Friday then, I don't want to take any chances so you will be having everything to protect you".

"Of course," he replied with a big smile

They finished up breakfast and Jasper loaded the dishwasher.

"If I pop out to get some things for the BBQ will you promise to behave yourself?" Jasper asked.

"Yes of course, I won't walk about I promise, "just leave me on the sofa with my phone and the TV remote and I will be fine"

"Okay I won't be long" he said,

He put on his jeans, grabbed his trainers and wallet and left them by the door. Carried Jane to the sofa and got her a drink, the remote and her phone.

"Does her ladyship require anything else?" he asked

"Cheeky, "no thank you, but you could get some ice cream" she smiled. "For the girls of course".

Jasper laughed, "of course"

He didn't want to leave Jane for too long just in case Graham and the girls arrived early, he dashed into the market and picked up some steaks, burgers, chicken, rolls, coleslaw, potato salad and a whole heap of other things including as many flavours of ice cream as he could find just in case Jane or the girls fancied anything, he grabbed some low alcohol beers for him and Graham too.

As he was walking out, he noticed a little shop with canes.

"That's a good idea" he thought, "just a bit of added support for Belle in case she needed it". He chatted with the vendor and picked one that could be folded up and shortened.

He headed back to Jane's loaded down with goodies, happy with what he had brought. He missed her while he was gone.

"How stupid" he thought, but it was the first time he had been away from her in 4 days. "

If I feel like this now god knows what it will be like if I need to go away soon", he said to himself. He knew he had a couple of day's away coming up, but he was just waiting to hear when, he didn't want to tell Jane until he knew.

He got back to the apartment and in true man style he struggled in with all the bags not wanting to look like a wimp, his hands were raw from the bags digging in as he stumbled through the door.

Jane laughed. "Trying to prove you are strong I see?", Jasper panted as he dropped the bags.

"I don't know what you mean" he replied laughing.

"You men are all the same" she laughed.

He went over to Jane and picked her up kissed her like he had been gone for days, she wrapped her arms around his neck and kissed him back, they were so passionate all the time, Jasper took her to the kitchen so she could help unpack and look at what he had brought, "Did you buy the market?" she asked "and leave anything for anyone else?"

"Well I wasn't sure so I just got everything I thought would be needed".

Jane laughed, "we are not feeding the 5000 only 5".

He grinned "oh well. I have something for you too".

"Oh really?"

He brought out the cane and Jane frowned.

"Well it's just in case you struggle this week, it's been a few days so you may feel a bit weak on that leg, we can set it up tomorrow".

She grinned and said "you think of everything don't you?"

"I just want to make sure you are ok Belle that's all". She grabbed his face and kissed him again.

"I could squeeze you Jasper, you are just too perfect".

"Far from that Belle" he said

As they finished putting everything away, the door buzzed, Jane was so excited, it would be great to see Graham and the girls

Jasper opened the door. The girls face's lit up when they saw the apartment.

Jane said. "Don't I get a hug today then?"

Both girls ran over to Jane and hugged her.

"Girls, Graham I would like to introduce you to Jasper".

"Hello Jasper" they said in unison. Graham shook Jaspers hand and they smiled. "Good to meet you" they both said.

"Hello girls, I hope you brought your swimming costumes?" he replied. They nodded excitely.

"Well you better go and look out of that window then" he said pointing to the patio doors. They both dashed to the patio window and saw the pool. They squealed with excitement.

"Can we go down?".

"Of course" Jane said.

"Go and get changed and we will take some drinks with us". Graham and the girls went to the spare room. Graham went into the ensuite and got changed. Jasper carried Jane to the bedroom. She put on her black bikini. shorts and a sleeveless t-shirt. She was kneeling on the bed in her bikini after just pulling it up and Jasper caught sight of her. "Do you think they will mind going along while I make love to you because I don't think I can stand to see you looking that hot all day" Jane laughed. "Yes, they will mind. You will just have to wait". He moaned and sulked like a little boy. Jane pulled him towards her and kissed his nose.

"Don't sulk Jasper". He kissed her lips hard.

"I can't help it if you turn me on so much. You shouldn't be so beautiful". She squeezed his face, so he did a fish face and kissed his soggy lips.

"You are such a charmer".

Jasper put on his long shorts. "They will hide any embarrassing moments I might have" he said and cupped his cock and balls.

"Seeing you like that all day is going to give me blue balls". Jane laughed. "Come on let's go".

They packed a bag of drinks, wet wipes, sun cream, towels and snacks and headed out. The girls loved seeing Jasper carry Jane. Melissa looked up.

"You look like a Princess being carried".

Jane laughed, "That's how I feel too".

They got to the pool side nobody else was out, so they had a choice. Graham and Jasper moved the sunbeds around and brought a table and umbrella over. They put themselves near to a BBQ so they didn't need to move later. The girls sat in front of Jane one by one and she covered them in sun cream and put their hair up. She did her own too much to Jaspers pouting and passed him the lotion to rub on her back and shoulders as the girls and Graham headed into the pool.

Jasper started spreading lotion over Jane.

"This is so unfair, you're teasing me".

Jane laughed "I don't know what you mean" she replied smirking. Jasper spread the lotion across Jane's back and shoulders slowly, teasing himself as well as her. He could hear her little moans. When he'd finished, he came and sat in front of her and she did the same for him. She purposely made it slow and sensual too. Jasper was moaning "you will pay for this later". Jane laughed "go play with the girls". Jasper got into the pool and the girls wanted to play and asked if they could get onto his and their Dads shoulders to play ball Jasper asked Graham if he was happy with that and he assured him it was fine.

Jane was laughing watching them squeal and laugh. She took some pictures too. She was sure Graham didn't have many of him and the girls together. Jasper asked if Jane wanted to get in, the pool had graduated steps at the far end and he was happy to carry her down, but she declined, she was happy watching them all play. Jasper looked so happy and relaxed.

Jane called them out after a while to smoother them all in lotion again, it was waterproof, but the sun was hot and she wasn't taking any chances with the girls.

Everyone agreed it was time to eat so Jasper and Graham went upstairs to collect all the food from the fridge. Jasper had picked up a cool bag too so the food wouldn't get warm before they had chance to cook it or eat it.

On the way up Graham asked, "Jasper I don't mean to pry but I wondered if Jane had shared any of her past with you yet, you are making her so happy I just didn't want anything to get in the way?"

"Not yet no, Jane felt she wanted to be away somewhere before she told me, so we are going away overnight to "somewhere seedy" as Jane called it a place she won't want to go back to. She didn't want to taint the apartment or my place with her past".

"Sounds like a good idea to me" Graham replied.

"I also agreed to go on the trike, it's a first for me and Im being kitted out on Friday".

Graham laughed "oh this I have to see".

"Graham I need to ask a favour, I know I will be going away for a few days, then potentially a couple of weeks pretty soon and I wondered if you would come over and spend some time with Jane, I know she has Shadow but I just want to know she has someone else around".

"Hey Jasper, it goes without saying, I do tell her when I am away so maybe we need to share diaries too, she is still nervous being on her own and I don't want to be away if you are too".

"Good idea" Jasper replied, "You know she will kill us if she finds out what we are doing".

"Oh, I don't doubt it but if it puts her mind at rest then its all for a good reason".

"I will be glad to know everything, I know something is bothering her and she is holding back a lot" Jasper replied.

"Well from the little I know from when we were on the plane you need to prepare yourself its not good Jasper".

"Thanks for the heads-up Graham I appreciate it. As Belle would say let's not spoil this afternoon with talk like that. Let's get this BBQ going".

"I'm with you their Jay, lets do it".

They collected all of the things they needed including plates and cutlery and headed back out.

"You took your time" Jane said, "you men are worse than women". They both looked at each other and laughed.

Graham lit the BBQ and Jasper prepared the salad, Jane sat like a Queen with the girls chatting about girlie things. Graham looked over "Jane is so good with the girls, they took to her so easily".

"Yes, she seems to get on with anyone".

"Have you thought about the future Jay, do you want kids?"

"Well to be honest up until now I hadn't really thought about it, my ex wife was against children she was more interested in herself, I don't know what I saw in her to be honest. But now with Belle I know it's only been a short time, I now think about it. I never thought I would find love like this, Christ I have been on my own for such a long time it didn't really bother me and then Belle came along and knocked me off my feet just by looking at me". He laughed and Graham smiled.

"I understand that, she is an incredible lady, she's like a kid sister to me. That first day I saw her cry it melted my heart. I am no threat to you Jay I promise. Not that any man could turn her, she isn't interested in anyone else".

"Thank you Graham I appreciate your honesty".

The food was almost ready so Jane and the girls started to lay the table and get napkins out and split the rolls. They boys came over with the first tray of food, they all tucked in it was a fabulous BBQ and everyone thanked Jasper for his great cooking and for supplying this wonderful feast.

"Next time you come to us" Graham said, the girls jumped up and down squealing.

Jasper replied, "well if that's an invite how could we say no?".

Jane looked around at everyone she was so happy and relaxed, she didn't feel like she had to look over her shoulder here. She always felt safe with Moses and G but being in another country really helped and she had some amazing people around her too, she was so grateful for these guys.

Jasper and Graham cleared everything away and took it upstairs so Jasper didn't have to do it alone.

The evening drew in and the girls started to yawn, Melissa was curled up with Jasper and Jane.

"I think it's time we called it a night don't you?" Graham said. The girls moaned, "oh Daddy please let us stay", they all laughed.

"No come on, you have school tomorrow you need to get sorted and ready". They moaned "okayyyy Daddy".

"Right say goodbye to Jasper and Jane, they both hugged them and thanked them for a lovely day before going to Graham for a cuddle ready to go home. Graham hugged Jane and shook Jaspers hand and reminded them "you need anything just shout", they had exchanged numbers whilst in the apartment and were going to be in touch in the next few days.

Jasper carried Jane back up to the apartment as they said goodbye to Graham and the girls. Confirming they would see them again soon. It was early evening and still warm so they were going to shower now so they could relax for the evening. It was Jane's first official day on site and she was looking forward to it. As long as she could get her boots on she would be fine. Jasper walked them both to the bedroom and put Jane on the bed. She started to undress and he stopped her when she got down to her bikini.

"Belle wear it in the shower please. I want to imagine you were in the pool and then take it off you. After all I have had to control myself all day".

Jane laughed "you are so hard done by Mr Mitchell" he pouted and nodded he was getting good at that. Jane loved it. She sat on her knees on the bed as Jasper stripped off. As soon as he pulled his shorts down his cock sprang out and started getting harder. Jane moaned she loved seeing him naked. She looked at him and wiggled her finger at him beckoning him to her. He climbed on the bed with her. Staring into his eyes Jane slid her hand round his cock rubbing the head with her thumb and rubbing him from top to bottom slowly. As soon as she touched him he was moaning in pleasure.

"Oh Jesus Belle that feels good. I've waited all day for you to do that." Jane opened her legs wider as Jasper slid his hand down the front of her bikini. And into her pussy.

"Belle your wet for me already". She nodded. "Mmmmmm come here" he said. He moved further towards her and pushed his free hand into her hair and pulled her head towards him. He took her bottom lip in his mouth gently and sucked it. He kissed her and their tongues found one another gently playing with each other. He sucked at her tongue and bit it. He wanted to taste every inch of this women.

"I thought you wanted to shower?" Jane said as their lips parted.

"I do". He jumped off the bed and picked her up throwing her over his shoulder. Jane squealed laughing. Jasper pulled her bottoms down and spanked her. She couldn't help laughing. He walked her into the shower and said.

"Would you like to stand for a few minutes see how you feel?". She nodded excitedly. He turned on the shower. The jets coming at them from every angle. Within seconds Jane was soaked. Jasper stood looking at her with a huge smile. The top had moulded itself round her breasts showing her hard nipples. He watched the water cascade down her body the droplets finding their way inside her bottoms. They moulded themselves too around her pussy. His mouth was watering to taste her. He bent down and grabbed her nipple in his mouth and sucked it, kissed her cleavage licking the drops of water from her skin. He undid the top he needed her nipple properly. He peeled the wet top from her skin. Watching the water cascade down her body was mesmerising. He bent down and grabbed her nipple in his mouth. He sucked hard pulling it into his lips He wrapped his hand around the rest of her breast and massaged it gently. His lips left her nipple and he started to suck the rest into his mouth. He took the other in his hand and pushed them together sucking and licking from one to the other. He moaned as he sucked Jane mewled. She was his addiction he would never tire of her. He bit her nipple gently again he loved hearing her moan in pleasure. It made him harder. His cock was aching to be inside her.

It was a huge tiled seat that ran the length of the wall the shower head was in the middle and smaller jets were placed along the wall to give maximum impact for those in the shower. Jasper pulled down her bikini bottoms and she stepped out of them. The water was trickling down her body and running off her pussy he got down on his knees stuck his mouth in its path and drank it. He slid his tongue inside her lips and onto her clit Jane caught her breath.

"Oh Jesus Jasper" she moaned as she grabbed his hair, her head fell back as he did it again teasing her. "Oh god I want you" she moaned, He got up off the floor and sat on the ledge, he pulled Jane down towards him she was facing away from him, he positioned his cock so when she sat he would slide straight into her tight hole, Jane opened her legs and spread them over his, he helped her sit down, she slid onto his cock with ease and fell back onto his shoulder as he filled her pussy. "Oh Jesus Jasper", she felt all of him fill her stretching her. She ground her hips into him as Jasper hissed threw his teeth, "Fuck

Belle yes", he had hold of her hips and lifted her up and down, he was biting the back of her neck which Jane loved, she moved her hand down to her pussy, she needed to touch herself and feel Jasper in her too. She rubbed his cock she felt him stiffen more, she loved teasing him, she could just feel his balls she wanted to squeeze them. She leant back against him and kissed him.

"Fuck me hard Jasper" she whispered, he held her tighter as she bounced up and down on his cock, Jane stood on his feet and and lent on his knees and pushed herself up and down, they were both ready to cum.

"Belle Im going to cum" Jasper moaned, "oh fuck Belle", she felt him explode inside her, as she came to, he felt her juices cover him as they mixed together.

He whispered in her ear "I want to taste that", he lifted Jane off and sat her on the ledge and knelt between her legs Jane was still trembling and throbbing from her orgasm as Jasper spread her pussy and caught there juices coming out with his tongue, he lapped it up as Jane squealed she was so sensitive but loving every moment, he came up to her lips and shared it with her.

"Belle I can't get enough of you. I could eat you all day" he said with a naughty look in his eye. Jane laughed and kissed him hard. "Let's get you washed and in bed, we have an early start". He said. Jane nodded stayed where she was so Jasper could wash her hair. She did his bottom half at the same time, he wasn't good at multi tasking she asked him to lift his leg while he massaged her head so she could wash his leg and foot and he almost fell over, they started giggling again, "not so perfect huh?" she thought, but was so glad about that.

They finished showering and Jasper carried Jane back to the bedroom, he wanted to dry her hair for her tonight.

"Fancy and drink Belle" he asked.

"Yes please tea would be nice", he smiled and went to make them both one and came back with biscuits and chocolate, he knew Jane loved her chocolate as he did too. Jane had dried herself off and sat naked on the bed, Jasper had his towel around his waist until he reached the bed and Jane pulled it off. He had no choice with his hands full, she leant forward and blew a raspberry on his tummy and fell about giggling, Jasper dropped the biscuits that were tucked under his arm and the chocolate that was sticking out of his towel was on the floor. Jane bent over the bed to pick up the goodies as

Jasper put the drinks down, he jumped onto the bed and grabbed her legs and blew a raspberry on her bottom, that started them both giggling again, Jasper moved up and kissed her tattoo, "my beautiful rose" he said.

Jane sat up and grabbed the comb off the bedside cabinet and passed it to Jasper. He pulled the towel off her head and rubbed her hair, he then ran his fingers through it as Jane relaxed back towards him. He ran the comb through her hair and kept touching it.

"I love your hair Belle, the first time I saw it out of the bottom of your crash helmet I couldn't believe it, then I looked into your eyes and knew I needed to meet you".

"Awww you big softie" she said.

"I think you stared back too if my memory serves me right" he laughed, "I wasn't the only one holding up the traffic".

Jane laughed, "well yeah okay".

He wrapped her hair around his fist and pulled her back into him, bent her head back and kissed her.

"Now feed me chocolate wench", she slapped his leg.

"Cheeky! Get my hair dried slave boy" she replied.

They both laughed as Jane bent across the bed for the hair dryer. She passed it to Jasper as he went to work drying her hair with his fingers. She opened the chocolate and broke some squares off and started to feed it to Jasper. It didn't take long before they were done and they both moved to the top of the bed, Jasper had his back against the head board and Jane laid against his chest. They finished their tea and biscuits and climbed into bed. Jasper set his alarm for 5.30am, they were a short drive from site, so a quick shower in the morning and breakfast they will be on site for 7.30am.

Jasper laid on his back and Jane cuddled into him, their legs entwined it wasn't long before they were asleep.

Chapter 15

First day at work

The alarm went off at 5.30am Jasper lent out of the bed not wanting to wake Jane too quickly and turned off the alarm. She was still snuggled into him, he really loved this, he managed to move Jane's arms and legs, she murmured but stayed asleep, he got out of bed, his cock hard as rock, he stroked it once, "fuck that feels good". He stalked across the apartment to the kitchen and made them tea, he placed it on his side of the bed, Jane had kicked the sheet off her she was laid with her right arm bent above her head and the left on his side of the bed her legs were open, her hair spread out across the pillow she looked so peaceful laid there he could see her pussy open and ready for him.

"Fuck I want you Belle" he whispered and stroked his cock again. He looked at the clock it was 5.45, just a quick one he thought grinning to himself, while the tea cools down, he stroked himself again and climbed onto the bed, he felt the first leak of precum, he spread it across the head moaning, this definitely wouldn't take long, her pussy was calling him. He bent over her and kissed her lips, he would be guided by Jane he wouldn't take her without her say so, he just hoped to fuck she said yes or he would have to take her over her desk later. He ran is tongue along her lips, she moaned again and opened her mouth for him, he pushed his tongue in and met hers, she put her arms around his neck her eyes still closed.

"Jasper take me" she whispered.

"Your wish is my command my lady" he said.

He opened her legs wider and kneeled between them, their tongues teasing each other, he left her mouth and moved across her cheek and onto her neck, he licked up to her ear and bit her gently, she ran her fingers into his hair and pulled it.

"Mmmmmmm, Im going to fuck you Belle" he whispered in her ear is that okay?"

"Yes" she nodded sleepily, he loved the way her voice sounded when she had just woken up, it was even cuter than normal.

He moved closer to her and moved his hand down her cheek, grazing his fingers across her face and down her neck, she moaned and moved her neck to feel more of his fingers, he moved down her shoulder and onto her breast running circles round her nipples he felt them pebble under his fingertips, he moved to her shoulder with his lips Jane spread her legs wider.

"Oh Jasper don't make me wait" she cooed, his fingers went across her tummy which tickled her and made her breath in deeply, he circled her belly button and went in a straight line to her pussy, his fingers slipping straight into her, she gasped.

"Oh fuck yes", he pushed in another and twisted them in and out of her, Jane was awake now, just how he wanted her. He took his fingers out and sucked her juices off.

"Share please" she begged, he went back to her pussy.

"Such a naughty Belle" dipping his finger back in, took it to her lips and joined her in sucking her juices off, both their tongues were licking his fingers and they were moaning, he kissed her as his cock slid inside her, she gasped again as he filled her pussy with his hard cock, her mouth opened and he bit her lip sucking it into his mouth. Jane moved her hands around Jaspers back and as he moved deeper inside her she sunk her nails into him, he arched his back into her.

"yes Belle", she did it harder and scratched down his back. He pushed harder in and out of her, lifting her legs onto his shoulders, he wanted to get as deep as possible inside her. He wrapped his arms around the top of her thighs and pulled her closer, he started to pump harder into her, "Fuck Belle you feel so good", she dug her nails into his arms.

"Fuck me harder Jasper baby please", it was like a switch being flicked whenever Jane said that to him, he was like and engine opening up, he fucked her harder for what felt like seconds until he felt his balls tighten and Jane screamed.

"Im cuming Jasper, he felt her cum all over his cock, he loved that feeling, within seconds he moaned loudy.

"shit, Belle Im cuming" as his cock stiffened like a rod and he shot deep inside her, he collapsed onto her after kissing her legs before putting them down, they were both hot and sweaty now and panting, Jasper kissed Jane, laughing.

"Better drink our tea my lady its back to work for us today", Jane groaned and covered her face, Jasper laughed and sat on the bed,

Jane sat up against the headboard and Jasper passed her the cup of tea.

"So what's the plan for the day my lord" she asked.

"Shower, dress, grab some breakfast and out the door on site for 7.30am, we have about a 100 being inducted today from the ground workers and then you can have them as you need them to do your bit through the week if that suits you? "

"Perfect small groups would be good",

"okay I will give you the list once Security have done the passes you can take your pick, just let me know what you need from me". She lent over and kissed him.

"I'm glad you are organised" she laughed.

"Im sure you will put me to shame once you get yourself settled". Jane smiled knowing full well she would be organised before the end of the day.

Jane got up gingerly, "promise me Belle you will take it easy today on your foot, any pains at all you let me know and I will bring you home, use the stick too please".

"Yes boss" she said saluting him, as she was getting off the bed, he threw his body across the bed and stretched his arm out and just caught the corner of her bottom as she moved away, she yelped and Jasper laughed.

"That'll teach you to be cheeky". They both laughed and Jasper followed Jane into the bathroom, he let her shower first he knew he couldn't keep his hands off her so he cleaned his teeth while he waited and watched in awe as she washed her body, it was so erotic watching her hands move across her breasts and down to her pussy, he was totally addicted to her. As Jane finished she came out and Jasper was waiting for her to wrap her in a towel, he rubbed her back helping to dry her off kissed her on the forehead and stepped into the shower, Jane went to clean her teeth and watched Jasper as he had watched her. She held his towel up too as he came out and wrapped him up.

They both went into the bedroom to finish drying off and get dressed. Jane wore black trousers and a red blouse with long sleeves and a plain collar, she would put her work boots on when she got to work for the ankle support but her bike boots would do for the journey. She wasn't going to ruin them at work.

By 7am they were both ready to leave, Jasper had trousers and a shirt on with his blazer, he took a spare pair of jeans which he would change into for when he went onto site. As they got to the front door he passed Jane her cane, and they left the apartment, he carried Jane's laptop bag and holdall for her. Jasper lowered the suspension so Jane could slide into the Range Rover with ease. She couldn't help but smile knowing the trick he played on her the first day. They chatted on the journey and within 20 minutes they arrived on site. They picked up their passes from the new guard Simon and went onto site by the time Jane reached her cabin she was getting the knack of this cane, Jasper had put it onto the lowest setting which was perfect for her.

He dropped Jane's laptop bag onto her desk and held her face with both hands and kissed her.
"I will be back soon with tea, I will get one of the labourers to bring in a kettle and tea and coffee for you later, we will organise a small fridge too. But if you need anything call me."
"Yes boss" she said laughing, "I'm a big girl, now go". Jasper laughed.

Before long Jane had unpacked her bag set her laptop up and had it displaying on the screen she opened up the shutters to let the light in and opened two windows to get the air flowing through. As promised Jasper came back with a cup of tea for her, he didn't stay long.
"Here is the list of the guys, we have set the induction room up for you with a nobo board and pens".
"Great, I have the sweets to bribe them with". he laughed.
"Can I come in to watch you?"
"If you like but you have to join in too" she said.
"Okay it's a deal, I will come into one later then".
He kissed her, "drop me an email with the list of guys you want and we will get them ready for 10am".
"Perfect Thank you" Jane said.

Jane emailed the list of names to Jasper of those she wanted in what group and by 9.50am she was in the Induction room ready for the first group.
As the guys started to arrive Jane said good morning to all, most of them answered, some just nodded, sadly mentioning Mental Health

to people always made them nervous they never knew what to expect.

Jane introduced herself and explained she was from the UK and had worked on sites for over 10 years and through her role she trained to be a counsellor and stay on sites, she gave them a few stats which made most sit up and listen.

"Okay this is where you join in, if you answer you get a candy or chocolate", they all smiled and nodded, "its as easy as that" she said.

"Okay, what I would like you to do is to give me the names you may have heard or used for someone who has a mental health condition", the room went quiet, everyone looked around.

"I know its sounds wrong but I promise you its for good reason, I will start". She turned to the board and wrote, fruit case.

"It's that simple, no offence will be taken for anything you say in this room, a voice from the back said nutjob, "great" Jane said and threw a candy, the guys laughed and a few more joined in, Jane had to write fast to keep up, candy was being thrown all over the room. The sheet was filled to the bottom in no time.

"Thank you all so very much, now the reason I asked you to do that is because this is the reason most people especially men won't put their hand up and ask for help because you think you will be classed as one of these" and she drew an imaginary circle around the names with the pen in the air, everyone nodded.

"Okay" she said put the lid on the pen and held it in her hand it gave her something to do with her hands. She went back to giving some information about Mental Health and how it can affect people, differently and everyone started to relax. Jane went on.

"When you arrive at site in the morning who do you speak to?", a few answered, "our mates".

"Okay how about those you don't know?", lots of shaking of heads.

"Right I would like to challenge you all starting tomorrow, when you arrive whoever you walk past say good morning or hello or whatever it is you say to your mates, but keep it clean", everyone laughed.

"And see what response you get".

A young lad around 20 put his hand up, Jane signalled to him.

"Yes, what's your name?"

"Its Tim".

"Hi Tim, go on".

"What if he looks miserable?"

"Even more reason" Jane replied, "none of us know what the person next to us is going through, you could be the only person that speaks to him/her that day, and the few seconds you give that person could change their whole day".

Lot's of heads nodded and people turned to look at each other.

"It doesn't matter if you speak to the same person more than once, I promise when you get a response it will make you feel good too". Everyone smiled. Jane continued with her presentation; a few questions were asked which made Jane happy. She finished off.

"Okay you will see my mug shot on site with my number underneath if you need to talk or you know someone who does give me a call, my phone is on 24/7 and no, not for that kind of call" she said laughing, pointing to one of the guys at the back that was pretending to suck a cock in the side of his cheek, he blushed but laughed.

"My door is always open. Take care of yourselves and I will see you later", they all clapped and got up to leave, each one thanked Jane as they left which was a great first result.

Jane took a deep breath tidied the room up and went to find a cup of tea before the next group arrived, she had three this morning to do and she loved it, the conversation always took a different path with each group. Not everyone was happy to be here either, so she didn't expect acceptance from everyone.

Jasper popped his head in and kissed her quickly.

"I will be in on the next one Belle".

"Okay great" she said, "just promise me whatever happens unless I ask for your input you will allow me to handle the situation".

"Oh, okay".

"Please Jasper".

"Okay love I promise, should I be worried?"

She laughed "not at all but some people don't want to be here that's all".

Okay, "see you in 10 minutes".

He kissed her on the nose before he walked out the door.

Jane checked a few messages on her phone and the next group started to arrive.

As with the first session she began, she didn't need notes she had done this so many times it was natural for her and it was better more believable. This group were a bit quiet to start then one of the guys got angry when Jane started talking about the different Mental Health conditions. He was huffing and puffing, Jane left him alone she knew he needed to talk to someone she spotted him after the first few minutes, he had become disruptive. Jane went on, she was talking about saying good morning to everyone, the guy got up and shouted "It's a waste of fucking time, who are you anyway to tell us what to do, you come over here with your posh accent thinking you know better you make me sick".

Jasper went to get up, Jane shot him a look and he sat back down, he was at the back screwing his hands together into fists. He would be over these chairs in a second if needed.

Jane looked over to the guy, he was mad he was up and down in his seat throwing his bag onto the ground and picking it back up again. Jane walked over to him.

"I'm sorry I didn't get your name?"

"Fuck off bitch" he said.

His mate pulled him into the chair.

"Leave it Stu, shes trying to help", he said.

He shrugged his mates hand off.

"Stu is it" Jane said quietly "shall we step outside?",

He shrugged and stormed out, Jane followed

If you don't want to be here you don't have to be, please leave if you want to.

He looked down at Jane and scowled at her.

"You're talking shit Doc"

"Okay Stu, we are all entitled to our own opinions and I don't expect you to stay if you really are not happy".

His Manager was sat at the back and was whispering to Jasper, Jane could see through the glass door.

"Look here is my card" she said taking one out of her pocket, "I don't expect you to take it but if you want to talk later about what you think is right, I will be happy to listen".

He sucked through his teeth and tutted at her, snatched the card and walked away.

"Bitch" he said under his breath.

Jane walked back into the room and continued like nothing had happened, Jasper was smiling he was so proud of her, his hands relaxed but this wasn't over, and she wouldn't be doing these sessions alone again, he wasn't risking it, someone would be in with her, he would do this week.

Jane continued, "so you got down to the bar on Friday night and you are with your mates after a few pints, your mate starts to talk He says it's been a tough week I've been staying away, the wife's given him a hard time, the kids need shoes, the dogs been sick, she's had no time to herself she wants spoiling and I just wants to relax", everyone nods, "he thinks I can actually talk to someone my mate is listening, then you turn and say, "Oh mate I know how you feel," your mate shuts up and changes the subject. "What should he have said?" Jane asked. Everyone looked blank.

Jane said its simple, "just say Im listening, everyone of us is different, regardless of our similarities with situations we all deal with them in our own way, and some of us get angry some drink turn to drugs, but don't say I know how you feel, because you don't, every situation is different".

Everyone started to nod. Jane wrapped up the session and said

"If ever you just need a hug because you are having a rough day then stop me and ask, it's amazing how good it makes you feel, it makes me feel good too". She thanked everyone again for their time, she repeated about her number and the room clapped as she finished. Jasper was grinning and on his feet looking as proud as punch, everyone left the room and Jasper came walked towards her.

"Belle I am so bloody proud of you, that was amazing, just seeing you up there talking, then handling that guy the way you did, I'm seriously impressed".

He grabbed her face and kissed her hard. They heard someone clear their throat at the door. They both turned to look it was Stu's line manager Ross.

"Hey Ross" Jane said.

He came in looking embarrassed.

"Jane, I have just rang my MD he said its your decision what happens to Stu but he wants him gone".

Jasper nodded "I agree".

Jane put her hand up, "no, let him stay, give him another chance, something is eating at him and by sacking him is not going to do him any good".

Jasper jumped in, "no Belle, he has to go".

Jane glared at him, "please both of you listen, I know what I am doing, this guy needs help, he took my card leave him, if he starts again then he goes".

Ross looked at Jasper, "it's Jane's decision Jay".

"Okay" he replied. "But any nonsense from him Jane and he's gone".

"I agree" she said, "now do you mind, I need a wee and a cuppa", they laughed and got out of her way as she hobbled to the toilet.

Jane was relieved she only had one session left her foot was aching now. She wasn't about to sit down doing a session it didn't have the same impact.

She was ready when the next session came in, Jasper followed and went to sit at the back, she frowned at him and then realised what he was doing and smiled.

"So protective" she thought, "silly bugger".

The final session took another pathway, a father and son came in and someone asked about suicide Jane gave the statistics and the father put his hand up.

"Hi" Jane said, "what's your name."

"Jerry" he replied.

"I would just like to say something if I may?".

"Of course" Jane said, "go ahead".

His son grabbed his hand, "this time last year I hit rock bottom, my business failed and I let my family down, I couldn't take anymore and tried to take my own life".

He had tears in his eyes as his son wiped his tears from his own eyes.

"I went through the house when the wife and boys went to work and found all the pills I could and sat with the family picture".

He took his wallet out and showed a smaller version of his wife and 2 boys to the group.

"I started to take the tablets, I was a mess, I couldn't see another way out, I thought they would be better off without me".

He began to cry his son hugged him, his friend who was sat behind him put his hands on his shoulders as he continued.

"Every tablet I took I found a reason to take it, I was a waste of space", a few of the other lads were wiping tears from their eyes, as he broke down and sobbed, "I then looked at the picture of my wife and kids and realised I was making a big mistake".

His son was cuddling him now openly crying with his Dad. His friend was crying too, Jane was fighting the tears herself.

"I picked up my phone I wasn't feeling so good and called my Son" he pointed to his Son Andy, "I told him what I had done and he called the ambulance. Thank god he took my call".

His Son laughed through his tears "yeah I normally say oh it's the old Man he can wait".

He sobbed again. Holding his Dad tight. Jerry wiped his eyes and looked round the room.

"Guys if ever you are feeling low sad or in need of a chat please see the Doc. Don't do what I did, I was lucky I got the help I needed because my boy here took my call".

The room erupted into clapping for Jerry and Andy, there wasn't a dry eye in the room, they all got up and came towards him, some shook his hand and others hugged him. They all went back to their seats and Jerry looked at Jane.

"Thank you for being here Jane, if you don't mind, I will come and talk to you at some stage this week".

"Of course Jerry it will be my pleasure".

Jerry got up and walked towards Jane, he said.

"Can I have one of those hugs you mentioned earlier?"

Jane smiled "It would be my pleasure Jerry, Im really glad you made that call and hugged him tight,"

One of the lads spoke

"I think you will have a queue Doc at the end", everyone laughed.

"Well I don't have a problem with that" Jane laughed.

She wrapped up the session and thanked everyone for their input especially Jerry and Andy, once again the room started to clap in thanks for Jane's presentation.

As they were all leaving they came to Jane for a hug, they had all felt for Jerry and Andy it had been one of the most emotional sessions she had done. She hugged Andy, Ross and Jerry again before they left and thanked them. Jasper waited and closed the door behind them as they left, he walked over to Jane and just wrapped his arms around her, she really needed that. He took her face in his hands.

"If I didn't understand before I do now love. Thank you for being here for them. You are one amazing lady."

Jane wiped her own tears away. She was exhausted hungry and in pain. Jasper walked her back to her room.

"Sit Belle please, let me make you a drink".

Jane did as he asked

"What would you like for lunch?, anything you fancy"

Jane smiled "yes you, and a nice foot rub".

He came over with her tea and kissed her.

"You can have me and the foot rub later. Now I need to feed you"

"Surprise me, I will have whatever you have as long as it doesn't have gherkins in, I hate gherkins".

He laughed "I won't be long".

He wasn't gone long and returned as usual with more than enough food to feed an army and Andy followed with a small fridge for her. She beamed at him and gave him a hug before he left. Jasper cleared the small table by the sofas and set out a picnic for them both.

"I could get used to this" she said.

He kissed her nose.

"Me too Belle, let's enjoy it while it's still quiet, it won't be long before we will be eating on the go."

"I know, thank you for spoiling me" she said kissing him.

They finished lunch and Jane went back to her emails for the afternoon, Jasper had to get back to the office for a meeting, so told her he would be back to take her home.

Jasper got back to the office to be met by Callum.

"I guess I know what this is about so let's get it over with where am I going?" Jasper said.

He hated the way Callum beat around the bush.

"Jasper take a seat, tea?"

"No Callum, I have to get back to site, can we just do this now?".

"Okay well, we have been asked to evaluate a job In Nebraska, its basically rebuilding the place after the tornado ripped it apart, there are several areas you will be looking at over a few days the first visit is leaving on Tuesday next week, you will be met by the local Government team and shown around, you have a lovely little place to stay you are flying business class then it's back to get the ideas drawn up, they are really open to our ideas, it's a blank canvas and then you and I go back for a week to present. There are a lot of hoops to jump through with them a lot of dinners to attend and the other bidders to meet, it's a huge job for us".

"Okay fine, thanks. Anything else?"

"No that's it Jasper".

Jasper got up to leave.

"Get Joan to email me the details please so I can plan my private life." "Private life, didn't know you had one"

Callum quizzed him "and that's why it's called private Callum"

Jasper snapped, he didn't need any snide comments from Callum, Joan was being discreet for him he could trust her.

He got back to site and went to see Jane. He wanted her to know first before anyone else said anything to her. He knocked in case anyone was with her, she called out.

"Come in"

Jasper opened the door and walked in. He went straight over to her and kissed her on the lips hungrily, she moaned as he pulled away.

"Mmm, what was that for" Jane asked.

"I just had too" he said, and I need to tell you something".

Jane looked at him concerned.

"Should I be worried?" she asked.

"No Belle not at all, but I have to go away next week for two days to Nebraska to look at a job, then once the proposal is done we need to go back, Callum is coming with me for a few days".

"Oh okay" she replied. "That's not too bad. I think I can cope without you for a few days" she laughed.

"Well I can't" he replied laughing.

He then remembered he needed to call Graham and let him know. Hopefully he would be around for Jane. Jane's phone rang it was one of her old clients.

"I need to take this love" she said.

"Okay I will be back at 5pm", he left blowing her a kiss.

Jane answered the phone to Bill, he had come to see Jane after struggling with his Mental Health a year ago, but they kept in touch still as and when Bill needed to talk. He was a biker and part of the club in the UK. Jane was fond of he would always give him the time he needed.

They spent time chatting and Bill poured his heart out to Jane, he was struggling again and just needed to hear her voice. Just needed the reassurance he wasn't crazy. Bill promised to keep in touch and said he would be over with Moses and G later in the summer.

Jane finished the day feeling accomplished but was ready to go home. Jasper knocked a few minutes later.

"You ready to go home Belle?" he asked,

"Yes I am love", she said sighing.

"Hows the foot feeling?".

"Sore if I'm honest".

"Would you like me to carry you?"

"No I will be fine I promise."

"If you insist" he smiled and kissed her.

He took her bags and her hand and walked her to the car.

"Belle if you want time alone you need to tell me to bugger off home or I won't go, I won't be offended. I will need to go home Monday night but you could come to mine and stay before I leave for Nebraska if you like. I would love to show you the house"

"I kind of like having you around but I will tell you if I want time alone, and yes I would love to visit yours", Jane replied.

"Great how about we go there Sunday night when we get back after our weekend away then?"

"Okay great",

"Then you can leave your toothbrush at mine" he grinned.

"I better buy a new one then" she replied smiling

They got into the car Jasper was grinning.

"I will miss you next week Belle"

"I will miss you too. It will be a long few days" she replied.

"I will make it up to you I promise as soon as I get back" he said looking at her with a naughty grin on his face.

"We can skype if you like?"

"Oh, that would be great" Jane replied.

They got home and Jane prepared dinner while Jasper showered, it had been a long first day they agreed dinner relax and bed early. Jane was going to join Jasper once she had prepared the salad and put it in the fridge, she was glad her foot was healing she loved the way Jasper had cared for her but she wanted to show him she could care for him too.

Jane finished the salad and went into the bedroom stripped off and went into the ensuite, Jasper was facing away from her as she walked in, she loved this man already and it scared her to death, she wasn't going to say anything in case he didn't feel the same way, he was stood washing himself the water running down his back, his perfect body, strong shoulders his muscles perfectly formed and into his narrow waist, he had the cutest bottom it was pert and firm, she got down on her knees quietly and got up behind him and licked up his cheek where the water was running down, Jasper jumped and laughed looking over his shoulder, Jane stayed their and continued to lick, then sunk her teeth into him, Jasper yelped and turned round.

"Perfect" she thought "just what I wanted".

His cock was hard and stood to attention, no hair at all just smooth beautiful skin, she looked up at him and smiled, she wrapped her hand around his balls and took one in her mouth sucking it gently.

"Fucking hell Belle"

He hissed through his teeth, Jane grinned while sucking and wrapped her hand around his cock. She started to stroke him up and down slowly.

"Oh Jesus" he said his head falling back.

"Don't stop Belle please".

She stopped sucking him and moved up to the base of his cock and licked it, Jaspers hands went into her hair.

"Oh fuck, oh fuck, do you know how fucking hot you are Belle?"

She just smiled, licked up his cock to the tip and across the top, she could see the pre cum already and licked it up.

"Oh Belle shit, do you know how I have dreamt about this?"

She ran her tongue around his cock head and into his slit, Jasper was coming undone, he knew he would explode pretty quickly but didn't want to. Jane ran her tongue down the top of his cock and he laughed nervously he was so turned on and his cock was as hard as steel. Jane moved her tongue back to the top and lowered her lips off the tip and just sucked it gently, Jasper shouted.

"Fucking hell women youre killing me".

Jane laughed, as his hands dug into her hair, he grabbed her grip that was holding her hair up and let it fall free, he pulled it up together into a pony tail and wrapped it around his hand, Jane started to move further down on his cock filling her mouth, he was overcome he was pushing her head slowly but didn't want to force her but in reality he did, he wanted her to take all of him and to cum in her mouth, Jane kept taking more of him, she knew he was close to cumming, his balls were rising and she was squeezing them.

"Oh fuck Belle"

She was sliding her mouth up and down him now and sucking harder, her tongue running around his cock, he couldn't take anymore, "Fucking hell Belle Im going to cum".

Jane nodded letting him know it was okay, he pulled on her hair and gently pushed her onto him further, Jane moved faster she wanted him to fill her mouth, she looked up at him and as their eyes locked he exploded into her mouth, his eyes went foggy his whole body was tingling down to his toes, Jane kept sucking as he came swallowing all that he had to give. He stroked her hair as he came back down.

"You are such a bad girl".

Jane licked every drop of Jaspers cum from his cock as she pulled him out of her mouth, he was so hard still. He pulled her to her feet and kissed her hard, his tongue invading her mouth forcing its way in to find hers. He pushed against the glass as he held her head kissing her, her hands were in his hair pulling him closer, he pushed her legs open with his knee and slid two fingers deep inside her wet pussy, she moaned deeply as he teased her in and out, he found her G spot and Jane bucked against his fingers trying to find her release, her pussy was clenching his fingers, she was panting and could feel her orgasm building as he continued to thrust his fingers against her pussy wall. "Oh Jasper please don't stop make me cum" she begged.

He smiled still kissing her and got down on his knees he wanted to taste her, he pushed her leg over his shoulder and devoured her, forcing his tongue into her with his fingers, teasing her clit as she screamed he knew it would be fast, she was so wet and ready, he thrust a few more times and felt her clench she came hard and fast, he was sucking her so hard not wanting to waste a drop, he loved the taste of her sweet juices.

Jane dug her fingers into Jaspers head and screamed as she came, she went light headed her eyes clouded over, her body was trembling, Jasper was holding her up she felt his tongue licking her out, every last bit, then she felt him smile as she came back to earth. He slid up her body and kissed her. They both smiled as they kissed feeling sated and exhausted.

They finished their showers and wrapped themselves in towels and went to eat. They got rid of their towels and sat wrapped in each other on the sofa chatting about their day. Jane could feel herself falling to sleep so Jasper picked her up in his arms and took her to bed, the dishes could wait. He just wanted to be near her and wrap himself around her. He laid her in bed, got in behind her and pulled her into him, he loved having her close. Jasper soon fell asleep with her.

Chapter 16

Being cared for

Jasper woke again first and went to make the tea, Jane was still sleeping, he loved to sit and watch her, she was so beautiful and looked so peaceful, he was concerned about what she was holding in from her past, after talking to Graham he grew more concerned, whatever it was he would prove to her nothing would ever happen to her again, he was falling hard for her and wanted to show her more every day.

He lent over and kissed Jane on the nose, she wiggled it like she had been tickled, which made Jasper laugh, he did it again and then kissed her forehead, Jane moaned and stretched, she was so cute when she did that he thought, he just wanted to hold her forever. Jane opened her eyes and looked at Jasper with a huge smile on her face, he bent and kissed her, he didn't care about morning breath neither did Jane, he moved her loose strands of hair from her face and tucked it behind her ear.

"Good morning my love" he said,

Jane smiled, "Good morning handsome, how did you sleep?"

"Like a baby thank you Belle" he grinned, Jane sat up with him and he passed her tea.

"Belle are you okay after yesterday, I was a little concerned, are you happy me having someone in the room with you?"I don't want you to feel I am pressurizing you into it, I am just worried that's all."

Jane smiled, "if it makes you happy as long as there is no interference unless I ask then its fine, I just don't want someone their looking like security they need to look inconspicuous."

"Agreed".

"We better get a move on or I won't let you out of bed". They both got up and quickly showered. Jane prepared yoghurt fruit and granola for breakfast, they sat on the patio eating, it was going to be another beautiful day.

They finished their breakfast and Jasper loaded the dishwasher while Jane cleaned her teeth. Jasper soon followed to do his. They were in tune with each other already they just did things without asking or needing to say anything. Jasper picked up Jane's bags grabbed his laptop and they headed out. When they arrived at work Jasper walked Jane to her office. Before he left he pulled her into his arms put his hands in her hair and pulled her in for a kiss. It was slow and passionate. He felt his eyes fog over when he kissed her. Jane had one hand on the back of his neck the other round his shoulder. When they stopped he kissed her nose.

"Now I have the taste of you on my lips for the morning. I will see you in a while Belle. Call if you need me. The first group of guys will be waiting for you at 8am".

"Thank you love" Jane replied. "See you later".

Jasper went off to talk to his team he wanted to make sure one of them attended Jane's sessions he wasn't going to leave anything to chance. If someone was going to kick off again he needed to know she was safe. He loved that she wasn't scared by it but as Jane had told him you never know how people will react. The guys agreed to take it in turn and cover every session including Jasper. He did find it a turn on watching her control the room. He was so proud of her.

All the sessions went well. Jane was getting some good feedback which pleased her, she noticed people were saying good morning. It made her smile when she heard it. She was getting horse saying it herself but she didn't care. Jasper was surprised and had to agree she was right it did change how you felt seeing someone's reaction when you said good morning. Of course there would always be the odd one who didn't reply. Lunchtime came around quickly Jasper went and picked up lunch again for them.

They enjoyed their lunches together. They were settling into a good routine. Everyone on site knew they were a couple but it didnt stop the guys flirting and having a joke with Jane she enjoyed the banter. A few of the lads were bikers and they were surprised Jane was too they were also impressed to know she had a trike. She would be taking it to work the following week with Jasper being away so she could show it off. He had suggested he leave the car with her but she declined. She wanted to ride. She missed it. She was looking forward to the weekend and getting Jasper out on it too and seeing him dressed up in leathers. That was a real turn on for her.

Her day went quite quickly as did the next few, all Jane's sessions went well and there were no more dramas. She was relieved deep down, she did get anxious when someone flew off the handle like that but that stemmed back to her past. She was used to being on edge.

Chapter 17

First Ride

Friday came around quite quickly and the site closed at lunchtime that gave Jane and Jasper time to get to the dealer to get his leathers sorted for the weekend

She was looking forward to the ride but not the chat, they were both going to open up about their past. They had booked a little hotel nothing special, it's somewhere Jane didn't want to come back to, she didn't want anything to taint what they had, so getting away from home would help.

They took Jaspers Range Rover to the dealer and Shadow spotted them as soon as they arrived.
He was chatting to a guy who was stood by a Road King special, it had some nice chrome on it and was a bright blue, he had leathers on head to toe, he was dark haired stood about 6ft, not that Jane was any good at heights, he was trim and had a gorgeous face, she could see his muscles under his leathers. His hair was swept back and he was ruggedly handsome. When he stretched out his hand Jane could see traces of tattoos, she raised her left eyebrow, and thought "he's kind of cute", then told herself off she had Jasper now, and what was her body doing betraying her like this, "reign it in women" she said to herself.

They got out of the car and walked over to Shadow. He crouched when he saw Jane and with his booming voice he shouted.
"Hey Doc, you coming to give me some more sugar, bring it on in here" as Jane walked into his open arms, Shadow lifted her off the ground and she squealed. He put her down and took Jaspers hand and pulled him in for a shoulder bump.
"Hey brother hows things?"
Jasper replied, "good Shadow, its good to see you again".
Jane turned to look at the leather clad hottie and Shadow said

"Sorry James brother this is the Doc, or half pint or Jane take your pick, shes here from the UK for a few years, she has a sweet Ultra classic trike, and this here is Jasper her fella".
James turned to Jane and Jasper and shook their hands.
"Pleased to meet you both".
Shadow went on to tell James that Jane was a counsellor and Jasper was an Engineer and they were working on the new village. James seemed impressed. Shadow continued,
"I don't know what this fella does but something in IT in the Army he tells me".
James smiled "yeah something like that".
Jane didn't believe a word of it, there was something about this guy, she would work it out she was sure, they stood chatting easily and Shadow said.
"So Brother are we converting you today?" Jasper laughed.
"Maybe, not converting but I have to keep this little lady happy so you better kit me out".

"Come on through let's see what we can find".
Jane piped up, "I know what he's having" and the men laughed.
"She certainly is sure of herself for such a little women" James said to Jasper.
"Don't mess with her" Shadow replied "Shes a sassy one", they all laughed.
"It's ok" Jane said "I'm used to being talked about".
James smiled "I suppose you must be used to it doing the job you do being around men all the time?"
Jane smiled back "yes I do, it doesn't bother me anymore, it did at first but I treat the guys like friends and they do the same with me. Respect is a two-way street but I enjoy the banter too. I know they respect me as I do them and they will look after me, but having just joined this site I have a lot of work to do to build trust and friendships".

"Well if you ever need anything and Jasper isn't about here is my card, give me a call, I take it you will be coming to the BBQ?"
"Yes we will".
"Great you can meet some of the others".

Jane saw his patch for Road Marshall, she was impressed, he didn't look the type, he was too clean cut. There was something about James and she wanted to know.

They chatted while Jasper tried on boots and dragging jeans, he came out of the changing rooms and she told him to turn around she needed to see his backside, he laughed as did Shadow and James.
"She has you under the thumb brother" shadow shouted laughing.
"I feel like a hoar" he laughed as James started wolf whistling at him.

Jane went looking at leathers and found the chaps, she pulled them off the hanger and found a nice jacket, he could pick his own crash helmet, but she wanted to choose the leathers and he had promised. Jane took them to him and sent him back to the changing room to put them on, not that he needed to strip off they went over his jeans anyway.
Once he was kitted out and he came out to show Jane, she almost wet her knickers she was so turned on he looked hotter than hot, she had all kinds of things going through her head that she wanted to do to him in those chaps. He knew what she was thinking as soon as he looked at her, he could tell, her breathing had changed she was pink in the cheeks and her nipples were hard.
He wasn't the only one to notice, James did too and it didn't do him any favours seeing them.

Shadow was packing up Jaspers things as Jane wandered over to look at the bikes, Jasper and James followed, Jasper said.
"I kind of like the idea of having my own", Jane jumped up and down squealing.
"It's a slow slippery path to an empty bank account brother" James said. "You won't stop at one and it wont stay standard".
Jasper laughed and swung his leg over the low rider, Jane nodded in appreciation, she could feel her knickers getting wet seeing him sat astride the bike. She had to move away before she embarrassed herself. She left the two men talking and went back to Shadow.
"So hightower, what do we need to bring to the BBQ next week?"
"Just your pretty little self Doc".
"The girls and boys have it in hand".
Jane handed over her credit card to pay for Jaspers things, it was the least she could do after all he had done and he agreed to get on the

trike with her. Jasper spotted her just as the payment went through and came dashing over.

"Belle" he shouted, "don't you dare", she turned and grinned.

"Too late".

James looked up "Belle?" "I thought…." As he was about to answer he said.

"I know, beautiful I get it, nice touch man" he nodded to Jasper.

"Time to get going Jasper", Jane said.

They were heading out early in the morning and Jane had a few things she wanted to do first. Shadow came over for his hug and made a big scene over Jane's hugs, He lifted her up again, and squeezed her tight. She thought her bones would break, when she got back onto the ground James said.

"So do we all get one of those then?"

"If you want one" she replied.

walking over to him, he looked round at Jasper for his agreement, Jasper raised his shoulders.

"Don't ask me buddy Jane's the boss" they all laughed.

James crouched as Jane walked into him and he squeezed her. He whispered.

"Please don't dig, I will tell you when and if I can".

Jane just nodded and James said out loud.

"You're right Shadow, this little lady gives out some good sugar", they all laughed.

They said goodbye and promised to be back the following Saturday for the BBQ, Jasper had spoken to James and asked him to let him know how much they normally spend on meat as he wanted to pay for it as a thank you for helping out with Jane and her move.

When they left Shadow updated James on Jane with as much as he knew, James said he had given his number to them both and if Shadow knew they needed help he wanted him to call him.

Jane was excited about all of Jaspers new things, she had got some new dealer t-shirts for them both and some neck gaiters. Jaspers leather was a speed distressed jacket, Jane loved it, he also had chaps and dark jeans, he picked lace up boots with a side zip and a dark grey helmet, with tan gloves, Jane was wondering if she could get him to dress up for her tonight, she got horny just thinking about it. She wanted to wash his jeans and their t-shirts and gaiters, before tomorrow. So she could get him in his chaps alone, she did have wicked thoughts she thought to herself. He just did things to her that she had never experienced before.

They got home and Jasper unpacked all of his things, he tried on his jacket and pulled all of the tags off that were on it, he looked in the mirror and didn't recognise himself.
"Belle I never thought I would see the day, me in leathers"
Jane smiled, "you don't know how happy you have made me" she said. They removed the remaining tags from all of the other things and put them in the machine Jane was stubborn when it came to washing new clothes before wearing them. Jasper laughed at her and said
"You are crazy women, but whatever you say, you're the boss".

All that was left was his chaps and leather jacket, Jane decided it was time to see him in just both.

"Honey"
she said looking up at him with her doe eyes, and twisting his t-shirt.
"Yes Belle", he replied with a caution in his voice knowing full well she wanted something.
"I would really, really love to see you with just your chaps on and your jacket".
"Oh really?" he replied smiling.
He knew what she was up to, still twisting his t-shirt and looking at him.
"Yes".
"And what will I get out of it little lady?" he asked.
"I will make it worth your while". He laughed again.
"Who can resist you? naughty girl".
He grabbed her and lifted her into his arms holding her under her bottom as she wrapped her arms around his neck and bent to kiss him. "Come on then, let's get it over with".
He lowered Jane to the ground and she clapped her hands like a little girl and skipped into the bedroom. Jasper came in and stripped off, he pulled his chaps on and his leather, Jane passed him his boots to finish off the look, watching him get dressed her knickers were soaking wet. Her pussy was throbbing and she needed to keep her

legs closed or she would be in trouble, Jasper pulled his boots on and stood in front of her, she wiggled her finger for him to turn around, he tutted and did as she asked, he grabbed her.

"Hang on, what about you, still dressed, not having that".

He went to the bottom of her blouse and pulled it over her head, then undid her trousers, pushed her onto the bed and lifted her bottom up to pull them down, they came off inside out as he pulled them off her legs and dropped them on the floor, Jane looked up at him with pure lust in her eyes, right in front of her was the whole package, even if he did have a beard and no tattoos she could live with that.

Jasper grabbed her legs and spread them, she still had her bra and knickers on, it was one of his favourite sets bright red and lacey, he knew what she was up to and he was going to make her wait.

He got down on his knees he could see how wet her knickers were, he loved that about her, she was always so hot and ready for him, he had never experienced that before and he wasn't normally the horny type but since she first looked at him all that changed, now he was like a horny teenager.

He kissed up Jane's leg as she mewled and put his mouth over her pussy and sucked, he could taste her juices and moaned as he sucked them up, Jane was pushing herself against his mouth wanting more. He pulled back her knickers and slid a finger down her pussy.

"Oh God she moaned".

Pushing at him further, he was smiling,

"What Belle?, is something wrong he teased?"

"Lick me baby please", she begged, so he slid his tongue up her once and pulled away.

"Oh god don't stop please baby".

He loved hearing her beg, she did it enough to him. He slid two fingers inside her and started to slide in and out, she was so wet, he wanted to eat her, but he wanted to tease her too. Jane writhed against him, trying desperately to push him further, she could feel him but not deep enough, she needed to feel him right inside her.

He moved his fingers further in and found her G Spot, he started to rub it just how he knew she liked it, Jane was moaning more.

"Oh yes, oh yes please don't stop".

But he did, Jane moaned like a child, It made Jasper laugh. He bent down and licked her once again, he couldn't take anymore he was done, his cock was throbbing to be inside her, all this teasing was doing him no good either, his cock was hurting as were his balls, he put his fingers into her knickers and ripped them off.

"I will buy new he thought", he pulled her up and undid he bra, Jane looked shocked but didn't say anything. He threw her bra on the floor, layed her back down as he kissed her, forcing his tongue inside her mouth Jane gasped this was really turning her on, he picked her up and turned her round.

"On your knees Belle" he demanded, with a playful tone. As she got on her knees he spread her legs, he bent over and kissed the rose on her bottom, he loved it, he slid his hand between her legs she was soaking, he ran his fingers down her pussy coating his fingers in her juice and sucked them making sure Jane heard him.

"God you taste good and now I want to feel how good you are", he spanked her right cheek.

"Open wider Belle"

He bent down and buried his head into her arse and pussy, her juices had moved round she was so wet sitting in it. He was licking round her hole.

"One day Belle" he said to himself as he licked her puckered hole, "I will take your arse" He sucked and licked her more, Jane's legs were trembling, he stood back up.

"I want to fuck you hard", Jane gasped, she wasn't used to hearing this from him, she loved it, she opened wider and her head rested on the bed, Jasper ran his cock up and down her pussy, he moved it round to her arse and teased her hole.

Oh fuck" Jane said under her breath.

Jasper smiled and sucked in air through his teeth, he moved back down to her pussy and slid in.

"Fuck, I love this pussy, mmmm that feels good" he said moaning, Jane moaned again, he slid into her so hard that Jane moaned loudly, he wasn't doing this gently tonight, that isn't what either of them wanted, he pulled Jane's hips towards him, spanked her again and fucked her hard, Jane begged for me.

"Yes, yes, fuck me hard Jasper please don't stop".

This turned him on more, he could feel his balls hitting her arse as he rammed into her, he licked his thumb and teased her hole again, he wanted her arse so much. Jane started to tease her clit, she needed the release, Jasper moved her hand.

"I don't think so Belle, that's my job!"

He spanked her again and pulled out of her, he turned her round and got onto the bed, he lifted one leg and put it on his shoulder, the other he held out straight he came in from the side and slid into her, he loved seeing his cock sliding in and out of her, Jane was moaning loudly again, as was he.

"Oh fuck, oh god" she moaned.

As Jasper got faster he knew he was going to make her hurt tomorrow but he would make it up to her, she wanted this too, and he enjoyed being bad for once.

"Jasper Im going to cum"

Jane screamed as he felt her pussy clenching around his cock.

"Oh fuck, yes Belle cum for me, I want to feel you all over my cock" Jane screamed as she came, Jasper was rubbing her clit too. He felt Jane cum as it hit him he felt his own build, Jane was clenching his cock, she knew how to tease him. He threw his head back.

"Oh fuck Belle I'm cumming" he yelled as he shot out so hard deep inside her, she clenched around him making him cum harder, Jane came again too harder this time, she felt her pussy clench around him and keep him inside her.

They were both panting trying to get air into their lungs, Jane's eyes were still foggy as she came out of her orgasm, and stroked the base of his cock before Jasper pulled out of her, she moved onto her knees and bent down, took his cock in her mouth as Jasper moaned.

"Oh fuck Belle, you are going to kill me", laughing she licked slowly down his cock and back up again before sliding her lips down the length and sucking every drop of their juices off him.

"Jesus Belle", he laughed.

Jane stopped and came back up to his mouth and kissed him pushing her tongue into his mouth giving him the last of their juices, he sucked on her tongue, moaning.

"Such a naughty Belle" he said as she pulled away.

He got off the bed. "Have you finished abusing me now Belle can I take these off?"

"I think it was the other way around Mr, you fucked me remember". Jasper laughed, "oh yeah I did, didn't I?".

He pulled his chaps and boots off and his jacket folding them over the chair. He was going to enjoy being the bad boy in those.

"Let's shower"

He said to Jane putting his hand out to her, they went into the bathroom and Jasper took Jane's hair grip off the side of the shelf and pulled her hair back into a ponytail and tied it up for her, she loved these little touches. They both showered and wrapped themselves in towels and headed for the kitchen to get something to eat. Jasper cooked a simple Prawn stir fry and they shed their towels and sat on the sofa together to eat. They agreed on an early night so they could get a good head start in the morning, Jane was feeling anxious about opening up old wounds but she needed to heal from it and be honest with Jasper. The ride would do her the world of good too, even more so having Jasper with her.

Jane was first up the following morning, she was excited about taking Jasper out for his first ride on a bike. She was packing things she knew they would need whilst waiting for the kettle, she made a mental note to get one of those one cup boiler machines, she hated waiting for the kettle.

She took the tea back to the bedroom put it on the nightstand and climbed onto the bed quietly, then sat across Jasper and covered him in kisses to wake him up, he woke laughing her hair was tickling his face and chest. He grabbed her arms and flipped her onto her back, knelt either side of her and did the same back to her instead he rubbed her with his beard until she was begging with laughter for him to stop.

They got up and showered. They were ready in the hour. They had scrambled egg for breakfast. Jasper washed and Jane dried the dishes. Jasper was feeling anxious and excited about being on the trike. They chatted about the journey Jasper knew where they were going so he could direct Jane on the intercom. He trusted Jane completely it was his first time and he wanted to enjoy it. Once they packed the backbox storage bag Jasper got into his leathers and boots and carried the bag down to the trike. Jane was checking the trike over making sure everything was okay. As he approached Jane wolf whistled at him. He shocked himself because he blushed. Which made Jane laugh. They were both grinning when Jasper got his crash helmet out. Jane lent over to kiss him before he put it on.
"Belle i have butterflies".
She giggled "me too".

They put their helmets on and Jane couldn't believe this was happening. Jasper got on the back and looked like the king of his castle. Jane got on the front plugged in the intercom.

"You can talk any time and it will cut in over the music so unless you can sing don't".

Jasper laughed. "Yes boss".

They had selected a range of music and added the playlist to his ipod and Jane started it. She pulled away and heard a little squeak from Jasper. It made her laugh.

"So cute" she thought. She could feel his legs squeeze her she loved that feeling already. She took her hand off the handlebars and touched his calf. He touched her shoulder.

"You ok Belle?" He asked.

"Yes, love, are you". "Great thank you". They got out of the town and headed onto the open roads this is what Jane had been waiting for. She felt Jasper relax behind her. They had been travelling for a couple of hours and Jasper spoke.

"Belle in about a mile is a cafe on the roadside shall we stop?"

"Sure" Jane replied. She was suprised he was so quiet she almost forgot he was there. When they stopped Jane got off first and turned to look at Jasper. "Dont move love"

she said and got her phone out to take a picture of him. He laughed, "come here I want one of the both of us", Jane went and stood next to Jasper and took a photo, he grabbed her face and kissed her as she went to take another.

"That's the one I want" he said.

Jane laughed. Jasper got off and they left their helmets gloves and jackets in the trike it was warm enough to not need them. The cafe was a small white wooden building with lots of windows. It had pot plants everywhere which really made it stand out. There were chairs and tables outside, and a separate play area for children, it was a really nice off the beaten track place. Inside there were pictures on the walls from a local artist, the walls were white and pale blue with blackboards behind the counter with an array of specials. There were 5 staff two young girls no more than 18. The chef and two on the counter doing coffees and payments. They were older in their 40's. All very smiley and welcoming. Jane was expecting to be asked to sit outside as you quite often got in the UK, but she was very surprised nobody bothered. A young girl approached and said good morning and asked where they would like to sit.

Jasper asked if they could sit in the window, the girl showed them to a table which was looking out into a wooded area. They sat opposite each other. Jasper passed the menu to Jane.

She just ordered a tea as did Jasper. They weren't hungry. Jasper took Jane's hand, this was the first time they had been out since there first night.

"How are you doing Belle is your foot ok?".

"It's fine baby thank you. I've had cruise on since we got out of town". "Oh great"

He lent down and kissed her hand.

"It feels odd looking at your back all the time, I am so used to you being beside me now". Jane smiled.

"You haven't said much on the journey "she said running her thumb over his fingers.

"To be honest Belle I felt so relaxed just sitting back I was enjoying the time and I didn't want to distract you. I have to say I am in awe of you, the first time I saw you sat at the lights in control of the trike I was amazed but being with you on it I'm in awe"

He had hold of both her hands running his fingers across her knuckles. Jane blushed she wasn't used to compliments.

"It's easy enough, is not like I have to hold it up you could ride it if you wanted too".

She meant it too, not just the ability but she would let him take control.

"I would like to try one day, James tells me it's addictive once you are bitten".

Jane laughed "he's right too, you either love it or hate it". Okay well you tell me when and I will give it a go".

"Okay" she said, "we can do that, just need a quiet place with a long road"

Their drinks arrived, two pots one with just hot water and two cups and saucers, with an additional plate of homemade biscuits.

"How lovely" Jane said.

"Belle can I hold onto you on the trike?"

"Of course, if you want too, you don't need to though, and you will be leaning down and bit".

"I know, I just want to be close that's all, and I have long arms to wrap around you".

She smiled she loved that. And hoped he would too.

They finished up their tea and biscuits, Jane went to the ladies and Jasper paid the bill, as she came out he was chatting to the ladies at the counter, she suddenly felt a burning inside her, they were flirting with him and she was jealous. She walked up and held his hand.

"Hi Belle, he said looking down at her, the ladies were just asking about the trike they thought it was mine, I was just telling them it's yours".

Jane scowled at the women she knew they were letching and she didn't like it. Jasper was a handsome man and in his leathers he looked even hotter, the women continued flirting with him which made her mad.

"That's so disrespectful", she had never felt like this before it was a new emotion for her. She needed to get it under control.

"Time to go" She said and gave the ladies a fake smile.

Jasper thanked them again and Jane took his hand as they walked out, she was just reminding them he was hers and to back off. She shocked herself, for her actions. Now she understood it. How people reacted.

They got back on the trike and headed out onto the road, Jasper moved closer to Jane and wrapped his arms around her, she couldn't help smiling it felt good. The road was so straight it was quite a boring road to ride, nothing was around them either just pockets of wooded areas on either side. It was getting warm so Jane undid her leather to get some air around her, she only had a small t-shirt on underneath. Jasper couldn't resist, he slid his hand inside and cupped her breast, Jane moaned and he heard it. He gently massaged it. He could feel himself getting horny and his cock was getting hard. He moved closer to her he wanted her to feel his cock, she did, you couldn't miss it, he was huge when he wasn't horny but when he was hard it was like steel. He found her nipple and rubbed it then got it between his fingers and pulled on it.

Jane said "You might need to stop that or I wont be able to concentrate".

He laughed, "sorry Belle".

He went to move his hand but she stopped him, she didn't want him to move, she didn't want to lose that touch, the closeness.

It wasn't more than an hour until they reached the town they were staying in, the hotel was quite central. It was a chain so nothing special but it's what she wanted. She needed to get her story out and hear Jaspers too. Then they could move on with their relationship.

Chapter 18

Laying themselves bare

Jasper grabbed the bag and they went to check in, he booked an executive room he wanted something decent, it was also at the quiet end of the hotel and sound proofed room, it made him laugh when he booked it. Knowing how noisy they were.

The hotel was a new build, it had underground parking, the lift took you to reception which was very minimalist. Lots of orchids on tables. There was a coffee shop to the side of reception and lots of metal, it had no character at all, they checked in and were given the ground floor, they went in search of the room and knew it was going to be out of the way, but didn't expect such a long walk. They were sure they would get lost, they finally found it and Jasper put the card into the door and opened it, inside the door on the wall was a slot to control the lights he dropped it in and walked in, the lounge area was first it had two big sofas and a huge 60inch TV on the wall, over to the right it had a huge cupboard and when you opened it there was a microwave fridge and sink with tea and coffee making facilities including a Nespresso machine. The room had big windows so they could see the landscape gardens, to the left was the bedroom which had double sliding doors to close it from the lounge, the bed was huge and high again.

"What is it about the US and high beds?" Jane thought, there was a nice bathroom on the left with white tiles with a double shower and a big bath.

"Nice bath" Jasper said smiling at Jane.

"Yes it is, maybe we could have one later".

"That would be nice" he said.

it certainly was big enough for the two of them. They unpacked their bags.

"let's go and explore then shall we Belle I know it's a nice place but at least it's not somewhere we would come back to, I wanted you to be able to relax in comfort".

Jane walked over to him and wrapped her arms around him, he held her tight, "its lovely Jasper thank you, and you are always so thoughtful. But no, we won't come back".

Jane was hungry so they headed out in search of somewhere to get a sandwich, she needed to eat before she started talking or she wouldn't be able too.

They found a small sandwich shop that had an array of choices, Jane went for ham salad on granary and Jasper had the same, they got some water and headed to the bike, Jasper knew just the spot to eat, it wasn't far away.
A few minutes later Jane pulled into a small park area, it had a lake with small pockets of secluded areas around it, they left the trike and walked round the lake with the blanket and lunch, they found a little spot and Jasper put the blanket down Jane unpacked the sandwiches and water, they both sat down next to each other, it was a lovely place, there were a lot of trees surrounding the lake, there were all kinds of birds ducks and a few swans bobbing about on the water, Dragon flies were hoovering around to, it was like a dance they were doing above the water it was beautiful. The sun was shining on the water leaving a lovely yellow hue.

They finished eating and Jasper lent against the tree, he patted his leg and Jane joined him, she sat between his legs but sat side on her legs dangling over his so she could look up at him. He bent down to kiss her nose then her lips. He could feel the tension inside her.
"Belle if you don't want to talk its okay, no pressure baby honest".
Jane took a glug of her water and shook her head.
"No It's okay, I want you to know it all".
He took a deep breath.
"Promise me you will wait until I finish before you ask any questions, then I will answer anything you want". Jasper nodded feeling anxious himself. He wanted to know it all but was scared of the feelings he would have.

Jane took a deep breath and explained she had met him when her Grandparents died she wouldn't use his name any longer, it made her gag to say it. She was in a vulnerable position and he could see that which is why she was easy to control. She knew that now.She went on "It was ok at the beginning he would say nice things but I always felt on edge and wasn't sure why, it came round to Grandads anniversary and I was a little sad he asked what was wrong and I told him, he flew off the handle and said I better smile he wasn't allowing a corpse to spoil his day and if I continued to be miserable he would give me something to cry for. We were in the garden and I was weeding and had a few tears, he came up behind me, grabbed my head and pulled it back, he could see my tear stained face and asked me what had he told me, he dragged me onto my feet and slapped me across the face, dragged me into the house as the garden was overlooked and then wrapped his hands around my upper arms and squeezed hard, he started to shake me spitting in my face telling me I was a miserable bitch and this was the last time he would allow me to be miserable. He slapped me again and threw me to the ground and kicked me in the stomach. He liked to hurt me where it couldn't be seen".

She went on telling him about the incident at the dealership when Moses had hit him and the subsequent beatings, she said I didn't tell Graham everything, but I want you to know it all, if you choose to walk away with what I tell you now I will understand, Jasper was boiling inside listening to Jane, he wanted to cry, could this get any worse he thought, she hadn't told him about the baby yet.

She continued, he began to get very controlling, if I was late getting home I would be questioned, he would look up the travel reports and call me a liar, he never believed anything I said, he would hit me for lying regardless. If I spent any money I had to give him the receipt as he would check the bank account daily and I had to prove everything I spent. I was never allowed to buy anything for myself, it was all handouts from friends. If I needed new shoes I had to wear them until there were holes in the bottom then it would be the cheapest pair he could find for me, I wasn't allowed more than one pair at a time. I had one coat which was over 20 years old and nothing else.

"He went out one day as I was working on the Saturday, he came too the office to make sure I was in and when I asked why he came he punched me in the stomach and squeezed my face, spat at me and said I will ask what I like don't ever question me again, if I talked to anyone he would beat me senseless. He kicked me in the back to

warn me what would happen later". She looked down and saw Jaspers hands clenching, she just rubbed his hands, he kissed her shoulder and she went on. "I couldn't tell anyone what was happening I was scared to death, I knew that was my life now.
One night he was drunk when he came to bed he started clawing at my body, I was trying to pretend I was asleep hoping he would leave me alone, that just made it worse, he forced me onto my knees ripped my nightie off me and raped me, when he had finished he punched me in the side and I collapsed on the bed, I knew he had caught a rib that time I was struggling to breath but I wasn't allowed near the Doctors. He told me never to deny him again".

Jaspers arms went round Jane and held her so tight, he didn't want to hear anymore he wanted to fid this guy and rip his heart out.

"I started to put weight on which I hated so I started to skip lunch and lose weight which he spotted so he told me if he had to force feed me he would. One night we were sat having dinner it was a roast and I had finished, I had left food like I had always done, he threw his meal at the wall and came round the table, he sat their with the fork and said you will eat this, I told him I had finished I didn't want any more, so he started to force feed me, he held my nose so I would open my mouth and pushed food in then closed my mouth, I was gagging as he made me eat it, it was falling out of my mouth as I was chewing he picked it up and pushed it back in, when I finished that mouthful he punched me in the face and told me never to disobey him again, I started to put on weight and look a mess, he didn't like me talking to anyone and believed if I was bigger nobody else would want me, he told me often enough". Jane started to cry a little. She was ashamed of allowing this to happen.

She took a deep breath and said "the bottom step in the house was broken, I had fallen off it that morning and asked when he would repair it, my friends daughter had also fallen so it was important to get it done. He told me that was another job that wouldn't get done now until he was ready and as I had nagged it would be a long time. I didn't say anything and walked away. I was upstairs cleaning the bathroom, it was my way of getting the frustration out, he came up and slapped me round the back of the head and asked what I thought I was doing, I answered back and said what does it look like, he grabbed my hair and pulled me along the ground out into the hall, he asked me if I was feeling brave because I had answered back, I shook my head, he unzipped his jeans and got his cock out, he told me to open my fat mouth as he pushed it against my lips I did and he pushed it in so far (he wasn't very big) but he pushed it in so I would gag and kept stopping and pushing again, I refused to suck it I was sobbing and I knew I would take a beating but I wasn't going to let him do this to me. He pulled his cock out and put it back in his jeans, he started to get verbal, and punching me, slapped me across the face, punched me in the eye and dragged me to the top of the stairs. He said he was sick of me and he was finished with me, I was begging him not to push me I was sorry and would do what he asked of me, he pushed me down the stairs regardless I was knocked unconscious he couldn't wake me so he called an ambulance, he told them I had slipped on the stairs, they took me in and he stayed with me all the time so I couldn't say a word to the doctors about what had happened, he broke three ribs, I had a blood clot behind my breast, he had broken my coccyx and lots of bruises, plus I broke my foot putting it out to try and break my fall. i was kept in over night for observation, the nurses were saying how lovely he was for staying through the night with me how kind of him it was he obviously loved me a lot, they didn't have a clue".

"Whilst on crutches I wasn't allowed to put my foot down for a few weeks but he still expected me to do everything and I had to find ways of getting the cleaning done and the washing to stop any further beatings. Things calmed down though, but he raped me most weeks and I just sobbed afterwards when I went to the bathroom. That's when I found out I was pregnant, it scared me, that meant I was stuck with him for life, but he didn't want kids so I would be in trouble for that too. I didn't say anything to him, then that was when all it kicked off again at the dealer and he put me in hospital". She went on to tell him what she had told Graham about him finding her in hospital and punching her so she lost the baby. The Doctors told me I would have trouble carrying a child now, and if I did I would need to be very careful.
"That was the end for me Moses wasn't letting me go back and has protected me since. I don't have social media and I stay off the grid as best I can as I know he will finish me if he finds me, he has vowed to do it".

"I spoke to the Police and I have an injunction on him not that he would abide by it. They had put me in touch with their counsellors and team who were great, I then went onto my own Counsellor who was fantastic, she really helped me, I started to like myself again but I am still not confident about myself, I have managed to get the weight off I put on and I am determined to keep it off, I have brought myself some more boots and shoes not that I have many and I have a few more clothes. I know I am still healing and it will take me time, it has been years now but still some things come back and haunt me. That's why I chose to become a Counsellor I wanted to be there for people like me that needed help. It was the best choice I had made".

Jasper let Jane finish and she turned and looked at him, he kissed her tears away from her cheeks which made her smile and then he took her in his arms and let her cry, she curled up on his lap he stroked her hair and held her tight, he whispered to her, "I promise you Belle nothing is ever going to happen to you again, I promise to love you and cherish you for the rest of our lives. You are an incredible lady, who deserves nothing but the best and I want to show you what being loved feels like if you will allow me". Jane sat up and looked at him. "You mean you still want me after all that? She was frowning, she had expected him to say he couldn't do this instead he was committing to her.
"Jasper looked at Jane you have no idea what an incredible person you are Belle, that's your past, your future is in front of you, let's take a day at a time, if you need time out from us that's okay I just want to be with you always".
Jane looked down she could feel the tears starting again but this time happy tears, he put his finger under her chin and lifted her face, he kissed her nose and her lips so gently, he wanted to tell her he loved her but not here not today. He would just show her. He wanted her in his life for the rest of time, he knew she didn't want spoiling but he was going to anyway he was going to get the size op f her shoes and her skirts and blouses and her bra and pants and go shopping, he knew she wouldn't go with him so he would bring it to her. But that could wait, he wanted to just hold her right now, she would never want for anything again. She was his and he was hers, nothing would come between them. He wanted to talk to Moses though and know what was happening there had this animal been seen. He wanted to

make sure he had no idea where she was, going away was going to be harder for him now, knowing how nervous she was, he was going to suggest she stay at his with the house alarm she could put different zones on and feel safer. That conversation would come tomorrow once she was there and saw the place. He would also ring Graham and let him know his thoughts and to let him know he knew everything.

The guys at the MC would also be around and he wanted to speak to Shadow to get some of the guys to keep an eye on her, he knew he was a bit over the top but he didn't care, he was going to do everything to protect her and make her feel safe.

Jane sat up and said "what are you thinking", she was worried now. "Nothing Belle", he smiled, "come here and kiss me" he said, Jane smiled and lent into his chest and kissed him, their tongues found each other and started duelling, he could feel his cock getting hard, this was not the time or the place, his old man really did let him down at times, Jane pulled away and said "oh someones horny".

"No Belle Im sorry, you know you turn me on but now is not the time or the place", she laughed and said "don't apologise knowing you are hard for me after all that is a compliment". She laid onto his chest and he hugged her, kissing the top of her head.

He knew he had to tell his story but that was nothing in comparison and it could wait until later.

They sat together for a while longer watching the birds and ducks, he felt Jane relax into him her shoulders finally back where they should be and not tensed up around her ears.

"Fancy a walk round the lake?"" he said to her.
Jane nodded "yes I would like that".
Tthey got up and packed the remains of their lunch and put it into the backpack, Jasper put it on and took Jane's hand as they walked round the lake, he put his arm around her waist as they walked and Jane did the same, he loved showing her off to people. This was a new beginning for Jane it was all out in the open and he wanted to get a picture of them both.
He stopped and said "I want a picture Belle".
"Ok" she said.

They stood with their backs to the lake to get a good background and Jasper said, "to new beginnings Belle" they both smiled, it was perfect, he set it as his screen background straight away.
"No secrets, no holding back Belle".
She nodded "I promise".
"That's my girl" he said kissing her gently as they continued their walk.

They got back to the trike in about and hour, both thirsty and hot, so decided to head back to the hotel for a shower.

Jane was feeling better for telling Jasper everything she was just nervous in case he started to pull away from her now he knew everything. He must have sensed it as his arms folded round her waist, "I hope you're not having silly thoughts Belle? I'm not going anywhere, I have so much respect for you". Jane relaxed in his arms. It was his turn when they got back to the hotel.
Jane parked the trike and they got off and walked into the hotel.
"Fancy a drink in the garden?" Jasper asked.
it was really quiet and they had lots of the wicker chairs for two so you could lose yourself in them.
"Only if we can sit in one of those?"
Jane said pointing to one, she had never sat in one but always wanted to, Jasper laughed.
"Of course, why don't you go and choose one and I will get the drinks, what do you fancy?"
"Whatever you're having" she replied.
"Okay love be right back".

Jane walked to the edge of the garden where the pool ended and the seat faced away across to the woods, it was a huge garden and it had been landscaped really well, with little areas to sit quietly and a huge pool near the building. Which was the other end of the garden. Jane pulled the canopy up over the seat it looked so cosy, some string lights had been put inside too for when it was dark, she thought how cool that was. She sat their feeling very regal as Jasper came back with the drinks, he pulled a small table over to put them on so they didn't have to be held all the time. He looked at Jane.
"My Belle looks cosy".

She grinned and patted the seat next to her, Jasper climbed in smiling. "This is nice" he said kissing her.

He cosied up to her and cuddled into her.

"How are you feeling Belle?"

"Better thank you, I want today to be the last time I cry over my past, is that okay?"

"He looked down at her "I think that's perfect love".

He kissed her head "let me get your drink"

He scooted over and grabbed the drinks, he got them both a lime and soda with ice and straws.

"Oh lovely, not had one of these for years".

"Well I knew you were thirsty and I know you wont drink as you are riding tomorrow, and I didn't fancy any tea".

"You did well then" she grinned.

They had a good amount of their drink and Jasper put them back down.

"I suppose I should share my past now".

Jane cuddled him "not if you don't want too".

"I do Belle, you have opened your heart to me it's my turn now".

He took a deep breath and started talking

"I met my wife Angela when I first arrived in America, she was the Daughter of one of the boss's friends. We got on well, she was an Architect, she was greedy, wanted the best of everything, very high maintenance. We brought an apartment it was ok, very her, I prefer a house and garden, she didn't. She told me early on she didn't want children I went along with it, never thought about it much as I go away a lot and she was always away".

"We had been married about a year and she started to go off me, we never went anywhere or did anything, sex was once a month and it was always what she wanted. I went off it quite quickly and just did it to please her in the end.

After two years we hardly saw each other I was either away or she was and it seemed to work for us, then I tried to call her one night and she didn't answer her phone which wasn't like her so I tried her PA who told me she wasn't in, she was on sick leave for a week, I then told her who I was and she panicked and hung up. I rang her back and threatened her job if she didn't tell me, she said Angela had gone in for a procedure that's all she knew.

I went to the hospital to see what I could find out, went to the desk to ask they told me after I proved I was her husband that she was in surgery and to go up to Maternity, when I arrived they showed me to her room and I sat waiting for her. When she arrived back she was still asleep, I was worried sick, I didn't know what was going on, anyway, the Doctor came in to check on her and I introduced myself, he said"

"we didn't expect you, Angela said you were away abroad and not to bother you".

"I asked what had happened and he looked confused", he said.

"I think I better let Angela talk to you".

"I was at my wits end, I thought she was dying or something. I know we didn't get on, but nobody wishes their partner ill. I sat with her until she woke up and when she turned and saw me she looked stunned and panicky. I held her hand and asked her how she was, she said she was okay, I said the Doctor wouldn't tell me anything, please tell me whats going on I have been going out of my mind. She moved her hand away, and said"

"I would like you to go Jasper", I sat back shocked, I said whatever it is we can work through it please tell me, she looked round at me and said in a vicious tone"

"I had an abortion, I was pregnant I told you I never wanted kids, I knew if I had told you then you would have forced me to go through with it so I got rid of it without you knowing".

"It was like being slapped across the face, I hadn't thought about kids for years and all of a sudden there had been a chance of being a Dad and she took it away from me. I got up and walked out. She came home the next day, I moved into the spare room and we barely spoke, every time I tried she blanked me. It went on like that for a few months then she started being nice to me, she wouldn't discuss the baby but we ate together and she was civil".

"I went away on a job for a few days and got back early, when I got back I came home it was quite early. I entered the apartment and noticed her bag and jacket, she was home too, I walked into the kitchen/diner she wasn't there, so I went towards the bedroom thinking she would be in the shower, she was but she wasn't alone, I noticed through the frosted glass the face of a man I knew, it was my friend. I waited until they had finished and when he stepped out it was like I had shot him the way he stumbled back against her, she was laughing at him until she spotted me, I threw their towels at them and walked out. I packed my bags and left; I didn't want to hear any excuses I was done. I moved into a place like your old one for a few months until she moved out and then sold the place and brought the house I am in now".

Jane wrapped her arms around him. She was lost for words.

"I'm sorry Jasper"

Was all she could say, he ran is hand up her arm and held onto her, she kissed him on the cheek and climbed into his lap, they sat for a while like it just holding onto each other.

Jasper took a deep breath. Jane lent back.

"There is more isn't there?".

He nodded, she moved back to look at him. She held his hand.

"2 years after I met another women, we were seeing each other on and off, more off than on, we had been dating a few months and she was like Angela, high maintenance, she expected to be wined and dined and brought nice things, I didn't mind, I love making people happy especially my partner, anyway she came to me one day crying telling me she needed money she was going to lose her house, she needed 200k I had it, I was doing really well, I gave it to her, I thought we were at the place where things were moving forward, yes I know stupid, anyway she took it. She came to my place one day, I was in the shower after working in the garden before she arrived. She must have rooted through my office drawer and took all my bank details and my credit card which I never used, it had a 50k limit on it, she made an excuse to leave soon after I came out of the shower and within a week I was almost bankrupt, she was a professional player, she had cleared my bank account out and my credit card. I was on my knees, I had nothing left just a bit of savings tucked away and my pension. I fell apart, I don't mind admitting I thought about ending it all, I couldn't believe I had been taken for a ride twice, I was honest and told the boss and Mr Black the Security guard only because his wife found me crying one night in the car, she called him out and we sat in reception and I told them everything, I have been close to them ever since, Mrs Black cooks meals for me occasionally and sends them in, she still thinks I need looking after. My friends knew and I just shut my emotions down, I haven't been with a women in 8 years now. Until this crazy biker women came along and changed all that", he said smiling.

Jane threw herself into his arms and knocked him backwards, she sat astride him kissing his hands.

"Im lost for words Jasper, you are an incredible man, so caring loving thoughtful, you should be a cold fish really".

"I was" he said, "I never thought about another women all that time, yes I got horny from time to time and had a play in the shower but never thought about anyone, just did it to relieve the frustration. It wasn't even enjoyable to be honest. Until the day I set eyes on you properly and spent the day with you. That shower scene was very different".

 Jane blushed. Jasper laughed.

"That took the edge off what he had told her, he was embarrassed to admit someone had taken him for everything. Jane looked at him.

"I know it's not worth anything, but I promise you I am not like either of them".

"I know you're not Belle, hell you are so far in the opposite direction", she slapped him.

"Are you saying I don't look after myself", he laughed.

"No Belle, you are already beautiful you don't need to be made to look it".

She grabbed his face and gave him a huge kiss. They had both had a hard day, they had held their past in for so long from others and now they both felt free and able to move on.

Jane laid down in Jaspers arms and flicked the switch on the lights inside the hood on the seat, it was almost dusk so they shone beautifully, she looked at Jasper he was smiling.

"If this was in my garden now Belle I would have my wicked way with you" he said.

"But as there are children about, I think I better behave myself".

Jane pouted pretending to be disappointed. He pulled her in and kissed her, forcing her mouth open so his tongue could play with hers, he bit her lip and sucked it into his mouth making Jane moan. He smiled and let her go, she moved her tongue into his mouth and he sucked on it hard, Jane was moaning and mewling at him, this was a turn on for her. He had his hands in her hair holding her head, she loved it when he did that. He pulled back and said.

"We better stop I don't want to be walking across the grass tenting in my Jeans and chaps".

Jane laughed and sat up, they finished their drinks and decided to go back to their room. Jane was ready to go home but she was too tired to ride. She wanted to leave this place behind now and say goodbye to the past.

Jasper looked at her.

"You look preoccupied Belle are you okay?" He asked as they walked across the gardens.

She smiled. "Yes, baby I am, I just want to go home now. I want to leave our past where it belongs and get on with our lives. But there is one thing I would like to do when we get home with your agreement, there are two things that should never be forgotten".

He frowned at her.

"You need to explain Belle Im sorry I don't understand".

She looked at him.

"There are two babies that should never be forgotten, neither of us got to know our children and I would like to mark their lives with a rose, what do you think?.

She said as she wiped a tear away from her cheek. He took her face in his hands and looked deep into her eyes.

"Belle you are one incredible very special lady".

As she shed another tear, he kissed it away.

"I think that would be perfect. We can plant it in my garden if you like", Jane nodded.

"That would be perfect. We just need to decide on a colour now" she said. "White would be nice, I didn't know if my child was a boy or a girl did you?"

Jane nodded her head.

"Yes a girl. But white is perfect".

"We will go shopping next week and find the right one".

"Great" Jane said.

She took his hand as they walked into the hotel room.

They stripped of their clothes and into their shorts and t-shirts. They needed to decide what to do for dinner.

"Anything you fancy for dinner Belle, do you want to go out or stay in and have room service?"

Jane smiled. Rroom service would be perfect, we can watch a movie if you like?".

"Sounds good to me" he said grabbing the menu off the desk.

Jasper opened the menu, it was vast.

"Belle come and have a look at this, we are spoilt for choice".

"Jane moved across the room to the sofa and sat in Jaspers lap, she took the menu from him turned to the back page and looked at the desserts, Jasper laughed.

"You really are a chocoholic Belle, you keep eating the way you are, and I will have to give you a beasting down at the gym".

Jane looked round smiling

"I would rather you gave me a beasting in bed".

without another word Jasper grabbed her, stood up put her over his shoulder while she screamed and took her to the bedroom, he threw her onto the bed he knew she loved it when he did that and he dived on the bed after her, he pulled at her t-shirt and blew a huge raspberry on her tummy, Jane was giggling, Jasper started to scratch her with his beard, she was screaming and laughing trying to wriggle away from him, she couldn't breath. Jasper loved seeing her like this, she was so very different to the other two. Jane made him happy, feel young again and alive.

He pretended to lose grip on her and as Jane thought she was free he pounced on her again, covering her in raspberries, Jane couldn't breath with laughing so Jasper stopped so she could catch her breath.

"Right women" Jasper said trying to be masterful "what do you want to eat".

Jane pretended to take a chunk out of his neck.

"You!" she said.

Jasper laughed, and picked her up in his arms and took her to the lounge area and put her on the sofa. He put the menu in her hands.

"Pick woman before I tan your backside until you can't sit down to ride".

Jane picked up the menu and started to look, she was bored with the choice and chose a cheeseburger with salad and onion rings, Jasper chose the big boy burger and chips knowing full well Jane would pinch a few, there was no point in her getting any she would only eat a few.

She also chose a big chocolate pudding for two, it had everything you could wish for in it, including chocolate sauce, flakes, ice cream sponge and sprinkles. Jasper phoned the order through and they were told 30 minutes until it would be delivered. Jane grabbed the remote for the TV so they could find a film to watch. She wasn't sure if she would stay awake through it, she was mentally drained after the day they had.

They found a film they would like to watch it was easy watching, no tear jerker they had enough of those it was a comedy called Paul, it was an old film but good fun, they sat snuggled up on the sofa watching the start when the food arrived. Jasper got up to let the waiter in, he unloaded the trolley onto the table and bid them goodnight, Jasper gave the guy 20 dollars tip, and he left with a huge smile, he told them to just leave the dishes outside the door and he would collect them later.

Jane was now hungry and couldn't wait to eat, Jasper squeezed the pudding into the fridge after removing the shelves as it was so big. Then sat down with Jane. Their burgers were huge, for once they looked like the picture, Jane looked at hers there was no way she would manage that. Jasper uncovered his and Jane laughed.

 "I know you have a big mouth darling but how are you going to get that in".

Jasper smirked "always a dirty mind Belle".

He picked up the cloth serviette and tried to tie it round Jane's neck, he knew she was an accident waiting to happen, but she refused.

"I can do this" she said,

Jasper laughed "if you say so Belle".

Jane cut her burger up into quarters to make it easier to hold and started to eat, her fingers were getting covered in sauce as the burger was slipping around and the salad was falling out, she was laughing trying to catch it before it fell. Jasper shook his head but couldn't help laughing at her, it was like watching a child eat. Jane got through a quarter and was happy nothing and gone down her clothes, she was pointing at herself looking smug.

As Jasper said, "early days Belle".

And continued eating watching her with interest, Jane picked up the next part of the burger and relaxed while eating it, as she bit into the bun the burger squeezed the sauce and onions out which fell out of the back, they dropped straight down her cleavage, Jasper was beside himself with laughter, her face was a picture of complete shock. He didn't say a word just lent forward pulled her top up and licked up her cleavage cleaning the sauce and onion away, put her top down and went back to his own dinner. Jane just stared at him, and burst into giggles.

"Will you do that next time we go to a restaurant too?" she asked. He tutted and shook his head, "if that's what my lady wants then yes".

Jane laughed and continued eating, she managed to eat the next bit without any incident but had managed enough she was defeated and of course had to leave room for pudding.

Jasper finished most of his dinner he was beat by the burger. They sat back and both felt very full, pudding would have to wait a while, he thought. They got back into the film and sat cuddled up, this was perfect Jasper thought. He felt Jane become heavy in his arms and knew she had fallen asleep he was happy she had, he was heartbroken for her and wanted her to sleep, tomorrow was a new day and a new beginning for them both. He didn't want to be away from her this week, not now especially, he wanted to be there with her always.

He watched the film until it ended Jane was fast asleep, he left her until he was ready to go. The pudding would be wasted but he didn't care, he knew Jane would scold him for not waking her though. He wanted to get home as did Jane away from here. She was right about going somewhere they could leave their past and not go back.

He picked Jane up and carried her to bed, he was used to this now, he loved watching her sleep she looked so peaceful. He pulled off her t-shirt and shorts and laid her down, she hated having her clothes left on. He undressed brushed his teeth and got into bed. He pulled Jane into him and fell asleep relaxed knowing there was nothing hidden from Jane now, they could both move on.

Chapter 19

Trike Fun

The following morning Jasper woke up and saw Jane looking down at him with a frown on her face.

"You didn't wake me for pudding" she scolded him. Jasper laughed "Good Morning Belle".

"Good Morning" she replied, "you didn't wake me".

He laughed, she had that little girl face on her.

"No Belle you were fast asleep you know I won't wake you up".

She folded her arms across her body and pulled out her bottom lip sulking, Jasper laughed and lent into her pulling at her lip kissing as she wrapped her arms around him.

"I hope you are going to make it up to me when we get home?"

"Of course, Belle you know I will".

"That's ok then" she said jumping out of bed.

They showered quickly and headed down to breakfast, they had woken later than they thought. They both had cooked breakfast with lots of tea. They finished up and headed back to their room to pack their bag for the journey home.

They packed the trike up and got on they were heading out onto the long straight road again. They were in a quiet area so Jasper asked if he could ride for a while, Jane didn't mind so they swapped over and he climbed on. It was very quiet Jasper was relaxed and seemed quite at home. Jane put her hand on his leg stroking it. He could feel it through his leathers. She was up close to him pressing herself into his back. Jane loved him in his chaps the way they pushed his jeans up around his cock it turned Jane on. They were chatting over the intercom and Jasper said laughing

"Belle you holding my cock is not the best idea, I'm supposed to be concentrating".

"Im protecting it. That's all".

He laughed "well I don't think rubbing it is protecting it do you?"

Jane mumbled under her breath about him being a spoil sport and moved her hands up to the zip on his jacket, she pulled it down and slid her hand in. Rubbing it over his stomach and chest. Purring as she did. Jasper just laughed knowing it would be that or back to his cock. Jane decided to tease him. she lowered her voice and as she stroked down his chest and tummy and said.

"Mmmmmm I love your body, I want to run my tongue down your chest and take your nipples in my mouth and suck them. Then leave kisses all over you before finding your happy trail to your cock. Lick your precum as it slides out of your hole"

Jasper kept moving in his seat. She laughed and said

"Whats wrong baby" do you need me to ride for a while?"

"Yeah why not. I might be able to get this hard on under control".

He said laughing. He pulled over to swap with her, before he got off and turned around Jane pulled the zip down on her jacket showing just her push up bra and breasts spilling out. He turned and had a huge grin on his face. He bent down licked her cleavage kissing both breasts before zipping her up.

"You are such a tease look what you've done to me"

He said sticking his hips out, not that he needed to as he was tenting in his jeans. Jane started to laugh. He grabbed her face and kissed her hard. His tongue invading her mouth before stopping to bite her lip.

"If there was somewhere to take you Belle I would do it right here. You are such a bad girl".

Jane climbed on the trike Jasper came on behind her and moved right up close she could feel his hard cock through her leathers pressing into her bottom. As they pulled onto the road he said.

"So how does it work? Oh yeah like this" putting his hand between her legs and the other on her breasts. They both laughed staying like it for some time. Jasper started to stroke her and in a deep sexy voice whispered.

"I want to run my tongue up your leg biting and sucking all the way to your tight wet pussy".

Jane tried to clench her legs together but his hand was in the way and she was trying to ride. He continued.

"I am going to open your pussy push my tongue deep inside you so I can taste your sweet juices".

Jane could feel herself getting wetter by the second.

"Then I'm going to tease that clit flicking my tongue across it. Sucking it until you can't take anymore and explode in my mouth. Then I will suck you dry and slide my big hard cock deep inside while you beg me for more". Her eyes were fogging over she couldn't take anymore, her pussy was aching and contracting she thought she was going to cum just listening to him. She quickly pulled into a park area and rode around the lake. It was quiet which was perfect. This wasn't going to be a quiet fuck by any means.

"What are we stopping here for Belle?"

He said in a knowing voice. "Like you hadn't planned it"

she replied. Jane got off and turned to see him sat in his seat rubbing his cock through his jeans with a huge smile on his face. She stood on the foot plates facing him and undid her jacket and let it drop to the ground. He pulled her closer and started biting and sucking her breasts.

"Such a bad bad girl" pulling her breasts out of her bra pushing them together biting her nipples in turn whilst making lots of silly noises. His cock was pushing hard on his jeans as she undid the buckle and unzipped him. His cock sprang out rock hard and ready to be fucked. Jane bent over and flicked her tongue across the top licking his precum his head fell back and he moaned.

"Fuck yes, suck it Belle"

she ran her tongue round the top as he pushed up towards her. His hands in her hair pushing her down slidding his cock slowly into her mouth.

"Oh Jesus, yes Babe" he said over and over growling at her. She ran her tongue round his cock as he fucked her mouth. He was so close, he pulled her off.

"not yet Belle I want that pussy"

He moaned. Pulling her head up and into him to kiss her. He started undoing her leathers.

"I want you to sit on me Belle".

They pulled her leathers off both desperate now, she stood in her bra and a thong as he sucked in through his teeth.

"Get that pussy up here now".

He said demandingly as he took his jacket off and pushed his chaps and jeans off kicking his boots away and pulled her towards him. She was straddling the seat as he kissed her pushing his tongue into her mouth like he was fucking it. She felt his fingers pull her thong to the side as he slid his fingers inside her.

"Oh Christ yes don't stop" she moaned with her mouth full of his tongue, which came out quite differently.

He slid his fingers deeper making her back arch and her moans louder. He stopped kissing her turned her round and pulled her into his lap. She used the arm rests to lower herself onto his waiting cock.

Oh the joy of it filling her so slowly she was in heaven, she couldn't get enough of this. They both moaned together as he filled her completely and Jane started to ride him. Their moans got louder not caring at all if anyone could here. Jasper pulled at her bra to release her nipples pulling and squeezing them as he fucked her faster. Jane was ready to cum. But Jasper stopped her pushing her hips down on him.

"No baby don't stop please" she begged.

"I want you to come in my mouth. I want to taste you first Belle" he said as he lifted her off. She was so close even the feeling of his cock leaving her pussy almost made her cum. He got up and patted the seat.

"Sit Belle"

She climbed on and sat down. He pulled her legs forward and over his shoulders as he laid down on the other seat pushing himself towards her.

"What was it I said. Oh yeah I remember".

He ran his tongue up her thigh sucking and licking and opened her tight hot wet pussy, ran his finger down as it dipped inside moaning as her juices soaked his finger. He put it to his lips and sucked it off

"mmmmmm you taste so good baby girl. I'm going to eat you up"

He said as he licked her pussy from the bottom up so slowly making her moan loudly.

"Oh god baby please suck me" she screamed pushing his head down. He laughed opened his mouth and devoured her. His tongue deep inside her fucking her. She was lifting off the seat in ecstasy.

"God this is naughty and damn hot he thought to herself as her head fell back.

"Oh fuck don't stop baby please". She begged. He slid his hands under her bottom lifting her higher as his tongue went deeper. Her nails were digging into the seat as he pushed into her.

"This is such a fucking turn on seeing your head between my legs she moaned. He flicked her clit as she screamed again.

"Oh god oh god. I'm cumming"

He sucked and licked harder her eyes closed all she saw was white light her body on fire her pussy pulsing under his mouth as she continued to cum. Another hit her as he teased her more.

"Oh Jesus baby I'm cumming again".

She screamed as she tried to push out of the seat she couldn't cope this was intense. He sucked drinking every last drop of her. She felt him smiling. Like the cat who got the cream. A few last licks as he looked up into her face his glistening with her juices. She pulled his head up to hers, her pussy still aching from the most incredible orgasm. She licked round his lips tasting herself on him.

"Mmmmmm you are so bad Mr Mitchell".

As he lent in and kissed her lovingly. He stopped. Looked round like he was looking for something got off and pulled her with him. Stopping at the rear storage box he pulled out the blanket and took her hand leading her to the tree. Laying the blanket down he dropped to his knees pulling her into him kissing her tummy and grabbing her breasts.

"I want you now, get down here before I get blue balls".

She got down onto the blanket. He laid on his back as she straddled him leaning forward, she kissed him. Bit his bottom lip and chin before moving down.

"What was it I said, oh yeah I remember".

She laughed as she moved down his chest to his nipples, biting and sucking. He was sucking through his teeth again as she smiled.

Get that pussy on my cock Belle" he growled.

She wasnt ready. She wanted to tease him as he did her. Jane moved down his body licking and biting down to his happy trail. Her tongue gliding down to his cock. She opened his legs and cupped his balls squeezing gently.

"Fuck Belle please" he begged.

She moved down and took his balls in her mouth sucking softly. Oh, Jesus Belle he yelled. His fingers grabbing her head. She grinded as she licked upwards from the base of his cock. Slowly all the way up to the tip. More pre cum waiting for her as she got to the top, she could see it glistening.

"Yummy" she moaned.

She suddenly felt his hands under her armpits as he dragged her up his body.

"You are going to be fucked so damn hard Jane"

he said trying to be masterful and forceful.

"I love it when you're so masterful. But you have the wrong person my name is Belle, I don't know who Jane is?"

She smirked sitting back with her hands on her hips.He sat up grabbed her around the waist and swang her down onto her back and sat on his knees. He pulled her legs up and apart onto his shoulders and moved in. Holding is cock running up and down her pussy. She moaned loudly.

"Belle I am going to fuck you senseless, but first there is something I need to do".

Smack, he hit her backside making her scream out.

"That's for being cheeky, now what should you have said?"

"Fuck me baby please" she begged.

He smiled pushing into her hard.

"That's better".

She screamed out in pleasure as he filled her again. He pulled her closer to him. His hips pushing hard and his cock going deep into her. Jane felt it rubbing her in just the right spot.

"Baby don't stop. Harder please" she begged him.

That spurred him on as he gets faster and harder.

There is no gentleness just need and she loves it. Jane screws up the blanket in her hands as his balls slap against her arse. Jasper is moaning loudly and getting faster. Jane clenches her pussy around his cock.

"Come for me baby" she says as he groans and hisses.

"Fuck yes" he yells and released inside her and she joins him cumming again. She feels him fill her up his cock pulsing inside her. Jane clenches around him again emptying him of every last drop. Jasper lays down on Jane his cock still inside her. She loved that feeling. Jasper brushes her hair off her face that had got wet and stuck to her as he kisses her softly.

"Wow babe. What are you doing to me? I can't get enough of you" he says as he wiggles inside her

"Mmmmmm" she moans.

"I'm ready for more if you are?" she says laughing.

Jasper kisses her again and pulled out of her laughing. He takes Jane into his arms. He grabs his leather puts it against the tree and lays against it as Jane snuggles between his legs and wraps the blanket around them.

An hour later they decide its time to get back. They get dressed and pack up the blanket. Walking back to the trike hand in hand. Jasper kisses Jane as he gets on.

She smiles and gets on in front of him. They were going back to Jaspers Jane was really excited to see his place and after him telling her everything she was even more excited to know other women had not lived or stayed at his. They got to Jane's first to pick up Jaspers

Range Rover and Jane followed him to his house. As they pulled up Jasper opened the garage door turned off the alarm and told Jane to reverse in next to the Ferrari. He then reversed into his space at the other end. He closed the doors and unlocked the house door. Jane was in awe. It was beautiful. He took Jane's hand and went straight to the bedroom he put the bag on the bed and took Jane in his arms and kissed her.

"Welcome to my home. I hope you can be comfortable here the way I feel at yours?"

Jane smiled. "I hope so too. It is lovely the little bit you let me see".

Jasper laughed, "Lets unpack this bag and then i can show you round".

Within a few minutes they were done.

"Come on then". He was excited for the first time ever to show Jane around.

When they got into the kitchen Jasper put the kettle on to make some tea. He thought how incredible it was to meet someone who was like him in so many ways including drinking tea. Jane was walking around the kitchen opening doors and having a good look.

Jasper smiled. "You like it then?"

"Its wonderful love, yes".

"Come on let's go in the lounge".

He carried their tea and put it on the table. Jane sat down on the sofa it was huge. And so comfortable. Her feet didnt touch the floor so she had to put them up. She snuggled into Jasper and he felt her relax against him. That was important to him. That's what he wanted to happen.

"Belle I need to ask you something?"

"Okay" she said looking up at him.

"While Im away would you stay here please. The house is alarmed you have the garden to relax in and i would feel happier with you being here".

Jane sat quiet and thought about it.

"We can come back here after work tomorrow then I will leave from here Tuesday. I'm home at the end of the week so it would be two nights".

Jane thought about it. "Are you sure. Do you trust me?" He looked down at her.

"With my life Belle". "Okay, thank you. It would be nice to sit in the garden with my tea in the morning. Ive missed that".

Jasper sighed and relaxed.

"I dont want you gardening though. I dont want to come home and find you muddy in the flower bed".

Jane laughed. "I might" she grinned.

He would let Graham, James and Shadow know she was staying here just in case she needed anything. He knew he was being overprotective but couldnt help it. He snuggled back into Jane it was 7pm they should really eat.

"You hungry Belle?"

"A little".

"Shall we have a look see what we can find".

Jane nodded and they walked into the kitchen. Jasper opened the fridge as Jane stood behind him her arms around his waist her head on his back.

"Not much in her Belle. Eggs. Beans in the cupboard bread".

"How about beans on toast" she said.

"Perfect" he agreed. Jane got the pans out Jasper got the beans and bread and together they made their first meal in his house. He couldn't stop smiling.

After dinner Jasper said. "I better introduce you to the garden then".

Jane clapped her hands.

"Took your time".

"Well i expected you to do it yourself" he laughed.

He unlocked the patio doors it was still light and warm out so perfect to end the day sitting out there. Jane walked out onto the patio. Her mouth dropped open. It was beautiful. The patio was stone with a wall built around it which had flood lights in. There was a lampost like in old London at the edge. The patio furniture was covered over so she couldnt see but she would in the next day or two. The patio led down onto the grass which was pristine. It must have been 500ft long at least and not a soul could see in. There were mature trees and bushes around the edge. The garden was split into sections, with beautiful flower beds.

Half the flowers she didnt recognise. She felt so relaxed like she could breathe. It felt incredible. She missed her garden she loved to potter. The first third of the garden was separated by heavy trellis and climbing roses and Jasmine. The smell was incredible. As they walked through the trellis into the next part it turned slighty to the left. More flower beds and incredible plants. Tucked away in the bushes was a small swing it was beautiful. It was wood which had been treated well. It wasnt straight lines but curved edges and had a rawness about it. Jane squealed when she saw it. There was a table and chairs along side it too. Jane thought how perfect to sunbath topless out here knowing they were not over looked. Jasper walked over to the swing and offered the seat to Jane.

"Belle would you like to be the first to ever swing on it?"

She jumped up and down clapping then dashed over. She took a seat and Jasper pulled her back.

"Is my lady ready?" He whispered.

"Yes, yes" she said nodding like a little girl. Jasper let her go and as Jane swung forward she put her legs out straight and squealed. Jasper laughed. He was so happy. Finally someone to make his garden come alive. He had spent alot of money making it right. He hired a gardener but spent alot of time working on it with him in the early days. Now he just pottered about. Ernie did a great job and enjoyed every moment. Jasper pushed Jane back and too for a few minutes until she stopped.

"Oh Jasper this is stunning" she said.

"Im glad you like it Belle. Come on there is more".

Jane could hear water as they went around to the right. She gasped at the most beautiful water feature. It was amazing. It was a small brook which ran down the last part of the garden and snaked off into the open land.

As Jane saw the water she felt emotional.

It was beautiful she could get lost in here for hours and probably would over the next couple of days.

"It's so peaceful".

Jane holds Jaspers hand, he looks down at her.

"Belle are you okay?"

She looks up at him

"Yes I'm ok, it's just perfect that's all".

He smiled.

"I think I must have had you in mind then when I planned it" he smiled and kisses her.

They wander back to the house and Jasper pulled the covers off the table and chairs, Jane helped him fold the cover up, there are 2 arm chairs that are wicker with foot stalls very large ones, Jane had never seen anything so big, he walked over to a box and pulled out the cushions and put them on the chairs, there was also a table and 6 chairs for entertaining, they are wooden too and look like they have been treated well. Probably by Ernie she thinks.

"Sit Belle, would you like a drink?".

"Oh yes please tea if you don't mind".

"Coming right up" he says pretending to tip his hat.

Jasper comes back out with 2 mugs of tea and sits next to Jane.

"I love the chairs Jasper, but I have one complaint".

"Oh?" he says frowning at her.

"I can't snuggle up to you on these".

He laughs at her. "well we will have to change that then won't we". He's already thinking now of something like they were in at the hotel. He could make love to her on that.

He holds her hand while they sit and watch the sunset at the bottom of the garden. There are lot's of noises from bugs and the wind gently blowing through the trees, Jane sits and closes her eyes. Jasper looks across and smiles, he loves how she is so relaxed here.

He lifts her hand and kisses it. Jane looks at him.

"Is Ernie coming in this week?".

"Not if you don't want him too" he says.

"No, its fine, I just wanted to know so if I come home and see someone here I wont be shocked".

"I will get him to pop in tomorrow night so you can meet him, so you know who he is".

"That's a good idea".

They finish their tea Jasper looks at Jane he can see she's tired.

"Ready to go in Belle?" Jane nods.

He grabs the cushions off the chair and puts them in the box.

"I will leave the covers off as the weather is supposed to be good for the week, it will save you worrying".

"Thank you baby, that's really kind".

They go back in doors and Jasper locks the doors and shows Jane the extra security on them.

"Ernie is just around the corner if you need him for anything, I know he will pop round if you want anything". Jane smiles

"thank you. Im sure I will be fine". Jasper goes through the list of others in his head and tells himself how crazy he is to worry about her.

They head to the bedroom and strip off, they need a shower after the long ride and al fresco sex.

They go into the shower together, Jasper takes Jane's hair grips from her and puts her hair up, he's getting used to doing it and enjoys it. He loves the feel of her hair. Especially when it's wrapped around his hand and hes taking her from behind.

Jaspers bathroom is huge, it has a bath in the corner which is big enough for two, and a shower big enough for a rugby team, the shower is one glass screen and similar to the one in Jane's place, but bigger. They enter and Jane feels the power of the water hit her, she moans it's such a lovely feeling. Jasper comes up behind her and kisses the back of her neck, it sends shivers down her spine and makes her tingle all over.

"Is my Belle tired?"

Jane nods, "yes you have exhausted me today".

Jasper laughs, "I kind of remember someone else starting this" he says.

Jane looks up at him "I don't know what you mean".

Laughing. Jasper washes Jane's body and she does the same for him, they are both exhausted and ready for bed but always want to wash each other. Jasper wraps Jane up in a towel and picks her up carrying her to bed, she loves it when he does that, she misses his arms as soon as she leaves them.

Jane was quite relieved he did pick her up when she realises how big the bed is.

"I hope you are leaving me with a step for when you are away?" He laughs, "what is it with the US and the high beds?" she asks, "is everyone tall here?"

Jasper can't help laughing she looks so stroppy when she says it, she even puts her hands on her hips.

Jasper leaves the bedroom and goes back to the kitchen he comes back a few minutes later with a kitchen step and puts it on Jane's side of the bed without saying a word.

Jane falls about laughing and launches herself at him. He grabs her and kisses her knowing it's going to be hard to leave her on Tuesday, he knows he has fallen for her, but he doesn't want to scare her away by telling her.

Jaspers grabs the bedding and pulls it up and snuggles in with Jane, He bends to kiss her "close your eyes Belle time to sleep".

She gets closer to him and mewls softly kissing his chest. She couldn't be happier, she feels like she is finally home.

Chapter 20

New friends

The next morning they woke together, Jasper turns and kisses Jane, "Good morning my Belle, how did you sleep?"
"like a baby, I love your bed can I take it with me?" she smiles.
"Well you will just have to stay here more then won't you?" Jane's heart skips a beat and her tummy is full of butterflies, "did he really just say that?" she asks herself, her whole body jumping for joy inside. "Right my beautiful lady it's times to get you in the shower so we can get to work, I have a full day. I need to finish preparing for this trip". Jane pouts which he loves, he bends and takes her bottom lip sucking it gently and kisses her.
"The sooner I go the sooner I can get home to you and believe me I can't wait to get back".
Jane climbs out of bed and makes a big scene of using her step which makes Jasper laugh, he comes around the bed and spanks her chasing her into the shower.

He turns on the water and ties Jane's hair back for her and follows her in. She grabs the shower gel and starts to wash Jaspers back, she wants to devour him but she would rather wait until tonight so she can have him for longer, just thinking about it makes her wet and horny, she tuts at herself. Jasper looks round at her with those beautiful big brown eyes.
"You okay Belle?"
She laughs "yes my body is betraying me that's all".
"Oh, like mine does you mean?"
He says turning round and looking down as his cock. It's ready and waiting for her. They laugh at each other.
"We need to get going we will just have to wait until later".

"Jasper growled as he grabbed Jane's face in his hands. He kisses her deeply, Jane kisses him again and picks up the shower gel.

"Come on let's get clean. They wash each other, finish showering and go back into the bedroom to dress.

Within 30 minutes they are in the kitchen eating toast and drinking tea ready for the day.

Jasper carried Jane's bags to the car as he does every morning. They set off for site, he was lost in his own thoughts, worrying about Jane being on her own, since she had told him everything. She was strong minded he knew that, but he also knew she was vulnerable he knew that side of her too. It was only two days this time but what about the next time. He needed to make sure she was safe always. He was concerned about this crazy ex husband of hers, if he meant what he said then she was at risk. He needed to talk to Moses properly about it. Find out what he knew about him and if anyone had seen him recently, he knew he was a member of the Skulls but stopped going after he beat Jane in the hospital and the club took Jane's side. He wasn't welcome and any one of the lads would have ripped him apart given the chance, but Jane had stopped them. That much he knew.

Jane touched his hand.

"Penny for them?" she asked.

He looked round and smiled at her.

"Nothing Belle, just going over things in my head for the next couple of days and thinking how much I am going to miss you".

He lifted her hand and kissed the back of it. She smiled and took their hands to her lips and kissed his hand.

"I am going to miss you too love".

Within a few minutes they arrived at work.

"Jasper let me help you prepare for tomorrow please, I have a quiet morning and it will make me happy knowing I am helping you. Just use me for whatever you need, you can sit at my desk if you like and I will use the meeting table, you must have packs to put together?"

He smiled, okay, okay, let me get my things together and I will be back, I do have a lot to prepare and the help would be great".

Jane clapped her hands, she liked feeling useful.

"I will go and do my presentation and join you afterwards, hopefully by then you will have lots for me to do". He kissed Jane and left her to get sorted.

Jane made her cup of tea in her new favourite china mug, she hated drinking out of thick mugs and Jasper surprised her with it when he went shopping. She grabbed her tub of sweets and headed for the Induction room to start the day.

Jane had a room full this morning she spotted at the back a young girl, she couldn't be more than 26. She smiled at Jane when she walked in, she was beautiful, big brown eyes curly brown long hair. How nice it was to have a lady on site, she thought. she could see she was a site worker too as she was in her PPE. She was looking forward to talking to her at some stage.

Jane started her talk the same way she always did and straight away the new girl was quick to jump in, Jane picked up straight away this lady had issues of her own, but she was feisty. Jane nodded to her to answer the question.

"sorry I didn't get your name?"

"Chikka" she replied with a big smile.

"Hello Chicca welcome, please carry on". Chicca gave Jane lot's of names for the board. "Thank you I take it you like chocolate? Boys I think we better pass the tub down to Chicca, she is wiping the floor with you all this morning".

They all laughed and looked round at her.

The session went well, the guys joined in today. Jane wrapped up as she always did. They gave her a round of applause and left. Chicca hung back as the guys went to work.

Jane closed the door.

"Hi Chicca, everything okay?"

"Yeah" she said, "I just wanted to say Hi, I noticed we are the only two girls on site".

"Yes, hopefully once we get an Office Manager and some administration, we may have a few more".

"I don't mind I'm used to it".

Jane offered her a seat and Chicca sat down. As she was chatting and sharing herself with Jane, she could tell there was a story there and hoped she could trust Jane and talk to her sometime. She noticed how she talked with an attitude when she spoke about being the boss on site with her contractors, it made Jane smile, but she knew there was more too it. She had a beautiful figure and a smile that would melt hearts. She told Jane she was 25, so Jane wasn't far off. She was single, she had split with her boyfriend as he didn't like her working on site. So she was trying to get used to being on her own. Jane warmed to her and wanted to know more about her, not for her job, but because she was nice, she made Jane laugh with her sassiness. She was a tall girl and in her site clothes and her hair tied up she was beautiful Jane was looking forward to seeing her off site, she could see her breaking hearts.

"I better get back, there is a briefing about my new area and the teams I will be looking after".

"Okay Chicca, I look forward to seeing you later".

Jane was smiling when she went back to her office. She knew this girl was going to be a force to be reckoned with on site and she was looking forward to getting to know her more.

Jane walked back into her office. Jasper was set up at her desk he looked sexy in his suit and pink shirt. She loved the way it showed the V of his neck when he didn't wear a tie and left it open, his chest muscles accentuated it too, he oozed sex appeal, she felt herself get wet just looking at him. He was on the phone, it wasn't a business call and she felt naughty, she walked towards him and undid the button on her blouse so her cleavage was on show, Jasper licked his lips, she went behind him, kissed him on the head and pushed her breasts into him, he shifted in his chair to sit up straight. He lifted his free hand and put it behind her head to pull her down, she licked round his ear and bit his lobe gently, he sucked in air as she moved down to his neck, moving her right hand down to his shirt and rubbed his chest and his abs, through the fabric, she loved the feeling of him, he was so taught, she moaned softly which made Jasper move more in his seat, trying to adjust himself he was stumbling some of his words trying to concentrate, whilst talking to Sam one of his friends about a weekend away in the summer and catching up generally, he had avoided the call a few times so had to take it this time.

Jane undid Jaspers shirt as she kissed his neck, she was running her tongue up and down pulling his shirt away from his shoulder, he moaned forgetting he was on the phone.

"Jay you okay man, what's wrong?"

Jasper coughed. "sorry Sam, I was trying to stop myself from coughing".

Jane sniggered. Same continued non the wiser, Jane moved her spare hand down to Jaspers cock, she could see he was getting hard, as she rubbed her hand down he bit his hand to stop himself moaning again, he needed to get off the phone he was going to have her over the desk, she was a real cock tease today. He loved it but she was going to pay for it. Jane continued rubbing him as he got harder. Jaspers head fell back into her breasts, he moved the phone round and ran his tongue up her cleavage and bit her softly. Jane was soaking and needed to feel him inside her. She turned him round in the chair and undid his trousers, his eyes opened wide, was she really doing this, she wouldn't he thought. This was a dream come true. Jane took his cock out, he stood rock hard, she pulled her skirt up while licking her lips, Jasper was lost completely now, not listening to Sam, he couldn't concentrate, once Jane had her skirt high enough she straddled him on the chair, Jaspers eyes were so wide he couldn't believe this, the excitement of being caught with someone coming in the door made it feel more exciting. What he didn't know was Jane had changed the sign on the door to do not disturb, Jane pulled her knickers to the side and lowered herself down onto his cock as Jaspers head fell back again.

"Fuck" he hissed

As he felt himself slide into her wet pussy she was soaking wet and ready for him. He suddenly realised what he had said.

"Sam, Im sorry" he said "I need to go, I have a situation here that needs urgent attention, I will call you tomorrow night".

"No problem" he replied.

Sam hung up Jasper threw his phone across the desk and grabbed Jane's arse with both hands as he lent down to kiss her taking her bottom lip and biting her.

"You naughty girl Belle" he hissed.

As she slowly moved herself up and down his cock, she moaned with him and nodded, he kissed her hard, pushing his tongue into her mouth.

"My dirty Belle" he said as he stopped.

He gripped her harder and said "fuck Belle faster", he was pushing her now faster he needed this he really couldn't get enough of her, he hoped this never stopped. Jane got faster, Jasper pushed her harder onto his cock.

"Fuck Belle Im going to cum, cum with me baby".

That finished Jane. she felt the tingle inside and exploded all over his cock, as she came Jasper felt it around his cock which was like flicking his switch he came hard inside her filling her with all he had, Jane slumped against his shoulder and bit him as she came, they were both panting, Jasper lifted Jane's face and kissed her with so much passion.

"And that is why I couldn't work close to you every day" he said laughing.

Jane climbed off and grabbed the tissues off the table, she had wet wipes in her drawer too, so they were both able to clean up better. They dressed themselves and Jane got rid of the evidence in the bin and tied the bag up. Jasper came up behind her snaked his arms around her, moving her hair. He kissed her neck.

"Mmmmm" he moaned "don't ever stop being naughty will you Belle?"

She shook her head. "No love, not while you look that good".

He laughed "I will have you on your desk one of these days".

"ooooh I look forward to that" laughing, Jane went over to make them a drink and Jasper went back to the desk. When Jane went over with the tea he pulled a chair round,

"Sit Belle, please and I will show you what I need you to do if you don't mind".

"Not at all" she replied.

They worked together well for the rest of the morning, Jasper was pleased how much they had achieved. He was going out to get some lunch for them it wouldn't be a picnic today just a quick 10 minutes then back to it, he didn't want to be here too late tonight, he wanted to chill out with Jane for the evening.

He was back within no time and they sat eating together chatting work and what was next to be done, the rest of the day went fast and they finally finished up at 6.30pm, he couldn't have done it without Jane and he took her in his arms.

"You are the best Belle, I can't thank you enough for today"

She grinned "you've never thanked me before".

He smacked her arse.

"Cheeky girl, get out of that door before I take you over that desk", Jane stood still, Jasper roared with laughter.

"You are so bad Belle". She smiled.

"Yes because of you".

She kissed him and walked out of the door Jasper grabbed her bags and followed her, they locked up and headed home.

They got in the car "Belle do you fancy a takeaway I dont want either of us cooking tonight?"

"That would be nice" she said.

"Great do you fancy Chinese?"

"Yes ok" she nodded.

"Anything in particular?"

"no I will let you choose".

He rang the Chinese as they drove and gave them the order as always he ordered to much, by the time they got there it was ready, Jasper jumped out to collect it and was back within a few minutes, as they got home they dropped their bags and Jane unpacked the food, Jasper started to strip off he went and grabbed a t-shirt for them both and as Jane started to dish up he stood behind her undoing her blouse, he took it off and slipped the t-shirt over her head and undid the zip on her skirt, as he pulled it down he bent over and kissed her rose, he loved that tattoo, then he bit her arse to make her squeal, it made him laugh. He put their clothes into the washing basket and helped Jane carry the food to the table in front of the sofa, they both sat forward and Jasper put the TV on, there was a house conversion programme on that Jane was enjoying.

"Busmans holiday again Belle" he laughed.

She nodded with a mouthful of satay chicken.

They sat listening more to the programme than watching and chatting, and feeding each other, it was a good job Jasper got them changed Jane had made a mess of herself as per usual, Jasper just shook his head when he looked at her once they had finished, Jane had some satay on the corner of her mouth that her tongue couldn't get to and her fingers were mucky, Jasper leant in and licked it off her, she just melted and kissed him. Jasper looked down at the leftover food.

"Belle there is so much", Jane laughed.

"And you are surprised? You ordered it, let it cool and I will have some for dinner tomorrow".

"Are you sure?"

"Of course don't waste it".

They took everything back into the kitchen got rid of what she didn't want and washed the dishes. Jasper looked at Jane laughing.

"Shower now madam before you get that food on your t-shirt all over the house".

Jane took his hand and led him to the bathroom. Jane jumped in the shower alone as Jasper packed some clothes and grabbed his spare toiletries, he didn't like having to take them from the house. He had smaller spare ones. He didn't need much, so it didn't take him long he just wanted to get it out of the way. As he went into the bathroom Jane was finishing, as she stepped out, he held out her towel and wrapped her up tight and rubbed her back dry. She kissed him and moved to the sink to clean her teeth as Jasper jumped into the shower. Jane grabbed her book and propped herself up against the headboard, she had found a new boxset of naughty books which she was going to start reading while Jasper was away, it was a Billionaire romance, she thought that would do to distract her. She would be talking to him in the evenings, but he also had to entertain the client too. She got bored with the TV unless it was something she could get her teeth into but she still wasn't sure here. Not that she had watched much TV. She started reading and heard the shower go off, she gave it a few minutes and continued reading until she heard Jasper finish cleaning his teeth, she put her kindle down and waited to watch Jasper dry himself, she couldn't get enough of that gorgeous body and she loved watching him dry off. She loved the way his muscles went tight across his back and shoulders. He was the epitome of gorgeousness. Jasper was bent over the bed with one leg up drying off and he looked up at her.

"You're staring Belle".

"Damn I got caught" she laughed.

"You shouldn't be so damn sexy and I wouldn't stare then".

He laughed and blew her a kiss. He finished drying off and climbed onto the bed with her.

"What are you reading Belle?"

"Oh it's just a new sexy novel".

"Oh really?, are you telling me you don't get enough of sex, so you have to read about it, or are you looking for ideas?"

Jane laughed

"Neither, I just thought I would find something to do while you are away?"

"Oh, so you're going to be thinking of another man while Im away, let me have a look at this filthy novel of yours".

He said taking Jane's kindle out of her hand.

"Hmmmm" he said, reading it aloud "he slid his hard cock into her wet pussy, she was tight and ready for him, she clenched her pussy as he slid in making him groan.

"Belle this is pure filth!"

Jane started laughing, "don't you play the prude with me Mr", he laughed.

"Well I think we can do better than that don't you?" Jane laughed and took the kindle back and put it on the bedside cupboard. Jasper moved closer to Jane took her face in his hands and kissed her, wrapped his arm around her waist and pulled her underneath him, he spread her legs lent on his elbows.

"He slid his hard cock into her wet pussy, she was tight and ready for him, she clenched her pussy as he slid in making him groan" as he recited, he followed with the actions, Jane laughed and did as he said. Jasper groaned on cue as she clenched her pussy muscles around him.

They made love slowly, neither wanting it to end, they would be apart for two days and neither was looking forward to it. It was only two days, but they had not been apart now in almost two weeks. To them it felt like years. Jasper kissed Jane softly and slowly brought her to orgasm as he slid in and out of her, he teased her clit with his thumb and Jane came like never before, she felt so content and so deeply connected to him, Jasper came very quickly as Jane was coming back to earth, her eyes were just focusing and she watched Jasper riding his orgasm, he looked so beautiful as he bit his lip and screwed his eyes up, his hands in her hair, the crinkles at his eyes more prominent. As he came back down she watched as he opened his eyes and saw deep affection for her. She was a little scared by it. She wanted him to love her, but she was scared to be loved.

Jasper kissed her softly, "you are insatiable Belle".

She laughed, "I didn't do anything you were the one reading the mucky book".

He tickled her until she giggled and begged him to stop, she was squirming all over the bed trying to get away from him. When he stopped she was breathless.

"I thought I was going to pee myself" she said panting.

Then realised what she had said, she blushed and Jasper started laughing, "Belle I have seen you sitting on the toilet enough times don't be embarrassed please".#

She laughed nervously.

"Yeah well saying is different, you might think Im an old lady".

He looked at her and traced a finger round her eyes, "well you are getting a few lines Belle", she smacked his hand.

"I'm not as old as you remember, after all I'm not the one who is 40 in a few months!"

He grabbed her arms turned her over and spanked her arse, "now say you're sorry Belle?"

She was screaming "ouch, ouch" as he spanked her again.

"I can't hear you Belle" he said laughing.

"Okay, okay Im sorry you're not old". He stopped and turned her back over. Leaning down he kissed her, so desperate to tell her he loved her, he loved the fun they had and the silly moments like this. Jasper sat up.

"Would her ladyship like tea?"

"Yes please", Jasper climbed off the bed and went to make it for them. Jane went into the bathroom to clean herself up again, she had never washed so much as she had the last two weeks, she wasn't complaining though, she looked at herself in the mirror, her hair was up she had no make up on and for once it didn't bother her, she was so happy and relaxed around Jasper. She got closer to the mirror and looked at her eyes checking for the laughter lines Jasper mentioned, she didn't hear him coming in behind her.

"Checking out your wrinkles Belle?"

He teased, she looked around for something to throw at him but then thought better of it, he had two hot cups of tea so not the best idea. He put them both down on his bed side table and climbed into bed, Jane climbed back in and snuggled into him. Her back against his chest. "So are you going to read more of your smutty book?"

"No not tonight I will wait until you are not here", she grinned at him, "any way when you have the real thing why read about it".

"Ahh but you were reading it."

"Cheeky, I was just getting started that's all". She said laughing.

"Okay then". He kissed her nose and it made her wiggle it as it tickled. Jasper pulled the covers up around her.

"So what would you like to do next weekend when I get back love?" he asked.

"I don't mind, we have the BBQ Friday night don't forget, I know, we will go and get the rose for the garden and then go out to dinner if you like".

Jane nodded "okay".

"Before I forget we have a black-tie event coming up, it's a charity event in aid of your favourite subject and all our clients will be there too".

Jane moved to look round at him, "am I going then?"

"Of course, you are silly".

"Oh, I don't have a dress".

"That's okay I am sure you can find something, I will come too if you like?"

"Hmmm, I will think about it".

He laughed and cuddled her back into him, he past the tea to her and they both sat drinking together.

"Tell me about the club Belle, what can I expect this weekend?"

Jane laughed, "Well if the ones at home are anything to go by don't put your prude pants on and you will be fine", Jasper pouted.

"Some one will get her arse spanked again if shes not careful" he laughed putting his hand on his hip.

Jane laughed, "It's loud rock music, I believe there is a band playing a friend of Shadows, and there will be lots of sex going on in corners and in tents, the club girls like to play".

Jasper nodded, "oh really interesting", he rubbed his beard being thoughtful, she slapped his chest,

"I don't think so! You're spoken for"

"oh, really so who do I belong to then?" Jane opened her month in shock and awe, and smacked him again.

"You cheeky sod"

He laughed and grabbed her squeezing her tight.

"Belle you are so easy to tease", he kissed her cheek as he squeezed her.

He passed Jane her tea and they sat drinking, Jane told Jasper what the Skulls were like in the UK and she expected the same and maybe a bit more here. She was looking forward to seeing them all again and even more excited that Moses, G and a few others were coming over.

Chapter 21

Absence makes the heart grow fonder

The following morning, they were up earlier than usual, Jasper was leaving for the airport at 5.30am, Jane was going into work earlier she had a busy day after helping Jasper the day before.

Jasper loaded his bags into the car and came back into the house to have breakfast with Jane before he left, she came out of the shower and got dressed, she walked into the kitchen as Jasper was making tea and toast. They sat down in uncomfortable silence both feeling sad. Jasper leant over to Jane and moved her tea away from her lips and kissed her.

"I have to go Belle". Jasper said looking solemn. Jane got off her stool and felt quite nervous. Jasper took her hand and they walked to the door. "Right you remember how to work the T.V. Jane nodded her head down both hands holding one of his. "Good and the alarm". "Yes, i do". "Okay and you have all the numbers in your phone in case you need anyone?".

"Yes, i do".

"Okay and where is the fob for the garage?".

"In my bag".

"Right. Call if you need anything. I will always take your call. I will call at dinner time anyway. But text me when you get to work. I will let you know when i arrive".

Jane nodded feeling emotional.

"Hell, girl what is wrong with you?" she said to herself.

Jasper pulled Jane towards him. She looked up at him with her big sad eyes. He got down onto his knees so he could look her in the eyes. She wrapped her arms around his neck laughing.

"You are silly".

"I just want to hug my girl properly".

Jane was fighting the tears. Jasper kissed her deeply like his life depended on it. He pulled her head back and just looked at her.

"You know you mean the world to me Belle".

Jane nodded, "as you do me Jasper" she replied.
He kissed her again and stood up.
"I have to go love".
She held his hand as he walked out the door. He blew her kisses and she stood waiting for him to pull away. He waved and blew more kisses and went around the corner. Jane stood at the door completely lost. Jasper had really gotten under her skin. He was part of her. She sighed and shut the door looked at the clock it was still early, she pottered around the kitchen washing up their dishes and put them away. She went and got her things together. Put on her leathers opened the garage door and rode the trike out. She went back to get her bags set the alarm and locked the house up. She went over things in her head making sure she had done everything then left. Jane got to work quite early she didn't mind she had so much to do anyway. Her phone beeped with a new message she looked down it was from Jasper she opened it quickly. Butterflies in her stomach.

*I don't know how to describe you, but if I should use a few words,
I'll call you romantic, cares with passion and you're the most compassionate human I know under the sun,
You're beautiful, you're amazing, you're gorgeous and you're the best feeling to happen to a man,
You're the kind of woman every man should dream about,
You're the greatest gift from God in heaven and just one smile from You my heart melts and gets softer than water...
That's how powerful and beautiful you are.*

Jane was almost on her knees reading the message, she didn't know what to say, she truly had fell for this guy, she was terrified of her feelings, but wasn't he trying to tell her the same as she felt, Mrs doubter had entered her mind and she was having lots of silly thoughts all negative. She needed to stop feeling this way. She thought "in for a penny in for a pound" and replied.

*I like you
You're fun to be around
You're smart
You're funny, you're (very) cute
You're crazy*

You're perfect in an Imperfect way
You have the best laugh
I like you, A lot
Like a lot a lot

Jane sent it and waited for a response; her heart was pounding out of her chest.

Jasper looked down at his phone and the smile that spread across his face was huge, his heart was pounding out of his chest too. He didn't know what to do now, he wanted to tell her face to face he loved her but not yet.
He replied.

I want to make you the kind of happy
That when you lay in bed at night
You're just like "Wow"
Who even knew this was possible?

Im boarding now Belle, talk in a few hours.
Your Mr M xxx

Jane replied
Take care, missing you already
Your Belle xxx

Jasper put his phone away grinning thinking of Jane. He had butterflies when he thought of her.
"Come on man pull yourself together. Butterflies at your age", he hadn't realised he said it out loud, the man next to him looked at him oddly and frowned. Jasper laughed.
"Sorry thought I was thinking that not saying it".
The guy shook his head and looked back at his book, Jasper smiled and closed his eyes thinking of Jane, and wishing the next few days away so he could get home to Jane.
Jane had a huge smile on her face for the rest of the morning, she skipped through all her meetings and felt so light.
A few hours later as promised she heard from Jasper

Hi Belle, I have arrived. Just getting into a cab to the client. I will text you later. Missing you.
Your Mr M xxx

Jane grinned and replied
Glad you arrived safely. Can't wait to talk to you later.
Your Belle xxx

Jane went towards the exit so she could go and grab a bite to eat. Chicca was coming towards her.
"Hey Chicca, how you doing?"
"Good Jane are you, Where are you off to?".
"Just popping out to get a bite to eat".
"Fancy some company? Chicca asked.
"Yeah great, not sure where Im going to be honest Jasper normally goes for us".
Chicca laughed, "the best place you need to drive to, I have my keys so let's go I will show you".
"Great thank you, I think I would have been walking around in a daze"
They got in Chicca's car When she turned on the engine the music blasted out, "oops sorry".
She said turning it down, "I love my music loud in the mornings it wakes me up".
Jane laughed "that's ok.
I'm the same when I'm alone especially when I'm on the trike, I blast it out".
Within a few minutes they reached a small shopping precinct, around the outside was a grassy area with benches and picnic tables, there were lots of couples and families sitting enjoying their lunch and the good weather. As they got out of the car all the smells hit Jane.
"Oh wow!" She said "it all smells so good. Now I know why Jasper brings so much food back".
Chicca laughed, "I can understand that".
They started at the beginning and investigated each shop at what was on offer, and there was hot food, from Thai to Jacket potato, salads and Sushi. Jane went with a chicken salad, Chicca had Sushi.
"Fancy sitting out here?" Chicca asked.
"Yeah why not".

They found a bench and sat down, Chicca started telling Jane about herself, she said she was single and looking for a good man, they both laughed.

"Well that's not easy. Anyone on site caught your eye?".

"No but its early days", they both laughed.

"Well there is some nice eye candy and I'm not just talking about Jasper" Jane said laughing.

Chicca chocked on her sushi, "I hope Jasper doesn't hear you say that Jane"

Jane laughed "I'm only looking, a girl is allowed".

Chicca smiled, "good girl".

They tucked into their food and chatted easily, Jane liked Chicca she was easy to get along with, Chicca asked about her and Jasper so she told her the story, she couldn't help laughing with her.

"Well I hope I get to meet someone like him".

"Fingers crossed" Jane motioned.

They talked about music and clothes and men again, Chicca told Jane about her Ex, he was an arse and didn't deserve her, Jane could sympathise.

"What about you?" she asked.

"Oh it's a long story. Maybe next time".

Jane meant it too, she was done with hiding her story, she didn't do anything wrong.

"I will hold you to that, we all need someone to talk to Jane even you".

Jane smiled, "it would be nice to have a girlfriend, it seems its all men around me now, I think there are some girls at the club, but I haven't met many of the gang yet".

Hey why don't you come with us Saturday? You might meet a nice biker?"

"Oh I don't know".

"Oh come on it will be fun, you can drive their and leave your car and grab a taxi home if needed. Dress code is as you please". Chicca thought for a few minutes.

"Hell, why not, but you can come shopping with me first to get some clothes", "deal" Jane said.

"I'm crap at clothes shopping so you can help me as I need a dress for a black tie event with Jasper".

Chicca clapped her hands together, "oh fantastic can't wait. When do you want to go, tonight?"

Jane laughed, "Yes why not we can have dinner out then too, if you like?"

"Deal".

"Right let's get back". They went back to the car chatting easily.

"Do you live local Chicca?"

"About 20 miles away".

"Do you have a change of clothes with you? You could always come back to Jaspers and shower there then we can go straight off".

"Are you sure you don't mind?". She said.

"Of course' I know he won't mind".

"Sounds like a plan".

Both girls were grinning as they got back to site, Jane was excited about shopping for the first time in a long time. She wanted something nice for her party with Jasper.

The afternoon flew by, Jane hadn't moved from her desk she was busy planning events. Before she knew it, Chicca knocked it was just after 5pm. Jane logged off and put her things away. She had to put her leathers on so quickly dashed off to her locker. Chicca looked at her when she came back and whistled.

"You look hot in those Jane, I bet Jasper loves you in these".

"Something like that" she said blushing.

Chicca laughed "deats Jane, I need deats". They both laughed.

Jane said, "what are deats", then she realised, they said in unison "details".

Jane said "oooooh yeah of course. Come on you, lets go, follow me, I will reverse the trike into the garage then reverse on in front of the other one". "Okay great" she replied.

They arrived back at Jaspers, Jane put the trike away and Chicca pulled up against the garages, she grabbed her bag and

followed Jane inside. Her mouth dropped open as she walked in.

"Wow this is lovely". Jane nodded.

"It is isn't it, not bad for a man living on his own".

They both laughed, Jane took her through to the guest room, it was a nice bright airy room, with a double bed, it was light blue on the wall behind the bed and white linen, Jane's favourite. There was a white wood wardrobe and chest of drawers at the end of the bed and a nice big window seat at the bay window.

Chicca nodded "this is lovely, thank you".

Jane left her to it and went to make them both a drink. Before Chicca had her shower. Jane took her tea into her and let her get on.

Chicca went into the bathroom and closed the door. She burst into tears. She was a happy girl most of the time, but she was lonely, she had girlfriends but nobody she was close too, she liked Jane a lot, she felt she could become good friends with her, she was welcoming. She was tired of her own company.

"I will go to the BBQ with them on Friday, I don't want to be like this anymore". She had made the decision.

She turned the shower on, the bathroom was dark slate tiles and a double walk in shower, with a wooden slated board as you stepped out to drain away. It had a beautiful white sink which was a bowl sat on top of a wooden table.

"Wow that man has class, I wonder if he has a brother or a friend?" she laughed at herself. The power shower was just what she needed it felt good. she showered and stepped out, wrapped herself in the big fluffy towels and went to get dressed. She was faster than Jane and walked out into the living room with her tea and sat down on the sofa, she was sat looking out into the garden when Jane came out a few minutes later.

"Ready to hit the shops Chicca?".

"Hell yeah, let's go".

They walked out to Chicca's car and left for the Mall. Jane told Chicca that she was no good at fashion that she had one little black dress and what she wears to work. She decided to tell her about her past later but wanted to enjoy the evening. She wasn't allowing this to control her anymore. While Chicca was parking Jane messaged Jasper to let him know she was out, and she would message him later when she went to bed. he told her to have a fantastic time and he would love to see what she had brought when she gets home.

They went off linking arms just like a pair of young girls. Chicca knew a little boutique she wanted to take Jane there she knew the owner and knew they would find something nice for the black tie event.

Jane had told Chicca about the girls back home when they dressed her up, she admitted feeling good and Chicca had plans, she grinned at her Jane was beginning to see the naughtiness in her eyes.

They walked into this little shop just on the outside of the Mall, it had quite a lot of racks along both sides of the shop, in the centre was an array of shoes, bags, wraps and jackets. Jane's eyes were going everywhere.

"I wouldn't know where to start".

The owner came across to them she air kissed Chicca,

"Hi darling" she drawled it came out as Darlink, "how lovely to see you so soon now tell me who this gorgeous lady is, I hope you are going to let me dress you both she looked at Jane".

Sophia was Old Russian, her family were from old money she was one of the last in the family to remember her parents and know the losses they had suffered with their parents. Sophia was a dressmaker for many years and still did alternations, but her fingers were bent with arthritis now so the beautiful wedding gowns she once made were no longer, she still carried a tape measure round her neck and a pin cushion round her wrist just in case. She had a mass of blonde hair now salt and pepper piled on top of her head in a bun, she had beautiful cheek bones and Jane could see she was stunning when she was younger, her skin was still perfect and Jane couldn't guess her age. She had a figure to die for still and wore a low heel and a form fitting dress which made her figure look hourglass.

 Jane was lost in thought about this beautiful lady and her past when Jane stuttered to answer her as Chicca had nudged her.

"Ermm, ohh yes… Thank you, well yes I suppose so I need a dress and shoes for a black-tie event, its for charity". Jane blushed answering her.

She looked Jane up and down and walked around her, making Jane turn.

"Stand still please darling" she said again.

She felt Jane's hips and pressed her chest in from the side, Jane blushed and looked shocked at Chicca who just laughed. Sophia rubbed her index finger over her lips, and hummed, she went off to the back of the shop to what looked like a very expensive rack, and she came back with a beautiful dress. Jane's mouth dropped open when she saw it.

"I can't wear that, it's too small for me", Chicca and Sophia laughed and nodded at each other.

"Come" Sophia said to Jane and took her arm, she was quite rough but kind. She pushed Jane into the cubicle.

"Undress child" she said. Jane did as she was told and Sophia came in a few minutes later and undid her bra, Jane was mortified, she could hear Chicca laughing outside, she had a dirty laugh and she could see her face all screwed up as she laughed so loud. Sophia held the dress above Jane's head, Jane put her arms up to have the dress put over her body, the dress was red and a fine fabric it felt like nothing she had ever touched, it had thin straps and the back plunged down to just above her bottom, if she moved wrong you would see her tattoo. From the neck hung a diamante long chain which tickled her back. The front wasn't low and cut across the bust, she was pert which is why Sophia pushed her bust in from the sides to make sure her bust were in good shape for the dress. It hung just on the knee, Sophia brought some stunning sandals in for her, they were diamante too barely any straps, they were 4 inches high, Jane put them on, Sophia then scooped Jane's hair up and clipped it so it still hung down her back but it was off her face and neck to give her height. Jane looked in the mirror and gasped when she saw herself. She opened the door and stepped out, Chicca's mouth dropped open when she saw her, the dress hugged every curve which was perfection, she had a tiny waist and a full hip like the old film stars, Chicca couldn't believe this figure had been hidden so long, she now understood what Jane's friends had meant too. She jumped up and down clapping.

"Oh Jane, you look amazing, oh my god that figure where have you been hiding it and why?? Jane laughed nervously.

"Jasper is going to fall over when he sees you in this, you look like a million dollars. He won't be able to keep his hands off you".

Sophie stood back looking very proud and just nodded at Jane, she gave her a wrap made of the same fabric in silver / grey which matched the shoes, the bag was the same colour, she gave her earings that hung low on her ears, she was ready. Jane wiped a tear away from her face, she couldn't believe she was looking at the same person in the mirror. She walked up to Sophia and hugged her. Sophia whispered.

"Heal child, you are beautiful". Jane frowned.

"How does this lady know?" she thought. She pulled away and Sophia stood smiling.

"Come back and see me when you need your wedding gown Jane, I will help you".

Jane laughed "oh I don't think that will happen", Sophia just nodded knowingly. Jane went and changed while Sophia wrapped up the dress and accessories. When she finished Jane was dressed again and came out to pay. Chicca took the bags from Jane and carried them outside for her. Jane was still stunned with how well Sofia had dressed her and how good she felt.

They walked back into the Mall and stopped at a lingerie shop, Chicca wanted new bras and pants and they found some wonderful lacey sets, Jane thought it might be a nice idea to buy some more too as Jasper had ripped a few pairs of her knickers, she chose a black and red set, it was very lacey with a thong, there was also a tiny nightie which was the same colours. It had little ribbons to tie up across the breast and a frill, at the edges, it was very pretty and good on the eye, Jane thought it would be nice to wear for Jaspers return home. She had that all planned out already.

Chicca found some lovely sets for herself and really splashed out she wanted to be prepared for the next man in her life.

"Just because I wear boots and trousers all day it doesn't mean I can't wear nice underwear".

Jane smiled "I couldn't agree more".

Chicca wanted to go to another small shop she wanted to blend in with the others on Saturday, when they went in Jane smiled, it was all short skirts leather denim, slashed t-shirts low cut tops.

"Perfect" she said to Chicca "anything you get in here will be fine", Chicca tried a few things on and settled for a leather mini skirt, She had the legs for it, she also brought a blouse with a frill at the button side, it was low cut, Chicca had a great chest and loved to show it off this blouse would be perfect.

Once they finished shopping, they went for something to eat. They found a chain restaurant and went in, it was the usual menu choices burgers pasta pizza, they were seated in a bay so had plenty of room for their bags, there was 50's music playing in the back ground, it was about half full so not to loud. The waitress came and asked what they would like to drink. Neither wanted alcohol so went for diet coke. Jane ordered a burger with onion rings and coleslaw and Chicca had lasagne. The food didn't take long to arrive, and they tucked in feeling famished after a good shopping trip.

"Jane can I ask you about your past, you did say you would talk about it, I hope you don't mind me asking?".

Jane shook her head trying to swallow the piece of burger she had in her mouth and wiped her face of the traces of sauce she had on her cheek, she laughed at herself.

She took a deep breath.

"I know I have to get past this it's something I know I will never forget, and I have hidden it for many years. Moses my best friend and G who you may meet in a few weeks when they come over, were the only ones to know for many years, I have felt ashamed of what I went through which is silly considering my job you would think I would know better", they both laughed. Jane went on to tell Chicca about her ex and what he put her through, she was trying to eat but the emotion got the better of her and she put her cutlery down, she wiped a tear from her eye when Jane mentioned the baby, Jane was quite emotional, Chicca was the first women she had told and would maybe understand how it felt to lose a child. Chicca grabbed Jane's hand when she saw the tears.

"Oh, Jane I am so sorry I didn't mean to upset you". Jane shook her head, "you haven't honestly, it feels good to talk about it if I'm honest, it has stayed bottled up for too long and its about time people knew what an animal he is". She went on.

"I suppose my only concern is the threat of him coming back, it has been 10 years, but I know how he harbours things. I have stayed off social media and not told many where I am, the only ones who know are those at the Skulls MC at home, and only a few know exactly where".

"Don't worry I got your back, if you ever need anything and JDubz is away you call me".

"Thank you" she said and squeezed her hand,

"it's nice to have a girlfriend again its been a long time.

JDubz?" Jane laughed when she said it.

"Well Jasper just seems a mouthful don't you think?" she said and they both laughed. The waitress came and took their plates away and asked if they wanted dessert, they both nodded and ordered a huge bowl of chocolate pudding to share. When it arrived a few minutes later they both giggled it was huge, they took a selfie and sent it to Jasper. He knew what Jane was like for chocolate he was as bad, and she knew he would love to be tucking into it too.

Jane paid the bill after fighting with Chicca over it under the agreement next time she would be paying, they headed off back to Jaspers place, Jane was excited about everything she had brought.

It was getting late by the time they got back, as Chicca was unloading the bags.

"Chicca you can stay over if you like, time is getting on and the company would be nice". Chicca smiled.

"I would like that".

"Great, I will open a bottle of wine one glass wont hurt us", Chicca laughed.

"sounds good to me".

Jane opened the patio doors to let some air in and they kicked off their shoes and went outside onto the patio, there wasn't much light pollution where Jasper lived so as it was getting dark you could see the stars. They sat drinking their wine Chicca was as amazed as Jane about the garden.

"Can we explore" she asked.

"Of course", Chicca went back into the house and got their shoes, they walked down and Jane was relaying to her about Jasper designing the garden, they walked round the corner to where the swing was, Chicca was like a little girl, she ran across to it and jumped on, push me, push me she giggled, Jane walked over and did as she asked, they were laughing as Chicca was saying higher, higher, Jane let out a deep sigh, she felt so relaxed. She felt she may have a good friend.

After Chicca had enjoyed her swing the girls went back to the house. They chatted easily. Jane felt good about having told Chicca her story it was like a weight had been lifted. She was a bit younger than Jane but had a good head on her shoulders. It was gone 11pm when they got back to the house and they decided to turn in. Jane was getting excited. Jasper was home tomorrow night. She wasn't sure what time yet but he said he would text from the airport before he boarded around lunchtime.

The following morning Jane woke Chicca with a cup of tea and headed for the shower. They sat and had toast together and chatted about Chicca's family. She had brothers and sisters who were scattered across the US. They only got together during Thanksgiving or Christmas. She was the youngest of 6. She wanted to make her parents proud, her other sisters married young and had children. Chicca wanted to get married one day but wanted her own life first. Her career was important to her and nothing was going to get in her way. Not even a man. Jane cleared their dishes away and they headed off to work. Jane reminded Chicca about the BBQ on Saturday night. They arranged to have lunch together again that day. They really were enjoying each others company and having a great time getting to know each other.

Jane's day went quite fast which she was pleased about, Jasper had called to say he was delayed and was hoping to be home for 7pm. She planned on getting home and preparing a meal for him, so she was leaving early to go to the market and pick up some fresh vegetables and meat. She was doing his favourite noodles.

Jane had a quick bite to eat with Chicca who suggested Jane wear her new lace nightie, they both giggled and planned an attack for when he arrived home. Jane could imagine what Chicca was like with her men, she was very sassy.

Jane went to the market on the way home and picked up all the bits she needed and headed home. She got changed into shorts and t-shirt before preparing everything for their dinner, she also brought some fruit and chocolate ice cream for pudding. But she was hoping she would be the pudding tonight.

Chapter 22

Silence is golden

At 6 o'clock Jane went to get showered and decided she would put her new naughty nightie on but cover up with his dressing gown it was thin cotton so she wouldn't get too hot cooking, she slipped the red nightie on and stood and looking in the mirror, she smiled at herself, she did look good and she knew Jasper would be pleased. The lace was sheer and didn't cover much, the lace holding it together was delicate and she felt sexy in it. The crutchless knickers were as sexy as hell and were turning her on. She couldn't wait for him to get home, she looked at the clock she still had 30 minutes, she went back into the kitchen and washed up the few bits on the side, she heard the door open and felt butterflies in her tummy, she was smiling, she didn't realise how close he was as she was still washing up until he snaked his arm around her waist and ran his fingers through her hair grabbing it, he smelt it taking in the scent and growling.

He moved it away from her neck kissed her underneath her ear and down her neck. Jane was moaning, her knees were weak. Not saying a word, he spun her round, grabbed the towel and dried her hands kissing her on the mouth. Still not talking but smiling. He licked across her lips pushing his tongue into her mouth to find hers putting his hands back into her hair. Her tongue met his and she bit it gently sucking it into her mouth. She felt him smile. He stopped, took her hand and led her to the bedroom. He began to undress her smiling, constantly kissing her nose and her lips. He pulled open the dressing gown tie and pushed it off her shoulders revealing her new nightie. He moaned in appreciation as he drank her in, she felt his cock stiffen, he just stared at her and licked his lips.

He lent forward and licked her left nipple through the sheer fabric making her moan, as she pushed her chest out for more. He moved his lips across her body never losing touch and licked the right one, sucking it into his mouth hard. Making her pant and suck in her breath.

Her pussy was soaking already at the anticipation of what was coming. He was leaving wet spots on the fabric from where his mouth had been. She was aching to be touched. she could see his cock pushing against his trousers desperate to get out. Each time she tried to touch him he moved away with a naughty grin. His lips left her nipple and he kissed down to her waist getting on his knees making her moan more.

His hand on her hip holding her, he caught the lace of her knickers as he went down and slid his finger between her legs to see how wet her knickers were, instead he found the opening in them as his fingers slid inside her. He groaned again loudy, still not talking, Jane felt like she could cum already, he bent and kissed lower passing her belly button and moving down onto the outside of her pussy, he slid his tongue down the rest of the way just before her clit and pushed his tongue in, her head rolled back. The silence was killing her, but it was so sexy. She bit her bottom lip and moaned deeply. Her hands grabbed his hair and she started pulling it. He stopped and sat back staring at her, knelt up and kissed her mouth, laid her on the bed but left her legs over the edge.

He started to strip off his shirt each button showing more of his gorgeous chest. She caught her breath. She could never get bored with looking at him. He shrugged the shirt off his arms and threw it on the floor, came to the bed placing his hands either side of her, his head hovering above her, he lent in and kissed her mouth. Smirking. She went to touch him, but he shook his head biting his lip. He kissed her nose. Her chin, neck, across her shoulders biting softly making her squirm. Her body begging for more. He moved to her nipples just a quick lick across the tops. Her back arching off the bed. He licked down to the top of her pussy and opened her legs. She was soaking wet. She could feel her juices on her thighs, no hair to capture it. It glistened in the light. He licked his lips and growled again. He undid his belt, button and zip looking into her eyes. She bit her lip in anticipation. She was desperate now. Her pussy was throbbing to be touched. As he pushed his jeans down he pushed his pants too so slowly, on purpose knowing it would be driving her mad. His cock sprang out of his pants standing to attention. Rock hard. He stepped out of his trousers and pants kicking them over to the others and pushing off his socks. Jane stared at him licking her lips and biting wanting to devour him. He stood in all his glory. He rubbed his hand across his chest. Knowing it would be driving her insane. He moved over his stomach and followed it in a straight line down to his cock. Jane held her breath. He ran his hand across the top and gripped it. Just the touch from his own fingers sent him spiralling with desire. He was doing this to tease her, but he was driving himself mad too. He pumped it once. With his other hand he ran a finger into her pussy collecting her juices then rubbed it onto his cock head. Her mouth was watering her pussy getting wetter. His head falling backwards, deep animal moans came from deep inside him. One more rub of his cock and he let go. He got onto his knees in front of her, pushing her knees making her legs open wider. He blew gently as her lips parted. She moaned loudy wanting to scream out but not wanting to spoil the quiet sexual tension. He grabbed her leg and sank his teeth into her thigh she yelped. Again and again he bit her as he worked his way to her pussy. His finger were at the top on the outside rubbing slowly on her pelvic bone. Making her moan deeply. She could feel his breath again and his skin against her as his hot lips touched her skin. Her body was on fire she pushed up towards him. She felt him smile again as his tongue found her lips.

"Oh my god"! She screamed in her head It was electric.

It was like he had never touched her before it was so powerful. He ran his tongue from top to bottom so slowly her body was trembling under his touch. She didn't think she could cope any longer. He pushed his tongue in deeper sliding deep inside her.

"Oh good god"!!! She was screaming silently, moaning loudy pulling his hair. "Yes, yes don't stop oh Jesus Christ" she screamed in her head desperate to scream out loud. This was incredible. She felt his finger slide inside her as he removed his tongue. "Ooooooooohh. Could this get any better? No"!!! She asked herself. She was panting, her chest rising up, her breasts heaving. Another finger slid inside her. "Oooohhh my god" she was chewing her lip desperate not to scream keeping her words in her head. He slowly pumped his fingers quickly finding her gspot. She thought she would cum. But he stopped. Smirking again. She was going out of her mind. His tongue moved to her clit. She moaned continuously. He flicked across the top.

"Oh, heaven was close, this was it" she thought. He was going to let her cum...... no, he moved away.

"Fuck, Fuck, Fuck" she screamed in her head again and groaned in desperation. He took his fingers out and sucked her juices from them. Then his tongue slid back in.

"Oh my god"!! She couldn't take anymore She thought she would pass out in pleasure. It must have been hours it certainly felt like it. He fucked her with his tongue pushing her to the edge once more. His thumb rubbing her clit.

"Oooh, oooh, ooohhh". She felt the heat of her impending orgasm building. And he stopped. Again. She was panting she couldn't control her breathing she was a mess. She heard Jasper let out a little laugh. "Oh, revenge would be sweet Mr" she said to herself. His tongue left her she felt the loss straight away. Her pussy was empty in desperate need of him again. His thumb went back to her clit and his tongue running up and down drinking her never ending juices he was causing. "Mmmmmm" he kept moaning as he drank her. She was gripping the bed desperate to touch him but not wanting to spoil this. He was sucking harder. Her hand went into his hair. "Please let me cum" she said again in her head moaning loudly. His tongue went to her clit joining his thumb. His fingers went inside her again finding her gspot. She could smell herself her scent was thick in the air. His fingers pushed against her this time not stopping. Her hips were pushing with him. His tongue against her clit.

"Please god let this be it" she said to herself.

The heat building again. Then it hit. Her head and body came off the bed. Her nails dug into the bed screwing up the sheets. Everything went white. His tongue moved off her clit, his thumb continued with the pressure as she screamed out not making sense at all. His lips at her hole tickling her teasing her skin. Catching her juices as they flooded out of her. He was drinking her so fast not wanting to miss any. Another hit her just as she thought she was coming down from heaven. Her body was trembling, it went on and on it was incredible. He kept drinking her. It was never ending. As the second subsided he slipped his fingers out stopped licking and stood up. His smile was beautiful. his beard wet from her juices. He licked his lips. Lifted her legs putting them against his chest. Kissing them both. His hand went to his cock. It was throbbing. She didn't think she could take anymore until she saw his rock-hard cock. He rubbed it against her pussy, oh boy she was ready. He looked into her eyes as he slid deep inside her. She felt every inch, his face full of pleasure as they moaned together. His balls hit her bottom she knew he had filled her already she couldn't get enough of him. Slowly.painfully slowly he slid in and out of her. Ohhhh the pleasure ripped through her she didn't think she could cum again, but her body was telling her different.

"What are you trying to do to me"? She thought.

He made love to her so slowly it was pure heaven. He was looking into her eyes intensifying it. She felt his balls tighten he was close. His thumb found her clit again. He rubbed faster as he thrust in and out faster and faster. Her orgasm building again. He let out a loud moan as he came. She felt it fill her up as hers hit her too. Together they were cumming she was exhausted she had never experienced anything like that before, it was all about her pleasure. He stopped and slid out of her. let her legs go and put them on the floor. He climbed onto the bed pulling her into his chest. She kissed him as she moved up to meet him. He bent down kissed her lips.

"Hi Baby. I'm home. How was your day?"

Jane started laughing as did Jasper. He brushed her cheek and kissed her again.

"My silly beautiful sexy man".

"My gorgeous sexy Belle".

They laid together talking for what seemed like forever. Jane patted his bottom.

"Come on, let's shower quickly and we will go and grab something to eat before I devour you this time".

Jasper laughed. "You think you will stay awake long enough?" he said getting off the bed.

"Cheeky" grabbing his outstretched hand for her to help her up. They went into the bathroom and Jasper put her hair up, she had missed that, he kissed the nape of her neck making her quiver and giggle. She pulled him into the shower.

"Come on you sex deprived man". He laughed.

"Well you would be the same being away from you for so long", "Ermm I have silly remember, you've been gone".

"No, I mean you, being away from you like I have".

Jane shook her head and turned him round to wash his back. They finished up quickly and Jasper grabbed the towels and wrapped them. Jane went into the kitchen and put the stove on, it wouldn't take long, she went back to the bedroom and grabbed her shorts and t-shirt so she could finish the dinner, Jasper was sat on the bed drying his feet, she went over to him kissed him.

"Welcome home baby, I have missed you".

Jasper smiled. "Ive missed you too my Belle".

Jane left him to get sorted and went to finish the dinner, by the time he came out in shorts and a bare chest which drove her nuts she had the table laid and was just dishing up.

"What would you like to drink Belle?" Jasper asked.

"Water would be fine baby thank you".

Jasper went to get the water for them and came back as Jane had finished. He kissed her.

"Thank you baby it looks delicious".

They sat down together and tucked in.

"So, tell me everything you have been up to".

"I found a dress in an amazing little boutique that Chicca took me too near the Mall. But I want it to be a surprise".

He smiled, "if that's what you want Belle, I'm happy with that". He knew the shop she was on about and made a mental note to go and visit, Sophia had her size, he had a cunning plan.....

"I brought more knickers too".

"Oh, let me pay for them Belle I ripped them".

She laughed "No its fine. I told Chicca about the BBQ, I asked if she would like to come along". Good idea.

"I'm sure she will enjoy it, she might even meet someone".

They finished their noodles and went to sit in the lounge, they curled up together on the sofa, Jane moaned as she snuggled into Jaspers chest.

"I really missed you" she said kissing his chest.

"I missed you too Belle", he replied squeezing her.

They sat chatting for a while.

"I told Chicca everything yesterday" she said looking up at him.

"That's good Belle, I'm really pleased you felt you could tell someone especially another women".

He wouldn't mind ripping the creature's head of though and he wasn't a fighter or an angry man but after what he had done anyone would want to do the same. Moses had told him it was really hard as he knew him, the club knew him, but Jane wouldn't allow it, she wanted to stay hidden. She knew his threats were real.

"Thank you baby", "What for Belle?" he said looking down at her kissing her head.

"I have never felt more relaxed since I arrived in Connecticut and met you. I love the UK and Moses and the gang of course but I always have that fear hanging over me".

Jasper pulled her in tighter, his heart swelled, he was feeling good, he wrapped both his arms around her and held her tight.

"I'm glad you feel that way Belle, you have made me so happy. I will do everything in my power to keep you safe. Just promise me when we ask you to do something or not then please do it, you know we just want to keep you safe".

Jane nodded "I know love, I will I promise".

They both went quiet but not an uncomfortable quiet it was more a relaxed happy contented quiet.

Jane jumped up.

"Oh we have pudding", Jasper laughed.

"You want pudding?"

"I think you will too when you see it"

She said pushing up off his chest, she bounced up and dashed into the kitchen, she came back with a spoon and the tub of ice cream wrapped in a cloth, she handed it to Jasper like a little girl as she couldn't get the lid off, Jasper read the lid.

"Ohh my favourite Belle, chocolate. Mmmmm".

He ripped the seal off and the lid, put it onto the table next to him and Jane sat back down with him, he put his arm around her as she started to push the spoon into the ice cream, it was rock hard, so you kept pounding it to get it soft, Jasper laughed at her.

"You are such a child Belle".

She looked up at him with those big blue eyes and silly grin he bent and kissed her nose. She ran the spoon around the edge and managed to get enough ice cream for Jasper on it, she fed it to him, he made a meal out of it moaning as she put the spoon in his mouth, she giggled at him.

"Now who's silly?" she said.

He laughed at her, "my turn", he took the spoon from her and managed to get a decent amount on the spoon, he moved it towards her lips and as Jane opened her mouth, he let the spoon touch her lip and took it away teasing her, she pouted he loved that face, he started laughing at her, he did it again and Jane went to grab the spoon as the ice cream fell off and slid down her chest, it was freezing and made her jump, it started to slid down inside her t-shirt, Jaspers eyes lit up, Here let me get it for you" he said with a naughty look on his face. He bent towards Jane as she laid back and lifted her t-shirt up and the ice cream was moving down her cleavage.

"Hurry up" she said "it's freezing"

Laughing, Jasper ran his tongue up her tummy just for the hell of it and caught the little bit of ice cream that had dropped, of course he didn't stop there his tongue continued over to her nipple as it was rock hard, he couldn't resist. He bit her nipple gently which made her squeal then ran his tongue around it, kissed it before coming back up. He was grinning as he did, Jane took the spoon from him, took some ice cream out and dropped it in the middle of his chest, he couldn't stop laughing at her knowing what she was going to do, Jane bent forward and did exactly what Jasper had done and ran her tongue up his body collected the ice cream and went onto his nipple. When she finished he grabbed her face laughing.

"You are funny Belle".

Kissing her hard. When he pulled away he looked at the ice cream.

"We better eat this before it's a pool of liquid in the pot", Jane laughed as they continued to eat feeding each other spoon after spoon. They finished half and Jane put the lid on and went to the freezer to put it away. She returned and sat on his lap snuggled in as he wrapped his arms around her. He was desperate to tell her he loved her but wanted it to be right. He decided he would do it in the next few days when his nerves stopped him from talking. He felt like a teenager.

Jane started to fall asleep, Jasper could feel her breathing change, he slipped his arm from around her and gently stood up, he scooped her up and carried her to bed, she just nuzzled into him as he lifted her. It made him smile that she was so relaxed with him. He laid her on the bed and slipped her shorts and t-shirt off, she hated being dressed in bed, when he had finished she rolled over to face his side, he went to the kitchen turned off the lights checked the doors and went to bed, he dropped his shorts and climbed in with Jane pulled her into him and soon he was asleep too.

Chapter 23

Retail Therapy

They woke to another beautiful day. It was Saturday BBQ day they had a few plans like unpacking Jaspers suitcase and putting the washing on, Jasper wanted to take Jane out for lunch and do a bit of shopping he wanted some more jeans for the trike, he also needed to pay for the meat for the BBQ it was due to be dropped off this morning. He could have paid over the phone but he wanted to pick some meat up for them too so it was easier to pay all together. More importantly they agreed to buy a rose for their babies no longer with them, they would plant them on the Sunday. He knew how important it was to Jane and it had become so to him too since he finally talked about it.

Jasper rang Shadow to confirm delivery of the meat. Shadow was still amazed by his generosity, but Jasper was eternally grateful, he wanted another favour too but this was personal. He walked away from Jane so she couldn't hear what he was saying.

"Shadow I need a favour, I want to surprise Belle with me riding a bike when the guys come over from the UK, What do you think the chances are?" Shadow laughed.

"You hooked already Brother?"

"I want to make her happy Shadow, and yes I did enjoy it. I won't get rid of my cars but it would be fun".

"We could do that, you will need to do the basic two day car park test but also do the I day with a radio and a rider behind you making sure you are happy in traffic and on the bike, we have plenty here you can use, come in and take a look".

"Great" Jasper said "I will pop in during the week, and we can discuss it then if that's okay".

"Of course," he said, "pleased to help out".

"Thanks Shadow, see you later".

He hung up and went looking for Jane, she was doing her hair, he loved it down, he walked up behind her and took the comb out of her hand, he started to comb it for her and run his fingers through it. Jane loved the feel of him doing that.

"Leave it down Belle please?" he asked.

"If you want me too, of course" she said.

Jasper finished and handed her the comb back, left a kiss on her shoulder and walked away to get his t-shirt. Jane pulled her summer dress on it was a nice flimsy dress white with small flowers it was perfect for the day she slipped on flat sandals too, they were going in the car so no need for leathers until later.

Jasper looked round at Jane he had never seen her in a summer dress, "You look beautiful Belle" he said coming over to kiss her.

He noticed straight away she had gone braless, he tutted at her.

"Bad girl Belle what are you trying to do to me", she grinned at him, "As if I would?" she said.

Jasper put his shoes on and they left the house, as they walked out of the door to the garage he slapped her backside and made her squeal, "That's for teasing me", she laughed and gave him a naughty grin.

They got into the car and headed to the market where they paid for the meat, "We will come back soon for the rest" Jasper said to the owner.

"Sure no trouble Jasper when you're ready".

They left and went over to the Mall, Jane headed for the little knicker boutique she wanted to show Jasper some Basques she had seen to gauge his interest, she knew he loved her naked but she wanted some sexy things to turn him on and have to take off her before he won his prize. They walked in and Jaspers face was a picture he just stopped and looked round, he had never been to a shop like it, Jane looked up at him.

"You okay?", he looked down.

"Oh yeah, but where do you start".

She laughed and pulled him along to where they had the things she wanted to show him, there were the basques, suspenders stockings of every colour you could imagine and every design, Jane knew what she wanted but wanted his thoughts too, the whole shop was an array of colour lace and knickers. There were rows of bras in different sizes then in colours, he was mesmerised. He needed to get Jane's size now and come back and spoil her. She pulled on his hand to get his attention.

"Oh sorry Belle he said clearing his throat".

He looked down to see what she was looking at, it was a wired basque in all different colours some were cupless others had a small cup most were all lacey.

"Which do you prefer Belle?" he asked, Jane picked up a black one, it had lace cups but was underwired. It had a lace panel at the middle of the stomach and suspenders, lace at the bottom which ran all the way round, it came with knickers and a thong.

Jasper smiled. "Mmmm, Yes Belle I love it, what stockings do you want?"

She picked up a pair which were seamed and at the top was a red rose, he grinned "perfect".

"Thought you would like that".

He nodded, and picked up some others looking at the patterns, he wasn't sure about those, then he found the fishnet.

"And these Belle" he said.

She grinned, "next you will want a school girl outfit like St Trinians!" he grinned and raised his eyebrow at her.

"You are naughty Mr M" she said blushing.

He bent and whispered in her ear.

"But you wouldn't need those knickers Belle".

"You're so bad" she said laughing.

"What size are you?"

he was a bit confused as some were cup sizes others were dress sizes, he wondered off with the information Jane had given him and a few minutes later came back with some knickers and bras. Jane shook her head as he looked like the cat who got the cream. They went to the checkout and Jasper took the basket from Jane and added the bits he had found.

"I will get these Belle".

"No Jasper.

I didn't bring you in here for that".

"Belle I'm not arguing you brought my leathers it's the least I can do", she grumbled under her breath at him, just because she could. He laughed at her she was funny. He paid for the items and they young man at the counter said.

"Sir can I remind you that these are delicate and need to be washed by hand, make sure all catches are done up so they don't catch in the lace", Jasper just stood amazed listening the young man, he looked round at Jane who just shrugged her shoulders at him. He paid for the goods and thanked him still stunned as he walked away.

"Did that young man just tell us how to wash your smalls?" Jane started laughing.

"Yes I think he did". He shook his head.

"I actually felt like I was at school again" he said laughing.

He took Jane's hand as they walked out of the shop.

"Where to next? She asked.

"I could do with some more jeans actually for when we are on the bike, so what do you suggest?"

"You could get leathers and jeans, its up to you where you get the jeans from, but the leathers you need to get from the dealer", "good idea, come on then lets go, lets see what they have and if they need any help setting up for later on".

They headed back to the car.

"Actually we can go to the nursery first if you like and we can see if we can find a rose we both like it's on the way?"

Jane nodded "I would like that".

Her heart hurt a little thinking about it, but she was glad they were doing this. Within a few minutes they arrived at the nursery, it was huge, Jasper said

"I brought most of the plants in the garden from here Belle".

"Oh good at least we know they are good".

They walked in holding hands and went straight to the roses, there were rows and rows, all different brands and all different types.

"Any thoughts on the type Belle?".

"I think a tea rose or Floribunda"

"Okay" he said looking up at the signs, "this way" he said walking in front of her taking her to where the sign was, there were 5 rows of Floribunda roses in every colour and so many different names, they were walking up the isles looking at the names, they split up and decided they would come back together when they found something that felt right.

Jasper was intent on a white rose, the names were wrong he knew what he wanted, he kept going, he loved roses and had so many, he saw a name first before the rose, it said "Angel eyes".

"That's it" he said out loud.

He turned the card round, it was a rose he had never seen before, it was the palest pink leaves with the most beautiful purple centre he loved it, but wasn't sure what Jane would say, he picked it up and walked down the isle, he stopped again at a yellow rose it was called "Sweet memories" "that's perfect for them too", yellow roses were

Jane's favourite and he was sure she would love it. He headed back as he saw Jane head over the top of the isle heading his way, as she got to him, she looked at the two he had, Jane frowned at him.

"What have you got there love?".

"Well this yellow one is for us, its called sweet memories".

"Oh I love that" she said, nodding her head with a little tear in her eye, he picked up the other which only had buds on.

"This is Angel Eyes Belle but its not white".

He showed her the picture and she felt the tears roll down her face, she nodded and croaked trying to say its perfect. Jasper put down the roses and wiped her tear from her face with his thumb and pulled her into him, he kissed the top of her head.

"Belle I'm sorry I didn't mean to upset you".

She smiled up at him. "You didn't, it just feels perfect. I will put this one back".

"No wait what did you find?"

She bent and picked up the rose.

"It's called "with love" and its white".

Jasper felt a tear roll down his face, Jane reached up and wiped it away, "it's perfect Belle, they both are. Lets take the three of them?", Jane nodded.

"That would be lovely".

They got to the checkout and paid for the roses and headed out to the car, they took some cardboard from the shop and Jasper laid it in the footwell behind the seats and sat the rose in securely, he moved Jane's seat back just a bit to make sure they were in properly. As they got in he looked across at Jane took her hand and kissed her.

"My Belle okay?" she nodded.

"I am baby yes" "Good, lets go and see the guys at the club then".

They got to the dealer in 10 minutes and there were already 100 bikes plus there, the adjoining field was full of tents from those who arrived the night before, music was playing, Jane thought just like home. They walked into the shop front and saw Shadow heading towards them, he crouched down and opened his arms as Jane walked into them.

"Hey Doc you're looking good enough to eat" and did his deep belly laugh.

Jasper walked over "Hey hands off Shadow", as they shook hands.

"She's all yours Brother, just teasing you", they both laughed Jasper knew he was joking as was he with his response.

"What brings you in early"?

"I need more jeans and her ladyship suggested I have leathers too so you know she gets what she wants".

Shadow laughed again, his laugh was so deep everyone in the shop turned to see what was going on.

Animal shouted across and waved as he is serving someone, and Jane sees James pull in, he waves at them as he parks the bike. They walk round to the clothes with Shadow and Jasper is looking at the leathers, he certainly won't be wearing them tonight its too hot he thought. He grabbed a few pairs that Jane liked and went to try them on, he came out of the changing room and Jane's jaw dropped, he looked so sexy, she pretended to waft her face.

"Smoking hot" she said as Jasper blushed.

Shadow spoke "behave Doc that poor man is blushing".

Jane laughed as James joined them.

"Oh she has you round her little finger Jay".

Jasper nodded "don't I know it".

The leathers were like his jacket they looked warn which is what he wanted and Jane's's face said it all so that was that sorted. Shadow passed him the jeans he found similar to what he brought before he tried them on and was happy, no need to do a floor show he thought until he heard Jane.

"You're taking your time?"

He tutted to himself, "it's a good job I love you women" he said under his breath. As he came out a few of the girls from the club joined them, Shadow was introducing Jane to them. One of them Alice wolf whistled at him and everyone laughed. Jane threw a t-shirt at him and said try this on love please, it was a new dealer t-shirt, he thought he would play her at her own game and pulled his t-shirt over his head showing off his chest grinning, he rubbed his hand down his pecks, the girls whooped as he did and started clapping, Jane laughed at him feeling proud, he was still smiling as he pulled the other t-shirt on, Alice twirled her finger at him to turn round he did as he was instructed and the girls continued to whoop at him. He bowed as he got back to the front and went back into the cubicle to get changed, the girls booed at him when he pulled the curtain closed, Jane joined in too as a bare leg came out from behind the curtain, everyone laughed and cheered. When Jasper came out the girls were talking to Jane, Alice and Chrissy were both members of

The Skulls MC they had their own bikes too and came down for the weekend BBQ.

Jasper went to see Shadow with his new clothes and while the girls were chatting and laughing, he had the opportunity to talk to James and Shadow about learning to ride. Shadow packed all the clothes up and Jasper paid for them then the three of them wandered over to the bikes. Jasper had his eye on a scorched orange softail. He wanted to sit on it, but he knew Jane would see him and it would give his surprise away.

"I will come back during the week Shadow and try it then if that's okay, I can get booked onto the training course too".

"No problem at all Brother", Shadow replied.

"You really going to do it for her" James asked.

"Yes, I am" he replied.

"I love that women, not that she knows yet and I want to show her. If that means riding with her and her friends, I will do it. I enjoyed it too, I enjoyed the freeness of it, you see so much, my car his high but this is different, you have the freedom to look round you without anything in the way".

Jane came up behind him and put her arms around his waist, he smiled feeling her and looked behind at her.

"Belle, you okay, have you done chatting?"

"Yes for now love, we need to get the meat from the butcher and get home so we can get changed".

"Okay," he said, he turned and put his around her shoulder.

"We will see you later guys".

Jane hugged Shadow and James, the girls came around as they were going outside to the BBQ.

They got into the car and went back to the butcher to collect the meat and headed back to Jaspers. They unloaded the car and Jasper took the roses outside and soaked them in water in the shade, they would plant them the next day. Jane unpacked all her presents from Jasper, she was taking the labels off as he walked into the bedroom.

"So when do I get to see you in these then?" he said picking them up.

"Once they have been washed love, not until".

Jasper pouted which made Jane laugh, she swatted him across the chest with one of her bras.

"Are you not going to try them on just in case?" he said.

Jane tutted "if you insist",

He grinned and took a seat in the chair. Jane bent over the bed and Jasper frowned, he noticed that Jane's dress had fallen between the cheeks of her bottom, he wasn't aware she had a thong on and it fact he hadn't felt any underwear, he got up out of the chair and walked across to her, put his hand on her hips and slid his hands down, Jane moaned.

"That's nice love".

"There were no knickers or thong. Belle…..?" he said questioningly rubbing his hand up and down her bottom, she turned slightly.

"Well you took your time".

He pulled her dress up her legs and looked at her, "You have been out all day like this?"

"Yes of course".

"Oh my god women, you didn't tell me?"

"Why would I?, normally you would notice".

"You mean I have missed out on this all day…?"

Jane laughed "yes love you have".

He pulled her dress over her bottom and spanked her hard.

"Ouch" she squealed, "what was that for?"

"Because I didn't know so couldn't tease you".

He bent over and kissed her where he spanked her.

"Such a bad girl Belle. In that shower now women" he said demandingly, Jane laughed and stood up.

"So you don't want to see my new underwear then?"

"Not now no" he laughed.

Jasper pulled Jane's dress over her head.

"Christ women I can't believe all that was covering you today was this little dress. Damn it".

Jasper peeled off his t-shirt and took his jeans and pants off, he grabbed Jane by the hips and led her to the shower, he stopped her in the doorway and put her hair up. Jane turned the shower on and they both stepped in, they washed quickly as they promised Chicca they would meet her there. They were taking the trike tonight; Jane slipped her leathers and t-shirt on. Jasper came into the room and grabbed her.

"Mmmm I love you in your leathers, I hope you have knickers on?"

"Yes of course silly" she said laughing. "What are you wearing love?",

"Jeans and chaps Belle", she went and grabbed his clothes.

They were ready to go in 15 minutes. Jasper opened the garage and Jane pulled the trike out. He looked over at Jane, he whispered to himself "I can't wait to ride along side you Belle".

He locked the garage up set the house alarm and climbed on the trike with Jane. He held her round the waist, he didn't need to be he just loved holding her.

They were at the club before they knew it and as Jane parked the trike Chicca arrived.

She got out of the car dressed in her leather mini skirt low cut t-shirt with high boots on, her hair was down, she had a lot of make-up on. She looked stunning, very different from her normal site clothes.

Chicca came across to Jane and Jasper, she smiled at Jasper.
"Welcome back JDubz.
Jane laughed and Jasper frowned.
"Tell you later" she said looking at Jasper.
Chicca hugged Jane, "you look gorgeous Chicca".
"Thank you, its nice to feel like a women sometimes" she smiled, "even if it is a sassy slutty one". They both laughed.
"Let's go get a drink".
Jane took Jaspers hand he suddenly looked out of his comfort zone even though he knew a few of the guys now. James came across to say hello first and handed Jasper a beer.
"I assume Jane you are riding tonight?" she nodded.
"Yes, I am, I will grab a drink in a minute".
James smiled at Chicca, "I don't think we have been introduced?"
Chicca put out her hand, "Hi I'm Chicca".
"James, nice to meet you. Can I get you a drink", they both ignored Jasper and Jane and headed towards the bar.
"That didn't take long" Jasper said, Jane laughed.
"No but don't be fooled Chicca is a picky lady".
They wandered out to the BBQ and Jane picked up a bottle of water.

The field ran down the side of the dealership, the shop was locked up, but it had its own facilities for the club, it had all the rooms they needed plus showers toilets and a kitchen. The BBQ was just outside the doors. The field was packed with tents bikes trikes and a few cars. There were small fires burning in metal pits, the remnants of the tops of oil drums that no doubt the mechanics had made. There were lights around the field, at the far end was a stage, a band were setting up and the music was booming out already. Jasper looked round in surprise, everyone was in leather or denim, there were some old rat bikes the owners you could tell lived for the road, there was an area fenced off for the bike show the following day, it had sections for the artwork which Jane was really interested in, custom bikes, traditional old bikes and the best in show. Jasper was impressed, he was glad he brought his small camera, Shadow spotted them across the field and shouted over, with his booming voice nothing could drown him out, he towered everyone else so could clearly be seen, gone was the dealer shirt and he was in his own jeans and t-shirt and leather waistcoat which had badges on, including the club emblem on his left breast side. He picked Jane up and hugged her.

"Hey Doc, glad you could make it".

Jane was laughing "put me down Hightower,

I'm scared of heights" she said.

He laughed loudly and put her down, he shook Jaspers hand.

"Hey brother, how you doing?"

"good Shadow thanks, thought we better come and sample this food", Shadow laughed again, "let me introduce you to a few people", they walked off together and stopped in a big crowd.

"Ladies and gents can I introduce you to Jane and Jasper, Jane is over from the UK, she is a member of the MC in Southampton and is a friend of Moses, Jasper is her partner". Lot's of hello's bellowed out and one guy shouted, "is the little arsehole still coming for the Vets run in a few weeks?"

Jane nodded "yes he is, I believe a few of them are coming this time". The guy raised his beer to them both.

"Cheers, catch you later guys" Shadow said as they walked away, they made their way round the field talking to quite a few people then the band started, they didn't have a chance now to speak to anyone it was so loud, everyone was on their feet and moving towards the front, it was a local band that rode with the MC. Jasper went and got them another drink and joined Jane on the ground to listen to the music, she was quite engrossed when he sat down, he looked round at her and smiled, she looked so relaxed and at home. He wondered how she would be when she met his friends. It was a completely different group of people, but it was important to him for her to meet them. He gave her the bottle of water and took a big mouthful of his beer, he surprised himself not being a drinker, he was really relaxed himself, he was surprised at the kinds of people he had met, bikers had a bad name he knew that and he knew there were some bad guys out there but to be honest to afford a Harley you needed a good amount of money, they had met a general surgeon, a solicitor, a banker and quite a few ex military guys. The Girls were around too, they came over to say hi and sat with them for a while. The band broke for food, the music came back on and those who hadn't already eaten wandered over to the BBQ, there was a traditional hog roast which Jasper fancied trying and Jane went for a cheeseburger, they were both impressed by how good the food was. There were pasta salads, salad leaves, rice, and all manner of sauces and accompaniments. Everyone was enjoying themselves, the bar was packed too, it reminded Jane of home, there were the typical couples who enjoyed giving floor shows, one couple were outside their tent which was up against the fence line, the woman was bent over holding on her leather skirt up round her waist and her partner pounding into her from behind, nobody paid any interest, a few people offered Jane and Jasper a smoke but they both declined, neither was interested. As they walked away from the BBQ they saw Chicca and James, they were very close up and personal, Chicca certainly turned on the charm with him, he was grinning as she was touching his chest, running her finger up and down and across his stomach, he was whispering something to her which made her laugh, he kissed her neck and looked up, they both knew where that was going to end, they nodded at them both as they walked past and smiled.

They walked over to look at the bikes in the show, Jasper wanted to take some pictures and Jane was eager to see the artwork on the bikes. The artist was with some of the guys talking so they went to speak to him. Shadow introduced them to him, he wasn't what Jane expected, he was clean cut and quite young, she had an image in her mind of someone older, his work was amazing though.

They started talking about what she wanted, she really didn't know so he asked about her passion and hobbies, She hadn't really done very much of her hobbies for such a long time she was struggling to remember. She mentioned Mental Health of course and bikes, photography, gardening flowers especially roses. She said she thought about having the club logo on the back.

He smiled, "I am sure we can do better than that Jane. Let me have a think about it" he said whilst writing some notes on the things she had given him, not that it was much but he would see what he could come up with, he gave her his card and said anything comes to mind give me a call.

Jane walked away with Jasper even more confused, he put his arm around her.

"Come on Belle, don't stress about it something will come to mind, I know you want the trike to be an extension of you and it is already".

She nodded, "I forgot something", she turned and rushed back, she stopped and blurted out "baby loss", the guy looked up confused, "Sorry, I just remembered. I lost a child some years ago, it would be nice to have something small even if it's just something I would know was there or the meaning of it".

He nodded and added to his notebook smiling.

"That's great we can definitely do something there for you".

Jane thanked him and walked away. Jasper was behind her and smiled, "Happy now?"

"Yes" she said, "I am". He hugged her.

"Let's go and have a look at some of the stalls see what we can find.

She nodded and they walked over to the other side of the field, there were all kinds of stalls, some were charity run, raising money for bikers injured on the road, others for the Veterans, and a childrens charity. There were clothes, boots, leathers, and a tanner sat adjusting belts and adding buckles.

"Ooh" Jane said "we need to get you a nice belt".

He smiled she was only happy when she was pleasing others, she dragged him across the field to see what he was making and what they could buy.

The Tanner was sat adjusting belts and adding holes, a guy was talking to him about his torn leathers where he had come off, he didn't want new ones he wanted a repair job, they walked into his little stall, there were huge amounts of leather waistcoats, chaps, full leather jackets, everything you could wish for. Jane wanted a new bag to go on her back, she started with belt buckles first. Jasper was pulling faces at some of them, "I will make a biker out of you, yet" she said laughing, Jasper smirked thinking.

"Just you wait and see Belle".

She found a nice one with a Harley on and decided that was it, it would look perfect with his chaps. They went around the whole stall and found Jasper a few more t-shirts and gloves for the winter. They gave the buckle to the tanner with the choice of belt and he put it together for them, they paid him and walked back towards the trike to leave their new bits locked up. Jane was ready to go home; she was missing her guys back in the UK being here was making her homesick for them. She turned and looked up to Jasper.

"Do you mind if we go home?"

He looked down at her, "of course not Belle, whatever you want".

"I better find Chicca and let her know, not that she will miss us" she laughed.

"Last I saw them they were still near the bar, let's go and have a look". They wandered back towards the bar and right enough they found Chicca and James. "Hey you two" Jane said, "we are heading home", will you be okay Chicca, silly question I know?".

"Yes of course" said James "I will look after her".

They all laughed "ok, give me a call tomorrow please?"

"Will do" Chicca replied and hugged her.

James hugged Jane and whispered "shes safe with me stop worrying", he shook Jaspers hand, "see you soon Brother, call if you need anything" and winked. Chicca hugged Jasper and they walked off back to the trike.

Jasper got on the trike and Jane joined him, they were only a short ride from home it was almost 10pm. He sensed there was more to her wanting to go home he would let her talk when they got there.

Jane put the Trike away and Jasper locked up and took their shopping into the house. Jasper grabbed Jane as she went to take her boots off, "Belle, talk to me" taking her in his arms, she sank into him hugging him tight she sighed.

"What's wrong Belle, tell me what I can do for you?"

Jane buried her head into Jaspers chest and started to cry. He held her, rubbing her back, and shhhing.

"It's okay baby let it go".

He cupped her head with his hand and kissed her head.

"Let it out Belle", Jane cried softly, she moved her head and looked up to him, he held her cheek and wiped her tears away with his thumbs, she talked through her sobs.

"I'm just missing home. Being at the BBQ tonight made me realise how much I was missing everyone".

Please don't think I don't love being with you I do, you make me so happy I feel like I'm at home with you, and I wouldn't swap that for anything. Like I said the other day, you make me so happy. I just miss the guys, they have been my constant for 10 years plus and now Im across the other side of the world from them". Jasper smiled.

"Oh Belle, I'm not surprised you are missing them, you have every reason too". He still had hold of her face, he bent and kissed her nose, "Don't you think they will be missing you too?" She nodded.

"Christ I was without you for a few days and I went crazy being away from you and we haven't known each other very long", she laughed and nodded.

"When did you last Skype them?" he asked.

"A week or so ago".

"Why don't you message Moses and arrange a good time to call so you can catch up". She nodded.

"I will".

"Anything else on you mind love?"

"I don't think so".

"Okay love, what would you like to do"?

"Can we just go to bed?"

Jasper smiled "of course baby come on, sit and let me get your boots off".

Jane sat on the stool in the hallway and Jasper knelt in front of her and put her foot on his knee, he unzipped her boots and pulled them both off, stood and took her hand and helped her up, he turned her round and pulled her leather off and hung it up. He shrugged his own off and unzipped his boots. He took Jane's hand led her to the bedroom. As Jane was getting undressed, he went and got them both a glass of water, left them on the bedside cabinet and followed Jane to the bathroom to clean his teeth. They got into bed, both had a drink of water and Jasper laid on his back. Jane laid her head onto his chest, her hand across his stomach. Jasper wrapped his arms around her and kissed her head, she looked up to him, kissed him softly.

"Good night baby".

"Good night Belle, sweet dreams my love".

She kissed his chest and snuggled in.

Chapter 24

Remembering you both

The following morning Jasper woke to Jane's bottom pushed into his cock, he wasn't sure how they ended up cuddling like that normally neither moved much.

"Jane must have had a bad night" he thought to himself. He gently rubbed his finger tips up and down her hip which made her moan gently, she must have been napping she wouldn't normally have felt that, Jasper was hard for her, it wasn't morning glory this was the fact the most gorgeous women who he loved desperately had her gorgeous arse pushed into his cock.

He pushed the hair away from her neck and shoulders so he could kiss her, at each gentle kiss she moaned softly which made him smile, he wouldn't continue if she were asleep, that just wasn't right to him, he kissed along her shoulder and up her neck, taking her ear lobe gently between his lips and pulling on it.

Jane moved beneath him and her hand came behind her onto his leg, he continued his soft kisses coming back down onto her shoulder and round her neck, he moved her face round towards him and kissed her cheek, Jane smiled, she craned her neck further so she could kiss his lips.

"Good morning my Belle"

She had a small stretch and mewled.

"Good morning baby".

He loved how she sounded first thing in the morning, she had a beautiful voice, but in the morning when she first woke it was even sexier. She moved her hand up towards his head and wrapped it around pulling him closer to her, his hand moved onto her breast and cupped it, taking her nipple between his index finger and thumb rolling it gently.

Jane pushed back into him making him groan, he cupped her breast and caressed it, he loved how soft her skin was, it was so soft like silk, Jane pushed harder into him and moved her leg so it was over his, opening herself for him. He moved his hand down her body over her tummy and slide his fingers down to her pussy making her moan more.

"Oh baby" she moaned

"yes?"

"Don't stop". He slowly pulled her leg further back over his and moved himself lower, he wanted to enter her from behind, his fingers found her pussy again she was so wet for him, he kissed her shoulder, sank his teeth in gently.

His cock was rock hard it was pulsing to be inside her. He lifted her so he could move his cock and ran it from her bottom to her pussy rubbing it on her outer lips.

"Oh fuck me baby please" Jane begged.

He slid inside her slowly, he wanted this to be gentle, he wanted to feel every inch of her as he slid in. He moved deep inside her and stayed still for a few seconds enjoying the tightness of her and the amazing feeling of being at one.

Jane clenched her pussy around him which made him moan loudly, "oh, fuck Belle, that feels so good".

He felt her smile. He had never enjoyed sex like this before but with her every time was amazing, their bodies just worked together and he couldn't get enough of her, or she him, he started to move slowly in and out, his lips still on her shoulder and neck, Jane's hand moved down to his bottom pulling him into her every time he pulled out, he made love to her slowly not wanting it to end, Jane turned her head and body slightly so they could kiss, it was intense, their mouths open, pulling at each others lips and sucking their tongues as he pushed in and out of her, Jasper didn't care if neither of them came this was just incredible.

His hand ran up and down her body stopping to squeeze her breast and pull on her nipple again. Jane started to increase the speed pushing into him, he knew she needed to cum, he moved his hand down her body again and onto her pussy, he opened her lips with his fingers and slid his middle finger onto her clit, it made her moan loudly.

She hissed "yes Jasper don't stop".

He slowed himself down he would cum as soon as she did. He kept rubbing her clit making her pant as her orgasm started to build, he rubbed faster and harder.

"Oh fuck, yes" she moaned loudly, "don't stop baby please", Jasper felt her cum as she exploded all over his cock, her body going rigid for a few seconds as it hit her, he kept rubbing her even though he knew she couldn't cope with it her pussy pulsing. He increased the speed of his cocking entering her and felt his balls go hard and his cock stiffen more as he came hard, his body quivering and his eyes fogging over, he pulsed inside her as he came over and over biting her lip and breathing hard into her mouth, she clenched around him again squeezing every last bit of his cum out of him, he smiled the feeling was incredible, he came back to earth, wanting to look at her, he pulled out of her slowly, rubbing her hip and turned her round to face him, she looked into his eyes and smiled.

H.O.L.Y by Florida Georgia Line

"Good morning my beautiful man".
"Good Morning love of my life" he replied.
Jane looked stunned as she realised what he said, he took her face in his hands, rubbing her cheeks with his thumbs.
"I love you Belle, I think I loved you the moment I set eyes on you the first time.
Jane looked shocked and didn't speak, a loan tear left the corner of her eye and ran down her face, Jasper caught it with his lips as he left a soft kiss just below her cheek.
"I hope that's not sadness Belle?".
She shook her head.
"No, its not".
Jasper smiled "good".
He pulled her into his chest, "I'm sorry if I have scared you Belle, I couldn't wait any longer to tell you".
She looked up at him, kissed his chin took a deep breath.
"Im glad you did Jasper, because I love you too".
Jasper wasn't expecting that. He now looked like the dear caught in the car headlights.
Jane laughed "breath Jasper".
He looked at her, "are you sure? You don't have to say it you know", she laughed.
"I know I don't, and yes I do love you very much, I fell for you the first night when you lifted me into your arms".

He grabbed Jane's face with both hands and kissed her hard. When he stopped he looked into her eyes.

"Oh Belle I am the luckiest man on this earth".

She laughed, "well that makes me the luckiest girl then".

They laughed, he brought her into his chest, for the first time in his life he felt at home, she was everything he had been dreaming about. She made the world right in everything she did.

They cat napped for a while wrapped in each other's arms, Jane was laid on Jaspers chest when she woke first. She looked up at him, he looked so peaceful and perfect sleeping, he didn't snore. His breathing was so quiet. She couldn't believe how things were changing for them both, she couldn't believe how lucky she was, this man loved her she thought.

"Oh my god", she gasped and put her hand over her mouth as she tried to stop herself from laughing.

"He said, he loved me", she let out a little squeal and a giggle, "ssshhhh" she said to herself, she was desperate not to laugh but what she wanted to do was scream, she slowly unwrapped herself out of his arms and went into the bathroom closed the door and started to jump up and down, her hand over her mouth to stop the squealing and giggling, she was ecstatic, what she hadn't heard was the bathroom door open, its something they didn't do, the door was always open, Jasper stood leaning against the door frame arms folded with a huge smile on his face watching Jane, his smile got bigger the longer he stood their seeing how excited and child like she was, he cleared his throat and Jane stopped dead with her back to him.

"You saw didn't you?" she asked without looking round.

"Yes, Belle I did" he said smiling.

"Oh god" she moaned and buried her head in her hands.

Jasper walked up behind her wrapping his arms around her pulling her into his chest. He kissed her shoulder and the back of her head, "Belle turn around and look at me".

She shook her head, he chuckled.

"Please Belle".

She shook her head, again, so he turned around, letting go of her and did exactly what Jane had done, he also punched the air and shouted "Yes, yes, yes she loves me, my god she loves me".

Jane turned and started laughing watching him. When he stopped she walked up to him and ran her hand across his back and walked round the front of him, they were both smiling, as she moved round the front he grabbed her face.

"That's what I wanted to do when you told me too Belle".

She started to laugh and wrinkled her nose.

"Really, you're not teasing me?", he loved it when she did that. "No Belle, I am serious I could scream from the roof tops you make me so happy". He pulled her face to his and kissed her again.

"Thank you for coming into my life. Now get your pretty arse in that kitchen women and make me a cup of tea" spanking her bottom hard making her squeal.

He laughed and rubbed it better, Jane turned laughing too and went off to the kitchen to make them tea. Jasper followed her and sat on the stool.

"Baby as we are planting the roses today would you like to shower afterwards, I was thinking we could have a tidy up while we are out their too, what do you think?"

"I would like that".

"Okay great, lets eat and we can throw on some clothes and get out there. I was thinking about saying a few words, and don't know how you feel about it?" he said.

"That sounds lovely, actually I do have a poem I thought it might be nice to laminate it and put it into each rose for a while". "I love the sound of that Belle, that's a beautiful idea".

"But if you want to add or change anything you can" she said.

"I will go and get the poem so you can have a read". Jane walked away and Jasper got the bread and eggs out.

"Poached he thought to himself for a change".

Jane came back with the poem as Jasper was cracking eggs getting them ready to slide into the boiling water.

She handed the poem to him and he started to read it, Jane went into his side and cuddled into him, she felt him gulp, she knew it would affect him too, all these years of not talking about his loss had affected him more than he thought. He cleared his throat.

"It's perfect Belle".

She looked up at him, "do you want to add anything?"

"I don't think so" he replied looking down at her.

"Okay".

Jane released herself from his arms and put the toast on while Jasper waited for the water to boil.

He had poached eggs down to a fine art, as soon as the toast popped, he would drop the eggs in and butter the toast, once that was done the eggs came out, they were soft and runny, perfect for breaking open all over the toast. A few minutes later the toast popped, he dropped the eggs in as Jane got the toast buttered and took it over to the cooker where he was waiting. They sat down to eat.

"These eggs are perfect! She exclaimed.

"Thank you Belle I aim to please".

She smiled "and you always do".

"Naughty girl".

"I was talking about the eggs honest".

"Yeah, yeah of course you were". He laughed.

They finished up eating and Jasper took the dishes to the dishwasher, he was cooking later so decided to use it today.

"You ready Belle?", he asked.

Yes love".

"Come on then".

They walked out into the garage and Jasper opened the back door, they had left their boots in his car, they booted up and went out to the shed. Jasper picked out the spade, fork, gloves, rose food and rubbish bag, wheeled out his little trolley, Jane squealed when she saw it, it was like a child's pull along, he loaded it up with the roses, "Get in then and I will pull you along".

Jane laughed "no, I want to pull it out to the rose bed".

Jasper laughed, "come on then, here you go".

Jane loved it, she was such a child at heart. They walked out into the garden. Jane inhaled deeply the smell in the garden was beautiful, everything was in bloom the colours were amazing, he had peonies that were deep red, it reminded her of her Dad they were one of his favourites. They got to the rose bed it was stunning so many colours. There was the perfect spot at the back of the bed near to where he had the empty space which he had big plans for and now he knew what he was going to do. Jasper unload the tools and roses, he placed them on the earth spaced out.

"What do you think Belle?"

He already had a yellow rose so chose to put the pink one close to it then the white in the middle and the yellow at the end next to a red one. Jane nodded "perfect".

Jasper left a space at the front, he decided he didn't just want a laminated sheet of paper on each rose he was going to have the poem of Janes engraved on glass and he would have it set at the front of the three roses. He knew it was her anniversary coming up for her loss and he wanted to give it to her then, he would get Ernie to do it for him so he could bring her out here on the evening to show her, he had a few more things to plan too so needed to get things in motion, if he was going to get them done for the day. He would make the calls in the morning and let Ernie know too.

Tears in Heaven, Eric Clapton

He started to dig the holes and Jane broke the soil away from the pots ready to drop in, she sprinkled the food in and filled the hole with water, they put all three in and stood back looking at them, Jasper put his arm around Jane's shoulder and pulled her in close.
"Are you okay my love?" looking down at her, she nodded.
"I am, thank you so much Jasper, I can't tell you how much this means to me".
He kissed the top of her head.
"Its my pleasure Belle, its important to you, so it is to me and to be honest I never realised how much it had affected me until I opened up to you. Somewhere up there, we have children waiting for us". he said looking up into the sky
They took their gloves off and Jane pulled the poem out of her pocket, she felt the tears ready to fall, she was desperate to get through this without crying, her throat was hurting forcing the tears away.
She opened the paper and shared it with Jasper.
"shall we read together?" she asked.
Jasper nodded, "I would like that. You start Jane and I will read every other line".
"Okay" She took a deep breath, fighting the tears, Jasper cuddled her tight.
"To our babies wherever you are always know that Mummy and Daddy wanted you so much, you will always be with us and never forgotten. No matter where life takes us". Jane chocked the last few words before starting the poem, she heard Jasper sniff too. She began.

Our beautiful Angels,
You were too beautiful for earth,
You are a thousand winds that blow.
The diamond glints on snow,
The love that surrounds us,
In every breath we take.
You will be remembered and loved,
As our hearts break.
We will visit you in our dreams,
Forever in our hearts.
Love Mummy and Daddy.

They finished reading the poem and Jane dropped her hand to her side, she never realised how much this would hurt. She looked up at Jasper and saw a tear fall, she stood on her tip toes and he bent towards her, she caught the tear with her lips and kissed it. He picked her up and held her tight not saying a word, she wrapped her legs around him, they stood for a few moments just holding each other tight, neither realised the loss they felt until today. Jasper pulled Jane's head out of his shoulder with both hands and kissed her, this kiss was different, it was filled with sadness and love, hunger and need for comfort. They never spoke a word, just held one another, their loss was evident and raw. Jane let her legs drop as Jasper let her down, she turned in his arms and stood against him, they stood silently looking at the roses and Jane read the names of each rose out.

"With love, Sweet memories our Angel eyes". Jasper kissed Jane on the head, hugging her.

"Thank you, Belle for giving me the courage and for seeing my child. I love you so very much".

She put her hand up and cupped his cheek, he turned his head and kissed the palm of her hand. He let go of her and she turned and looked at him.

"I love you to Jasper Mitchell".

Jane kissed her fingers and placed them on one bud on each rose bush. Then bent to pick up the pots and watering can, their hearts feeling heavier than they ever expected. Lost in their own thoughts.

"You ok love?"

"Yes" she nodded, "are you baby?"

He nodded too "yes Belle, thank you".

They walked around the rose bed and Jasper started to dead head the roses, Jane got onto her knees on the pad and started to pull out the weeds that had come up. It was a huge bed and she got caught on a few of the thorns trying to get through to the middle, she kept tutting and saying ouch as another scratched her, Jasper started to laugh, "Belle, do you want to swap?"

"No" she huffed "it's fine, these little beggers won't get the better of me".

He laughed again "okay love, just say if you need help".

"Thank you, I will".

They worked round the bed until it was clear and moved onto another, it had the most beautiful cottage garden flowers in it, Hollyhocks at the back standing tall, Delphiniums, Geranium, Lupins Verbena to name a few, the smell was like nothing else and the colours were just perfect.

Blues yellows, pinks purples oranges and white. There wasn't much room for weeds, these flowers had been packed in tight, Jasper couldn't take credit for it this was all Ernies work. He was the master.

They both knelt and cleared fallen buds and petals with a few weeds. They looked round at each other and smiled, Jasper looked at Jane her cheeks were flushed red and she looked beautiful, he could see she loved being out in the garden, it woke something in her. They moved down the beds together until they came to the end. Jasper helped Jane up and they brushed themselves down. They looked round at their work and smiled.

"That will save Ernie a bit of time Jasper thought" I have plans for the next couple of weeks for him. Jasper loaded the bin into the trolley with the tools and they walked back to the shed. They unloaded everything and Jasper threw the weeds into the compost bin. He kept the rose pots and put them in the shed, Ernie liked to keep the empty ones you never knew if they would be of use later.

They walked up to the garage door and undid their boots, leaving them outside to dry off from the morning dew as they stepped into the garage in their socks. They went into the kitchen and Jane headed for the kettle.

"Tea time I think" she said.

"Great idea", "then shower"

Jasper said as he stripped off his clothes ready to wash them with Jane's, he came up behind her as she was making tea, he took hold of the hem of her fleece and pulled it up over her head, then her t-shirt, she laughed.

"I can undress myself you know!"

"I know, but this is more fun" he replied laughing.

She didn't have a bra on, she saw no sense in it they were at home anyway alone. Jasper turned her round as she was taking the tea bags out of the cups and kissed her nose, pulled the button on her jeans and undid the zip, he bent down and pulled her jeans off her, he tapped her leg.

"Lift please".

Jane lifted her leg so he could take her leg out, then the other, he pulled her knickers down and did the same. He kissed her nipples and moaned as he did then scooped her clothes up taking them into the utility putting them into the washing machine. Jane watched him walking away, she groaned to herself, she loved that body, it was an offensive weapon, she knew she couldn't resist. He knew she was watching so when he got to the door of the utility room he bent forward and shook his bum at her, she burst into a giggle, as he disappeared around the corner.

Jasper put the washing on and came back out to Jane, just seeing her stood there naked and finally at ease with her body made him happy, she was stunning but didn't see it. He walked up to her and took her in his arms.

"Hey love of my life what are you thinking about?"

She looked at him, "nothing much really just that your body is offensive", he laughed.

"Oh, I thought you liked it".

"Oh, I do" she said.

"It's still offensive".

He laughed at her, "come on you, shower time", he grabbed the mugs and walked with her into the bedroom.

Jane was going to wash her hair so left it down and grabbed the comb so she could condition it as they walked into the shower. They stood under the jets and Jasper turned all the others on, so they were being hit from all angles, Jane picked up the shampoo and Jasper took it out of her hand.

"My job Belle", she turned away from him as she squeezed it into his hands and started to rub it through her hair. Jane loved his fingers in her hair she moaned softly as he massaged her head, she had shown him how to do it on his head, he had mastered it well. When he finished Jane turned and told Jasper to sit down so she could do his too. She massaged his head from the nape up circling her thumbs up the back, he moaned too and put his hand around her to hold her close to him, he loved the feel of her body against his. When he sat her breasts were in the right place just at the top of his shoulders. He turned around as she got to the top of his head and her nipples were right in his face, he shrugged his shoulders.

"Would be rude not to" he said.

Jane laughed, "you are so bad", he tried to talk while sucking one, Jane thought she heard him say.

"What would you do if my cock was at face height" and continued to suck and squeeze them.

Jane finished massaging his head not really focusing properly and as she pulled away his mouth made a loud popping sound as he let go of her nipple and he laughed. He pouted pretending to be sad.

"No sulking allowed" she laughed, "you only had me a few hours ago", he slumped his shoulders like a grumpy teenager which made her laugh, he grabbed his cock which was rock hard.

"Tell him that! you shouldn't walk round with that body either".

Jane laughed and kissed him, "well let's see how long you can wait" turning away from him and washing off the shampoo. Jasper stood under the other ceiling jet and washed his off, Jane conditioned her hair and Jasper combed it through for her.

They washed each other down and Jane was teasing Jasper, she was going to make him wait, she loved teasing him. He knew he could have her whenever he wanted too but loved letting her tease him. When they finished in the shower they put on some shorts and t-shirts, no knickers or pants, they had no plans to go out. Jane sat with the hairdryer on the dressing table stool and Jasper combed it while it dried off. He loved her hair it was so soft; he ran his fingers through it to make sure it was dry and wrapped it around his hand, pulling her back into him, her head fell back, and he kissed her.

"All done Belle". He said letting her go. They finished off their tea and went back into the kitchen.

"Are you hungry Belle?"

"Not sure to be honest, happy to eat if you are?"

He grabbed his cock through his shorts.

"Here you go", she laughed and slapped his arm.

"It's true isn't it? you men think about nothing but sex every thirty seconds", he laughed, and put his hands up.

"Oh, I beg to differ Belle, I think about your body every second", she laughed at him.

"You are silly".

"Fancy a ham salad roll?"

"Yes sure" she said, they prepared the rolls and went outside and sat on the patio, it was getting really warm they were being promised an Indian Summer this year and he could feel it getting hotter. "I might put my bikini on and sunbathe what do you think?"

"If you want to love, go for it, we have no plans".

Jane finished her lunch and went back in and changed, she left her top off just went out in her bikini bottoms, she grabbed the sun tan lotion from the bathroom and a couple of towels, as she walked out Jasper was putting the sun beds on the patio in the sun, He looked up and whistled at her.

"Was it worth putting it on you tease?"

Jane laughed he was probably right.

She sat on the sunbed and Jasper started to put suntan lotion all over her back she had her hair up out of the way, when he finished she turned and Jasper sat down so she could do his back too, once they were all covered they laid on the beds and they both got there kindles out.

They laid in the garden for a couple of hours, enjoying the time out.

Chapter 25

Naivety

Helen was one of the new girls at the club, she worked with Linda and Jax in the kitchen, she had been around a few years, but she was always going to be the new girl. She was quite gullible and didn't have a man to speak of, she bounced from one to another when other clubs visited, she wasn't a club whore she just couldn't settle. The club was quiet they were having a good summer in the UK too, they were making plans to go over to see Jane and join the Veterans run with the Connecticut boys and girls. They had called a meeting to discuss it and Helen was helping Linda with food.

Moses said they would be gone for two weeks so they could spend time with Jane and do the run. They didn't know if she would be joining them yet he would call her later to find out.

Moses, G, Matt and Steve were going, Jax, Gwen and Linda would also go but be pillion so they needed four bikes from Shadow. They would take their own leathers and helmets. The date was set Kevin and four of the girls would stay back to look after things. The dealership would still be open and so would the café.

When the meeting was finished Helen said she needed to go and get a few things from town, it was Sunday, so opening hours were limited, she left around 1pm and went directly to town.

She parked up and was leaving the car park when she bumped into Mark, she knew he was Jane's ex husband, he had been to the dealership a few times and noticed not many bothered with him. She had no idea what had happened between him and Jane only Moses and G knew that.

Mark stopped her, "Oh Hi Helen, how are you?"

She smiled "Hi Mark, I'm good, how are you?"

"Yeah okay just out for a bit of retail therapy"

"Yes, me too" she said.

"Fancy some company?" he asked.

"Oh, "okay sure" she replied.

He held the door to the car park open for her.

"A gent, she thought that's nice".

"So, where do you need to go Helen?" he asked

"Oh, just need to get some underwear" she said blushing, "and some things for the bathroom", "ok great", they walked through the Mall and got to the store Helen wanted, Mark walked in with her.

"Do you want me to wait out here?"

She felt guilty for saying yes.

"No, its ok, as long as you won't be embarrassed"

"Not me love, no". "Okay great". they walked in and he was looking around, his mind ticking over.

Helen found what she was looking for and Mark was giving her all the compliments making her feel good about herself, she was quite taken by him, he was a tall man, he had shaved his hair off years ago due to hair loss, he was big built but looked after himself, he had a huge chest and looked good, he had a lovely smile too. Helen was enjoying the flirting with him and was taking all the compliments he gave. She picked a few new sets of underwear and headed towards the checkout.

Mark said, "shame I won't get to see how good you look in these Helen", she blushed not knowing what to say.

"I always thought you had a great body, you should show it off more".

"Thank you" Helen replied. "I thought you had a girlfriend anyway?".

"No, I'm single what about you?"

"Me too" she said, "well let's get together then" Mark replied.

"Okay" Helen said. "Come on let's grabbed some lunch my treat.

You can tell me all about you". They found a quiet table in a restaurant and Mark was ever the gentleman. Helen was really loving the attention, she couldn't work out why Jane had left him, he was lovely, such a gentleman and seemed really caring, he said he loved cooking and would love to cook for her, she was excited about it and agreed. Mark wooed her most of the afternoon really pulling out all the stops. He knew she was naive and could in time get information out of her. He couldn't believe his luck. They spent the rest of the day together in town and Mark followed her home. Once in the house Mark turned up the charm, he needed to be careful but knew the Vets run was in a few weeks and hoped Jane wouldn't be going.

Helen went to make a drink for them both and Mark followed her, he came up behind her and kissed her neck, she was a tall slim girl with dark hair a great figure, she wore her hair up all the time in a ponytail. She jumped when he did it.

"Sorry Helen I didn't mean to make you jump", he said and placed his hands on her hips.

"It's okay, I just wasn't expecting that".

He kissed her again and this time she leant back into him, he wrapped his arms around her, while she finished the drinks.

"Need any help love?" he asked.

"No, I'm done now thank you".

He let go of her and took the drinks into the lounge, he sat first and patted the seat next to him for her to sit down. Helen sat with him and he put his arm around her shoulder, she cuddled into him. He put the TV on to watch some football. She didn't like it much but thought you need to do things to please a man, so she let it go. She stayed quiet and watched with him. After the match had finished he said. "Right I'm off, I will call you".

He took her phone off the side, "password", he demanded she told him he opened her phone and added his number. He sent himself a text kissed her and left.

Helen felt a little annoyed, but let it go she didn't expect to hear from him again anyway, "at least I didn't sleep with him" she thought.

She went off to bed and forgot about him. The following morning she had a text from him.

"I will be over tonight at 7pm see you then".

She was surprised but replied.

"Okay I will cook", he replied.

"Don't bother we will order take away".

She went off to work, not sure how she felt about it him, she decided not to say anything to anyone in case nothing came of it and she knew they didn't really like him anyway.

She got home and made sure the house was clean and tidy and at 7pm she heard the bike pull up outside and opened the door for him, Mark walked in, bent and kissed Helen and sat down on her sofa, he patted the seat next to him again and Helen joined him.

"So what we having then?" he asked her.

"What do you like Helen?"

"I don't mind, whatever you prefer".

"Indian it is then" he said and got his phone out of his pocket and logged onto the website, "what do you eat?" he asked.

She looked at the screen and opted for a Jalfrezi and rice. He selected several things and placed the order, he sat back and beckoned her into him again, she laid against him. He said.

"So, do I get to see you in your new underwear tonight?

I think while we are waiting you should go and put some on for me".

Helen got up and went into the bedroom, she came out a few minutes later looking sheepish with a purple set of underwear on, it was all lace, a small pair of knickers that sat high on her hips, the bra was a cleavage enhancing bra, which Helen loved as it made her look bigger than she was, she stood in the middle of the room and Mark got up walked round her, slapped her bottom, pulled at the lace on her knickers to look at her properly then walked round the front, he ran his fingers down her body, then over her cleavage, he spun her around and kissed her neck, undid her bra and threw it onto the floor.

"On your knees Helen, we have just got enough time before the food arrives" he said, he undid his belt, took it off his jeans and told Helen to put her wrists behind her back, she did as he asked and wrapped his belt around her hands to stop them moving, he undid his jeans and dropped them to the floor, they were in the middle of her lounge still. He got his cock out and slapped Helen round the face with it, "you will do as I say, do you hear me?" he said.

Helen nodded, he put his hand on her pony tail and pulled it back so she was looking up at him.

"Open your mouth", he ordered.

Helen did as she was asked and he pushed his cock into her mouth, he pulled her head towards him and made her gag as his cock hit the back of his throat.

"Don't you dare throw up on me, do you hear me?"

Jane nodded tears rolling down her face, "suck it now" he said softer, Helen started to suck him and he stopped forcing it to the back of her throat. She sucked him as he squeezed his balls.

"Suck harder, and make sure you swallow"

Helen nodded as she felt him get harder.

"Fuck that, I want your arse", he slid out of her mouth and pulled her up by her wrists.

"Bedroom now" he demanded, Jane walked to her room and he pushed her to the bed, he pulled her knickers down and pushed her onto the bed on her knees, he undid the belt and let her hands go free, "stay on the edge and push your arse in the air".

Helen did as she was told and he came behind her dropping his jeans again, he bent forward and spat on Helen's arse and rubbed it into her hole, he slid his finger in as Helen gasped.

"Hmm someone has been here before I think"? He said out loud, Helen didn't say anything.

"I don't care it saves me being gentle", he ran his cock over her hole and pushed in hard.

"Helen screamed, Mark moaned with pleasure. He grabbed her ponytail again and pulled her head up.

"You are mine, do you hear me?" Helen nodded.

"When I tell you I want to fuck you I expect you to get into this position and do as you are told". Helen nodded.

"Cry and I will hurt you, do you hear me?"

Helen tried not to sniff in fear of being hit or worse. He continued to fuck her hard, Helen was in pain as he forced himself harder into her, within minutes he came hard screaming loudly.

"Fuck yes you little hoar, you are mine".

He spanked her and pulled out of her.

"Turn round", as Helen turned round on the bed he demanded.

"Open your mouth", she did as she was told and he pushed his cock in, "suck it clean now".

He pushed her head down onto him as she closed her mouth around him sucking him clean. Just as she finished the doorbell rang.

"Get some clothes on" he growled and walked out of the room pulling his jeans up heading towards the door.

Helen sat on the bed hugging herself, trying not to cry.

"Where are you?

Get out here now this food needs dishing up" he yelled.

Helen grabbed a t-shirt and shorts got dressed and walked out of her room. She went into the kitchen as Mark was unpacking the food containers, Helen got the plates out and started to put the food out. He grabbed his and walked into the living room sitting on the chair and taking control of the TV. They sat and ate their food in silence and when Helen had finished she took Marks plate too. When she came back into the lounge Mark grabbed her hand and pulled her down onto his lap, she cuddled into him feeling really confused. One minute he was aggressive the next he was nice, there was no happy medium with him.

They sat together late into the evening and Mark said just before midnight.

"Bedtime come on"

Helen got up "are you staying over?"

"Yes, is that a problem?"

"No, not at all"

"Good" he said and walked into the bedroom.

Helen picked up the cups from the table and took them into the kitchen and put them on the side. She went into the bedroom as Mark was undressing, she had never seen his body before, he had huge shoulders with very pronounced muscles around his chest, he tapered into the waist and a defined V down to his cock. He stepped out of his jeans and turned around, his back was all muscle too and Helen knew he could hurt anyone he wanted too. He walked round the bed and pulled the bedclothes back. Helen undressed and left her clothes on the stool at her dressing table.

As Helen got in Mark pulled her across to him and she laid on his chest, Mark fell to sleep pretty quickly as Helen laid awake thinking of what she was getting herself into. She thought how nice he could be when he wanted too, but she didn't understand his anger over sex. She let out a huge sigh and closed her eyes ready to sleep.

When Helen woke, she could smell bacon, she dressed and walked into the kitchen, Mark was cooking bacon and egg.

"Morning sleepy head" he said.

Helen was even more confused, she never imagined he would do this not after the night before.

"Morning, you should have woke me up, I would have done this" she said.

"No need I thought you might like some breakfast. Sit he pointed to the table", Helen sat down as the toast popped, he put it in front of her, Jane buttered the toast and put it on the plates as Mark placed the bacon and egg on top. He put the pan next to the sink and came and sat down.

"This is really kind of you Mark thank you"

"You're welcome"

He said tucking into his breakfast. Helen cleared the dishes away after they finished and Mark left.

"I will be back later". Okay Helen replied.

"I'm not going anywhere", he didn't kiss her just left.

Chapter 26

Fun in the sun

The following day was a hot one again and Jasper was up early setting up the sun beds for them, he wanted to chill out again with Jane. He loved seeing her so relaxed. They had breakfast and showered together, Jasper went out to water the garden before it got to hot and checked the roses, he knew Jane would be out to check them too she was treating them with kid gloves.

He watered the plants and packed the hose away, as Jane came out of the house. She saw Jasper putting the last of the things away.

"Oh have you watered already?"

"Yes love, they are fine"

Jane smiled and walked down the garden to look for herself Jasper followed, catching her hand and walked with her. She stopped at the roses and crouched down. She stayed there for a few minutes and Jasper stood behind her with his hands on her shoulders. She kissed her hand and placed it on each rose and stood up. `

Jasper took her in his arms.

"You ok Belle?"

"Yes darling I am"

"Good"

They turned and headed back down the garden to the house.

Jane went back into the house to make tea for them, she brought it out and they sat the on the patio just chatting together. Jasper held Jane's hand rubbing his thumb over her knuckles while they talked about the week ahead.

"When is Moses arriving love?"

"Not for another two weeks" Jane replied.

"Okay and they are staying in the hotel near the dealership?"

"Yes they are"

"Great, happy to help if needed love"

"Thank you love, they are sorted they do this every year and they have a discount where they stay"

She brought his hand to her mouth and kissed him.

"Thank you baby I do appreciate it".

"Anything for you Belle you know that.

Come on let's go and get changed it's getting warm already I want you laid next to me on the sun bed so I can stare at you for ages". Jane laughed, "Pervert!"

"How can I be a pervert when it's the woman I love I am staring at?" Jane went to mush inside, "Mr smooth talker" she said and they both laughed.

They went into the house and got changed Jane put her bikini on and a pair of shorts Jasper put on his shorts and t-shirt.

They went back outside Jane grabbed the sun cream and Jasper got water for them both. Jane sat on her bed and passed the suncream to Jasper as she took off her t-shirt. Jasper sat behind her and sprayed her back rubbing in the lotion.

"Hair up please Belle".

She did as she was asked and tied her hair up smiling, they were so relaxed around each other she loved it. Jasper finished her back and arms, Jane took it from him turned round as did Jasper and she did his back. They both then smothered their arms and legs before laying back on the sunbed.

They were laid reading but holding hands twiddling fingers.

"Would you like a fresh drink?"

"Yes, please love"

He said and she thought it was time to cool them down. She came back into the garden with an extra glass of ice cubes and their drinks. Jasper was laid on his back his hand under his head legs crossed. Jane knelt beside him and popped a small ice cube into her mouth. She took his book away and went to kiss him. As she did, she ran the ice cube over his lips. He smiled and had a small moan. Jane continued with her quest. She straddled him, lent forward and ran her lips and ice down his chin and let the water pool into the V on his neck. She sucked it up and continued across his shoulders and down his right arm. He was moaning softly and could feel the water tickling him as it started to melt and run down the sides of his arm. She worked back up to his arm pit which she loved to kiss when it was smooth and run the ice across it. Jasper laughed and spanked her which spurred her on. Jane thought I'm sure this isn't cooling us down though. She came across his body to his nipples.

"Oh I've waited for this moment." She thinks to herself. She slowly pushed the ice out of her lips a bit further and ran it around his nipple which stiffened straight away. She felt her pussy getting wet as his cock got harder beneath her. She ground her hips into   him.

Jasper pushed her body down, so she was sitting against his cock sucking in air through his teeth, whispering.

"You are such a bad girl Belle".

She continues with her nipple quest teasing with the ice then sucking them both.

"God I love teasing you" she whispers.

The ice is melting so she discards it and grabs another peice and moves down his legs pulling his shorts down as she goes, just so they stop at the start of his cock. She rubs the ice down his body to his happy trail as he moves under her pushing his cock up towards her moaning desperate to be sucked. She rubs the ice slowly side to side on the waistband of his shorts, to make it run down inside. As he feels it trickle down, he begs.

"Fuck baby more".

She starts grinning, she gets up, picks up the ice and wiggles her finger at him beckoning him to follow her in doors. Even though they are not overlooked the last thing they need is anyone catching them. As he walks into the bedroom Jane is bent over the bed laying a couple of towels down to catch any stray water. She hears him pad into the room and kick off his shorts. He comes up behind her with his cock in his hand pushing it into her bottom.

"Just where i like you Belle".

he says as he pulls her bikini down and pushes her legs apart. He spanks her arse and climbs onto the bed. He lays on his front and Jane climbs on and sits astride him. She picks up where she left off putting the ice in her mouth. To get him to relax she massages his head from the nape making circles with her thumbs until she feels him relax beneath her. Then she starts at his shoulders keeping the ice in her mouth, so he gets the warmth of her lips then the cold of the ice. Every time water escapes, she finds it and licks it from his beautiful body. She moves down as she gets to his arse; she holds the ice at the top and lets it melt.

She opens his legs wide enough for her to kneel between as the ice melts and runs down between his cheeks. She lets it reach his balls as he squirms, moaning loudly, she runs her tongue slowly from his balls to the top of his arse watching the water taking time to suck any excess off his balls and hole. It's making her so wet. Jasper moans as she continues to lick the water from him.

"Roll over baby" she says in her sultry voice, she straddles him again and slides her tongue around his belly button. She works her way down to the start of his cock and bypasses it. Going down his leg. He lets out a huge sigh and she grins.

"Yes, you thought i was going for your cock" she thinks. "Not yet baby boy" she laughs

The ice is melting on his leg and it runs down to his balls. She swaps to the other leg and does the same. He moans as he feels the water hit his balls again. It makes Jane smirk. She moves the ice, running It up and down his chest again teasing his nipples just to get him all hot, Jane's nipples stiffen at the thought of him doing this to her. She runs the ice down his body further her head getting nearer to his cock. She circles the ice just above it and lets it run down his legs again and catches it with her tongue making long strokes back up to his cock and over his balls.

"Fuck Babe, suck my cock please" he begs again.

Jane just grins and continues teasing him. He blows air through his teeth in frustration. It doesn't stop her.

He tries to grab her, "Im going to spank you lady".

She runs her tongue back up his cock to the top. Jane grabs another small piece and puts it into her mouth, grazes it gently over the top of his cock. He takes a sharp intake of breath grabs the bed clothes, "Fuck baby what are you trying to do to me?" She continues down his rock, solid hot cock as it twitches, he screws the bed clothes up moaning loudly. Jane moves back up and slides her mouth over his cock the ice melting quickly which changes the whole feel of her sucking him. His eyes stare into hers as she sucks him slowly up and down. The heat from her mouth is melting the ice but still giving him a great feeling. He is hissing through his teeth and grabbing at the bedclothes.

"Fuck Belle, I want you, I need to be inside you now" he says demandingly.

Jane stops grabs another piece and traces her route back up his body round his nipples to remind him how it feels. Then she moves up to his mouth. She runs the ice over his lips, he opens for her as they kiss, moving the ice between them. Jasper takes it and stops kissing her. Instead he sits up straight keeping her on his lap and leans forward taking her breast in his hand, caressing it, his lips find her nipple as he sucks it teasing her with the ice as she did to him. Her head drops back as she feels the sensation, she starts to moan loudly.

"Oh my god this is incredible" she moans. Her pussy responds getting wetter and coating his cock in her juices. Jasper whispers.

"I want to taste you". She runs her fingers into her pussy which makes her clench around them. She slides them out and puts both fingers into his mouth. They are thickly coated with her; he sucks them like it's his last drink and cleans every drop. His cock is throbbing beneath her, she grinds into him a bit more. He lifts her by the hips to release his cock and slides into slowly filling her with his cock. It takes her breath away every time feeling the fullness of him. She starts moving her hips and he follows her as they grind together. Jane leans down to kiss him and before she realises, she is on her back. Jasper laughs and slide out of her.

"Now it's my turn".

He opens her legs, grabs some Ice and begins to tease her with it, first pushing his finger inside her she moans loudly. She loves the feeling of him touching her. He gets on his knees and blows over her pussy. She shudders in pleasure. Then she feels it. She screams out.

"Oh my god. oh fuck…"

She can feel the ice on her pussy. she instantly pushes to feel more. Jasper teases her bringing her to the edge so many times then he stops.

"On your knees Belle" he demands. She does as he asks, as he spreads her legs open. Jasper bends over her back and lets the ice make its way down and licks it up. He pushes his fingers into her pussy collecting more of her juices and rubs it onto his cock sucking the rest off. He slides into her pulling her hips into him. Jasper pushes hard into her which she loves. He gets faster, his hand goes around to her pussy. He kisses and bites her back leaving his mark on her.

"Oh, baby Im going to cum" she screams.

He stops rubbing and pushes harder and faster her pussy clenches around his cock.

"I will milk you" "wait for me baby" he groans.

"Oh god im cumming" she yells as she feels it hit her as he does too. Jane keeps clenching around his cock milking him as he gasps and moans. Her body has floated away somewhere as she rides through her orgasm with him. "Pure heaven" she croons. As their bodies slow Jasper pulls out of Jane she moans as he does and turns around his cock covered in their juices. She bends forward and takes him in her mouth, sucking all the juices off saving some for him as she comes up to kiss him.

"Are you trying to make me hard again baby girl." He laughs as Jane nods. He smiles laying her down, pushes between her legs, his cock rock hard again and slides into her. He puts her legs onto his shoulders and slowly makes love to her. They move together not looking from each other's eyes. Jasper moans.

"I will never get tired of you and your pussy Belle, it feels so good everytime. I love you".

Her hands go into his hair and she pulls him down into her for a kiss. She bites his lip.

"I love you too baby". Slowly they build up speed and cum together. Exhausted they wrap themselves in each other's arms and fall to sleep.

Chapter 27

Give me the information

Mark goes back to Helens for the night, he knows he needs to treat her nicely if he is going to get what he wants out of her, but he is struggling, he is repulsed by her and most women they are just toys to play with and she is another in a long line of them. He gets off the bike and locks it up and heads to the door, he takes a deep breath and says to himself, "you can do this, it's a means to an end, and if you want to end Jane then you have to do this".

Helen opens the door with a huge smile.

"Hi Mark, come in, I wasn't sure if you were coming but I brought dinner just in case", she says tiptoeing to kiss him. He leans down and kisses her on the lips and smiles.

"Yeah sorry I got held up".

"That's okay, you have a choice anyway, steak and salad or potatoes and veg?".

"The last one will do me" he says sitting down on the sofa.

Helen goes into the kitchen and gets the food out ready to cook, she comes back in.

"Are you staying the night, if so, would you like a beer?".

"Yeah ok", he grunts.

"How do you like your steak?"

"Rare".

She heads back into the kitchen grabs him a beer and brings it in to him, he takes it off her and stands it on the arm of the chair holding it in place, he still has his boots and jacket on which annoys Helen. Mark didn't care, it wasn't his house and he wasn't paying the bills to replace or repair anything. Helen put the food on to cook and came back into the room, she knew the steak would take no time at all to cook when the potatoes and vegetables were done. She sat on the chair.

"What are you watching?"

"What does it look like?" he barked at her.

Helen felt her cheeks flush "sorry", she stood to go back into the kitchen and Mark grabbed her hand, he pulled her to him.

"What's the fucking face for?"

"Nothing Im fine"

She replied feeling like she wanted to cry. He pulled her down into his lap and took her face in his spare hand, he pulled her to him and bit her lip hard making it bleed before kissing her.

"Stop reading into things, you can see what Im watching, you know I don't like stupid fucking questions".

Helen didn't know she had only ever met him at the club and hadn't got to know him but didn't argue.

"Okay, I better go and finish dinner", he let go of her and she climbed off his lap and went into the kitchen.

She finished off the food and took his in on a tray with the cutlery and condiments. He thanked her and she sat across from him while they ate.

Once he had finished he put the tray on the floor and went upstairs to the bathroom.

"Where are your spare towels? I want a bath" he yelled.

She pointed to the cupboard outside the bathroom.

"In there", he opened the door and pulled two towels out went into the bathroom and turned on the taps, he stuck his head out of the door and yelled.

"Bring my beer"

"I will in a minute I am just finishing my dinner".

"Now" he barked at her.

Helen put her dinner down and grabbed his beer heading for the stairs. She was scared of him and didn't know what to do about it. She thought I will just do all he asks and then hopefully he will be happy.

She went into the bathroom and he was undressing, he took his beer and took a mouthful.

"You can go now" he said turning away from her. Helen went back downstairs and collected the dishes and went back into the kitchen, suddenly she wasn't hungry anymore.

Mark was in the bath for an hour, she heard him turning the hot tap on several times to heat the water back up. He yelled down to her, "Come and wash my back", she jumped up and dashed up the stairs. She walked in and he was laid down in the bath with his phone in his hand watching porn, there was a women on her knees on a sofa surrounded by men with their jeans round their ankles as one was fucking her from behind another had his cock in her mouth and she was holding another going from one to the other.

Helen didn't mind watching porn, but this wasn't her kind of thing, the women was gagging and trying not to be sick. He looked up at her and moved the screen to show her.

"Fancy some of this Helen, I can get some of the boys round if you like, after all you are the club bike".

She felt the tears well up again and the back of her throat was burning where she was fighting the tears back. He lent forward laughing loudly. Jane picked up with cloth on the side of the bath and soaked it in the water. She squeezed the body wash onto it and started to rub it on his back.

"Harder" he shouted, Jane used two hands to scrub up and down him, she was sure it must hurt but he didn't seem to care.

She finished his back and rinsed him off.

"Go and shower and get into bed, make sure that pussy his smooth I don't want any fucking hairs in my teeth".

Jane turned away and went to the ensuite shower in her room, she got out a new razor and started to shave herself, she did it regularly anyway there wasn't really much there but she didn't want to anger him. Once she washed herself she got out of the shower wrapped herself in a towel and went to the bedroom, Mark was already in their laying in bed his damp towels on the floor where he had stepped out of them.

He was watching more porn on his phone, Jane looked across at him and could see he was playing with himself.

"Come here" he ordered beckoning her round to his side of the bed, she went round to him.

"Open your legs", he pushed his hand between them and felt her, he looked up.

"That will do I suppose, get in". Helen walked back round the bed and got in.

He pushed the bed clothes back and was laid rubbing his cock still watching porn on his phone.

"Get your lips round this"

He said pointing his cock in Helens direction. She did as she was told and leant over, he took his hand away as she started to suck him, he grabbed her pony tail and pushed and pulled her head, he forced her head down making her gag on him again, the tears sprang into her eyes and she was choking, water was escaping her mouth either side of his cock, she knew she was going to be sick any minute, suddenly he pulled back on her hair.

"Enough, lay down with your legs open". Helen did and he put his phone down laid across her, his cock near her face and buried his lips into her pussy.

Helen thought "well he can't be all that bad if hes prepared to eat me I suppose".

Mark was rough with Helen there was no passion in his touch, she did as he wanted and sucked his cock until he had enough, he didn't finish Helen off but not all men liked that she thought, she had started making excuses for him which wasn't a good sign. Mark climbed off Helen.

"On your knees" he demanded as he sat on his haunches rubbing his cock, Helen did and opened her legs for him, he pulled her hips into him and rammed into her as he did every time, Helen was used to being used by men, so she didn't expect anymore, she would love to have what other women have but it wasn't meant to be for her. Mark took less than a few minutes to get himself off in Helen and he pushed her away once he had done. She climbed off the bed and went to clean up, she came back a few minutes later and Mark was already sleeping, she got into bed and curled into a ball feeling used and cried herself to sleep.

The next morning Helen made coffee for Mark before he left for work, he kissed her cheek and didn't say when he would be back. Jane stood at the door and watched him ride away then showered dressed and headed to work.

Mark rang her during the day and asked if she was free that night, she was excited he sounded in a good mood, she said she was and went around the rest of the day with a skip in her step. Helen got home showered and put on a dress she felt good and wanted to look good for Mark. He arrived a short while later, when she opened the door he picked her up in his arms and swang her round kissing her passionately, she didn't want to comment in fear of upsetting him so enjoyed the attention.

"Come and see what I got". He pulled her hand and took her outside, he pointed to his new bike, Helen worked for the Harley dealer but wasn't knowledgeable with what bike was what, but she did like them. "It's a custom Street Glide, I had extras added".

Helen nodded in appreciation, "it's this years model too, do you like the colour?".

It was bright blue and looked good with the chrome on it.

"yes I do, it's lovely".

"Get your boots on I will take you for a ride" he grinned. Helen went back in quickly put her jeans jacket and pulled her boots on as she was locking the door, she was excited and enjoying seeing him so happy, he always seemed happy when he had something new. She jumped onto the bike and Mark pulled away with some speed, Helen held on tight, they were out for about an hour and Mark stopped at a steak house.

"Are you hungry?" he asked, Helen nodded.

"I am yes", "great come on lets eat"

He grabbed her hand and headed in, it was an old shack of a place, wooden and looked like if you blew too hard it would collapse, it had a great reputation and got quite busy in the summer months with the fair weather riders. Once inside they were seated in a booth and handed menus, they both had a long lemonade and lime and ordered a sharing platter of spicy wings ribs, onion rings, and nachos, Mark was very chatty and Helen was enjoying this side of him, she relaxed and started to enjoy herself.

"So, when do the guys head out to the US for the Vets run?".

"Two weeks" Helen replied. "They are looking forward to seeing Jane when they get there".

Mark was trying not to look too interested.

"Oh, really?", "yes she has been out there now a few weeks working",

Marks ears were wide open, he needed to be careful he thought, not let on he was plugging her for information.

"So are they going to Connecticut as usual?", "yes they are, Jane lives local to the dealer and she will be spending a few days with them before they head off".

"Oh great Moses will enjoy that, Im sure" he said. He changed the subject for a while as they finished their starter, their steaks arrived shortly after, Helen was talking about her day and the guys getting ready to leave. He knew he needed to rethink his plan now, he didn't realise she was in the US, that would take more planning. He needed dates too, he would go softly and dig later.

He asked Helen about her, he made the evening all about her, made her feel wanted, he kissed her hand at the table, and wooed her.

Helen was loving the attention and really relaxed. After the meal they headed back home to Helens and as they got to the door Mark swept her into his arms and carried her to the bedroom, he laid her on the bed, bent over over her kissed her, then moved down to her boots, he pulled them off and threw them on the floor, removed her jeans jacket and t-shirt, he stood back looking at her body.

Helen felt embarrassed but was also loving the change in him, he pulled her legs open got on his knees going straight to her pussy, he started to lick her out quite roughly then held back, he needed to treat her gently he had been too rough, Helen began to moan his soft tongue flicking over her clit was amazing, she grabbed at his head pushing him deeper.

"Oh yes Mark please don't stop".

She begged, as she pushed her pussy against his face, her juices covering his chin and mouth, as his tongue licked up her pussy, he sucked as he went collecting her juices. He was sucking hard because for once he was enjoying it and wanted to please her.

Helen was almost going out of her mind with pleasure. Mark slid his finger inside her and rubbed against her pussy wall.

Helen crumbled and felt her orgasm hit. Her body trembled her eyes fogged over it was just a bright light, she hadn't experienced this before not to this intensity. It took a few minutes for her to recover when she did, she opened her eyes to see Mark looking at her smiling with his face wet from her juices. He came up to her kissed her.

"Lick my face taste yourself on me".

Helen did as he asked, as she was doing so Mark pushed his cock inside her and fucked her hard until he came, he then rolled onto his side and went to sleep. Helen wasn't surprised.

The following morning Mark was still in a good mood, Helen got up showered and dressed then went to make them a drink, they sat at her breakfast bar and chatted. Helens house was small, she didn't have room for a big table in her kitchen she had a small 4-seater and a breakfast bar for two, her kitchen area was small, off to the right was a door to the garage.

"So Helen wouldn't you like to be going to America to see Jane?", "oh yeah it would be nice but someone has to stay behind don't they. I'm the new member too I don't know her as well as the others".

"I understand" he said. "So where does she work".

"Oh I don't really know to be honest, Moses and G talk about things themselves they don't share. She does Skype though from home or from her new boyfriends occasionally".

"So you get to see that?"

"Yes we all do" she replied.

"Okay, so where does she live then?"

"Near to where she works apparently. Not far from the dealership where the guys are going to meet Shadow. She has her trike there too".

Mark just nodded he was taking it all in, he stopped asking questions he didn't want her to register he was asking so much.

"Well Im glad she has found someone else it looks like we both have" he said taking her hand, he needed her to believe what he was saying.

"Right I better get off to work, do you want a lift?"

"No it's fine I have my car".

"Okay", he kissed her and left, "I might see you later, depends how my day goes" he said as he put on his crash helmet. "

Sure, just let me know I will be here".

Helen went to work with a big smile on her face, when she arrived Gwen stopped her.

"You look like the cat that got the cream, did you get laid last night?"

Helen didn't want them to know who she was seeing, she just nodded and walked away humming to herself. Gwen just smiled.

"It's nice to see her happy" she thought.

Helen got home that night hoping to see Mark, but he didn't arrive, he didn't call either, they weren't really an item so she couldn't complain. She just sat back and enjoyed the time to relax and catch up on her TV programmes.

Mark was at home researching Connecticut; he had enough information to start with and would keep asking questions until he knew where she worked. He found the dealer, no doubt Moses had warned them. if so, he couldn't get help from there, but he could arrive a little earlier and wait for them, he could then follow Jane when she turned up. Helen hadn't given him the date they were leaving but she would even if he had to beat it out of her, in the meantime he found a cheap apartment block close by and a car rental firm who took cash he was going to rent a 7 seater it would be easier to get Jane into once he grabbed her. He was getting excited, he needed to calm down and plan this military style, he hadn't been in the military but believed he knew more than most of the men that did. He was very sure of himself which made him very arrogant.

The apartment he was booking wasn't quiet, but it was cheap, nobody would ask questions he was sure. He needed to get a few things when he arrived so found the local hardware shop and noted the address. He had a week or so he thought to go before he flew out so started a schedule of what he had to do, once there he could sort out timings, he would just sit and watch outside the dealership. He rubbed his hands together, he looked at the background on his screen it was a mass of pictures of Jane, he looked down at them "Soon you will be mine again Jane and you will pay for leaving me, I didn't say you could".

He slammed the lid down and thought he better go and see Helen, he needed her onside, he wasn't going to miss this opportunity to get to Jane.

Helen was sat watching the TV when she heard the rumble of the bike outside. It was almost 10pm, she smiled though, it was nice he thought about her. Before Mark had the chance to knock Helen opened the door to him, he didn't kiss her just walked in with his helmet in his hand and put it down next to the chair. He pulled off his jacket, "sorry I was a bit busy".

Helen smiled "that's ok. Would you like a drink?"

"Sure, a beer will do".

Helen went to the fridge and got a bottle for him.

"Have you eaten?"

"Yes, thanks at work". Helen sat down on the sofa next to his chair.

"You didn't have to come over if you were busy".

"Why not?" he asked. "Don't you want me here?"

"No, no I meant I am flattered but if you are busy its okay".

"Well I wanted to" he replied.

"Okay thank you"

"So what have you been doing today, how was work, many in the café?"

"No, not really, the boys are busy getting services done before they go away then the garage will be on emergency work only as there is a big gang going over this year for the ride out, a lot of the old vets have decided to go there is going to be a big party too".

Mark started to listen harder she was giving information without him asking.

"Oh, ok that's great, when is it again, I know you did say"

"Oh did I? I don't think I did"

Mark looked round at her, his face growing tight with anger.

"I think you did Helen" he scowled.

"Ummm, I think it's a week Thursday they fly out, the run starts on the Sunday".

"Okay" he replied.

He made a note in his head, he needed to get there before them so would leave the end of the week.

"I have to go away too" he said.

"Oh", Helen looked round, "why?"

"Training, I am going to be away 3 weeks, were going to Spain. Then a week of relaxing getting to know each other".

"Oh, okay". "I leave the end of this week. I won't be over much as I need to get ready".

"That's okay" Helen said, "I know you have an important job to do. Can I text you while you are away?

"Sure, but I don't know how often I can reply"

"I know. That's ok, whenever".

Mark finished his beer.

"I think its bedtime, you coming?"

He said getting up out of his chair pulling up his jeans, Helen jumped up taking the bottle from Mark and picking her empty cup taking them to the kitchen. Mark turned out the lights and followed her stopping at the bathroom, cleaned his teeth and went to bed, he was asleep in no time, Helen got in and cuddled into his back.

Helen woke with a start Mark had his hands around her throat, she was gasping for air and pulling at the bed clothes, Mark had murder in his eyes, but he looked vacant, she couldn't breath, she was trying to grab him.

"Mark, Mark" she tried to scream but nothing but a whisper came out, she grabbed at his hands scratching him trying to breath, Mark was shouting at her.

"You fucking bitch I told you I would find you, you are mine you wont get away this time".

Helen kicked her legs trying to get free when suddenly he let go, he sat back on his legs and looked at his hands, he had woken up from a dream, he looked at Helen she was holding her throat gasping, trying to get air into her lungs her eyes were wide she looked terrified.

"Oh shit, fuck I am so sorry Helen please forgive me" he said grabbing her hands, Helen scrambled onto her knees moving away from him, terrified.

"I am so sorry I had a bad dream".

"Who were you talking about?" she said with a whisper.

"I don't know" he said lying.

Helen got off the bed and turned the light on, she started pacing the room.

"You said she, who is she?"

"I don't know what you are talking about" he said trying to cover his lies, "it was a dream I told you".

Helen sat on the bed, right on the edge.

"Let me see" he said touching her hands, Helen gingerly let go and allowed him to see, she had red hand prints round her throat.

"Fuck, fuck I am so fucking sorry Helen, I would never hurt you" he lied.

He touched the red marks he could see his finger marks. He thought how good that necklace of marks would look on Jane. But her death wasn't going to be that quick.

"Please say you forgive me Helen?"

"I forgive you" she said lying.

"Come to bed please, let me hold you".

Helen got into bed and went into Marks arms not sure she was doing the right thing. Mark held onto her, kissed the top of her head and forced himself to stay awake while she slept, he couldn't risk doing it again, he wouldn't stay again just in case he didn't wake up next time.

By morning Mark was exhausted, he called into work sick and went home to sleep. Helen looked in the mirror, the bruises were around her throat, she tried to cover it with foundation, she couldn't wear a scalf it would be seen. She had to get her story straight. They knew she liked sex so she would say a game went wrong with a new boyfriend. She put on a blouse with a high neck and went to work.

Gwen spotted straight away that Helen had a lot of makeup on which was unusual.

"Got a date after work Helen?" she asked.

Helen put her head down.

"No why do you ask?"

"Just you have makeup on which you don't normally wear to work. Is everything okay?"

"Yes, fine thanks" she replied keeping her head down and walked into the kitchen to get on preparing food. Gwen wasn't satisfied but wouldn't press her.

At lunch time the café got busy and Helen was out front, Moses saw her and spotted the marks on her neck too.

"Hels, you ok love?"

"Yes, fine thank you?" why do you all keep asking me that".

Moses put his hands up.

"We just care Hels that's all"

"Well nothing is wrong" she snapped back.

"Fine, fine I will keep my nose out".

He took his sandwich and walked away, G came in.

"Watch what you say to Hels she has a right mood on her today, don't ask about her neck, for god's sake".

G nodded as he walked past and saw what Moses was on about, he watched Helen with interest as she moved around. He could see she was keeping her head down.

"Hmmm" he said under his breath. "Hels how are you?"

Helen tutted, "Im fine, why can't you all just leave me alone" she snapped. G wasn't going to take this attitude Helen was quiet and never snapped at anyone something was wrong. He waited for the queue to go.

"Hels can we talk?"

"Why?" she snapped back, he stepped behind the counter took her hand and led her out looking over her head at Gwen who nodded. He led her to the other side of the room and sat her down.

"Hels, we are all worried about you, talk to me please. What happened to your neck and don't say nothing".

She took a deep breath.

"Look Hels, if someone is hurting you? We need to know, we will sort him out for you, do we know him?" She shook her head.

"No, you don't. He didn't hurt me ok, it was an accident".

"Hmmm sure if you say so. Just hear me out Hels. We care about you like we do all the other girls and we won't let anyone hurt you. You need anything you come to us, do you hear me?"

She nodded. Fighting the tears, she got up.

"Is that all?"

G sighed, "yes that's all".

Helen went to turn as G stood up and hugged her.

"Always here for you Hels".

"Thank you"

She said accepting his hug and enjoying the warmth from him. He was a straight man, you got what you saw, she watched the love he showed to Jane and believed every word he said. Helen walked away and went back to work. Gwen looked over at G he shook his head, she smiled and turned around, she would keep a closer eye on Helen before they went to the US.

Helen went home exhausted from trying to hide her neck from the others, she decided to text Mark and say she was feeling unwell and going to bed, he replied straight away and said no problem, it got him off the hook too. Helen went to bed early and hoped the following day would be better, she laid in bed and cried herself to sleep. How could she tell anyone what he did to her, this was Jane's ex after all.

Mark got his laptop out, he booked the flight apartment and car, he was sorted, he would have 5 days to work out his plan when he arrived, he would watch the dealership, he needed to see who was about now and sit tight for when the others arrived and Jane. He knew there would be a couple of days before they set off so he could follow Jane back to her place in case he needed to grab her there. He was set.

Chapter 28

Playtime

Jane was getting excited in 10 days her friends would be here and they were having a huge party at the dealership. She couldn't wait to see Moses. She missed him. She missed G and the others too especially Gwen.

They had a black-tie event tonight they had to attend for work then the following Friday the guys would arrive.

Jane was day dreaming in her office and didn't hear the door knock, it was Jasper, the sign on the door didn't say she was busy so he walked in, Jane was at her desk, hands under her chin staring out of the window in a world of her own.

"Earth to Belle, come in Belle" he said laughingnothing...

he stepped closer.

"Earth to Belle, come in Belle".

Still nothing, He walked right up to her and stood in front of her, she jumped out of her skin and slapped him hard.

"Hey what was that for?"

"Why didn't you speak to me?"

"I did try Belle, but you didn't hear me", he was still laughing.

"You made me jump!"

She exclaimed as she held her chest, her heart beating fast, Jasper bent down to kiss her. She grabbed his face and bit his tongue as he ran it along her lips.

"Ouch, someone wants her arse smacking" he said grabbing her out of her seat.

Jane squealed as he turned her round and bent her over her desk.

"If you didn't have these jeans on your arse would be getting very sore right now".

He said as he landed a smack on her cheek.

"Ouch" she screamed, and another landed, "please stop Im sorry" she begged.

"Are you sure?"

"Yes, yes I promise".

"Okay" and stood her up. Jane rubbed her cheek screwing her face up.

"You hurt me"

"I'm sorry love shall I kiss it better?"

He asked as he bent towards her arse.

"No later you can" she smiled.

"Are you ready to go home and get ready for tonight?"

"Yes love, let me grab my laptop and bag".

Jane packed her things away and Jasper took her laptop bag and they walked out together.

When they got home, they went straight to the shower. Jane had done her nails the night before while they watched the TV. They were deep red to match her dress, she was excited about wearing it, but nervous too. She knew it looked good but showing off her figure again was nerve wracking, the guys at home knew her, not many did at this event only Jaspers co-workers and his friends, who she was going to meet for the first time tonight, they were all on different tables too. She knew she would be the only women between him and his friends and expected some leering from one of them especially, Jasper had warned her. She needed to keep him from getting jealous. He was very protective this could be an interesting evening.

Jasper came into the bedroom.

"You ready to shower Belle?"

She nodded, "I need to wash my hair, I don't mind going into the other room if you want me too?", she said pointing towards the spare room.

"No, I won't hear of it, we have plenty of time".

"Okay" she said smiling and walked into the bathroom with him.

They behaved tonight as time was getting on, Jasper washed Jane's hair for her and her body, she had been to the salon to have her arms and legs waxed the day before at lunch time, she had her pussy done too instead of shaving it.

They got out of the shower and dried off, Jane stayed naked until Jasper was ready and had left the room, she wanted everything to be a surprise for him, she dried her hair and put half of it up but left some length as he liked it, applied her makeup feeling good. She put on her dress, she loved the feel of the fabric as it fell down her body, it was soft and clung to her, it made her feel very sexy. She looked in the mirror, she was still shocked it was her. She felt confident and sexy, especially with her hair and makeup done.

Speechless by Dan and Say

Jasper was sitting on the arm of the chair dressed in his DJ, he was leaning back, his body saying come and get me girl all seductively.

Jane walked out of the bedroom and Jasper just sat staring at her, he looked her up and down, twirled his finger for her to turn, she smiled and did as directed. As she turned facing away from him she heard his breath catch. He got up off the chair and came towards her. Jane could already feel the heat between them. She was still facing away from him as she felt his finger run along the top of the dress against her bottom. He pulled the fabric away and saw her rose, he bent down and kissed it. Letting out a long groan. As he stood, he ran his finger up her back to her shoulder and into the nape of her neck moving her hair away, brushing his lips against her skin, breathing in her scent, he peppered kisses down her neck and onto her back. Jane felt the heat go straight to her pussy and moaned as he gently continued trailing his finger around her bare skin.
Her pussy was on fire her nipples stiffening. He ran his hand across her bottom and spanked it hard making her yelp. He snaked his hand around the front of her waist pulling her into him. As their bodies touched, she felt his hard cock pushing into her back. Jane loved it when Jasper didn't talk, she felt the heat intensify between them. He bent and kissed her just below her ear sending thunderbolts to her pussy and tingles across her skin. As he reached her ear he bit it. She sucked in air desperate to touch him. She knows better when he is in charge like this. He whispered in her ear.
"I want to fuck you right here and now. You are so beautiful Belle".
He spun her round kissed her forehead and ran his fingers across her breast, circling her nipple, making it harder, making him smile. He moved across to the other and did the same.
"That's better I can see what i will be sucking later. Any other man looks even for a second longer than is acceptable and you will pay dearly" he said playfully with a glint in his eye.
He ran his hands up her sides and stood back with a questioning look.
"Where are your knickers Belle?"

"I can't wear them baby, VPL is not a good look". She replied smiling naughtily. Knowing full well she could if she really wanted to.

"You are such a bad girl". Do you want me hard all night"?

"I don't know what you mean" She giggled.

He got onto his knees pushed up her dress and demanded.

"Open your legs".

She did as he asks, she felt his finger first slowly running up and down her pussy and pushing inside her, she was soaking wet already. Her head fell back.

 "Oh Christ" she moaned. He leant in and kissed the outside of her pussy; she could feel her juices running down inside her.

"Oh god oh god".

She moans loudly pushing his head to where she wants it. He licked the hood of her pussy sliding his tongue inside finding her clit. She almost came her whole body was on fire. A knock came to the door. It was the car service to take them to the venue. Jasper stood. "Damn cars early" he said. Wiping his face "I haven't finished with you by a long shot".

Jane adjusted her dress checked herself in the mirror.

"Just popping to the loo" she said.

Dashing off, within a few minutes she was back.

"I'm ready".

He took her hand and kissed her nose. She could smell herself on him as they headed for the door.

"Don't you want to wash your face? people will smell me" she asked.

"Hell no!, I want to taste and smell you all night".

They got into the back seat of the car, Jane's dress rising up her legs showing the tops of her stockings. Jasper licked his lips.

"You are such a tease Belle. I may have to play with you under the table".

He groaned as he trailed his fingers up her leg stroking softly.

Jane decided as the driver couldn't see or hear them due to the partition now was a good time to surprise him further. She opened her clutch and took out a small controller, putting it into his hand.

"Belle?" he said frowning "whats this?" She grinned at him.

"Turn it on low"

She replied and instantly her pussy throbbed as the eggs vibrated inside her. She then opened her legs took his hand and slid his fingers inside her. The look of shock and pure pleasure appeared on his face as he felt her body vibrate. He turned up the speed which made her moan loudly not helped by him teasing her with his fingers too.

"Maybe not wearing knickers was a bad Idea I will be wet all night". She said laughing.

"Oh no you did the right thing baby. I'm going to tease the hell out of you tonight and make you want to cum at the table. I will leave you so damn horny you will be begging me to finish you off" he replied laughing.

He lent in kissing her. Her hand moving up his leg to his cock which was straining to get out. As she touched him a deep groan escaped. "He hissed as she cupped his balls.

"Fuck Belle. Let's go home instead".

She laughed and shook her head. He pushed his fingers into her more and bent them up scooping her juices, pulled them out and sucked them slowly.

"Jesus women I want to eat you".

They pulled up outside the hall he lent over and kissed her.

"Ready Belle?"

He climbed out took her hand and helped her out, wrapped his arm around her waist as they entered the building. They were greeted by staff and told where the table was and headed over too it. They would catch up with his friends once they knew where the table was. Jasper waited for Jane to sit pushing her chair in and sat next to her. He leaned across and whispered in her ear.

"Let the games begin" with a wicked smile on his face.

The hall was huge very ornate, there were tables enough for 500 people, there were beautiful lights hanging from the rafters. Each table had more glasses and cutlery than a Royal table. In the centre was a beautiful tall vase filled with cream peony's roses and draped in beads, it stood proud in the centre. The table filled with people they didn't know but who knew of Jasper. Dinner was served quite quickly, and they started to chat with people. Jane was chatting to an older man to her right he was a retired surgeon, very charming too, suddenly Jane felt a light vibration in her pussy it made her jump, then moan. She was trying not to let on to the man she was chatting to as he looked quizzically at her. She could feel her face flushing as she excused herself, she stood as did the old man, Jasper did too and asked if she needed help. Jane smirked and shook her head at him she walked away feeling his eyes bore into her and the vibration get faster. Her legs almost gave way as she headed towards the ladies. She suddenly felt a hand at her waist as she turned to push the hand away, she found Jasper by her side. He laughed.

"I told them you were feeling unwell".

As he held her firmer round the waist. As they rounded the corner to where the toilets were in a darkened area Jasper pushed Jane against the wall and kissed her hard. His tongue pushing into her mouth, he bit her bottom lip gently and duelled with her tongue, the passion building between them. Jane felt her nipples go hard and her pussy clench. Her hand moved down his body her nails teasing as they moved down onto his cock. He was hard already.

They stopped kissing Jane couldn't breath with lust for him. She could feel his cock pressing against her as he bent his legs to be closer to her. The vibration in her body from the eggs and his cock was driving her mad. She pushed him back slightly and opened the door to the toilet to escape for a minute or two. She leant against it feeling flushed and wanted desperately to cool down. She couldn't go back to the table in this state. She heard the door open behind her and lock as she looked round Jasper was stood behind her.

"Jasper" she exclaimed "what are you doing?"

She asked shocked that he had come into the ladies, he strode across to where she was stood grinning.

"Nothing, just here for my girl".

He pulled her close to him her chest against his at the mirrors he hitched up her dress picked her up and sat her on the countertop and spread her legs. Her pussy was throbbing. Jasper pushed her legs open further and got down on his knees. Her juices glistening against her skin and her lips, he sucked in air through his teeth with a loud moan.

"What if someone wants to come in" she whispered through her moans as he buried his head between her legs, running his tongue down her pussy licking up her juices, that sweetness the taste of her he loved. The smell of her He lent back.

"Tough".

Before returning to her swollen aching pussy. Jane lent back her hands behind her taking the weight of her as her head rolled backwards moaning loudy.

"Fuck baby yes don't stop" she begged him.

The eggs and his tongue were sending her almost over the edge. Then he stopped. Jane must have looked frantic as he came out from between her legs, he had a huge grin on his face.

"I told you the games were about to start Belle".

He kissed her, desire raging through her body she couldn't go on much longer and would have to take things into her own hands literally. As if he read her mind Jasper wiggled his finger.

"Oh no that's all mine Belle dont even think about it".

He lifted her down off the top and onto her feet straightening himself up and brushing down his trousers. Jane straightened her hair and dress the best she could before they walked back out into the party. Jasper slid his hand inside his pocket the other was round her waist as he turned up the vibration. Jane jumped and Jasper gripped her waist tighter kissed her ear and whispered.

"All mine Belle. You started this remember" grinning as they headed back to the table.

Just as they arrived back a tall man stopped in front of them.

"Well finally we get to see you, now I know why you have been missing, you did right to hide this beautiful lady from us"

He said looking Jane up and down and undressing her with his eyes, Jane felt the vibration stop suddenly and when she looked at Jasper his jaw went tight.

"Are you going to introduce this beautiful lady then?"

"Tom may I introduce Jane my girlfriend", Belle this is Tom, Sam and John".

Tom took Jane's hand and kissed the back of it.

"So good to meet you Jane, if this man doesn't give you what you want give me a call", he smirked as he said it.

Jane could tell he was a player. Sam came forward.

"Hi, I'm Sam, pleased to meet you Jane. Ignore this dick he thinks every woman will fall at his feet".

Jane smiled "thanks Sam, not this woman, pleased to meet you".

He seems nice she thought. John was next.

"Hi, Jane, I hope this man is towing the line and treating you well", he shook her hand.

Yes he is thank you" she smiled up at Jasper.

"Catch you at the bar after deserts" Jasper said.

"Okay man, Tom said as they walked away.

"I'm sorry Belle I would rather you met them elsewhere, please ignore Tom, hes an arse as soon as he sees a woman regardless of

what she looks like he turns on the charm or not as the case maybe".
Jane's head spun round.
"Are you saying I am not worth looking at?"
Jasper laughed. "Sorry Belle that came out wrong". She laughed,
"Just teasing".
Jasper pulled out her chair as Jane took her seat. The old man next to
her laid his hand on hers and asked.
"Are you feeling okay dear, your husband said you were feeling
poorly?"
"I'm fine thank you. Just a bit hot". He smiled as the waitresses
returned to the tables.
Deserts were being served and a bowl of Eton Mess was put in front
of them. Jasper poked his spoon into the cream picking up a good
amount and slowly sucked it into his mouth looking into Jane's eyes
he lent into her and whispered.
"I am going to fuck you senseless when we get out of here. You in
that dress is doing my cock no favours at all".

Watching him suck that cream was far worse for Jane as she could
still feel his lips and tongue on her pussy. As dinner ended the drinks
were flowing around the table. Jasper said
"We better go over to the bar and see the guys shortly before Tom
has too much to drink".
Jane nodded.
"When you are ready".
 The music started and it was a slow dance. Jasper stood up, grabbed
Jane's hand kissed the back, bowed and said.
"My lady, may I have this dance?"
Jane smiled, "yes my King you may".
He led her to the dance floor away from the table. He took her in his
arms his left hand resting on her bottom, half skin half dress the
other was wrapped in hers held against his chest. He kissed her on
the forehead and nose as she cuddled into him, he guided them
round the floor. His thumb was caressing her skin which sent shivers
through her. She was getting used to the soft vibration as Jasper had
turned it back on at the table, but she wasn't about to tell him that
especially out there on the dancefloor. Being in his arms dancing the
heat from his hand on her skin felt delicious.
She could feel him get hard as he pushed into her.
"What a mess we are" in she thought to herself.

She had never felt like this before, never been turned on by someone as much as Jasper did, he was her addiction. The song ended and the next was faster they started to dance naughtily gyrating and spooning Jane started it, she was so turned on and wanted to tease him. She was pushing her bottom into him as they danced around the floor.

Jasper was running his hands up and down Jane's thighs and pulling her into him. Jane raised her hands over her head and pulled his head down to kiss him. They were both laughing and enjoying the silliness and fun. As the song stopped, they were both hot, they returned to the table for a drink. As Jane bent over to put her drink back on the table Jasper grabs her hips, spins her round and kisses her hard turning up the vibration.

His tongue found hers and she felt him smile her legs buckle under the pressure of the vibration and her pending orgasm.

Their kiss grows hungry and needy.

"Enough Belle I have to have you" he moans.

Jane grabs her bag as he pulls her towards the door. The car is outside all the drivers have been waiting all night. Jasper opens the door and holds Jane's hand as she gets into the car, he climbs in after her and pulls her into him.

The screen goes up in front of them as he starts to rub her nipple through her dress. Her nipples are so hard already and the softness of the fabric of her dress isn't helping. Jasper bends his head down and bites her left nipple sucking it into his mouth.

"I've been wanting to do that all night"

He says with a grin on his face moving to the right one. It sends pleasure straight down to her pussy which has been wet and on fire all night. His hands are squeezing her breasts together making Jane moan. Jasper is trying to eat her through her dress. He pushes her hands behind her back stopping her touching him. Jane moans in pleasure and frustration. Before they realise the car stops outside the house.

Jasper climbs out pulling Jane with him. He pushes $50 into the driver's hand as he holds the door open and thanks him, before walking into the house. As the door shuts behind them Jane is heading to the kitchen for a drink and Jasper is prowling towards her like the lion who's about to pounce on his pray.

"Now you are all mine Belle" he says as he licks his lips. Jane stops at the kitchen door and Jasper leans his hands flat on the frame either side of her caging her against the closed door. He looks into her eyes and pulls her towards him. His hands run down her body and he spins her round.

"Bend over Belle"

He whispers into her ear as he inhales the smell of her pushing his nose into her hair. She does as he asks. He runs his hands down her body and pulls her dress up pushing it up over her bottom before opening her legs. He crouches between them. Inhaling her scent again and turns on the vibration. Her hands are on the door, she has nothing to grab as the intensity builds.

"Oh, christ baby please lick me. I need to cum".

She begs and pleads him. Her pussy is vibrating madly and throbbing her legs are going to give way soon. Then she feels his hot breath against her bare skin. It sends a shiver through her as he blows air onto her pussy and bottom. She lets out an almighty scream trying to dig her fingers into the door wishing it was his head.

His tongue flicks out into her pussy hood making her arch her back.

"Mmmmmm Belle you taste so good".

He moans as he licks and sucks her. Jane feels like she is going to fall, her body is red hot she can feel her orgasm building its about to hit her.

"Jasper please baby I'm going to cum she yells don't stop".

Her mind is scrambled. Suddenly the vibration stops Jane is left panting her pussy fluttering and pulsing.

Jasper turns her round and gets up off the floor comes behind her and slides his hand across the front of her pulling her into him. He pushes his cock into her side which makes her pussy pulse with desperate need to be inside her. He walks them slowly moving his cock so it's pressing into her bottom. As they walk towards the bedroom Jane starts to swing her hips so her bum rocks on his cock.

"Mmmmmm" he groans pulling her even closer.

"Such a bad girl. I love it" he says.

As they get into the bedroom Jasper moves Jane's hair from her neck as she pushes back into his cock her hands behind her travelling down his trousers, down to his zip over his rock-hard cock which makes him hiss as he inhales through his teeth. He kisses her neck moving up to her ear as she squeeze his balls. His teeth sink into her neck as he growls at her. In a really low voice.

"Turn around Belle".

She grins knowing she has him right where she wants him. She takes control and pushes him back towards the bed. She kisses him, his lips parting hers to find her tongue. They are so hungry for each other. She undoes his shirt slowly looking into his eyes and pushes it off his shoulders. "Mmmmmm " she moans in appreciation of his body.

Her hands come up to his nipples as she leans in and sucks them hard. His hands pull her hair at the nape of her neck as he hisses "Fuck Belle bite me".

She does as he asks, placing her teeth around his nipple and biting gently, but just a bit on the hard side. He yells out.

"Oh fuck, yes Belle". She stops and teases it with her tongue.

"Bite me" he hisses again.

Jane continues to suck and bite him as her hands go down to his trousers. She undoes the zip and the clasp at his waist, she pushes them down. He pushes off his shoes almost falling over as they grab at each other. His hands move down her body pulling at her dress gathering the fabric in his hands he pulls it up, he pulls away for a second.

"Arms up".

He whispers and slips it over her head and up her arms holding them together for a second as he kisses her again before throwing the dress to the ground. She is stood in front of him naked apart from her shoes and stockings. She pulls at his pants wanting his cock. As she pulls the front of his pants down his cock springs out, stood so proud, rock hard. She wraps her hand around the shaft as he moans loudy.

"Fuck yes"

Sucking air in again. She pushes him down onto the bed and he uses his elbows to move up to the top and lays on his back. She grabs his socks off and throws them onto the floor. Bends to his feet and kisses his toes. He wiggles them as she kisses down his foot and onto his ankle, she runs her tongue up his inner thigh. His breathing gets sharper as she holds his hands down so he can't touch her or take control of the eggs. She knows he could fight her, but he doesn't. As she reaches his knees she starts to nibble gently. He is hissing through his teeth and moaning.

"Fuck yes. Oh, christ dont stop".

She can see his cock twitching. She puts her hand into the bedside drawer stretching her arm to grab her little surprise she left earlier. Jasper looks round quizzically as Jane has stopped and she just smiles, the only light is that from the hallway so he can't see what she is doing. She continues with her teasing him and biting up his leg. She pushes his other leg wider, so his balls hang free for her. As she reaches the top of his leg she moves across to the base of his cock and licks it gently. Jasper arches off the bed.

"Fuuuck" he moans loudly.

She circles her tongue around his cock licking up, he is as hard as steel. It's such a turn on for Jane. As she reaches the tip she licks around his hole and the tip dipping in and out waiting to taste his pre cum. The tip is almost purple he is so hard and horny. She runs her tongue back down the shaft, flicks it round and back up to the top. Discreetly she pops his little surprise in her mouth to make it wet and slowly slides her lips over the top of his cock.

Pushing the cock ring down as her lips take him. He feels the tightness as it gets close to the base.

"Oh, fuck Belle, what the hell......" His voice trails off as she continues sucking him. She moves the cock ring into place properly and turns it on. The vibration pack springs into life as she pushes it into his balls. He yells out.

"Fucking Hell Babe, what the...."as he grabs her shoulders and pulls her towards him. Jane can't help smiling and lets out a little laugh as he jerks with the vibration. His cock pulsing. He kisses her harder than ever like he is trying to devour her.

Jane suddenly feels herself being flipped onto her back. Jasper pulls her legs, she slides down the bed making her giggle. He's so masterful. He kisses her.

"Revenge is sweet Belle".

She tries to speak to remind him about the torment all evening, but he hushes her with his finger on her lips and kisses her again. Jasper opens her legs and sits between them, leans over and grabs the remote off the nightstand. He switches it on low as the hum moves through her body again.

"Oh Christ" she moans.

He kisses down her face round to her neck which he knows drives her nuts and down onto her shoulder. Her pussy is soaking wet. She can feel it on her legs. His cock is leaning between her legs on the outside of her pussy. She pushes towards it trying to get it inside her she is desperate to feel the fullness of him and cum. His lips continue kissing her until he reaches her nipples and he licks around the outside, bites them making her squeal. She feels him grin as he continues down. Jane is still moving her hips trying to get him to push his cock onto her clit but he's pretending not to notice how wet and turned on she is. He's enjoying the torture. He reaches her tummy and his tongue trails down to the top of her pussy; he runs it along the edge and traces it around. Her moans get louder. His tongue slips inside so gently and glides up and down her juices sticking to his tongue and lips, she is drenched. He starts to lap it up in slow strokes skimming passed her clit which makes her mewl at the loss each time he moves away.

"Oh, baby please let me cum" I beg you".

"There is plenty of time Belle".

"You tease".

The vibration gets faster as her gspot is being teased by the eggs.

"I'm going to explode she thinks to herself".

His tongue gets faster. Her moans are louder, her body is moving against his face. Pushing into him, trying to get the relief she desperately needs.

"Ooooh god Jasper I'm cumming".

She screams as it hits her harder than ever before, everything goes white as his lips lock onto her he's sucking at her hungrily licking it all up. Her body is trembling her pussy pulsing. As it slows, he stops, hooks the eggs and pulls them out. He lifts her legs up onto his shoulders and pulls her towards him looking into his eyes as he slides his hard cock into her waiting hot tight pussy. Her eyes widen as always as he fills her up, he slowly slides in and out. Trying not to cum, the vibration of the cock ring hitting in the right place. Jane's nails dig into his arms as she pulls herself closer to try and reach his back. He leans down and kisses her gently her hands moving onto his back as he gets faster controlling the urge to cum, they are still looking into each other's eyes.

He picks up speed as Jane feels herself ready to cum again, he stops.

"On your knees".

Jane quickly gets up and onto her knees as Jasper comes up behind her, rubbing his cock down her arse she pushes towards his to tell him its okay if he wants to try, he is tempted but wants her pussy he wants to feel her round him as she cums again. He slids back into her with force this time, pulling her hips against his body and thrusts in and out of her.

"You are such a bad girl Belle, such a tease".

He slaps her hard, she squeals as he rubs the red mark on her bottom and spanks her again. Jane squeals this time it stings.

"Tell me you are a bad girl Belle" he demands.

"I'm a bad girl all for you".

She says pushing back into him, he fucks her harder now, sucking through his teeth.

"My bad girl, nobody else's, you hear me Belle?".

She nods her head overcome with the feeling of being fucked hard and her impending orgasm.

"Say it Belle" he says.

"All yours baby" she moans.

Squeezing her muscles in her pussy. Jasper gets faster as his orgasm hits. "Arghhh fuck Belle, I'm cumming" he yells, "cum with me baby please".

His cock pulsing as he cums deep inside her. Jane feels hers hit as his cock rubs her gspot.

"Oh god, oh god Im cumming" she yells, Jasper feels her cum as it washes over his cock mixing with his cum.

He keeps up the pace until Janes slows, his focus coming back feeling exhausted from being so turned on all night, his balls aching, he puts his hand down and turns off the cock ring before it sends him crazy. Jane opens her eyes and smiles at Jasper, he leans over.

"You never fail to amaze me Belle. I love your naughtiness. You are such a bad girl. I love you".

He slides out of her; Jane is moaning about the loss of him. He chuckles.

"You are so bad Belle".

She nods her head like a child. She feels their juices leave her body as Jasper grabs the tissues off the bedside cupboard and wipes it away for her. Then wipes himself. He sits back.

Do you need the bathroom?, Jane nods and he smiles, "come on then", he extends his hand to her and pulls her up kissing her. They both go to the bathroom and clean up before they return to bed, Jane cuddles into Jasper wrapping her legs around his and laying on his chest. He wraps himself around her as they fall asleep together.

Chapter 29

Perfecting his riding

Jasper took Jane to work and made his excuses with her and headed of to the dealership, he had a week to perfect his riding skills and get confident. He hated telling lies and he promised himself he would never do it again. Even if it was for good reason.

Shadow was waiting for him when he arrived.

"Hey man you ready? The Doc not suspecting anything yet?".

"No nothing, thank god".

"Good, let's make sure it stays that way".

Jaspers phone rang as they were talking, it was his boss.

"Excuse me a second Shadow?"

"Sure" he said and walked off.

"Callum Hi, whats up?"

"Jasper the job has come off, we need to get back out West for a week, we leave in 10 days, hotels and flights are being sorted so be ready please".

Jasper punched the air, it was great to get the job but he was frustrated he had to go away again from Jane, he was hoping Moses and the gang from the UK would be around for the whole time he was away, he would have to check with Moses, he was due to speak to him later that day anyway. There was something he needed to ask him and only he could help. He hung up from Callum and agreed to see him the following day in the office. This had to be special now he thought.

He wandered back to Shadow helmet, gloves and jacket in hand. Shadow had wheeled his bike out, he really was enjoying this. Shadow looked up.

"Sorted?"

"Yes, thanks Shadow, I have to go away again in 10 days for a week this time. Im not sure if Moses and the gang will still be around".

Shadow did some mental calculations.

"Fraid not man, we head out just after you leave".

"Fuck" Jasper said, "Okay I will speak to Graham I need to invite him to the BBQ anyway hopefully he will be around that week".

Well if not Chicca will be, Im sure she will be around like the last time".

"Probably yes of course" Jasper replied.

"I just hate being away from Jane and leaving her on her own, especially with you all being away too. I will let the guys know who are staying behind and give them Jane's number".

"Okay man, that would be great.

If they text her their numbers she can at least call if she needs anything, the stubborn woman won't use the car she insists on the trike all the time".

Shadow laughed "oh she's stubborn all right".

They both laughed.

"Let's go, I thought we could go up the coast road, traffic is quite light today, we will go past your site though".

"That's ok, she wouldn't even think of me on a bike and she's too busy to be looking out. She never looks this way either until its time to go home".

"Great", they put their jackets and helmets on and got on the bikes, Jasper had passed his test and got his licence it was more about confidence than anything else. He put his gloves on and was ready.

He fired up the bike as did Shadow and nodded to let him know he was ready. They pulled out of the dealership, Jasper went first so Shadow could keep an eye on him and give him tips if he saw anything in his riding that needed changing.

Shadow was pleased at how well Jasper was doing he was ready to be on his own he just needed to be confident about it. All those years being in a car had made him comfortable, especially in the Range Rover, you couldn't fail to be seen in that.

Not so much the Ferrari though. Shadow was a biker through and through. He didn't get in a car unless it was necessary. He enjoyed the freedom the bike gave him and enjoyed the journey wherever he was going.

They rode out past the site, Jasper smiled when they stopped at the lights, remembering the first day he saw Jane, how weird it was now to be sat here on a bike. The lights changed and he pulled away, he loved this road. The last time he was out here was with with Jane when they first went out on her trike. He couldn't wait to show her his bike and take her out, downside she couldn't ride it she was too short, but he was sure she could go pillion with him.

They rode out 50 miles and stopped for a drink, there was a great little café Jasper and the boys stopped at from time to time when they went away for weekends with the cars.

They did great cakes and pies, Jasper pulled in and got off the bike, Shadow pulled along side, he smiled at Jasper as he got off and said "Hey Jay you don't need me anymore brother, you have this done and dusted and let me tell you that smile on your face says it all." Jasper brushed the sweat off his brow with his hand and over his face still grinning when he looked at Shadow.

"Thanks fella, that means a lot, I have to be honest my opinion of bikers was very different a month ago, now…… I get it. I love this bike and I just hope Belle does too, she will go crazy at me for keeping it from her but I'm glad I did"

Shadow laughed deep from his stomach, his laugh was deep and loud. "That little lady is sure going to kick your arse and I am glad we will all be around to see it".

"Thanks Shadow, I thought you were on my side" Jasper replied laughing.

"Where the Doc is concerned, I'm on her side every time", he laughed again as they walked into the café.

The owner was an older lady, her husband did the cooked food she baked all the nice cakes and pies. She looked up as they walked in from behind the counter.

"Anywhere you like boys, the menu is on the table and the specials are around the room, take your pick I will be over shortly".

They took a seat in the window and picked up the menu, it was vast. It was almost lunch time, they looked at the meals first. Shadow decided on a huge 8oz double burger with cheese, bacon fries and onion rings, Jasper went for the 8oz single with bacon and cheese. Plus a bowl of onion rings. They both decided on a coke too. The owner came over.

"So boys what can I get you both?"

They gave their orders and she went off to get their drinks. A few minutes later she returned with two large glasses of coke, cutlery and napkins.

"What brings you boys out during the week she asked looking at Jasper, we don't normally see you until the weekend and on a motorbike?.

Wow I'm impressed. Jasper replied.

"I haven't seen you before" she said looking at Shadow. Jasper laughed.

"You don't miss a trick, do you?" he said.

"Women don't miss a trick darling" she laughed back.

"Im getting in some miles on the new bike to build my confidence". Jasper said "This is Shadow a friend of mine", Shadow nodded, "Pleased to meet you ma'am".

"Likewise. I will leave you boys to it, shout if you need anything, I will bring your food over once it's ready". They both thanked her as she walked away, Jasper took a big gulp of his drink and looked out of the window.

"Hey brother, you all set for Saturday?" Shadow asked.

"Sure am".

"Great, the guys arrive Friday night, I know you will be coming along to see them".

"Do you think I could keep Belle away?"

Shadow laughed again, "I would like to see you try". "It will be good to meet them all, I have seen them enough on Skype but much better in the flesh".

"They are good guys" Shadow said, "It will be good to see them again. Jane not going on the ride out?".

"No, she has a lot on to be honest so decided not to, she will next year I will make sure of it, we will go together".

"Great, sounds like a plan" Shadow nodded.

They both looked round in unison when they heard the old man shouting for his wife, she yelled back.

"You don't need to shout its only the two boys in here you know". They both laughed as she came across carrying their meals. The plates were huge, Jasper was glad he went for the smaller burger, he couldn't fit Shadows in his hand, but then Shadow had hands like shovels, he didn't have any trouble.

"I sure hope you are going to eat all that?" she said as she put Shadows plate down in front of him. He laughed.

"Sure will Ma'am can't waste a decent burger and this looks mighty fine". She smiled and tutted.

"Can I get you boys anything else, ketchup, mayo?".

They both shook their heads as they dove into the food. It fell silent between them for a few minutes while they devoured the plate full in front of them.

"Damn these are good" Shadow said, as he wiped the juice from his chin. Jasper just nodded as he still had a mouthful, it was going down to easy and he wasn't stopping. They finished up minutes later and both sat back rubbing their stomachs and wiping their mouths.

"Wow, now I could do with a sleep" Jasper laughed.

"Hey good plan me too". Shadow replied.

"So how do you want to play it on Saturday, have you spoken with Moses yet?"

"Yes I have he knows what we are doing".

"Okay great".

"I will suggest we come over on the trike so I have my leathers and helmet, then later on I will go around and jump on the bike and ride round. Is the stage ready?".

"Yeah man the guys are primed and ready. You just give us the nod and we will get the crowd to move for you, there is a ramp ready for you to go up onto the stage too".

"Fantastic, and you have the band ready to play the song too?"

"Yes, we do Brother".

"Brilliant".

"Nervous?"

"Hell yeah, she is gonna kick my arse".

"Lol hell yes brother".

"I've been thinking there is this farmhouse I have been to with the boys and I am going to book to take Belle there, it's so beautiful and relaxing, the owners really spoil you too, I think Belle would enjoy a week out there".

"Great idea man, will you take the bikes".

"Yeah, I think so, it will be a great chance for us to have a decent ride out together. I think I will give them a call and get it booked, Jane is pretty busy at the moment but once all the guys are on site and the big influx of guys is out of the way she wont have any presentations to do for a while she can still take calls while we are away if anyone needs a chat".

They finished up their drinks chatted for a little longer until their food had settled, they were no longer feeling so bloated and sleepy, settled up the bill and headed out to the bikes.

"Ready to head back Jay?" Shadow asked

"Yeah sure, I need to get back to work anyway, Jane thinks Im at a meeting, I don't want her to get suspicious".

Shadow just laughed, they kitted up got back on the bikes and Jasper pulled away first Shadow right behind him.

They got back to the dealership and Jasper left the bike for the guys to put away.

"We will get her cleaned up for you ready for Saturday, don't worry she will be gleaming".

They hugged and shook hands.

"Thank you for everything you are doing for us Shadow, I really do appreciate it".

"Hey man you never get in the path of true love".

They both laughed and Jasper went to get changed back into his suit trousers, hid his bike kit in the back of the car and head back to site.

It was mid afternoon when he got back, he knocked on Jane's door and headed in when she called out.

"Hey Belle, you ok?" He asked as he walked in, Jane had her head down taping away on her laptop.

"Hi love, yeah good its been busy, how was your meeting?"

"It was great, productive, went better than I could have hoped".

"Oh, brilliant, Im pleased for you". She said looking up from her laptop. "I just popped in to let you know I was back" he said as he rounded the desk and bent down to kiss her. Jane looked up and grabbed his face. They kissed softly and Jane made silly noises which made Jasper pull away and laugh.

"Daft as a brush Belle" he said as he walked away.

"Right Im off onto site. See you when you are ready to go home".

"Okay love". Jane replied blowing him a kiss, he caught it and smiled walking back out of the door.

They left for home at 6pm, Jane had been busy with new starters all day and she was shattered. She was hoping for a few days off, but the time wasn't right, so she had to wait. Only a few days to go and she would see her friends again she couldn't wait. She loved her new friends, but it was going to be great to have the guys around for a couple of days. She had a lot of catching up to do with Moses. It wasn't the same over the phone.

Chapter 30

Trouble ahead

Mark arrived in Connecticut and had rented an old apartment. It wasn't anything special which is what he wanted, he would be coming and going and didn't want anyone asking questions. Especially when he brought Jane back, he couldn't fail this time. He picked up his rental vehicle at the airport, it was a good size with a side door, perfect for a struggling women, he knew she was going to fight like a cat but he knew how to handle her. One punch and he would quieten her down.

He got up, knew he had to get to the dealership again. He needed to see Shadow, he expected he would be going on the run, he needed to know who else was there. He packed some snacks and a bottle of water and headed out. It was a busy road, he didn't have any issues about being seen. He saw Shadow yesterday go out with a guy who had come in driving a Range Rover, then go out on a bike, he assumed it was a test ride, but they had been gone a few hours. They looked like they knew each other well too. He wasn't going to worry about him now, he had bigger things on his mind. His phone went off it was a text from Helen, She was up early.

Hi stranger just wondered how you were doing and how the trip was going? Speak soon Helen x

He replied
All good thanks, I should be back in a couple of weeks. I will text when I can. See you when I get back.

He threw his phone onto the seat. I will finish her when I get back too, I don't need her telling any stories either.

He sat for most of the day at the dealer nothing much happened, it seemed a quiet week, he needed to find out where she was. He knew it was a new village being built and he had been given an address, he decided to go and look. It took no time at all to get to the site and when he turned at the lights, he saw the Range Rover that was at the dealer the day before. He pulled up out of the way and sat waiting. He didn't wait too long before people started drifting out. He hadn't seen her yet. He sat and waited, just after 6pm he saw her.

His blood pressure rose as soon as he set eyes on her, then he saw him too. The rage inside him almost made him get out of the van, He was shaking in temper, his skin was prickling, he started to beat the steering wheel.

"Fucking bitch, I'm coming for you, just one moment alone that's all I need, you are mine".

He started to laugh, a deep evil laugh. He knew he had to calm down. He watched as they got into the Range Rover, Jasper held Jane's hand and lent over and kissed her.

Mark screamed out at the top of his voice the rage building again. "You are going to fucking regret that kiss. I am going to make you suffer so badly".

He screamed, beating the dashboard. He watched as they pulled out and stayed behind them as far back as he could, he needed to see where they went. He turned on the sat nav so he could program the location when he got there. He couldn't take her from site it was too open and there were cameras. Hopefully wherever they were heading was a little easier he thought. He started sweating in temper and the air con wasn't cooling him down. He knew he was so close to taking her the excitement was pushing the adrenaline round his body, he was ecstatic.

After 20 minutes they came into a housing development, the houses were very nice, the street was tree lined all the homes were big with nice driveways and garages.

"Must be his place" he said out loud. "Little hoar, not been here 5 minutes and already shacked up with him".

He rubbed his hands together as they pulled up outside a house, he watched the garage door open.

"Not long now Jane, not long now".

He programmed the address into the sat nav. Waited for them to go into the house before he drove past. He heard an alarm beep as they entered the house. He made a mental note of that. He looked round at the other houses, not many people about at this time. No nosey neighbours looking out at his van, perfect.

He drove away satisfied this would be the place he would take her, he just needed her to be alone.

He got back to the apartment and decided to go over everything he had, he wanted to make sure when he got back here with her he had everything. He didn't want to go out for anything until he needed to move her body.

He would feed her soup, it was easy to get into her, and he knew that already. Hold her nose and she can't help but swallow. She was a stubborn bitch he remembered that much. She was in the beginning anyway, until he had her where he wanted her, and she conformed. She looked so confident again, like when he first met her, he would soon knock that out of her before he killed her. He wanted her begging for her life and for him whoever he was. He went to get some food and was planning in his head what he was going to do when he first got her back to the apartment. He had butterflies, the grin on his face showed how excited he was.

He showered and went to bed, he needed to be up and ready at the site in the morning, wanted to see what time she arrived and know what options he had.

He laid in bed with the window open listening to the city noises, his hands behind his head, his legs crossed. He was laid in the dark playing a waiting game. He wasn't tired the adrenaline coursing through his body was keeping him awake, he turned over onto his side, letting out a huge sigh, he closed his eyes again and shoved his hand under the pillow squashing it into his head. Finally, he dropped off but tossed and turned all night, he woke grumpy the next morning. The birds singing made him angry, he walked over to the window and shouted.

"Shut the fuck up" before slamming the window. "God help any fucker that gets in my way today" he grumbled.

He packed his ruck sack and walked out of the door ready for another day sat in the van.

Chapter 31

Old friends

Jane woke up so excited, today was the day everyone arrived from the UK. She was full of life, she threw back the covers, shook Jasper, "Please tell me it is Friday",
he laughed wiping his eyes and yawning.
"Yes Belle it's really Friday" Jane cheered and bounced out of bed. Jasper watched Jane as she lept around the room jumping up and down, arms in the air shaking her head like she was doing a war dance.
"Woo hoo" she screamed, excitedly "what time is it baby. How many hours do I have to wait?"
Jasper laughed it was so good to see her so excited.
"Its 5:30am they arrive with Shadow around 2pm."
Jane whooped again, she was working until lunchtime then heading to the dealer where they were arriving to collect their bikes. They were getting a minibus from the airport, Jane really wanted to pick them up but it didn't make sense so she would have to be patient.

"Get up, get up", she bounced "let's shower".
"Okay, okay" he laughed "I'm getting up".
He couldn't help laughing at her. He walked round the bed Jane was still bouncing, he smacked her arse.
"You keep bouncing around like that you won't have any time to shower".
Jane stopped and giggled like a little girl,
"I am so excited Jasper". He laughed.
"I hadn't guessed".
They headed towards the bathroom, Jane stopped in the door and Jasper grabbed her hair, twisted it and put it up, Jane walked forward and turned the shower on, she turned and looked at him smiling at her.
"What's so funny?"

"Nothing Belle, I just love seeing you look so happy".

"I'm always happy she frowned".

"I know love, but you are super happy today and it's wonderful to see". She grinned.

"Thank you love".

They showered quickly and dressed, Jasper went to make tea and toast as Jane finished her make up, she didn't bother with much but needed to feel confident.

She sat at the table.

"So whats the plan Belle?" He knew exactly what the plan was he just wanted to see the excitement on her face when she told him.

"They collect their bikes and later go off to their apartments, then Saturday a full day together and the BBQ in the evening. Sunday a chill day here, then Monday they head off on the Vets run. You leave on Tuesday and come back Friday?"

"Yes love", "then in a few weeks I have to go back for two weeks, but hopefully you can fly out for a few days to see me, even for the long weekend?"

Jane nodded frantically, as she took another mouthful of tea and toast.

"Yes, definitely, I can't go two weeks without you".

Jasper smiled, "so glad to hear it. We will talk every day and skype too, though right?" he asked.

"Of course, we will. I want lots of messages when I wake in the morning too, you know all those romantic ones".

Jasper laughed "oh do you now? Well, you will just have to wait and see won't you".

Jasper stood and took their plates to the sink.

"You ready to go Belle?"

She nodded taking the last mouthful of tea. She stood and walked to the sink putting her cup in and turning to Jasper.

"I think you have gone off me you know" she said tiptoeing to kiss him.

He frowned looking down at her.

"Where did you get that silly idea from?"

"Well we haven't had sex for 24 hours"

Jasper laughed, "tell me you're kidding Belle?"

"No! Im deadly serious".

He grabbed her by the arms and lifted her kissing her hard. As he put her down.

"I fancy the pants off you but it doesn't mean we have to have sex for the sake of it, yes I could rip those jeans off you right now and bend you over the table, I always want you Belle".

She nodded, "that's ok then", she turned away and he swatted her arse. "I will make it up to you tonight, if you are not too tired after seeing your friends", she span round.

"I am never to tired"

He laughed, "Oh really I think I can tell you otherwise. Come on or we will be late".

Jasper grabbed their bags set the alarm and they headed into the garage. He opened the door and helped Jane climb in, the doors opened as he started the car and drove out. The doors shut behind him and he set the alarm. Jane lent across her seat resting on the arm rest.

"Do you really want to rip my clothes off all the time?" He laughed again.

"Yes Belle I do".

Her hand was resting under her chin.

"Do you really think about me all the time when we are apart?"

"Yes Belle I do, why don't you think of me?"

"Yes of course I do".

"Good".

"So, is it true men think of sex every 30 seconds?"

Jasper was really laughing now she was sat staring at him asking questions like an inquisitive child.

"Well I wouldn't say every 30 seconds Belle, I can't answer for all other men, but until you came along I hadn't really thought about if for a long time. But now, yes I think about it a lot, but I think about you and what I want to do to you, but then I could get myself in trouble if I do that too often".

"Why?" she asked just like a child.

"I think you know the answer Belle"

"No, I don't" she replied. Jasper sighed.

"Because I get turned on when I think of you, it's not a good idea to walk round with a hard on is it?"

Jane laughed and covered her face.

"Oh sorry. So how do you get rid of it then?"

Another big sigh from Jasper.

"Are we really having this conversation?"

"Yesssss" she replied.

"Well I have to think of something else, or put pressure on it, like the heel of my hand, or flick the top if I can get to it".

"Does it hurt?"

"Yes it does, they ache Belle when I want you and I can't have you".

"Do they ache now?"

laughing he said "no Belle they don't".

"Oh", she said disappointingly.

"So, if I was to do this", she lent across and rubbed her hand over his crotch, "will that make you hard and make them ache?"

He groaned, gripping the steering wheel.

"Belle stop that".

"Why?" she said again.

"You know why", he looked round at her as they sat in traffic, she had that naughty girl look on her face. She rubbed him a little more.

"Tell me what you thought when you saw me the first time?"

"You better stop that Belle or I will have to pull over and take you over the bonnet of the car in front of everyone", she laughed and stopped.

"Okay. Tell me?".

"The first day I saw you at the lights I was taken aback, all I saw was those beautiful eyes looking at me and that hair hanging down your back in those leathers, I could tell you were smiling at me. For the first time in a very long time I felt a flutter in my stomach and a twitch in my pants", he lifted his hand and brushed down her hair.

"Ohh, really? Wow, go on".

"I was so happy all day, I was desperate to see you again and when I saw the trike at the market that night I searched for you, I didn't know what I would do if I found you but I just needed to see you again, I never thought you would put your hair up and I walked straight past you. The next thing I saw was you pulling out. I never in my wildest dreams expected to see you again, and certainly not on site". Jane smiled.

"I love this, tell me more".

Jasper took a deep breath.

"Seeing you get off the trike that morning, so many thoughts went through my head, I was scared, I was turned on, Christ I was like a child again, a bit like you are today" he laughed.

Jane was grinning.

"Being with you all day was a killer, I was so horny, I wanted you so much".

"Do you still want me like that?"

"Yes, I do love, but more so, but differently too. As we have got to know each other more and we enjoy each other it is more intense, it means more too".

He turned and stared at her.

"You are everything and more Belle, words can't describe how I feel about you".

Jane felt her cheeks go pink, he placed her hand onto his cheek.

"I love you so much baby, more than I ever thought was possible".

He took her hand and kissed her palm.

"Infinity and beyond Belle".

They pulled into the car park of site, Jane looked into his crotch.

"I think you are safe to get out now".

He laughed, "yes I think so, cheeky".

Jasper walked round the car and opened the door for her, he lent in and kissed her running his tongue along her lips first, then forcing his way in.

"You are mine" he thought for ever and always. Jane wrapped her arms around his neck and he lifted her out like he did when she hurt her leg, she laughed.

"I miss that",

"Me too Belle".

He swung her round, kissed her quickly on the nose and put her down on the ground. He shut the door and went to the back to get their bags. Hand in hand they walked into site, other people began to arrive, they chatted to them as they walked in. Jane was so happy she loved teasing Jasper. She looked down at his watch,

"6.45am".

"You clock watching again Belle?" she nodded. "It will go quick enough", she shook her head.

"No it won't".

Jasper walked Jane to her office left her laptop on her desk kissed her on the head.

"I will see you later love, got a lot to get through before we leave. Shout if you need anything".

Jane nodded. "I will love, see you later".

Jane sat responding to emails and made a few calls, she had a couple of people to catch up with. Chicca knocked and stuck her head in the door, "Hey you, all set for later?"

"Yes, I am, so excited, I am driving Jasper nuts", she laughed,.

"I'm sure you're not. I will be over tomorrow night for the BBQ".

"Okay great". "You meeting James?"

"I think so, if he's back, he had to go away suddenly"

"Oh really?"

"Yeah something to do with his job, I am not an IT nerd so couldn't tell you".

Jane thought about it for a second, "yeah right, IT my arse", one day she would get it out of him.

"Right I'm off, see you tomorrow, have fun tonight".

"Thanks Chicca, I will".

"Oh, before you go are you still okay for a night out when Jasper goes away?"

"Of course, wouldn't miss it", she replied.

"Great, see you tomorrow".

It was 1.45pm Jane started to pack her things away, she had butterflies in her tummy, she was so excited. Jasper walked in.

"Ready to go Belle?"

"I was ready first thing this morning".

Jasper laughed, "I know you were. Come on then, what's the hold up, give me your bag."

Jane was packing as fast as she could, the excitement was making a mess of it, Jasper came around the desk and took her hands off the bag and finished packing it for her.

"Grab your phone and let's go." He smiled.

They got out to the car, Jasper opened the door and helped Jane in. He closed the door and got in himself.

"Right then let's go and meet these friends of yours."

Jane was smiling from ear to ear, rubbing her hands together then rubbing her legs with nerves. The short drive took 10 minutes the roads were clear as it was just after lunchtime. Jane looked over at Jasper.

"Please forgive me if I cry today, when I see everyone. Especially Moses."

He looked round and saw tears in her eyes waiting to spill out.

"Belle I know how much Moses and the guys mean to you, I will probably have a few myself."

Jane laughed and wiped her eyes.

"Okay then", Jasper grabbed her hand and kissed it.

"Not long now my love."

They pulled into the dealership just before 2pm, it was all quiet. Jane felt a dark cloud move over her head. Jasper squeezed her hand.

"It's only 2pm now Belle, don't worry, they will be here soon."

Jasper knew they were already there. It was all planned. They wanted Jane to be in the building and Moses was going to creep up behind her and give her his normal beard rub to annoy her. They walked in and met Shadow, he bent down to cuddle her.

"Hey Doc, I bet you can't wait?" he said laughing deeply.

"No, I can't," she said hugging him tight.

"Won't be long now I'm sure" he replied.

Jane had her back to the door which Shadow had purposely planned and Jasper was stood next to her. The music was playing a little louder than usual to cover any footsteps. Behind her led by Moses and G were the gang. Moses crept up behind Jane as Shadow was talking to her, as he got to her he grabbed her round the waist, bent her backwards towards him and started to rub his beard against her neck and face. Jane screamed loudly giggling trying to get away from him, she tried pulling his hair but found none, she stopped struggling as Moses stood her up and turned her around. She grabbed him hard and cuddled into him, the tears started as she lost control. She looked up to see G stood with his head to the side staring at her the others behind him all waiting their turn, Jane wiped her eyes. Spreading mascara all over her cheeks.

Gwen shouted "Didn't I teach you anything girl about Panda eyes, don't you listen to me at all?"

Jane laughed through the tears. She grabbed G and brought him into the cuddle, everyone else came in and had a group hug, Jasper stood back with a huge smile on his face and Shadow patted him on the back.

"Well done Brother. Just perfect".

The group broke up and Jane stood staring at Moses, she was holding his arms and couldn't believe the change. His beard was trimmed up nicely, he had lost his beer belly and had almost a flat stomach, his hair was cut short, she couldn't believe it.

"What did you do? Where did my Moses go?" she asked.

"Well I couldn't come and see my girl looking a mess now could I?" everyone laughed.

Matt shouted "someone had to be honest, the old bastard was looking a mess so we took him in hand, the haircut and beard was compliments of my gorgeous lady, the rest was the gym, day and night", everyone laughed.

Jane hugged him again, he whispered.

"It's good to see you beautiful. I've missed you".

Jane started crying again.

"Oh god here we go" they all said in unison.

Jane laughed and pulled away, walked forward and looked at her friend Gwen, they both started crying, Gwen grabbed Jane and hugged her tight,

"God I've missed you lady".

"Missed you too" Jane chocked out through her tears laughing at the same time. Matt broke them up, pulling Jane away from Gwen.

"My turn".

Gwen laughed and tutted, Jane laughed as Matt hugged her too.

"We have missed you half pint, it's good to see you".

The others came in again and Jane went to each of them and hugged them all. Once she had finished she turned round and walked up to Jasper kissed him on the cheek cuddled into his side and said.

"Guys I would like to introduce you all to Jasper".

Moses went first, he shook his hand and pulled him in for a hug, "good to finally meet you brother" he said.

"Same Moses". "Let's chat later".

Moses finished and moved back, Jasper nodded and went around the group meeting everyone.

When he reached Gwen she had her hands on her hips.

"Don't even think about shaking my hand come her and hug me, I want to feel what Jane is getting", everyone laughed as they hugged. As she pulled away Gwen looked at Jane.

"Hell girl, he hugs well, fancy swapping", everyone broke into laughter again. Shadow came forward "come on guys let's go sit down and catch up".

They all went away chatting heading into the café, a few more of the Connecticut guys and girls had arrived and the guys went around saying hello to each other. They had a lot of catching up to do. Moses took Jasper away for a chat.

"Hey brother we all set for tomorrow?"

"Sure am".

"How you feeling?"

"Okay I think" Jasper said laughing.

"So where is this beast of yours?".

They walked out to the show room, Shadow had put it back inside with a sold ticket on it.

"The orange soft tail over there" jasper pointed to it.

"Beautiful man, beautiful". The bike stood in all its glory polished ready for the next day. The chrome was sparkling.

"I don't think Jane will like that seat much, she's used to luxury you know". Jasper laughed.

"I am sure for the odd trip I can persuade her. But I would imagine she will stick with her Red Robin".

"How has she been, since she told you the truth?"

"She's doing okay, has her moments, she will probably want to show you the roses on Sunday when you are over, I told Belle my past too, it seems we have a lot in common".

"Well if there is one thing I learned from her it's talking is good. But it's a shame she hasn't told the rest of the club".

"Oh, I think you will be surprised, she's started to open up about it and she wants to tell everyone, she will probably tell the guys while you are here".

"Oh fantastic, it's not been an easy 10 years keeping it from people and trying to protect her at the same time. We are a family after all, but it's what Jane has wanted".

"Well let's hope she will give you the okay to tell everyone back home."

"Let's hope so". Moses replied, patting Jasper on the back

"We better head back before her ladyship spots us talking, she will be demanding to know what's going on".

"Good point" Jasper laughed.

They headed back to the café, everyone was chatting loudly and catching up, G was playing the fool and Gwen was trying to get him to shut up. Jane looked up as the boys approached.

"I know what you have been talking about, both men looked at each other their hearts in their mouths, pumping like crazy.

"How do we get out of this one they both thought".

"You don't need to hide it from me".

"Belle listen".

Moses grabbed Jaspers arm to stop him from telling her about the plans for the following day. He jumped in.

"I was only asking how you were, because you wouldn't tell me anyway and I wanted the truth".

"See I knew it" she replied.

Jasper sighed heavily and Moses looked at him and winked.

"Thank Christ" he said under his breath.

"I thought she had sussed us". Both men laughed.

"Fancy a walk Jane?" Moses asked.

Jane got up, placed her hand on Jaspers chest and kissed him, "won't be long love".

"Take as long as you need Belle".

They walked off outside and sat on the benches, Shadow followed with some drinks for them.

"Save you going back in guys".

"Thank you, Shadow," Jane said smiling at him.

"So, tell me what's new Jane? How have you been?"

Jane cuddled up to Moses and put her head on his shoulder.

"I love it here Moses, but I miss you guys. I have made a few friends and of course I have Jasper, but something is missing".

Moses squeezed her tight. "It will all work out Jane you need to give it time. We all miss you, damn it I look round for you every bloody day when I want to tell you something, I head out to your place to see if you are okay then remember half way there you are across the pond now".

Jane laughed, "I think you're getting old" she said patting his chest, "cheeky mare" he replied and kissed her head.

"So, tell me Moses why the change in lifestyle, what scared you".

He smiled, "you did half pint leaving like that. I knew I had to do something and not having you around to kick me in the pants I decided to do something about it.

She grabbed his beard, I like this a lot, it's much nicer".

He smiled, "well it was getting out of hand and it was just to annoy you half the time".

Jane hit him in the stomach, "uhh" he said holding his stomach like he had been winded. Then laughed.

"Don't pretend that hurt either, you big girl", they laughed together.

"I have missed you half pint, the place isn't the same without you".

"I've missed you too". She pulled on his beard.

"Tell me about the ride out. How long are you gone for and how long do I get to have you around before you fly home?".

"Well we planned on being away two weeks, there are a few runs we can do and events in the calendar, but we decided to do a week as you can't make it and head back here, we have a good apartment why waste it, when we can spend time with you".

Jane cheered, "Yippee, Oh I am so pleased. You have made my day twice"

She said hugging him hard.

Moses laughed "so pleased to hear that, you will have to get some time out if you can even a day or two and take us on a ride".

"I would love too" Jane smiled.

"That's sorted then. Shall we grab Shadow and see what rides he has for us?".

"Yeah great idea". "Are you bringing the Red Robin tomorrow night?"

"Can do, Jasper can have a beer with you then too".

"Good idea. Well if Shadow hasn't got me something decent, I may take it off your hands for a week, I am getting old after all".

Jane thought about it for all of a second.

"You can take her if you like, she could do with a proper run out".

"I may take you up on that love, let's see what Shadow has".

They walked back inside and found Shadow with the others chatting, Moses put his hand on his shoulder.

"Hey brother can we look at the bikes you have for us, I think we could do with heading off for a while and getting showered and some sleep, I know her ladyship will want to be here early tomorrow?"

He said looking across at Jane as she joined Gwen.

"I don't know what you mean".

Both girls laughed. Jane turned to Gwen.

"I wanted to talk to you while you were here, you first and then the others".

Gwen looked worried," "okay...should I be worried?"

"Not really, no. I just think it's about time you all knew the truth and since I told Jasper it feels better to be honest and talk about it. I go on about being honest and opening up all the time yet for 10 years I have hidden from you".

Gwen hugged her, "I'm so pleased Jane we have all worried about you and not been able to help you. If you want to talk later come over. The boys won't mind".

"That would be good".

"It's a date then, give us a couple of hours to sort ourselves out", "Shall we pick up a takeaway on the way over?"

"Great idea" Gwen replied.

"What are you two cooking up over there?" Matt asked.

"Jane and Jasper are coming over later for a chat, they are bringing take away with them", "and beers I hope?" he said.

"Yes, okay if I must Jane laughed.

She looked at Jasper, "shall we head off now and come back around 7? Let you get the bikes sorted have a few hour's sleep?"

"Good idea", Moses replied.

"Chinese?"

"Sounds good" they all said at once.

Jane knew what they liked, it was just about everything off the menu. They all stood and hugged.

"Oh, before we go I want a picture of us all".

 Jane said, "All?" Moses asked.

"Yes is that a problem?"

"I suppose not" he said turning round laughing.

"You heard her, come on guys, gather round", everyone jumped across the tables from both sides of the pond, they were all laughing, "big ones at the back little ones at the front"

Jane bellowed. "That's you on your own then half pint" G shouted.

Jane turned and poked her tongue out. He walked to the front and got on his knees next to her. Jasper went behind her and Moses knelt the other side. Luckily Gwen had her selfie stick, she never went out without it, Jane held the camera.

"Smile you miserable lot" she shouted.

Everyone laughed as she started taking pictures, G and Moses wrapped their arms around her and kissed either side of her face, Jane grinned. They all stood and went back to their tables, more hugs and Jane and Jasper left. She was so happy, all her favourite people together in the same place.

As they left the building Moses said.

"Right Shadow what do you need us to do for tomorrow?".

Well, we are pretty much sorted, the ramp has been built, and we just need you all to ride in together with Jasper at the back. He will then go up onto the stage, we have made it lower and wider to take the bike. She hasn't got a clue which is pretty amazing really".

"Okay we will help set up in the morning, how many are invited to the BBQ?".

"The normal crew will be here, so a good 150 plus some".

"The food is arriving around 10am".

"I'm on it" Gwen put her hand up.

"Thanks Gwen, I'm sure the girls will appreciate some help".

"We will help get everything else done", Moses said.

"Just be bloody careful what you say around her tomorrow she isn't daft". They all laughed.

"Damn right, she can sniff a rat at a 100 paces" Matt shouted.

They all laughed again.

"Right then bikes, come on let's get you sorted so you can get off for some rest".

Jane and Jasper got home, she hadn't stopped smiling all afternoon, Jasper was so happy.

"Belle what do you want to do now?"

"I could do with a shower to be honest"

"Okay sounds good, tea?".

"Oh yes please" Jane replied.

"Go and get sorted and I will bring it in, its 4.30pm we will order the food from the place around the corner from Shadows at about 6.45pm, that gives you a couple of hours".

"I think I will wash my hair then save me doing it tomorrow".

"Okay love, I will be in shortly"

Jasper went off to make the tea and Jane headed to the bedroom. She sat on the bed and got her phone out, she was skimming through the pictures as Jasper came in.

"Let's have a look love" he said sitting next to her. They both laughed looking at the pictures, they were all fooling around, pulling faces, they were perfect. Jane sent them to Gwen, Moses and Shadow.

"We will have to print a few off and put them up" Jasper said.

"Oh I would love that, yes please" Jasper smiled.

"Anything for you Belle. Come on if you are showering move that backside".

She turned and put her hand on his cheek, kissed him hard making mmmm noises like a little girl which made him laugh. Jane stood and started to undress.

"You going to strip for me" he asked grinning.

"Not today, maybe later, don't want to rush it do we?"

"No we don't"

Jane finished undressing and Jasper joined her throwing their clothes into the washing basket.

Both naked they headed for the shower, Jane turned it on and turned to Jasper.

"Thank you, I know it was you who set that up today".

Jasper grinned taking her by the hips.

"My pleasure Belle, it was great to watch, you might want to take a look at my phone after your shower"

She looked up at him shocked.

"Why what did you do?"

"Wait and see".

"You can't say that and make me wait".

He laughed, "I had one of the boys video it all, I handed him my phone when we arrived".

She slapped him on the chest, "you sly old dog".

He grinned and thought, "if only you knew Belle, if only you knew". He kissed her nose and turned her towards the shower and smacked her bottom.

"Get in there now". Jane walked into the shower holding onto Jaspers hands which were on her hips. She stood under the water and let it run down her body, her hair was getting wet as Jasper started to smooth it down, he grabbed the shampoo and spread it onto her head making lots of bubbles, Jane turned round to face him and picked up the shampoo and did the same to him. They washed each other hairs out and Jane put conditioner on her own, Jasper combed it through for her, grabbed the clip off the ledge and pilled it on top of her head so he could wash her body. He bent towards her shoulder and kissed her.

"Mmmm, that's nice" she moaned.

His hands moved from her waist up to her nipples, he started to roll them in his fingers as Jane moaned more. He felt his cock stiffen, he pressed it into her moving closer. One hand moved down her body and parted her legs, he slid his hand between them and found her pussy, he pushed his middle finger in, she was wet already, she arched her back moaning loudly, he bit into her shoulder and whispered.

"Turn around Belle" She did as he asked as he removed his fingers, he grabbed her face in his hands and kissed her lips, the water cascading down her face into her mouth. He let go of her face and grabbed her legs and lifted her up, she wrapped her legs around his waist and he moved to the wall to support her, as he lent her against it she winced with the cold tiles, it made them both laugh, she held his face kissing him, he lifted her a little more and felt his cock slide into her waiting pussy, she clenched her muscles as he slid in. Her eyes opened wide as they always did when he entered her. She took a deep breath and sighed into his mouth as she held onto his face kissing him, he slowly raised her up and down, they both moaned into each others mouths as they bit and licked at each others lips.

"I love you Belle" Jasper moaned.

"I love you too" she groaned.

Trying to catch her breath as he slid in and out of her getting faster. "I want you bent over Belle" he said as he lifted her off his cock, "Ohhh god", she moaned as he did, and slid down his body and stood up, she turned round to face the wall and bent over leaning on the ledge. He bent and kissed her rose.

"Mine all mine" he said as he opened her legs and crouched to take her, he slid back into her easily, his cock knew her body well and the curves of her pussy. He grabbed her hips as she pushed back into him, he started slowly then got faster.

"Fuck Belle".

He hissed as they got faster, his cock rubbing her pussy wall, Jane could feel her orgasm building already, she was ready for it.

"Oh Jasper don't stop baby please I'm going to cum".

He sucked in through his teeth and gripped her, fucking her harder. "Yes Belle, let me feel you cum".

That was Janes undoing, she felt her muscles tense around him as her body got hotter, the water pouring down on their bodies lubricating them even more. She felt herself tremble as her orgasm took her, her eyes closed, she could only see white she grew weak her breathing got faster and her knees giving way, her juices covering his cock. Jasper put his arm around her waist and held her up as he felt his building.

"Fuck Belle yes I'm cumming" he moaned as his balls went hard and his cock stilled, he pounded into her the feel of her helping the wonderful sensation he was having, he felt his body tremble too as he filled her full of him. He was breathing erratically too as his took hold of him. Their juices merging together. He slowed down and stopped as his orgasm subsided.

"Christ Belle, I love you" he said leaning down and kissing her back, she placed her hand over his on her waist and stood up, her legs still weak, she turned into him, his chest wet from the shower, she rubbed his pecs and kissed him.

"I love you too lover boy".

He laughed. "Oh, lover boy really?"

She nodded, her hands travelling further down his body, he tensed under her touch, he was more ticklish after an orgasm, she watched as his muscles clenched as she moved further down.

"Mmmmmm I love this body" she moaned drinking him in.

Haven't you had enough?"

She bit her lip and looked up at him giving him her naughty look, "Never".

He laughed. "Well I'm sorry you will have to wait a little while".

Jane pouted teasing him. He spun her round and spanked her. "Shower gel now you bad girl before we end up all wrinkly".

Jane did as she was told and picked up the shower gel and his body puff to wash him. She put plenty on it and spread it all over his body, "Turn around"

she said as she continued scrubbing his body down.

When she finished Jasper grabbed her puff and did the same, then took her clip out of her hair and washed out the conditioner, he turned off the shower and they both smoothed the water of their bodies before stepping out, Jasper went first and grabbed his towel wrapped it round his waist and then waited for Jane, she bent over and pulled her hair forward as he wrapped the towel round her head. She stood and he wrapped her body, pulling her into him and kissing her.

"Come on then let's get dried off and I will do your hair for you".

Jane smiled "I am the luckiest girl in the world".

"That you are Belle" he replied smirking.

"Cheeky".

They went back into the bedroom and dried themselves off. Jane sat on the bed when she was done and combed her hair, Jasper climbed on behind her with the hair dryer, took the comb from her hand and began to dry it for her. He loved the smell of her hair and enjoyed drying it for her, it gave him an excuse to indulge in it. It was one of the first things he noticed about her. That and her eyes.

When they were finished they went through the menu and chose a huge selection of food and added lots of rice noodles prawn crackers, and sauces. They got ready and headed out in the car. Jane was going to sit with Gwen and tell her everything tonight and then tell the guys but keep out the details, they didn't need to hear that, it would give Jasper some time to get to know the guys too while her and Gwen chatted.

Chapter 32

Time to tell the truth

Jane and Jasper head out to collect the Chinese.
"I think the takeaway can close once we leave tonight" he laughed.
"Well they are a hungry bunch as you will see. It won't go to waste"
They collected the food, the bags kept coming out of the kitchen and one of the staff helped them to load it into the car. Jasper thanked them and they got back in the car. The smell was overwhelming, their stomachs started rumbling.
"Oh my god can we just pull over and start now" Jane said laughing.
"You better call Moses and see if a few of them can meet us outside to help take it all up".
Jane grabbed her phone and rang Moses.
"Hey love, you okay?" Moses asked.
"Yeah good, we will be with you in 5 minutes please could a few of you come and meet us? The car is packed with bags of food and beer".
"On it love. Guys get your shoes on Half pint and Jasper need help with the food and beer, see you outside".
 He said and hung up.
"Sorted"
Jane said putting her phone away. Within minutes they pulled up outside the apartment block and the guys were all outside waiting. G came around and opened the door for Jane, he held her hand as she slid out. She grabbed him for a hug.
"Hey Doc, sorry I haven't had time to chat today, how you doing?"
"I'm okay thank you", she said kissing his cheek".
"So good to see you. I'm going to talk to the guys tonight, it's well overdue".
"You ready for it?"
"Yes, I should have done it along time ago and I owe all the guys a huge apology, will you please tell everyone back home when you go. I don't want to hold anything back anymore?".
"Sure Doc if that's what you want".

She nodded, "come on let's grab some of this food before it gets cold" G said.

They walked round the back of the car as the last of the bags were being taken. G grabbed a couple from Jasper as he locked the car and they all walked in together.

"You will have to leave your windows open for a day Brother" G said laughing "to get rid of the smell".

"You're telling me, I didn't want to open the windows on the way in case it got cold".

They laughed walking into the apartment, everyone was opening bags and stacking the food as Gwen walked in.

"Can we have some order please, lets spread them out on the worktop and we can walk along and take what we want" Gwen suggested.

"Good idea" Jane said.

They had borrowed plates and cutlery from the other apartment and brought chairs in so they could all get around the table. Beers were opened and they all sat together. The table was full of laughter, Jane sat back watching, it was so good to be back with these guys, she turned and looked at Jasper, he smiled at her and winked. She nodded, he knew she was good.

After they finished then men moved into the lounge and sat chatting with more beers, Jasper had a few too, Jane was driving tonight.

Gwen took Jane off next door to her the other apartment, they sat in the lounge, Jane was feeling a little anxious, she was taking deep breaths trying to calm herself down.

"Tell me about that gorgeous man of yours Jane, is he as hot in bed as he looks".

Jane spat out the mouthful of tea she was about to swallow. "Gwen!" she exclaimed.

"Oh, come on don't hold out on me".

Jane laughed, "yes he is, if you must know".

Gwen squealed and started jiggling about in her seat.

"Details pleassseee" she begged.

Jane told Gwen the details of all the naughty things her and Jasper had done, Gwen was squealing, covering her face, clasping her hands together.

"I am so thrilled for you Jane", she lent over and hugged her.

"It's about time you found someone, and he is pretty damn hot" they both laughed.

Jane took a deep breath.

"Okay, firstly I am so sorry I never trusted you enough to tell you what that arsehole did to me, I suppose it was shame that I allowed it, I didn't see it coming and when it did I forgave him every time thinking I could change him". Gwen sat quiet and listened. Nodding as Jane spoke. She went on and told Gwen everything from the beginning, all the details of the beatings, rape, the mind games and the abuse. Gwen lent across and took Jane's hand as Jane wiped tears away. She was desperate to not give any more tears to this animal. She went on and told her about Moses and G finding her and getting her into hospital. Losing the baby when he got into hospital and beat her again. Gwen was wiping tears away as Jane continued.

"Jane I'm sorry".

She said clearing her throat and grabbing both her hands, she squeezed them so tight fighting her own tears. Jane finished telling her about the roses and a little about Jasper. Gwen lent across and hugged Jane tight.

"I'm sorry Jane, truly I am. I don't know what else to say, I am so glad you are now with Jasper and everything is going so well".

"Thank you Gwen I really appreciate it, I love him so much, I know he loves me too, I couldn't see my life without him anymore, I know it has only been a short while but this is real Gwen, Jane couldn't stop smiling when she spoke about Jasper. "He makes me melt, he is so thoughtful and kind, romantic, silly, funny".

Gwen was smiling she could see how much in love Jane was with Jasper.

"I'm sure he feels the same, you can see it when he looks at you"

"What are you going to tell the guys?"

"Not everything, I don't think they need that much detail".

"I agree, I will tell Matt when we get home if you don't mind?"

"Of course, it's up to you what you tell him, I just won't embarrass anyone giving them the details. You know what will happen otherwise and I don't want to bring trouble to my door". Moses and G know everything, well almost I think a few embarrassing details were kept back but they saw the bruises and cuts they don't need to know the rest".

Gwen hugged Jane again.

"I'm so proud of you Jane, truly I am".

"Thank you Gwen, I really appreciate it and again I am sorry for not sharing with you sooner".

They hugged again.

"Shall we go back to the guys?".

"Yes lets, I want to get it over with tonight and then no more".

They walked back to the apartments where the guys were. Jane smiled as she saw Jasper laughing with everyone. She walked up to him and he sat back so she could sit on his lap.

"Hello ladies" Moses said as Gwen sat on Matts lap.

"You all caught up?"

Gwen laughed and looked over at Jasper.

"Oh yeah" she laughed.

Jasper looked at Jane, she touched his face, "don't worry love I just gave away a few of your secrets".

Everyone laughed. As the laughter stopped Jane spoke.

"Guys there are a few things I need to tell you".

She took a deep breath, firstly I want to say I am sorry to Moses and G that they have had to carry this for 10 years or more.

G touched his heart and blew her a kiss. Moses lent across and grabbed her hand and kissed her knuckles.

"Secondly none of you have ever questioned them when you have been asked to help and for that I am eternally grateful. But now I owe you an explanation. I don't want to take away from the fun of tonight but I just wanted to share it with you all tonight so we can then enjoy the time together. Moses G and Gwen know everything as does Jasper, she felt his arms tighten around her, but I felt I could tell you all without nasty details"

The guys nodded, she could already see knuckles turning white. She took a deep breath and started. She kept it short, told them the basics of what Mark had done to her, she stumbled a few times as she looked around the room at the faces of the guys in front of her who had been her friends for many years. She finished off as she did with Gwen and told them about the roses they had found and planted in the garden, she looked round at Jasper and he nodded giving her permission to mention the child his wife aborted without telling him. Everyone sat quiet for a few minutes. Matt cleared his throat and spoke first,

"Jane please don't ever feel bad about not telling us, to be honest had we have known we would probably all be inside now for murder a very slow murder and where would that have gotten us?"

Jane smiled at him.

"Thank you Matt".

"Jasper Brother, I am so sorry for what your bitch of a fucking wife did to you, I hope you both find peace with each other, you both deserve happiness".

A few others spoke and it ended with everyone standing and hugging Jane and Jasper, forgiveness wasn't needed she was part of the family, they understood, it helped them all to know now though. Moses grabbed Jane and hugged her.

"I promise you if I ever see him again I will rip him apart, hearing you talking tonight has reminded how far you have come. I love you half pint".

Jane chocked back the tears. "I love you too Moses".

"Right more beers are in order me thinks" G shouted.

"Lets get this party started", everyone groaned.

"I think its bedtime actually" Moses said "we have a party tomorrow and then a full week of drinking". Jasper and Jane nodded.

"We will make a move home now leave you in peace to get some rest. We will be back tomorrow late afternoon. We will let you relax, we need to get sorted for Sunday when you come over".

They all hugged Jane and Jasper and said goodnight. Little did she know they all had work to do to get things ready for the following night's events.

Jasper and Jane left taking the rubbish with them from the Chinese so they didn't smell the apartment out. They got to the car and before Jasper opened the door he hugged Jane.

"Have I told you tonight how much I love you Belle?"

"You hadn't no" she replied.

He smiled and put his finger under her chin and lifted her face towards him, he lent down and kissed her.

"You are my world". Jane went to jelly as they hugged each other.

"As you are mine" she replied cuddling into him feeling so happy and content.

They got home and went straight to bed, Jane was mentally shattered, she curled into Jasper and laid in her favourite place, on his chest. They both went off to sleep very quickly.

Chapter 33

My Girl

Jasper woke early, full of nerves, this was it. Jane was going to be kicking his arse later for not telling him but hopefully thrilled to bits knowing he can ride.

He had a few calls to make to ensure his friends were coming along, it would be very different for them. Like it had been for him the first time. But he needed them here. He was calling Graham too, he had become a good friend to them both. He wanted everyone there for Jane tonight.

He needed to keep her away from the dealership as long as he could to let all the plans come together. She would only be asking questions about the stage and ramps etc, once everyone was there she wouldn't even realise. He needed to get his own nerves under control too.

He made tea and went into the bedroom with Jane's, she was still asleep, but restless, he kissed her on the head, she woke up stretching out all over the bed, her hair was laid across the pillow, he loved looking at her first thing in the morning, she was so beautiful.

"I promise to always love and care for you Belle and make you the happiest girl in the world"

she looked up as she opened her eyes and smiled. She put her arms out to him, he climbed onto the bed and snuggled into her.

"my favourite part of the day" she said.

He kissed her nose, "mine too Belle.

There is a cup of tea here for you. Anything you would like to do today apart from shopping for tomorrow."

"Yes, stay in bed with you all day, watching movies and eating popcorn and ice cream".

Jasper laughed. "If that's what her ladyship wants that's what we will do".

"Would you really?"

"Of course Belle" he replied kissing her.

"Thank you, maybe next weekend, but we better get up and get sorted everyone is here tomorrow and we have to be ready".

"Do you really mind them all coming here?" she said sitting up in bed and taking her tea.

"Of course, I don't silly, it's about time this house was made into a home, its been just me and it for long enough, you being here has brought it to life and the guys coming round will just liven it up". Jane laughed.

"They will do that all right".

Jane jumped out of bed.

"Come on then let's get showered and go shopping".

Jasper saluted her and laughed,

"Yes boss".

He followed her into the bathroom, grabbed her hair as she went in and tied it up. They showered dressed and decided to have breakfast out. Jasper wanted to take her to the diner him and the boys meet at for their weekends away. It was great food and a real introduction for Jane into an American diner. They pulled up outside, Jane smiled.

"Oh wow this looks great".

"I thought you might like it"

They walked in the 50s music was playing and the waitress came across.

"Hello Jasper, how are you? Where are the boys?

"Hi Jenny, they are not coming in today, this is Jane my girlfriend. We popped in for breakfast before we go shopping I wanted to show her a real American Diner".

"Welcome Jane" she said.

"Thank you Jenny.

"Right lets get you seated, how about the normal table in the corner" she asked looking at Jasper.

"Perfect thank you"

She gave them menus and they walked over and sat in the booth. Jane was looking round smiling.

"This is really nice, I like it".

Jenny came back to take their orders and brought drinks back soon after. Jane went for pancakes and bacon, Jasper decided on the same. Jane was in awe especially when she saw the size of the plate of food Jenny brought over, her eyes were out on stalks. Jasper laughed and tucked in to his. Full and satisfied they left to go shopping. They decided to have a buffet style lunch, they would be all barbecued out over the next week anyway. They brought lots of meats, cheeses, breads, salads and a few deserts to go with it. They loaded the car up and headed back home.

They unpacked the car put the car away and went to get changed, it was time to head off to the dealership and meet the guys. Jasper had received a text to say everyone had arrived the field was full of people and the barbecues lit. It was time to go.

Jasper got Jane's leather trousers out for her and his own, a couple of t-shirts too.

"That should do it, god I love her in those trousers".

He felt his cock twitch, remembering the first time he saw her in them getting off the bike and bending into the boot of the trike.

"Behave"

He said looking down at his cock.

"We don't have time, I need to stay focused".

Jane came out of the bathroom.

"Who was that love?"

"Sorry Belle? "

"Who were you talking too?"

"I wasn't, I was talking to myself as I got our things out".

"Oh okay, sounded like you were having a conversation".

He looked down at his cock and gritted his teeth.

"You are really going to get me locked up one of these days"

he whispered. He grabbed his leathers and pulled on his t-shirt, he looked up as Jane was pulling hers on. She bent over to adjust the bottoms, Jasper groaned, and walked towards her, he grabbed her hips and pulled her back into him.

"If you don't want to be late you better not bend over like that Belle", Jane looked up at him and smiled.

" I'm game if you are?"

"For once Belle I am going to say no, I promised we would be there by 4pm so we better get going".

Jane pouted and stood up. They got their boots on at the garage door, Jane pulled the trike out as Jasper locked up. They were at the dealership shortly after 4pm, Jane parked up as the guys came out to meet them, and she was surprised so many others were there.

They all went out onto the field to grab drinks and a table, a few of the others Jane had met the last time were there. She saw Chicca walk in with James, she came over for a hug.

"Hey how are you two?"

James came over and gave Jane a hug shook Jaspers hand and Chicca hugged them both, Jane looked round.

"Chicca, James please can I introduce you to my friends from the UK?"

They went around the table introducing each other. Everyone moved round as they all joined the table. The band started playing and everyone got up and went to the front to watch. The girls stood next to Jane to distract her when the guys moved away. They were dancing and singing together as the song changed, everyone turned round and the group split in two as the band started playing "the boys are back in town" The noise of the bikes coming towards them was intense, the twin cam engines vibrated the ground as they rode in. Jane recognised Moses, Matt, Shadow, G, and James, the others she didn't really know, the group parted, she saw an orange and cream Harley softail come through the middle and go up onto the stage as the music changed again.

Queen – I was born to love you

Jane watched as the bike came to a stop on the stage, she suddenly realised it was Jasper, he pulled his helmet off as the crowd roared, clapping and cheering, she stood there with her mouth open. Jasper looked straight at her and beckoned her to join him on the stage with his finger. Moses and G came up to her and lifted her up. Jane was in shock, Jasper was grinning from ear to ear, she stumbled to talk.

"Did you really just ride that?"

He nodded. Jane held her hand at her mouth.

"I don't understand Jasper?" she was frowning, she could feel tears welling up in her eyes, she looked out into the crowd as everyone was clapping. The lead singer from the band came up to Jasper and handed him the microphone as the band stopped singing.

"Belle"

Jasper said, "You have made me the happiest man on this planet, I could never have dreamed I would meet someone as incredible as you. I now eat more, sleep more, hell I even smile more".

Everyone laughed.

"Belle, I know we have only been together a short while and you probably think I am crazy, actually don't answer that.

"He got down on one knee, pulled open the box that had been burning a hole in his pocket for days, the crowd went silent, apart from a single gasp from Jane.

"Please would you do me the honour of becoming my wife? Take my name and make me the luckiest guy alive?"

Everyone held their breath. Gwen held onto Matt as Moses felt his heart break a little, Jane looked straight at Jasper and burst into tears, she grabbed him round the neck nodding her head shouting.

"Yes, yes, yes, if you are crazy then so am I".

The crowd erupted, everyone cheered, hollered and whistled. Jasper slipped the ring onto Jane's finger. She looked down at the ring with her mouth still open. It was a beautiful pale blue oblong aquamarine with a smaller diamond either side set on white gold. She touched it gently running her finger over the top, it was stunning, she felt tears slide down her face. Jasper cupped her face and brushed her tears away with his thumb. The band started playing again as Jasper stood up, grabbed Jane round the waist picked her up and spun her around kissing her like crazy. When he finally put her down she said.

"So, can you really ride that bike?"

He laughed, "I hope so because I brought it".

She swatted him hard across the chest. He hugged her again.

"God, I love you Belle".

She grinned, "I love you to fiancé".

Jasper jumped off the stage and grabbed Jane, everyone was greeting them as they walked back up towards their friends. Gwen was crying as was Chicca, the boys were cheering, clinking their bottles.

"Let's get this party started" G shouted, he was determined to have a party, they all cheered. As they got back to the table Jaspers friends were stood to the side. James had joined everyone as Jasper went onto the stage.

"Well, well you are a dark horse".

Tony smiled. He grabbed Jasper and hugged him.

"So thrilled for you man", Sam and John came in and hugged him too, patting him on the back, in turn they all hugged Jane congratulating them both, and Tom without fail offered his services if Jasper was never able to.

Moses came across to Jane.

"No more tears of sadness Jane, only happiness from here on in".

Jane hugged Moses tight.

"You knew, didn't you?" He nodded.

"Jay rang me, asked if I thought he was crazy, of course I said yes".

Jane smacked him in the stomach.

"That's not very nice"

She replied pouting, Moses laughed.

"I told him he was crazy not too, it is clear to see you two are in love"

Jane felt the tears again. Moses wiped them away.

"I love you Jane, I just want you to be happy, I will always be here for you, don't ever doubt that"

Jasper came up behind them both, he shook hands with Moses and hugged him.

"Thank you for everything Moses".

"Hey brother, it's a pleasure. I know you will look after her, I am always here for you both".

Jane looked up at her two-favourite people, feeling so emotional and happier than she had ever been.

Jane and Jasper were tapped on the shoulder when they turned Graham was stood there. Jane hugged him, fighting the tears again.

"So happy for you both, truly I am, the girls will go nuts when I tell them, you know they will want to be flower girls"

The three of them laughed.

"Oh, I'm sure there will be a queue for bridesmaids too.

Jasper laughed in response. Jane put her hands up to her face pretending to be dreading it secretly ecstatic, her mind was working overtime already.

The drinks flowed for the rest of the night, everyone danced and drank until the early hours of the morning. Jane and Jasper were the first to leave. Jane hadn't drank all night, she never took the chance. They got their jackets and helmets on and headed home, Jasper spoke to her through the intercom.

"Hey Mrs Belle Mitchell to be, you doing okay"?

Jane was smiling, and nodded, she was still so emotional and knew if she answered the tears would start again. She heard Jasper laugh softly. He squeezed her tightly, he was so glad it was a short journey home. They arrived home at 2am. Jane shut the engine of as quick as possible she didn't want to upset the neighbours. They took their boots and jackets off and left them in the boot room before stepping into the house. Jasper stopped Jane as she went to step in.

"Oh no you don't, come here".

He said as he scooped her up in his arms, Jane squealed she loved the time he carried her everywhere, she wasn't going to rush him to be put down. He nuzzled into her and bit her neck, she was still squealing as they went into the house. Jasper hadn't shut the door to the garage in the excitement of the evening and playing around with Jane. He carried her into the bedroom, put her down on the bed and and lent over her, kissing her deeply.

"You have made me the happiest, luckiest man in the world Belle. Thank you for coming into my life".

As he was kissing her Jane felt a presence in the room, before she had chance to scream Jasper fell to the floor, he had been knocked out, Jane screamed calling out for Jasper as Mark grabbed her grinning at her. He pulled up her neck warmer and pushed it into her mouth, "scream any more and it will just make things worse Jane".

He picked her up like she was a feather threw her over his shoulder and carried her out through the garage. He closed the door behind him and threw Jane into the back of the van.

He got into the driver seat, he couldn't believe his luck, he was prepared to wait, but seeing the door open, he couldn't waste the opportunity.

To be continued.

About

Grace Williams

I am a new Indie Author, my books are from a few genres including Contempary Romance, Erotic Romance.
When not writing and researching I enjoy learning more about Mental Health and how to help others. Spending time with my friends and family.
Of course spending time with my followers and friends on Social Media.

Links

Facebook – https://www.facebook.com/gracewilliamsauthor

Instagram – Grac.e2609

gracewilliamsauthor@gmail.com

THANK YOU

Thank you for reading the first in the "For the love of Jane" Trilogy. I hope you have enjoyed it as much as I have writing it. I promise not to keep you waiting too long for the next book "Jasper" where the story continues.

Gaining exposure as an independent author relies mostly on word-of-mouth, please consider leaving a review.

G x

Next book in the series.

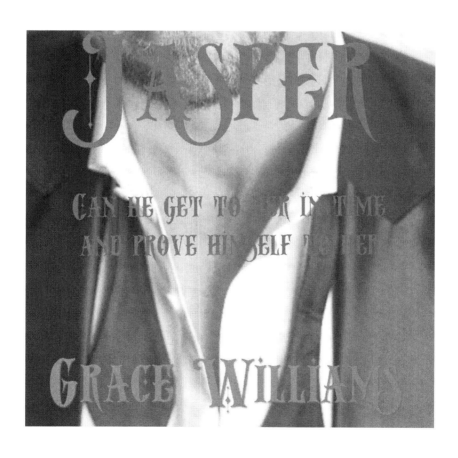

Printed in Poland
by Amazon Fulfillment
Poland Sp. z o.o., Wrocław

50280256R00204